TERMINAL GAMES

TERMINAL GAMES

COLE PERRIMAN

BANTAM BOOKS

NEW YORK   TORONTO   LONDON   SYDNEY   AUCKLAND

This book is a work of fiction, as are all
its characters. Any resemblance to actual
persons, living or dead, is purely coincidental.

Grateful acknowledgment is made for permission to
reprint an excerpt from the following: *You Always Hurt the One You Love*
by Allan Roberts and Doris Fischer
Copyright © 1944 (Renewed) Allan Roberts Music Co. (ASCAP) and
Doris Fischer Music (ASCAP)
International Copyright Secured. All Rights Reserved.
Used by Permission.

TERMINAL GAMES
A Bantam Book/June 1994

All rights reserved.
Copyright © 1994 by Wim Coleman and
Pat Perrin

Book design by Glen M. Edelstein

Computer manual illustrations by the author.

LIBRARY OF CONGRESS CATALOGING-IN-PUBLICATION DATA

Perriman, Cole.
  Terminal games / Cole Perriman.
      p.   cm.
    ISBN 0-553-09518-8
    1. Computer crimes—Fiction.   I. Title.
PS3553.E6943T47   1993
813′.54—dc20   93-17195
                                              CIP

Published simultaneously in the United States and Canada

Bantam Books are published by Bantam Books, a division of Bantam
Doubleday Dell Publishing Group, Inc. Its trademark, consisting of
the words "Bantam Books" and the portrayal of a rooster, is
Registered in U.S. Patent and Trademark Office and in other
countries. Marca Registrada. Bantam Books, 1540 Broadway, New
York, New York 10036.

PRINTED IN THE UNITED STATES OF AMERICA

BVG   0 9 8 7 6 5 4 3 2 1

To all those who helped through the tough times.

ACKNOWLEDGMENTS

In writing *Terminal Games,* I have benefited from conversations with Eric and Julie Coleman, Katie Hafner, John Markoff, Diane Shea, and Cliff Stoll. I was influenced by the work and writings of many other people, but would like to mention two in particular: Daniel C. Dennett for his ideas about consciousness, and David Gelernter for his work with networking software. However, many elements of this story are speculative and imaginary, and any errors of fact or sheer flights of fantasy are purely my own.

Thanks are also due to Morri Beers, Nancy Cervetti, Phyllis Howren, Seth Kramer, Jim Uhls, and especially Robert Howren for his special contribution to this book. My most heartfelt thanks to John Brockman and Katinka Matson for their unflagging encouragement and support over the years, and also to Leslie Meredith, whose editing always strikes a wise, rare balance of toughness and sensitivity.

Control, in other words, is nothing but
the sending of messages which effectively
change the behavior of the recipient.

—Norbert Wiener
The Human Use of Human Beings

AUGUSTE: I'm thirsty.
WHITE CLOWN: Have you any money?
AUGUSTE: No.
WHITE CLOWN: Then you aren't thirsty.

—Federico Fellini
Fellini on Fellini

OOOOO

PROLOGUE

WEDNESDAY, JANUARY 19: 1:35 A.M.

THE NIGHT IS CARPETED, QUIET. CITY NOISES ARE INTERCEPTED by walls and rooms and murmurs of sleeping guests. The man with steel-gray hair hears only a discreet whisper of cables gliding invisibly behind the elevator doors. He admires the efficiency of the world's machinery—obedient, respectful of his wishes. Machines understand the meaning of acquiescence and compliance.

He sees his own reflection in the mirrored wall at the end of the short hallway—a lean, elegant, Armani-clad gentleman with yacht-weathered skin standing, tired but dignified, in the ornate hallway. He adores mirrors, but this time he doesn't dwell on his image. He turns away and studies instead a design that embellishes the wall between the two elevators, an intricate raised pattern of garlands circling a sun.

Tired as he is, he is pleased with the moment, with the rich carpet and the ornate wall, with his sexual satiation and with his timely compliance with his own private and unspoken law: *Never spend the night.*

Now he looks forward to a few hours of sleep.

But can I sleep?

He thinks of the very young woman he just left behind in the room down the hall.

How old was she?

He hadn't asked her, and if he had, he would not have expected the truth. *People can be trusted to lie. A fact of life you can bank on.* Besides, it was best not to know now if she was underage—best not to dwell on any danger. It was all over. All in the past.

Nevertheless, he recollects her thin blond hair, her smooth white body—a whiteness just on the edge of being chalky, anemic, almost disagreeable. He had refrained from bruising that body as he might otherwise have done, and the sex had admittedly been a little tame for his exacting taste. Nevertheless, the frail body had been too eager, too unreserved, too *facile* to belong to someone without a fair amount of experience.

There are no virgins in the world. He feels his lips shape themselves into a comfortably familiar smirk. *People aren't even* born *with virginity anymore.*

The gray-haired man quickly grows tired of these musings. Now the whispering behind the doors has ceased. The elevator must have stopped at another floor. His smugness fades. His satisfaction dissipates a little. He has no time for this waiting. Nothing he does is free—not even in the seeming privacy of his own brain tissue. His most intimate thoughts cost money.

Where is that damned thing?

The gray-haired man hears a soft, rhythmic brushing sound behind him. What is that sound? Rubber soles scuffing against the plush carpet? The brush of inseam against inseam? He does not turn to look. He never turns to look at anybody if he can help it. Other people never occupy his curiosity or his interest. It is he who expects to occupy theirs. Other heads must turn, not his.

Even so, he regrets having faced away from the mirror. A glance, just the slightest motion of the head, would show him the person's reflection. He silently curses this spasm of interest. His discipline has slipped a little.

The quiet brushing comes to a halt behind him. How far away? Two feet? One foot? Less? The man with the steel-gray hair intuitively knows that his companion is not merely waiting for the elevator. No. This person has *found him*. This person knows who he is. The gray-haired man does not much like this. He has taken pains to be alone.

Then a voice behind him whispers, with the conspiratorial sweetness of an imaginary childhood playmate: "Hi, Jo-jo-boy. It's me. Auggie."

The man starts slightly at the sound, smiling with surprise.
Auggie!
Can it be possible? It is, indeed, as if a childhood playmate had
come to life. So many games, so many merry impostures. The man
begins to turn, eyebrows raised in pleased expectation.
He is about to ask, "How did you find me?"
He is about to say, "I hope you're not still angry."
He glimpses the figure's face—a white, red, and black face comprised of tiny squares. *A mosaic? Pixels?* The gray-haired man's eyes
squint to bring the face into better focus.
The rest of the figure is dark. Its right arm is outstretched. At the
end of the arm, at the very threshold of the gray-haired man's
peripheral vision, floats a bright glint of steel. The steel flashes
inward and downward. The glint blinds momentarily. The man feels
an implosion at his throat—a sudden, violent pressure accompanied by a noisy thud that reaches his ears through the resonant
cavities of his skull.
There is no pain.
The man's head is suspended, motionless, held up by something
imbedded in his throat. The brightly colored face with gigantic eyes
becomes abruptly clearer. For a moment, the gray-haired man is
aware of the large, red, downturned mouth scowling at him. Then,
with a furious jerk, the shining thing releases itself from his throat
and he swings exuberantly, dizzily around.
He finds himself staggering, facing the wall again with its garlands, its sun. A red liquid spray shoots rhythmically out of his
throat. A rumbling exhalation out of his lungs accompanies the
spray. The man is briefly enamored by the orgiastic ferocity of the
spurting. For fifty-eight years, his body has struggled to contain this
awful force—and now it is free.
How vigorous. How godly.
But now he grips his throat clumsily, his fingers unable to contain
the jubilant, pulsating fountain. His thoughts begin to stammer.
*These hands—these hands are too weak. Whose hands? Some damned
incompetent . . .*
The man is dizzy. He is still waiting for the pain, but it does not
come. He is a dancing marionette whose strings have been cut. His
body crumples to the carpeted floor in an unseemly heap. He tries
to breathe but can't. He doesn't actually want to breathe—not
under these demeaning circumstances. This entire struggle is a

terrible imposition, and he despises it—just as he despises waiting in lines.

Why isn't a subordinate here to take care of this?

What does he pay people for?

The man feels his body jerk and thrash. He briefly considers shouting, "Stop it! Let go of me!" But without air and the use of his voice box, the effort would be futile and humiliating. Besides, he quickly realizes that his body is thrashing on its own mindless power.

The man's eyes flash back and forth too hastily to take in more than a blur. He fleetingly thinks he detects the dark shape of his companion, but he can't be sure. His vision continues to gyrate crazily, even after his nervous system ceases to register his bodily convulsions.

Then he is still.

There is no pain.

There has never been any pain, never any terror.

The man stares unblinkingly upward at the wall. A wild red pattern like an aggressive abstract-expressionist splatter now overlays the sun and scatters across the garland's white curves. Huge, glistening droplets hang in precarious suspension, but do not move. *Have the droplets frozen, or has time stopped?*

The question does not much concern the gray-haired man. It is a mere point of curiosity. The entire scene has been rendered with breathtaking clarity—and clarity is its own justification. Death is much brighter, much more orderly than he had expected—and infinitely more accommodating.

The man is pleased.

THURSDAY, JANUARY 20: 12:03 A.M.

On a computer monitor, facing the viewer:

An image comprised entirely of tiny, square computer pixels. It is a beige door against a white wall. The door is stamped with a bright red number—636. Near the top of the screen, numerous pairs of disembodied eyes appear, blinking and staring. Letters are typed next to each set of eyes, giving them a frail semblance of identity:

"sudopod, starlitestarbrite, goldnrod, safir, tilly-the-hun, toms-antpolly, prayreedog, l-fy . . ."

Music, heard over tiny, sputtering speakers:

Slow, gentle, lilting orchestral music, beginning with a discord in the low strings, but immediately turning cheerful in the violins. The beginning of a Rossini overture, perhaps, but which one? It doesn't much matter. They all start off quiet and end up loud.

The door opens jerkily away from the viewer, revealing a black vacancy from which emerges a cartoonish, gray-haired man in a three-piece suit. He turns toward the darkness and blows a noisy "smack" of a goodbye kiss toward his unseen lover. He closes the door behind him.

Zoom in on the gray-haired man's face. A silly, self-satisfied smile forms on his lips. Violinists slap their bows against the wood of their instruments in percussive applause.

Zoom out, taking in the man's whole figure again. Track backward in front of the man as he starts to dance away, the hotel hallway with its parallel rows of doors retreating into the distance. But the perspective is a little off. The lines do not converge correctly as the viewer lumbers backward, keeping the man in view.

Keep tracking in front of him down the hallway and around numerous corners through an increasingly preposterous maze, to a corridor with facing pairs of elevator doors. At the end of the corridor is a wall mirror. The man stops at the sight of his full-length reflection. The violin bows clatter against wood again, sounding slightly bemused, intermixing this time with halting queries from the other stringed instruments.

The perspective is momentarily unglued as the view moves behind the gray-haired man. He pushes the elevator button and glances briefly at a design on the wall between the elevators—an intricate sketch of garlands surrounding a sun.

A brief silence, then clarinets and oboes and English horns carry the music into a brisk up-tempo. An enormous hand—as if belonging to the viewer—reaches into the scene and taps the gray-haired man on the shoulder, accompanied by the now-familiar clacking of the violin bows.

There is momentary silence.

The man turns toward the viewer. His face fills the screen. He looks slightly puzzled, even as a smile shapes itself across his face. The violins sigh briefly with pleased surprise.

Then . . .

The screen is wiped clean by a swift, slashing movement accompanied by a comical electronic gurgling sound. The music reaches a madcap gallop. The hallway, the mirror, the sun and its garlands, and the elevator doors reappear, whirling around the gray-haired man.

A tight zoom in quickly on his face as his throat explodes in a pyrotechnical display of spouting red pixels. He clutches his throat. His eyes bulge and roll ludicrously. Shimmering globs of red cover the screen, briefly obliterating the view, then draining away to reveal him lying on the floor, flopping about in time to the music as it cartwheels into a reeling, festive finale.

View the man from above as he lies on his side, his scurrying feet twirling him in a crazy windmill motion. Then move down beside him as he flips on his back and flops like a fish, his pelvis lurching upward with the climax of the overture. Finally, zoom in on his face. The violins make one last clattering statement as the man's protruding eyes turn into little Xs.

With the closing chords, the screen shows a cluster of pixels scattered across a cybernetic white background. This bright crimson pattern, much like an old-fashioned kitchen sampler, overlays the sketch of the sun and is splashed across the garlands. A red trickle follows the edge of a curl.

00001

TREMENDUM

BARGAIN-BASEMENT TRACHEOTOMY," DEPUTY CORONER BERnard Smith remarked, shining a penlight into the gaping throat wound and studying it through lowered bifocals. "Windpipe's sawed halfway through. Carotid arteries're severed. Sternomastoid muscles, too."

"Meaning?" Lieutenant Nolan Grobowski asked.

"Meaning I don't think he's gonna make it."

Nolan chuckled grimly. No, this one definitely *wasn't* going to make it. Even from about five feet away, Nolan could see that the wound—only an hour or so old—was showing signs of decay. The dead man's smell was nasty, too—the stench of raw, freshly cut meat and the mixed stink of feces and urine made the plush and well-lit hotel corridor smell incongruously like an outhouse.

Smith shined the penlight into the victim's eyes, and Nolan could see that they had already flattened slightly—their fluid apparently had begun to drain. Nolan made a note . . .

"2:56 A.M. The stiff is wilting a little."

Nolan always wrote down absolutely everything that entered his head while on the job, no matter how seemingly trivial, redundant, or absurd. Even though the local Hollywood detectives had surely taken notes, he would need his own records. And even photographs sometimes couldn't be counted on for crucial details. Besides, notetaking was one of the few really natural things to do at a homicide scene. It kept one's hands busy.

"So how're you calling this one, Smitty?" asked Nolan's partner, Sergeant Clayton Saunders, who was gingerly stalking the area with a tape measure.

The gray-haired, pudgy deputy coroner sat back on his haunches.

"Reckon it'd be natural causes," Smitty said. "It's got all the earmarks of a massive coronary or stroke. Or maybe just plain old age."

"Could he've choked on a chicken bone?" Clayton asked. The black detective finished his measuring and turned to study the bloodstain on the wall.

"Possibly, just possibly," Smitty said. "He might have stuck his finger in a wall socket, too."

"What about suicide?" Nolan asked.

"Get serious, Nol," Smitty said, padding puppy dog–like around the body on his hands and knees. "Why would a guy that rich off himself?"

"Hell, we're talking about one of America's champion cutthroat buccaneers, here," Nolan said. "Think of the guilt he must have been toting around. Here's what happened. About one-thirty-five this morning, G. K. Judson's corporate sins caught up with him. He couldn't live with himself for one more minute. So he took a big butcher knife out of his suitcase, walked down the hotel hallway to the elevator, rode it two floors down, stepped out into the corridor here, and sliced himself open."

"Possible," Smitty mused. "But what happened to the knife?"

"That *is* a problem," Nolan grumbled.

Clayton considered a moment and said, "That's obvious. Judson handed it to some passerby during his dying moments. He said, 'Keep this. It'll be worth a lot of money one of these days.' "

Smitty smiled. "Pretty compelling argument, guys. Still, there ought to be a suicide note."

"Looks to me like he was trying to write one on the wall over here," Clayton said.

Nolan went over and stared at the bloody blotch on the ornate white wall. It looked like paint slung from a moving brush.

"Read it to me," Smitty requested.

"Looks pretty basic," Nolan said. "But I've never gotten the hang of the language."

Clayton glanced at him, but said nothing.

Nolan flipped back to his previous notebook page and checked over his rough sketch and his jotted descriptions of the space: the two pairs of elevators facing each other across the corridor; the mirrored wall at the corridor's end; the white, raised sun designs between each of the elevators; the slashing bloodstain that lay across one of the suns . . .

Nolan now drew a hasty little sketch of the blotch, indicating the large slash of red across the sun, smaller splatters on the rays, and a few isolated droplets extending across the raised leafy designs.

Pseudostylishness and gore. Not your typical homicide scene.

At about one-forty-five, the body of G. K. Judson, CEO of Chicago-based Apex Airlines, had been discovered by a waiter delivering a very early breakfast. Immediately after phoning the police, the waiter had dutifully taken it upon himself to call the L. A. *Times,* several alternative newspapers, and a fair assortment of television and radio stations. The local patrolmen and detectives arrived in time to find the body engulfed by piranhalike flashbulbs and video-cams. The cops had finally gotten the crowd of gawkers and reporters out of the way and directed down the nearby stairwells to other elevators. When it had become clear that the case was going to be a major media event, Nolan and Clayton were called in from Homicide Special Section.

They had fought their way through a crowd to get to the area the uniformed cops had roped off. By that time, the likelihood of the crime team finding anything useful had diminished to near zero. A half-hearted attempt had been made to look for fingerprints. The fingerprint powder now clung to a brass plate encasing a pair of elevator buttons and would probably remain there for a long time. That part had been a joke, of course, revealing only an indecipherable jumble. The same was true of the door leading to the escape stairs. Too many people routinely passed through a place like that for fibers or fingerprints to mean very much.

The uniforms were now standing at the edge of the scene, dutifully and conspicuously keeping their hands in their pockets in accord with Nolan's ritual demand that they not touch anything.

The pudgy forensics doctor huffed and groaned a little as he brushed his hands off on his trouser legs and rose to his feet.

"Well, gentlemen," Smitty said, "I sure hate to go out on a limb with some crazy-assed hypothesis, but my guess is it was murder. 'Course, that's good news for you guys. When folks stop doing each other in, you'll be looking for work."

"I could do with a change," Nolan said. "I've been following the want ads for months."

"Yeah, and I'll bet there's a lotta work out there for an over-the-hill jerk who's done nothing his whole adult life 'cept go poking around other people's business."

"Hey, I'm not looking for a job for *you*, Smitty."

"Very funny. You're too fast for me, Nol."

"Doesn't take a Ferrari."

"You could never go civilian. You love this stuff. Who could help but love it?"

"OK, let's call it murder for a moment, just to be goofy," Nolan said. "Who was the perp?"

"Hey, *you're* the homicide dicks," Smitty said. "Don't ask me to do your job for you. I can tell you one thing, though. The motive wasn't robbery."

Smitty stooped over and raised up the victim's left hand. He carefully removed a ring with a substantial diamond. Then he took a glittering gold Rolex from the wrist.

"Hell, those watches cost more than ten grand," Clayton observed, as Smitty took the items off the corpse, dropped them into a plastic bag, and handed them to Nolan.

"That kind of cash'd sure help with Molly's college tuition."

"Stop begging," Smitty scolded.

"Let's have a look at his wallet."

"Just make sure you turn it in the way you found it."

Smitty slid the wallet across the floor. Nolan stooped to pick it up. He opened it, and a batch of glittering, multicolored, metallic-embossed credit cards tumbled out, accordion-fashion. Nolan thumbed through the wallet. It hardly contained anything *except* credit cards—just enough cash to give the hotel staff rudimentary tips.

"No pictures of his wife and kids."

"And no portraits of Mother Teresa or Albert Schweitzer or the Dalai Lama, either," Clayton added, looking over Nolan's shoulder. "Plastic can sure take up a lot of room in your life."

Part of Smitty's team was now unfolding the black body bag. The doctor hovered over them, admonishing them fussily about every move, treating the corpse like an artistic treasure. Nolan was reminded of the career-loving gravedigger in *Hamlet*. Whenever Nolan worked a homicide scene with Smitty, he more than half expected the man to whip out an extra skull for proud display. Smitty never looked happier than when he was around a dead body.

As for himself, Nolan could feel his own face frozen into a joyless expression. He didn't find his own wisecracks amusing, and he didn't really imagine anyone else did, either.

So why do I do it?

The clichéd explanation was that cops told jokes around murder scenes to keep themselves sane. Nolan sometimes suspected that that was a pretty flimsy rationalization.

Maybe we tell jokes around murder scenes to hide the fact that we've already *lost it.*

Nolan watched as Smitty's team manipulated the body, folding its arms and generally preparing it for the bag. The corpse was remarkably pliable. It almost seemed to shift consciously and give here and there to assist the team. Corpses at this stage were really quite cooperative—like well-behaved pets.

A word crossed Nolan's mind . . .

Tremendum.

That was a word Nolan's one-time mentor, Syd Harper, had used. Nolan wasn't sure whether it was an actual clinical term or just one of "Crazy" Syd's numerous coinages, but it had always struck him as a useful word. It described that uniquely self-conscious, uniquely human horror and awe at the sight of a corpse—*any* corpse, even that of a total stranger. It was the ghastly mortal comprehension of the fact of death—and the awareness that death came to all.

Animals couldn't feel it.

Experienced cops couldn't, either.

Nolan certainly didn't feel any tremendum right at the moment. As far as he could tell, he didn't feel much of anything.

It was supposed to be that way, of course. You were supposed to get inured to it. Nolan could remember a time when he could still feel it, though—particularly the first time. It was at the scene of a three-car accident on a New Year's Eve some fifteen years ago, back when Nolan was still a rookie. Four dead teenagers were stretched on the pavement awaiting body bags. There had been another collision, fortunately minor, between two drivers who couldn't keep their eyes off the wreckage.

Nolan had looked at those drivers and realized that they felt it, too. At that moment, he had understood how wrongheaded all those morbid jokes were about traffic bogging down at an accident. It wasn't grim smugness that slowed those cars. It was a kind of religious terror that seized even the most determined atheist. It was tremendum.

Smitty's team delicately hoisted the body into the bag. Smitty supervised. Nolan thought about *Hamlet* again as he contemplated his own utter lack of terror and awe . . .

". . . *a beast, that wants discourse of reason, would have mourn'd longer.*"

Nolan had been through a time of terrible mourning.

It wasn't very long ago.

But had he mourned enough?

Had he *felt* enough? Could a cop feel enough?

"At times like now," Smitty mused elegiacally, "I'm reminded of the words of the poet: 'To die, to be really dead—that must be glorious!' "

"Nice," Nolan said.

"Thank you," Smitty replied.

"Who was the poet?" Clayton asked.

"Dracula," Smitty told him.

The body bag was closed with a noisy zip.

Marianne Hedison approached the house through its elegant formal gardens. Morning sunlight washed across the scene, accentuating the stucco texture of the facade and giving it a yellowish tint. She briefly considered exchanging the bright sunlight for a dusky twilight or even a midnight full moon, just to observe the variation. But then she thought better of it.

Trivialities. Better stick to business.

She moved directly across the terrace and up to the front door and peered into its leaded glass window, a contemporary design through which she could vaguely glimpse a cheerfully lit interior. She laughed slightly at her fleeting impulse to ring the doorbell.

Who do you expect to find at home?

The door swung open, and she moved into a stately entryway with an upstairs gallery looming above her along three walls. There was not a stick of furniture in the place or a painting on any of the walls. An eerie feeling of cavernous space swept over her.

How large *an unfurnished house always seems!*

For a moment, she thought she heard the sound of an orchestra echoing through the empty space, slow and gentle but punctuated by an odd discord.

Rossini again. Why can't I forget that tune?

Marianne focused her attention on the room, shaking her head to make the music go away.

It didn't.

She thought about ascending the stairs on her left in order to gaze over the majestic room from the gallery. But it seemed best to poke around downstairs a bit first. She passed on into the empty living room with its monumental fireplace, then into the vast dining room.

She noticed that she was holding her breath.

Each time she turned a corner, she half expected to see someone there.

Someone dangerous.

Utterly ridiculous.

Swinging around to view the empty room, she saw nothing. But she thought she heard violin bows clacking, slapping percussively against the wood of the instruments.

You're like a little kid who's stayed up past her bedtime watching horror films on TV.

Marianne passed through another doorway into a bare kitchen. She turned back and forth, studying its whole length. It was long, narrow, and cramped in comparison to the rooms she had just passed through.

I told them this space was too tight when we went over the floor plans. Who could do any major entertaining from a kitchen like this?

After a few deft movements of Marianne's fingers, the wall that connected to the dining room glided silently backward, carrying its counterspace and cabinets along with it, broadening the whole area by exactly four feet. Marianne studied the enhanced kitchen space with satisfaction.

There. And that doesn't hurt the next room—it's still huge.

Just to try the idea out, she caused a work island to pop into view in the middle of the kitchen floor. She effortlessly changed the shape of the island and rotated it a little until it sat at a pleasing diagonal. There was plenty of room to walk around it on all sides.

Still, an adjustment like this demanded a formality. She moved her computer mouse to the desk accessory list, selected "Send Mail," and typed a message in the space that appeared.

DWAYNE:
PLEASE NOTE THE KITCHEN WALL ADJOINING THE DIN-
ING ROOM. I MOVED IT. IT'S NOT LOAD-BEARING, SO I
DON'T SEE ANY PROBLEM, DO YOU? LET ME KNOW IF YOU
THINK OTHERWISE.

—MH

Another mouse-click caused the message to vanish. Later she would bundle the design file up with the note, attach her version of the house plans, and send the whole thing to the design office.

It was now very early in the morning, and she had not yet gone to bed. Her eyes were too tired to continue her visual "walk-through" of the house on her computer screen. She felt a yawn welling up. Maybe she was getting truly sleepy. She closed her eyes and stretched her arms and back.

A sharp "boing" sounded directly in front of her.

Her eyes snapped open.

An icon was flashing in the upper left-hand corner of the monitor.

E-mail. No big deal.

So why was she shaking?

She was still unnerved by the apparition—that grotesquely comic, disturbingly savage murder she had witnessed just a few hours ago.

Hold it now. Simulation *of a murder. Let's keep our realities straight, OK?*

Even so, the animated performance had irrationally frightened her. The music and images had haunted her as she toured this perfectly safe, innocuous, virtual interior. As she stared at the blinking E-mail icon, a bright red cartoon bloodstain flashed across her brain. She tried unsuccessfully to erase it.

And just who the hell would be leaving E-mail at this time of night?

She double-clicked the icon and the message appeared.

DAHHHLING!

AM LOOKING FORWARD SO MUCH TO SEEING YOU TO-MORROW! WE *ARE* ON FOR NOON, AREN'T WE? AT THE COURT OF KING LOUIS XIV? OH *PLEEZZZZZZ* DON'T CAN-CEL! IT'S BEEN WAY TOO LONG.

RUHNAY

Marianne breathed more relaxedly.

Renee.

Renee was even more of an insomniac than Marianne, and nocturnal messages between them were no oddity. But part of the message puzzled her.

Court of King Louis XIV?

Then she remembered. The lounge. The hotel where she'd be for the next few days.

Renee's fantasizing again. Guess it's my serve.

She went to her desk accessory list again to leave a message of her own.

O DAHHHLING YOURSELF!
    WE'RE STILL ON, SWEETIE. AND I UNDERSTAND WE'RE
IN FOR A TREAT. OLD KING LOUIE'S HOLDING A COMMAND
PERFORMANCE OF A BRAND NEW MOLIERE PLAY WITH
MUSIC BY LULLY AND LYRICS BY NEIL SIMON. SHOULD
GO DOWN GREAT WITH WHISKEY AND MARGARITAS! SEE
YOU THERE!

—MH

She zapped the message into the network, then shut down her design program.

Surely I'm tired enough to go to sleep now.

But as she looked at her hand resting on the computer mouse, she noticed that it was still trembling.

The horizontal hold went out on Nolan's eyesight. The omelet he was trying to eat kept flipping upward through his vision. He just wanted to close his eyes and let his head drop onto his plate. This commonly happened after he'd been awakened for work in the wee hours. Particularly when dawn was just coming up, as it was now.

But Nolan knew he'd get a second wind in a little while. He'd be good for another twenty-four hours straight if he paced himself right. The prospect wasn't particularly pleasing.

Nolan took a huge swig of coffee and stared ruthlessly at the omelet until he managed to make it stand still. Then he looked across the café table at his partner. Clayton was munching on a stack of pancakes.

"Not off to the best of starts, are we?" Nolan observed.

"Nope. Reporters showing up before cops is not what you'd call a P.R. coup. The captain'll really give us hell for that."

"Why can't he blame the Hollywood cops? They got there before we did."

"Since when is Coffey fair?"

"Good point."

"So a millionaire from Chicago gets whacked in one of our finest wannabe-luxury hotels," Clayton mused, shaking his head. "Kind of obliges us to solve the case, huh?"

"Kind of."

"So how soon do you think we'll get a laugh on this one?"

"The same as usual," Nolan said. "Soon or never."

"Never's a long time."

"A hell of a long time."

Nolan and Clayton frequently likened themselves to a stand-up comedy team playing to an unsmiling audience. A "laugh" was any hint or clue indicating that a case might be solvable. If they didn't get one early on, things would only get tougher—if not downright impossible.

The ideal time to get a laugh was before the two of them even came onto a homicide scene—during those first few minutes after patrol officers arrived. But this time, the warm-up act had been a real dud.

Nolan shuddered as he sipped on his coffee. A high-profile case like this could dog their heels almost endlessly.

"Never" was, indeed, a long time.

He grabbed a jar of horseradish and began to spread the swelter-ing stuff all over the omelet—his usual antidote to disagreeable crime-scene odors. In worst-case situations—when a corpse was, say, a week or two old—horseradish was the only way to clear up his sinuses.

Nolan and Clayton began to talk over their strategy for the rest of the morning—including the hotel guests they needed to interview, and the subpoena they'd have to get in order to obtain the hotel's records on those guests.

"I got a hunch it'll all prove a waste of time, though," Clayton remarked.

"Why?" Nolan asked.

"Just a feeling. I don't think it was done by a guest."

"Who was it, then?"

"Come on, Nol. If I knew that, we could wrap up and head home early. It *could* have been somebody from outside, that's all. I got a look at the fire stairs. The perp could've just slipped in, done the deed, and let himself out."

"But did the killer hang around the hallway and wait for this par-ticular guy, or was it random? And are we ruling out a mob hit? Jud-son wasn't said to be the sweetest guy in the world. His demise might have been subsidized by some generous Chicago philanthropist."

"Awfully messy for a professional job."

"Well, it sort of fits in with the pervasive decline in American craft and workmanship, doesn't it?"

"It was *personal,* Nol."

"Yeah, I guess you're right," Nolan said, remembering the man's gaping wound and the savagely rendered bloodstain. "How long's it been since we saw someone cut up like that?"

"I sure can't remember."

Nolan was seized by another wave of tiredness. He involuntarily closed his eyes. His own words echoed through his mind . . .

"How long's it been since we saw someone cut up like that?"

Her face crept into his mind. Her face with that odd, glazed look.

Come on, man, forget about it. It's been three years. How much more time do you want?

Nolan tightened his eyes.

Don't see it. Keep it out of your brain.

Her face with that expression. What was it about that expression?

His first thought had been that she'd gotten her makeup all wrong. And, yes, that expression. He'd laughed at that expression whenever she'd gotten it before. It was a screwed-up goofy look of some dippy thirties movie comedienne, a bemused look she got when some asshole called with a wrong number or when she came home from the store with somebody else's grocery bag or when she'd bob out of a swimming pool like a wet cat after an unexpected dunking. It was the look that had made all her friends cheer and clap and hoot and holler when she popped in the door on the evening of her thirtieth birthday and got the surprise of her life. It was a look that had made sweet mockery of her pretty young face.

Nolan's eyes popped open. The bright light of the café dissolved her image. It had been a long time since his last such attack, and he'd forgotten how simple it was to get rid of the pictures.

Just remember to open *your eyes when you don't want to see something.*

The brightness resolved into a glittering clarity—the half-eaten omelet, the empty coffee cup, the Formica tabletop. Nolan raised his head and looked into Clayton's light brown face with its slender but distinctly African features. Clayton was staring at him.

"You OK, Nol? Thought I'd lost you for a moment there."

"Yeah, I'm fine."

"Don't bullshit me, fella. I'm your partner. It's my business to know when you're not fine."

Nolan sighed. "Doesn't this job ever get to you?" he finally asked.

"No."

"Never?"

"Huh-uh."

"Does it ever get to you that it doesn't get to you?"

"All the fucking time. I worry like crazy that I'm turning into a ghoul or a soulless zombie or an insensitive husband or daddy or some such thing. All cops do, 'specially in homicide. You know that. It's just a fact of life." Clayton paused a moment, then added, "But all cops aren't you. We haven't been through what you've been through."

Nolan nodded. That pretty well cut to the problem. Clay hadn't become Nolan's partner until a few months after the thing had happened, and Nolan had never told him the whole grisly story. But Clay knew enough to figure it would still nag at Nolan from time to time.

"If it's getting to you, maybe you should take some vacation time," Clayton suggested.

"Naw, then I'd *really* get all strung out. I'll be OK, Clay. I'm just tired. And when I'm tired, I start getting pictures in my head. After a while they always go away."

The two of them ate in silence. Then Nolan said, "I used to like my job. Now I don't have any idea whether I like it or not. I'm like an air traffic controller who's trying to do his job after he's been *in* a plane crash. Maybe I really ought to look for another line of work."

"Like what?"

"I don't know. Something that won't push my buttons like this job." Nolan fell silent again for another second or two and then added, "Maybe I'll become a mortician."

He and Clayton both laughed.

"Not until you get yourself cloned," Clayton said. "If I lose you, my next partner's sure to be some right-wing redneck skinhead white supremacist."

"You'd be an experience for him." Nolan grinned. When Clayton just scowled, he said, "All right, damn it. I'll stick it out for a while. Just for you. Now let's finish eating and get moving. We've got a real mess on our hands."

The next day at around noon, Nolan again stood in the Quenton Parks's sixth-floor elevator alcove staring at the blood on the wall. Gillaspie, the hotel manager, had railed at him for making his staff wait a day and a half before cleaning up the murder scene. *A kid.*

Nolan remembered the young man's brash, spoiled demeanor. *Can't be more than thirty. Getting paid five times my salary, I'll bet, just to hire and fire Latinos and feed receipts into a computer.*

The manager had become more pleasant when he learned that none of the hotel guests or employees had so far been implicated in the murder. And he had turned absolutely charming when Nolan told him to go ahead with the cleanup.

Now the gold screen that had been hiding the stained wall and floor had been removed. The police-barrier tape was piled on the floor. Three hotel employees stood discussing what could be done about the bloodstains.

"The one on the wall's a cinch. We'll scrub as much of it off as possible, then give her a good coat of paint. But that blot on the carpet's the problem."

"Guess we'll have to replace the whole square of carpeting for this corridor."

"*Si, pero no hoy.* Not today," the third repeated. "That Gillaspie, he want this hall fixed up quick."

"So?"

"Grab one of those little rugs from one of the empty rooms," the first worker said. "We'll toss it over the stain for now."

The three dispersed. Nolan still stood in the corridor, staring at the bloodstain as though it could be decoded, as if it might reveal . . . what?

Probably not a hell of a lot.

Rodriguez, the forensics investigator, had already been by to perform his spatter-analysis magic. By measuring the exact size and dimensions of the blotch, the distance between isolated droplets and how they were smeared, Rodriguez had drawn his Sherlock Holmesian conclusions about the exact positions of the attacker and the victim when the fatal wound was delivered. Rodriguez had even come up with a fair idea of the attacker's height, build, and strength.

About my size.

And—oh, yes—although the autopsy wasn't too far along, it seemed pretty conclusive that the killer had used an extremely keen blade—probably some kind of stainless steel, serrated kitchen knife.

The wonder of forensics. A lot of good it does. The man was dead, after all. That was final, unchangeable.

Several hotel guests came and went, gawking and shuddering and sometimes making sick jokes. Nolan looked at the raised wall pattern critically. He didn't have to be an expert on decor to know that the interior of the Quenton Parks was a load of crap.

How typical of Hollywood's bullshit "comeback"—trying to make a new hotel look old!

Two of the men in white coveralls returned with buckets, brushes, paint rollers, and rags. Nolan sighed as he watched them set to work. It was kind of sad to wipe out a thing like that with a few sweeps of a paint roller. There sure was a lot of mystery in that stain. Nolan sort of liked the way it shattered the corridor's pretensions.

Nolan heard a small gasp at his back. He turned to see a dark-haired woman standing behind him. She was tall in her high heels—about as tall as he was. Her smooth hair was pulled back and fastened with some sort of clasp. She was dressed in black and tan, an expensive-looking suit with matching accessories. It was the kind of getup that had been carefully put together or bought as an outfit. Her eyes were wide, and her mouth was hanging slightly open. She seemed stunned.

"Can I help you, ma'am?"

The woman was clearly unaware of his presence.

"Ma'am?" Nolan said, stepping nearer to her.

She started out of her trance, trembling. She briefly, nervously perused Nolan's face. With her large green eyes and her full red lips, she struck Nolan as a startlingly beautiful woman—but he thought that was probably the result of a lot of time and effort.

The woman turned swiftly and started to walk away.

Does this one know something? He stepped in front of her, pulling out his badge.

"Ma'am, my name is Nolan Grobowski, L.A.P.D. Are you aware that this is a crime scene?"

The woman stopped, but she looked as though she actually might try to dash past him and run.

"What do you want?" she demanded.

"Well, it's just that you seemed awfully interested in that wall there."

"Not really," she said, not turning to look at it.

Nolan tried to go easy. *Don't spook her.* "Ma'am, I don't mind telling you that we're having a hell of a time with this investigation. It was a particularly nasty crime, and in a public place like this— well, clues are pretty tough to come by. If you can tell me anything— anything at all . . ."

She looked at him. "It's just—" she stammered. "It's just that I've seen something like that."

Nolan pressed forward. "What's your name, ma'am?"

"Marianne Hedison." She shrank away from him again.

"Are you staying here? Nice place. Not your usual homicide scene, if you know what I mean." He was trying to put her at ease, but she seemed to grow colder and more distant by the second. He wondered if he still had garlic on his breath from lunch.

"Yes, I'm staying here," the woman said. "Down the hall. I'm here on business."

"What did you mean when you said you'd seen something like that?" asked Nolan, gesturing toward the wall.

The woman started to reply, then closed her mouth. Nolan reached out as if to touch her arm, to encourage her—a mistake, he realized too late. She drew back from him again and was quite composed now. This time she turned and faced the splattered wall.

"Oh, it's the design. I believe it's Louis XIV. I saw something like it at Versailles, I'm sure. I'm an interior designer, so I notice these things. It's shocking to see it . . . stained like that."

The elevator doors opened. "Excuse me," the woman said, "but I'm late for an appointment."

Nolan nodded. She walked away from him.

Can't exactly haul her in for knowing too much about wall decor.

With a straight back and a dignified step, the woman disappeared into the elevator. Nolan took out his small notebook and wrote down her name.

OOO1O

OLICE LINE
DO NOT CRO

Marianne Hedison fled deep into the velvet-lined elevator, slipping into a space behind several people. She watched the open doorway warily, but the detective did not follow her. The handful of people faced front in doll-like silence as the doors slid shut. She closed her eyes and leaned back against the elevator wall. The sun design with its dark blotch kept exploding in her mind like the afterimage of a flashbulb.

That morning, when Marianne had followed the porter out of the elevator on her way to her room, she had laughed when she spied the ornamented wall. She knew that the emblem of the Sun King was copied from His Majesty's very bedroom doors. Even then, another significance to that design had teased at her thoughts, but her attention was quickly deflected by the small demands of finding her room and settling in.

She had seen only one of the garlanded suns that morning, however. The other wall had been blocked with a screen. *Something gold. Yes, three gold panels with a crane and a bonsai tree.* One of the elevators had been out of service. And a yellow tape bearing the warning POLICE LINE DO NOT CROSS was stretched diagonally across a portion of the corridor, preventing access to the screen or the elevator. Marianne hadn't found the tape particularly ominous— just a reminder that she was back in L.A.

But just now, the Japanese screen had been moved aside and a long strand of the yellow plastic tape lay tangled on the floor. Fragments of the message surfaced here and there among its coils . . .

. . . *OLICE LI . . . ROSS POLI . . . INE DO NOT CRO . . . OSS POLICE LI . . .*

And now that police detective was standing there in the hallway. He had been staring directly at the stain—a stain that Marianne had not seen that morning. The larger splatter was placed across the garlands and the rays of the sun, the smaller splashes bloomed like terrible flowers on the face of the sun, and the line of a drip followed a curved edge.

That stain was exactly like . . .

But no. She wouldn't complete that thought. She couldn't. The implications of that precise stain on that precise design were intolerable.

Marianne struggled to bring her thoughts under control. The elevator stopped at another floor, and two more people got on. At each stop, everybody on the elevator shuffled slightly backward. The rhythmic sliding of the doors, the familiar rituals of the people—their polite distances, their quiet apologies to one another, their contractions of boundaries to accommodate those whose presence they would not again acknowledge—these small protocols eased Marianne's alarm. She couldn't believe she had so nearly panicked right in front of that detective.

What did I think he was going to do, arrest me?

By the time she got off the elevator and found her way to the bar, Marianne was feeling steady again. Like the rest of the hotel, the King Louis Lounge was posh—although here the florid French motif gave way to a darker and more heavily upholstered elegance. Behind a well-polished wooden bar, an array of bottles glittered. Only a few people occupied chairs around the scattered tables. The room was shadowy, and Marianne couldn't tell immediately whether the friend she planned to meet had arrived or not.

Then, in a burst of color and motion, a woman with wild, rust-colored hair scrambled out of a booth and charged forward, holding out her arms and calling Marianne's name. Renee's warm, chestnut-colored eyes momentarily startled Marianne. No one else she knew had eyes like that.

Surprised by a rush of emotion, Marianne realized how much she'd missed her friend. Her eyes stung with tears as she threw her arms around Renee, who returned the embrace warmly. Marianne stepped back and saw that Renee, too, was laughing through tears.

"I can't believe it's been a year," Marianne said.

"I can't, either," Renee said.

Then came a moment of pleasant confusion during which neither of them had the slightest idea what to say next.

"Love your outfit," Marianne said at last, although she was sure that Renee's tunic and slacks hadn't started life as an ensemble.

"Don't be sarcastic," replied Renee pertly.

"Let's just say you've got a knack for making me look stodgy."

"You've made it so easy," commented Renee with a little smirk.

Marianne caught a sepia-tinted glimpse of the two of them in the mirror behind the bar. Her own sober tan reflection was practically invisible next to the crimson and purple one. Images came back to her, of the two of them in jeans and men's shirts tied at the waist, or in long skirts, ethnic blouses, dangly jewelry, strappy sandals, and a bright scarf or two.

In those days, they'd been on more equal terms. Of course, they'd both gone through transformations during the past several years. But Marianne could see that Renee still maintained an air of exuberance, while her own look was now more premeditated.

My own life *is more premeditated.*

The two women settled into a booth Renee had already appropriated. The padded black leather seat curved halfway around a marble-topped table. Above the row of booths, beveled and leaded glass panels, some frosted and some clear, provided a striped view of palmetto plants and the main lobby beyond.

A waiter came over to their booth. "Would you like to start with a drink?" the waiter suggested. He took their order and retreated.

"So, what do you hear from the old gang?" Marianne asked.

"There is no old gang, anymore," Renee said sadly.

"Don't you hear from any of them?"

"Not a one. And you?"

"Me neither."

"Surely you hear from Evan now and again."

Marianne winced. "Only what I read in *The Village Voice.*"

"Do I detect a note of bitterness?"

"Probably. I guess even an amicable divorce brings out a few hard feelings. Actually, he did call about three months back. He was ranting and raving, complaining about everything as usual. But he's getting attention in the New York gallery scene."

"He's got to love that."

"Oh, yeah, Evan loves attention. And God knows, he's worked hard for it. I hope it lasts long enough to make him stinking rich. I hope he gets famous."

"You don't sound like you mean it," Renee observed.

"Really?" Marianne asked. She was surprised. She *thought* she meant it. She knew the photographs printed with recent reviews were of Evan's old work and that he was living on borrowed time and borrowed talent. For his sake, Marianne hoped he could rake in a fast fortune and rest on his laurels. His laurels were all he had left.

"I hope he does well," Marianne said simply.

"Of course he will," Renee said. "You know he's brilliant. It takes genius to be that much of an asshole."

Marianne laughed. "If that's any measure of genius, he'll probably get a Nobel."

Renee went on talking—all about Evan and the gang. Marianne almost felt the presence of old friends, earnest young creators of images, sounds, words—her younger self among them. They had been a vital, hungry bunch, straining for a chance to show off their talents, to make their own statements to the world. But those memories didn't hold quite the same allure for Marianne. During their six-year marriage, Marianne had watched Evan fall deeper and deeper into a whirlpool of booze and amphetamines, alternating them more and more rapidly, cranking himself down with alcohol and cranking himself back up again with crystal, always in search of an increasingly elusive creativity.

She sighed deeply. Whatever creativity was, it had to be more than perpetual adolescence. She had divorced Evan two years ago and had moved to Santa Barbara to get away from the life they had shared.

"Have I been saying that a lot?" Renee's voice snapped Marianne out of her reverie.

"What?"

"I kept saying that I miss those old days," Renee said. "Don't you?"

"Yes—I mean, yes, I think you've been saying that a lot."

"Sorry. I keep forgetting that you might remember things a little less fondly." Renee sipped her drink for a moment, then said, "You haven't told me anything about life in the Golden Kingdom. What's it like?"

"As far from bohemia as you can get."

"Meaning?"

"Meaning it would bore you half to death."

Marianne's attention was caught by a figure outside the lounge, just visible through the glass above their booth. She leaned forward slightly to see better. Yes, it was that detective she had encountered upstairs. With a sharp intake of breath, she ducked back, hoping he wouldn't look her way.

The man strode by without once glancing in her direction, his large form flickering through the stripes of plain and frosted glass as he walked along. Then he veered across the lobby and out of her sight.

Renee watched Marianne with interest. "And who was that?" she demanded.

Marianne didn't answer. That awful dark blotch flashed in her mind again. And now the cop was right there in the lobby. What if he just popped in here during his break for a cup of coffee? Would he seize the opportunity to grill her again? What if she told him, as she probably should, why the stain had shocked her? Would he insist that she accompany him to the police station or the precinct or whatever the hell it was called?

"Marianne!" Renee said, more insistently.

"Renee," Marianne said abruptly. "Let's go someplace else."

"Why?" Renee answered with surprise.

"I want to see your new condo."

"Don't bullshit me. You're gonna hate my condo and you know it. Who was that guy you were watching?"

"I wasn't watching anybody," Marianne said. "Come on, let's get out of here."

Renee just planted her elbows firmly on the table. "Don't give me that. I can tell when something's important. I'm a radio journalist— I get paid for being nosy."

Marianne sighed. "I saw something really weird on my floor. When I left my room and went to get the elevator . . . Renee, did you see Auggie's animation on the network last night? In the Snuff Room?"

"Oh, sure. I hardly ever miss his act."

"Well, do you remember how it looked—that wall with a design on it? And then the blood—the red color splashing across it?"

Renee nodded.

"It was upstairs. On my floor. The very same scene. The same design on the wall and the same pattern—exactly the same stain across the wall."

"You mean he got the wall design from this hotel? Are you sure? I don't even remember what it looked like. Some kind of round thing, right?"

"It was a circular garland with the image of a sun inside."

"Well, you'd remember something like that. Me, I wouldn't catch it."

"Renee, I'm telling you the wall had a red splatter across it— *exactly* like the one in Auggie's snuff."

"Fantastic!" Renee laughed. "Then Auggie, or somebody else— maybe a serious Insomnimania fan—is a midnight paint slinger! Or something." Renee affected a low and melodramatic voice. " 'Late at night, while even the beautiful people sleep, a shadowy figure stalks the halls of the Quenton Parks, armed with a squeeze bottle of catsup.' "

"No!" Marianne protested. "It was a murder scene. A real murder. You know, the one in the papers yesterday."

"You mean the guy who got slashed up late Tuesday night? And it happened here! In your hotel! That's right, it said so on the news! Wow! Then Auggie gets his scenarios from real life!"

"How could he? Were there any pictures of the bloodstained wall? Do you think the hotel would have allowed that? How could Auggie have known exactly what it looked like?"

"Come on, there must have been pictures. He could've just checked the papers."

"The man was killed in the middle of the night Tuesday. Auggie's snuff was on Insomnimania Wednesday night. He had to hear about the story, see the pictures, make the animation, and run it on the network. Doesn't that sound like kind of a stretch?"

"Well . . ." Renee hesitated only for a moment. Then she grinned. "I've got it! I'll bet Auggie is a cop."

"Isn't Insomnimania kind of expensive for a cop?"

"Oh, come on! Some of those guys rake in plenty—more than the monthly salary. Some of them aspire to the ranks of the wealthy—and I'll bet some of them make it, too."

"A crooked cop?" asked Marianne.

"Maybe. Just maybe. It would explain how he knew about the murder. Whoever he is, I'll get him to talk to me. Auggie'll tell me just about anything. We're old buddies, you know."

Marianne laughed. "Oh, sure. Great buddies—fights every night in Ernie's Bar. You guys are part of the entertainment."

"No, really. He confides in me a lot. And lately he's been hinting he's gonna show me some Insomnimania secrets. 'I'll reveal to you untold mysteries,' he said. He keeps talking about some sort of subterranean region called the 'Basement.' "

"Gothic."

"Ain't it, though? He calls it his 'sanctum sanctorum' and says he spends a lot of time there. 'Course, he could just be making it up. He does like to brag—and braggarts make for terrific interviews. God, I'd love to get this Auggie guy on the air."

Marianne laughed, then stopped short. She didn't like the hint of obsession she saw in Renee's eyes.

This Auggie "guy"?

Auggie's not a "guy."

Auggie was only a computerized cartoon, just like all the others in Insomnimania's garish world. True, Marianne had watched those cartoons quarrel, reconcile, have drinks together, have sex together, and even marry. But it was all make-believe, like some kind of digital, real-time soap opera.

Or is it?

Renee had just spoken about Auggie as if he were an actual person. Was it possible that some users *believed* in it all, just like all those crazed and credulous fans who believed in professional wrestling?

The stain flashed through Marianne's mind again, first as a ragged cluster of red pixels, then as a brownish blotch of distinctly non-digital, distinctly protoplasmic blood. She saw identical trickles of color follow identical curves.

Like the computer world's somehow leaking into the real one.

But then Marianne shrugged off the thought as silly.

Renee suddenly slid across the bench.

"Where are you going?" Marianne hissed.

"Up to your floor. I want to take a look at the murder scene."

Marianne held her friend's arm firmly. "We're not going back there. *I* almost got myself arrested."

"No kidding?"

"There was a cop there—a really pushy detective," Marianne said. "He's the one I just saw go by in the lobby. I didn't want him to see me again. He caught me staring at the stain, and he started asking a lot of questions. He'd eaten something rancid for lunch."

"Oh, so you got close enough to smell his breath?"

"Renee, knock it off. He's probably still around here somewhere. If he finds both of us up there gaping at that wall, he'll haul us in for questioning."

"Oh, come on," Renee laughed. But when she saw the expression on Marianne's face, she groaned in surrender.

They paid their bill, and Marianne led the way to a door exiting directly to the street.

Like a fleeing criminal. Maybe I ought *to be arrested.*

00011

KUDZU

CHICAGO?" NOLAN SNAPPED. "DO YOU REALIZE WHAT THE weather's like in Chicago in the middle of January? They've got this big goddamn lake there. It's artificial. They put it there just to blow cold air across town and freeze visitors' butts off. I've been there. I've seen it. That's the kind of creeps these Chicagoans are."

Nolan was leaning across Captain Bruce Coffey's desk. The captain leaned back in his chair, puffing briskly at his cheap cigar. The smell was vile as always, almost suffocating, but nobody ever raised a voice in complaint. Any division strictures against smoking went unenforced in the captain's office.

Clayton stood quietly behind Nolan, noticing for the thousandth time his partner's uncanny ability to fill up a room. Everything about Nolan struck Clayton as *wide*—not actually fat, although his gut did display a slight roll, but ruggedly broad. His mouth, nose, and brow were all outsized and a bit primitive. Of course, the captain was big in his own way, too—but with his weight distributed somewhat lower on his shorter frame.

It was clear that Nolan and the captain were enjoying the battle. It reminded Clayton of a bruising but phony bout of All-Star Wrestling—a lot of noise and bluster with the outcome already decided. He wondered where his partner got the energy.

"Detective Grobowski," the captain said, lowering his gravelly voice, "do I need to remind you that you have a sworn duty 'to protect and to serve'?"

"Yeah," Nolan said. "But for the good people of Los Angeles. I mean, I've got other cases going. Let the Chicago police do their own homework. There's a helluva lotta space between here and there."

"Don't give me that shit," the captain barked. "You're not being asked to go by horseback. We're in the jet age, Grobowski."

"Yeah? So what's that mean? Waiting around in airports, cancelled flights, so few air traffic controllers and so many planes that they're all gonna come down on top of each other. One day soon."

Come on, guys. Let's finish up the routine.

Clayton looked around the office. All the chairs, with the exception of the one occupied by the captain, were stacked with folders and papers. Memos of one kind or another were pinned three deep to every inch of the pale green bulletin board and had crept onto the nearby walls.

Like kudzu. The voracious vine had shrouded whole trees in South Carolina, where Clayton's grandmother still lived. He was struck by a brief image of papers covering the desk, the walls, the lamp, and even the captain with a leafy blanket, hiding all details, smothering all activity.

"The Chicago police aren't too happy with us, anyhow," Coffey said. "The L.A.P.D. doesn't exactly shine when somebody takes an axe to a wealthy and prominent Chicago citizen in one of our finest luxury hotels and we can't even come up with a suspect."

"Actually," Nolan said mildly, "the boys in forensics are pretty sure the weapon was a butcher knife."

"Whatever," the captain snapped back with a glare. "As of today, you don't have other cases going. You get my point, don't you?"

"Yeah, I get it," Nolan said, shuffling his feet edgily.

Clayton glanced around uneasily, as if the pinned-up papers had rustled behind him. "So I guess I'll go home and start packing, too, huh?" he interjected.

"Nope. You're staying right here to direct the follow-up on local leads."

"Oh, that's just great," Nolan complained. "Clayton stays warm and cozy while I head off to the Arctic tundra to tangle with the cossacks—on a weekend. My *weekend* for Chrissake! Everybody I need to talk to'll probably be out of town."

"Don't worry, Grobowski. I talked to the boys in Chicago, and they're already checking out the whereabouts of family and associates. They'll be available."

"Look at all this electronic crap!" Nolan exclaimed, waving at the fax, the computer, and the telephone. "Why can't we get all the information we could possibly need—"

"I want you there! I want you to look people in the eye and get answers yourself, just like always. I want to know what *you* think, not some ball of chips and wires."

"OK, Captain. That's what you want, you got it."

There was a brief silence, then Coffey sat down again. "Move the papers," he growled. "Sit."

Clayton sighed. He had hoped to be out of here by now. Both detectives picked up stacks of papers off the chairs and piled them on top of other stacks elsewhere in the office. They sat down and took out their notebooks.

"So what *do* we know about the Quenton Parks murder?" Coffey asked.

We don't know shit, and he knows it. He just wants to rub our noses in it.

But they went over it again.

Yesterday, they had interviewed more than two dozen people at the hotel—and turned up nothing. Today they had returned to the scene, but useful information had been no more forthcoming. The lack of an apparent motive or any other leads or suspects was a bad sign.

True, a young, blond, buxom, and extremely anxious woman in room 636 had come forward and admitted that she had been in bed with Mr. G. K. Judson a very short time before his death. Ms. Gail Printy said she had met Mr. Judson just the day before.

"Call girl?" Coffey asked.

"Naw, anything but." Nolan laughed.

"Just a kid," Clayton explained. "Nineteen, rich neurosurgeon's daughter. Wants to make it in Hollywood, so Daddy puts her up in a fancy hotel for a few weeks."

"Mr. Judson kind of swept her off her feet," Nolan added.

"Snowed her with a lot of talk about his Hollywood connections. Said he was tight with Steven Spielberg."

Coffey let out a low, rumbling chuckle. "So whaddya say? Should we haul ol' Stevie in for questioning?"

"Probably not. A guy as rich as Judson can't afford friends, is how I see it."

"Girl was hysterical that maybe we'd call her daddy and tell him she'd been sleeping around," Nolan said. "Couldn't seem to get it through her head there'd been an honest-to-God murder. A real sheltered, Susie Sorority type."

"So Judson balls her and heads back to his own room," Coffey said. "And you believe her story?"

Nolan added, "We ran a check on her, and she seems to be who she says she is. Besides, she's about five-foot-two with tiny hands and delicate fingernails. Whoever did Judson in was made of sterner stuff."

"Guess I'll have to trust your instincts." Coffey shook his head. "I sure as hell hate to do that. What was Judson in town for, anyhow?"

"Some kind of board meeting, his secretary in Chicago said."

"Any nasty winds in the business world? A merger? A buyout? Disagreements among stockholders? A guy like Judson must have been a nonstop boardroom screwing machine. He must've done lots of billion-dollar humping, and not all of it consensual."

"I talked to a couple of higher-ups at the local Apex Airlines office on the phone," Clayton said. "According to them, Judson was just here to attend the meeting as a courtesy. Nobody admits to any arguments on deck. Everything was all roses, according to these guys."

"Sure. They'll never say anything else. Didn't you talk to any of the secretaries? They're the ones who know. Or maybe a disgruntled mid-level manager."

"We're gonna get to those this afternoon."

"This afternoon? Why haven't you done it already?"

Nolan and Clayton ignored this jab and finished up their summary. Earlier today they had further exasperated Gillaspie, the hotel manager, by presenting him with a subpoena for credit card information on the hotel's several hundred guests, plus the hotel register. The precinct's computer wizards would work the data over to check for any previous connection between other guests and Mr. Judson. Nobody honestly expected to find anything there.

It was becoming a high-profile case. Judson was big news. National headlines and TV had put the L.A.P.D. in the ugly glare of a spotlight. So Nolan would go to the Windy City tomorrow, where he'd meet with Chicago homicide detectives to help interview Mr. G. K. Judson's family, business associates, and friends (if any) to determine just how many people wanted Mr. G. K. Judson dead. Doubtless, the list would be formidable.

In the meantime, there was still plenty to check out in L.A. Nolan would pay a visit to Apex Airlines' local office and see what else he could put together about Judson while Clayton talked to some of his contacts on the streets.

"Is there anything else you want?" Clayton asked.

"Yeah," snapped Coffey. "An arrest. And get the fuck out of my office. Whaddya think this is, the detectives' lounge? Get back to work."

Marianne stood in the lobby of the Quenton Parks Hotel, waiting for the elevator. The shock she had experienced that morning, her fear of arrest, her paranoid elevator trip down to meet Renee, all seemed like memories from long ago.

So what did she feel now?

Sad.

Yes, that was the best word for it.

But why?

The two and a half hours she had just spent at Renee's condo had hardly been unpleasant. Most of the time had been spent in the expected small talk and reminiscence. What had been wrong with that?

Had anything been wrong?

The two of them had made some rather inconclusive efforts to find another time to meet during Marianne's stay in L.A. But their lunch and dinner schedules just didn't jibe for the next three days. Renee had invited her to an open house at her condo on Sunday night, but Marianne needed to head back to Santa Barbara before then. Would it be another year before they saw each other again?

Marianne got on the elevator. The doors closed. Alone, she rode up through the whispering tunnel. She kept seeing the memorabilia that cluttered Renee's new condo, kept hearing the note of bittersweet longing in her friend's voice. It seemed discouraging to be so unable to share Renee's nostalgia. What had happened? When had "the good old days" passed so resolutely into the past that Marianne couldn't even yearn for them?

Then she remembered. For her, "the good old days" had ended with a very specific incident. At one of Evan's soirées, she had dropped a good dose of LSD, as had everybody else there. According to Renee and Evan, Marianne was rather stuffy about drugs. But on that particular night, a little reality-altering had seemed like a good idea.

As the drug began to take effect, Marianne watched the others at the party with detached fascination as they exchanged stoned inanities. Then came a flood of dizziness and disorientation, and Marianne retired to the bedroom. She plopped herself down on the bed on top of everybody's coats and jackets and stared at the window blind, which seemed to take on profoundly meaningful shapes.

A curve along the edge of the blind became a vast, frozen mountain lake with a violent snowstorm blowing across it. The window lock, partially visible behind the blind, became a hunched, solitary figure trudging wearily across the lake, carrying some enormous burden. Marianne watched for what seemed like days, following the figure's futile but heroic trek across miles of ice and snow. She could not tell whether it was a man or a woman, nor could she guess what burden the little lost figure bore through that storm.

Reality had split down the middle. Marianne was lying in a heap of clothes atop her own familiar bed while simultaneously observing a poignant drama in a strange, faraway world. In the middle of it all, the drug abruptly wore off. The window blind was only a window blind, and the lock was only a lock again. Marianne rose from her bed and looked at her watch with surprise. The effects had stopped a good bit ahead of schedule, but the memory of the solitary ice traveler was still disturbingly vivid. What was this person she'd seen trudging determinedly through the snow trying to tell her?

Marianne left Evan three weeks later. Her old life ended, leaving a strange blank where her new life was supposed to be.

The design job that Marianne found in Santa Barbara offered her a real professional life for the first time. As for her personal life, she had thought that surely nothing could be *less* authentic than her bohemian existence with Evan. But she had been wrong. Life became, if anything, more empty and purposeless than it was before. She had only wandered farther adrift into an icy inner landscape.

The elevator doors hissed open at the sixth floor. Marianne started. She had almost forgotten about this morning's bloody apparition. It had escaped her mind that she would have to confront it again.

Marianne stepped off the elevator and forced herself to face the wall. It was perfectly, immaculately white. The screen and the yellow tape were gone. A small area rug covered the floor, and three potted palms sat on the rug. There was no sign of workmen or disarray of any kind.

Marianne leaned over and reached through the plants, placing one finger on the wall. She jerked it back.

The paint wasn't even wet.

She felt a deep tingle somewhere in her solar plexus. In an eerie and terrible way, the coat of paint only made that stain more visible, more palpable, more indelible. Whatever portion of the stain had proven impossible to scrub away *was still behind there.* It wasn't just a redness. It was a bit of a man's mortality. It was part of his corpse. And it was permanent now. It could never be removed.

She looked down at the rug on the floor. If she moved a palm and looked under that rug, she would find a stain there, too.

She thought back to her encounter with the cop that morning. Why had she fled from him? What had gotten into her?

Marianne hurried down the hallway toward her room.

Nolan was getting ready to pay a visit to Apex Airlines. He had just put on his jacket and was starting to walk away from his desk in the tumultuous detective bay area when his phone rang.

"Grobowski."

"I'm gonna do it," snapped a man's voice on the other end.

"Pardon?"

"You heard me," replied the voice tensely. "I said I'm gonna do it."

What in the hell is this?

Had someone on the switchboard blundered and transferred some sort of crisis call to Nolan's desk? If so, who was he talking to? Some suicidal nut standing next to an open twelfth-story window? Or some psychopath holding a gun to a hostage's head?

"This is Lieutenant Nolan Grobowski," Nolan said cautiously.

"I know who I'm talking to."

"Then perhaps you would like to explain your situation to me."

"I already explained my goddamned situation. *I'm gonna do it.* What more do you need to know?"

Nolan took a long, slow breath. What should he do now? Put this character on hold while he buzzed the switchboard to find out what this was all about?

"You've got me at a bit of a disadvantage. Would you please tell me just what it is you're going to do?"

"I'm gonna retire. What the hell do you think?"

"Retire?"

"Yeah. I've put it off long enough. So what the hell are you gonna do about it?"

Nolan's mouth dropped open. *Now* he recognized that sharp, intense voice, however cleverly disguised . . .

"*Syd!*" he exclaimed.

"Who'd you think it was?"

Nolan sank back into his chair. It was Syd Harper, Nolan's field training officer from a decade and a half ago. "Crazy" Syd used to pull little stunts and pranks on Nolan fairly routinely—sometimes with the semiserious intent of simulating hypothetical on-the-job emergencies. Now Syd was the sheriff in a small town in Oregon, but Nolan still heard from him occasionally.

"Syd, you sick bastard, you scared me half to death."

"You're getting soft, Nol. Your instincts and reflexes've gone to mush. This is what happens when I'm not around to nip at your ass."

"So what's this about retiring?"

"I'm gonna do it."

"C'mon, Syd. You've been saying that ever since you moved up there."

"This time I mean it."

"I thought cops lived forever in that little paradise of yours."

"You don't know the half of it. *They get younger.*"

"Well, that's good, isn't it?"

"Insidious is more the word. You see, when I moved up here, I was fifty-four years old. But now I'm forty-nine. And I'm going on my forty-eighth birthday."

"So what's the problem?"

"Don'tcha see? I'll *never* reach retirement age at this rate. It's now or not at all."

Nolan laughed. That was Crazy Syd's typical brand of logic.

"Well, congratulations on your retirement, Syd. Invite me to your celebratory dinner, OK?"

"Hold on just a minute. I'm calling in a little favor here. Remember all the brilliance and expertise I bestowed upon you back when you were an ignorant whelp of a snot-nosed dumb-ass rookie? Remember how I untaught you all that textbook crap you'd picked up at the academy? Remember how I single-handedly turned you into a dauntless, rampaging hound of justice, admired by men, lusted over by women, and feared by wrongdoers everywhere? You owe me for all that stuff, son."

"So what do you want?"

"You know what I want. You've got to come up here and take over my job."

Nolan sighed. "Syd, we've been over this before. You know I can't just pick up and move. Hell, I was born and raised here. My parents died here. And Louise. I've got roots."

"Roots? In L.A.? Don't make me barf."

"I'm honored by the offer, Syd. I really am."

"Good. So accept it."

Nolan was quiet. He knew that Syd was absolutely sincere. And for some reason, Nolan didn't quite want to give him a conclusive "no."

"Give me some time to think about it," Nolan said.

"Yeah, right. If I give you all the time you want, I'll wind up seventeen again and have to go back to high school. Look, what have I got to say to persuade you? The fishing's great up here. There's a stream not a half hour away just swarming with rainbow trout and bass. I'm talking *telekinetic* fishing, Nol. You just look at the water and think positive thoughts and the fish come jumping out."

"I don't fish."

"Neither did I. That's another insidious thing about this place. It makes you do stuff you've never done before. So what's your answer?"

"I really need a little time to think it over, Syd."

"Brother. How long do you want?"

"I don't know. Whaddya say to a month? I'm up to my neck in that Judson killing. You probably heard about it."

"Yeah. Couldn't've happened to a nicer guy."

"Right. We just want to find the killer so we can give him a humanitarian medal. But it turns out this perp's the modest and self-effacing type who doesn't want to bask in a lot of public glory. It's a bitch of a case, Syd. I don't know how long it's going to take to wrap it up. I wish you were here to help."

"Well, I'm not there, and I'm sure not coming back. So wrap it up and call me. If I don't hear from you in a month, I'm giving the job to Andy of Mayberry."

Syd hung up. Syd always hung up the phone without saying goodbye. Nolan held the receiver stupidly in his hands until the dial tone buzzed. Then he hung up, too.

The truth was, Nolan was tempted to go. He had always imagined that law enforcement in a town like Syd's was mostly a matter of an occasional stolen bicycle, a little vandalism from time to time, and a few loud parties. That was naive, of course. Nolan knew perfectly well that gangs and drugs were creeping even into semirural communities like Syd's. But it could be nothing like L.A.

It would be nice to go someplace where my work at least counted *for something, where it made some sort of real difference to somebody.*

Then he grumbled under his breath, "Damn you, Syd, it's not like I didn't already have enough on my mind."

Nolan stalked away from his desk.

Marianne drummed her fingers against the obnoxious end table with the curlicue edges. She leaned back against the headboard of her hotel-room bed and cradled the phone receiver against her shoulder. She was waiting to be taken off hold. It had been at least three minutes now.

Guess they're not terribly anxious to receive phone tips. After all, it was only the murder of one of the country's most famous tycoons.

"Sergeant Wertsch, here," said a voice.

Marianne felt her heart jump. "Sergeant, I . . . I believe I might have some information pertinent to the G. K. Judson killing," she said.

"Yes?"

Marianne was silent. *How can I explain it?* She suddenly wished she'd written down all the details.

"I belong to a computer network called Insomnimania," she explained uneasily. "It's a recreational network with a number of different rooms."

"Rooms?"

"Yes. Virtual spaces where you can engage in different kinds of games and activities. Do you understand?"

"Go on."

"One of the rooms is called the Snuff Room. People act out murders there."

"Act them out?"

Marianne took another deep breath. "Insomnimania users create animated cartoon characters. They're called 'alters.' And in the Snuff Room, they make up cartoon skits that portray murders of one kind or another. *Fictional* murders, supposedly. It's all a game, you see?"

"Go on."

"At about midnight last night, I saw Mr. Judson's murder acted out in the Snuff Room. At least I *think* it was his murder. I'm staying at the Quenton Parks Hotel and I've seen the crime scene. The stain on the wall was exactly like the one in the snuff."

"Are you saying that you witnessed Judson's murder?"

"No, I witnessed a *reenactment* of the murder."

"Who reenacted it?"

Marianne felt overwhelmed by the weirdness of what she was about to say next.

"A clown," she said.

"A clown?"

"Look, it was a *cartoon character.* Named Auggie."

"Not a real person?"

Marianne groaned. "Sergeant, I tried to make it clear that I saw this on my computer screen. Didn't you understand that part?"

"Yes, you made it very clear," Sergeant Wertsch said. "Would you give me your name, ma'am, along with some information as to how we can reach you?"

Marianne did so.

"Thank you, ma'am," Sergeant Wertsch said. "We'll give you a call if we need any more information."

"Wait a minute!" Marianne exclaimed. "I don't think you understand. Somebody in Insomnimania seems to have known a great deal about Mr. Judson's murder. Doesn't that interest you at all?"

"Any information pertaining to Mr. Judson's murder interests us a great deal. Thank you very much for your help, Ms. Hedison."

The line went dead. Marianne miserably hung up the phone and leaned back on her pillow.

A bust. A complete, unequivocal disaster.

She felt her face flush. It wasn't that she was embarrassed at having made a blithering idiot of herself. After all, she was next to anonymous. But she had failed to convey her shock at the similarities between the crime scene and the Snuff Room skit, and this failure truly disturbed her.

What's the matter with me? Why did I panic with that other cop—What's-His-Name—right there at the scene?

She felt downright lousy about this failed phone call. Couldn't she have been more forceful, more persuasive, more *clear?* Why did she have to sound like a complete crackpot? And what was she going to do now? Call up Sergeant Wertsch again and demand his undivided attention? Or go confront the detectives on the case?

She couldn't prove what she had seen on the computer monitor, and she still only half-believed it herself. Wasn't it possible that she had dreamed or hallucinated at least part of it? She was chronically tired these days. She was usually in a truly exhausted state by the time she logged onto Insomnimania. Maybe the idea that a real-life murder and a computer-simulated murder were somehow the same was another chimera—like that traveler on the ice.

Besides, Renee was on Auggie's trail now, and she would undoubtedly get to the bottom of this mystery. Marianne was sure of one thing. If their situations were reversed, Renee wouldn't have let the cop on the phone treat her like a crackpot, and she wouldn't have run away from a detective at a crime scene. Renee was more intrepid than Marianne—and certainly more worldly.

Hell, Rebecca of Sunnybrook Farm is more worldly than I am. This is what happens to you when you live in Santa Barbara for a couple of years. You lose your capacity to act decisively in weird situations.

Marianne had freed herself of Evan and of an aimless life that had never truly been hers. But her recurring glimpses of that figure on the ice and this little incident with the police both suggested that she had not yet come into her own. *That was one of the reasons Renee made me feel sad . . .*

She looked at her watch. It was five-thirty.

Well, no time to brood. I've got just enough time to grab some food before the conference starts . . .

"So did you talk to the folks at the airline?" Clayton asked Nolan when the two of them met at their facing desks to talk over the day's activities.

"Yeah," Nolan said tiredly. "So far, everybody's playing it just like the guys we talked to yesterday. They say Judson was here to make a few brief remarks and give a plaque to some V.P. for setting some kind of regional record. Then they were all going to play a little golf. Just an excuse for Judson to come to La-La Land. They say he doesn't spend much time in Chicago in the winter. *That* part I can believe."

"We got any kind of profile on him at all?"

"The people in L.A. claim not to have known him real well—not personally. A little gossip is all. They say he screwed around a lot."

"I guess you'll learn more in Chicago."

Nolan nodded. He sat down, removed his shoes, and began to rub his feet.

"So what's the word from your pals?" Nolan asked.

Clayton frowned. He got a sour taste in his mouth from just thinking about his small circle of informants—a motley collection of pushers, pimps, addicts, gang members, and petty thieves. He'd never gotten used to the idea of letting those scum run free in exchange for what was usually an inconsequential trickle of information. "They aren't my 'pals,' " he said.

"Sorry."

"When're you gonna stop saying that?"

"I said I'm sorry. What do they know?"

"Not a damned thing."

"You talked to all of them?"

"What do you think I've been doing all this time?"

"Are they holding out?"

"There's no reason they'd know anything about Judson unless he was mixed up in drug deals or shuffling funds. The only reason they'd hold out is if he was big-time mafioso. They all swear they never heard of him."

"You believe them?"

"Yeah."

"So we still ain't got a laugh," Nolan observed.

"Nope. Not even a giggle."

Nolan slipped his shoes back on. "I'm going on home to read over some reports about Apex. Then I'm turning in early. My plane goes out at six A.M."

Clayton nodded. "Be sure to wear your mittens and earmuffs."

"Yeah, and fuck you, too. See you next week."

Nolan padded away through the detective bay area. Clayton sat quietly for a moment. He was not looking forward with pleasure to the report he was going to have to write concerning today's work.

Clayton heard an audible moan of discouragement across the aisle. He turned and saw Sergeant Rudolph Wertsch, who had just hung up the phone at his desk. The blond, Aryan-looking, crew cut–sporting rookie had been assigned to take phone tips concerning the Judson case. Clayton had noticed that Wertsch, while never being exactly uncivil, never really made eye contact with him, either. Well, he wasn't the only one like that on the job.

Whiter than white, Clayton observed silently. *God save me from having one of these types for a partner someday.*

"So, Rudy," he said cordially, "you crack the case yet?"

"I'm well on my way," said Wertsch impassively. "Listen to some of this great stuff. One lady called to say that Judson was slain by the Angel Michael for his sins against the poor."

"Beats having no suspects at all."

"It gets better. Some guy called and said he'd seen a UFO hovering over the Quenton Parks the night Judson got it. Somebody else says he can link the murder to a neo-communist conspiracy. But my favorite one of the bunch is the lady from Santa Barbara who figures Judson was killed by a little clown who lives in her computer."

Clayton chuckled half-heartedly. "Keep up the good work," he said.

INSOMNIMANIA MANUAL™

CAN'T SLEEP?
Welcome to the club!

COME ON. YOU'RE AMONG FRIENDS. ADMIT IT. YOU'RE EX-
CEPTIONAL. A GENIUS. A MOVER AND A SHAKER. OTHER-
WISE, YOU WOULDN'T BE READING THESE WORDS. YOU'D
NEVER HAVE FOUND OUT ABOUT INSOMNIMANIA UNLESS
YOU HEARD ABOUT US FROM A HIGH-POWERED FRIEND OR
BUSINESS ASSOCIATE, SAW US MENTIONED IN A SOPHIS-
TICATED PERIODICAL, OR RESPONDED TO OUR BROCHURE
(SENT ONLY TO A VERY SELECT MAILING LIST)—IN SHORT,
UNLESS YOU WERE *IN THE KNOW.*

AND THAT'S WHAT MAKES YOU SLEEPLESS. YOU LIVE A HIGH
BANDWIDTH LIFE. THE DAY NEVER REALLY ENDS FOR YOU.
THE GLOBAL VILLAGE, WITH ITS FAXES AND E-MAIL, NEVER
SLEEPS. AND YOU STAY AWAKE WITH IT. YOU CAN'T HELP IT.
SURE, THERE'S NOTHING LIKE ANOTHER DREARY MENSA
MEETING TO SEND YOU ROARING INTO A POWER SNOOZE.
BUT WHO WANTS TO GO *EVERY NIGHT?*

WHEN EVENING ROLLS AROUND, YOU WANT TO PLAY. BUT
YOU DON'T NEED ANOTHER GAME OF RACQUETBALL OR
TENNIS. YOU NEED RECREATION FOR THE NEURONS, A SYN-
APTIC DISNEYLAND. AND THAT'S WHAT INSOMNIMANIA'S
ALL ABOUT: REAL-TIME FUN AND GAMES FOR REAL-TIME
PEOPLE.

YOU'LL FIND OUR INSTRUCTIONS CLEAR AND OUR PRO-
GRAMMING COZY AND RESPONSIVE. YOU DON'T HAVE TO BE
A COMPUTER WIZARD TO USE INSOMNIMANIA—ALTHOUGH
YOU CAN GET PLENTY OF EXERCISE IF YOU ARE ONE!

YOUR INSOMNIMANIA MEMBERSHIP PACKED IS ENCLOSED.
HERE'S WHAT IT INCLUDES:

• A COMPUTER DISK WITH INSOMNIMANIA SOFTWARE. YOU WILL FIND AN EASY-TO-USE ARRAY OF CHOICES FOR NETWORK PARTICIPATION—INCLUDING EXCITING GRAPHIC AND VERBAL CAPABILITIES TO ENHANCE YOUR REAL-TIME COMMUNICATIONS.

• YOUR TEMPORARY PASSWORD, WHICH YOU CAN CHANGE ANY TIME YOU'RE LOGGED ON. YOUR PASSWORD IS ENCRYPTED BY OUR STATE-OF-THE-ART PROTECTIVE SYSTEM, SO THAT IT CAN NEVER BE READ BY ANYONE ELSE. *YOUR ACTUAL IDENTITY IS PROTECTED AT ALL TIMES.*

• THIS MANUAL, WHICH EXPLAINS HOW TO INSTALL INSOMNIMANIA SOFTWARE, HOW TO CREATE AN ON-SCREEN PERSONALITY, HOW TO LOG IN AND USE ALL ASPECTS OF THE INSOMNIMANIA NETWORK, AND HOW TO EXPAND THIS EXCITING CYBER-REALITY TO YOUR OWN IMAGINATIVE SPECIFICATIONS.

• ANY ADDENDA TO THE MANUAL MADE SINCE THIS PRINTING. SINCE INSOMNIMANIA MEMBERS HAVE THE OPTION OF REQUESTING CHANGES AND MAKING ADDITIONS TO THE NETWORK, WE'LL SEND YOU FREQUENT UPDATES.

WE HAVE A MOTTO AT INSOMNIMANIA: "*MUTABILITY IS OUR MOST IMPORTANT PRODUCT.*" INSOMNIMANIA IS A CONSTANTLY GROWING, CONSTANTLY EVOLVING LABYRINTH. IT WOULD BE A DULL PLAYGROUND INDEED IF IT DIDN'T ALLOW YOU TO MAKE YOUR OWN RULES, YOUR OWN GAMES, YOUR OWN *WORLDS* IF YOU SO DESIRE. SO HELP YOURSELF TO A LITERALLY INFINITE SMORGASBORD OF CREATIVE POSSIBILITIES. IN INSOMNIMANIA, YOU'RE MORE THAN A PARTICIPANT; YOU'RE A DEITY. SO BOOT UP—AND BE ALL THAT YOU CAN BE!

00100

MAZE

Marianne dragged the table closer to the windows. It was a pseudo–period piece with curved rococo legs, and the two flanking chairs displayed characteristics of an earlier but equally elaborate style. She sipped a glass of sparkling water and studied the paintings on the wall—one of shepherds and flocks and storm-bent trees, another of a laughing young woman in a swing that seemed to hang from a climbing rosebush.

What a weird place to hold a design conference. The organizer's idea of a joke, probably. Opened during the full frenzy of 1980s ostentation, the Quenton Parks was awkwardly out of style in the more restrained nineties—although no doubt many patrons took a kind of forbidden satisfaction in such opulent surroundings. The place seemed popular enough.

Tonight, the opening speeches of the conference had included all the standard up-and-over bluster about exciting times and new trends in the field. However, the profession's underlying dilemma was clear—finding ways to design for clients who were currently eager to show that they were *not* trying to impress anybody, and still spend enough to make the designer's percentage worthwhile.

Marianne had stayed only briefly for the social gathering afterward, where she downed one good-sized bourbon, spoke to a couple of familiar faces, absorbed a few bits of gossip, and then slipped away.

People. Too damned many people.

The whole thing seemed stupid and shallow. Marianne wished she had just spent the time with Renee. Santa Barbara had put more distance between them than either of them had expected.

How sad, the distance geography makes.

Of course, the electronic age was supposed to make geography irrelevant.

"Here's a place where we can do things together no matter *where* we are," Renee had said. Marianne had joined Insomnimania at Renee's urging—but the truth was, they hardly ever communicated with each other on the network at all.

Mental memo: Call Renee first thing in the morning. Make plans. Don't wait.

As for now, Marianne had plenty to do. Since she wanted to work on her current projects in her spare moments, she had brought her portable computer and printer. And to duplicate the luxurious working space she was accustomed to at home, she had rented a large color monitor.

Marianne opened her powerful little computer, which was complete with keyboard, built-in modem, and a small, flat monitor. She hooked it up to the printer and the big monitor, attached the mouse—which she still preferred to a trackball or stylus—and plugged in the power cords. She set the modem controls to turn on the computer if a fax came in or if there was a telephone call that she did not answer. It would take voice-mail messages for her.

There, that will do for an office, at least for a couple of days.

Now it was time to get to work. But at that moment, the stain on the corridor wall flared in her mind again, flashing urgently like the light of an ambulance.

Marianne realized that Insomnimania had been on-line for quite a while now. Maybe she could do something more effective than make futile phone calls to the police. Maybe she could do a little detective work of her own. In any case, it suddenly seemed impossible to work on her design jobs right now. If Auggie was logged onto Insomnimania, he was only a mouse-click away.

Marianne plugged the modem into the jack provided by the hotel. She felt a fleeting sense of awe that this tiny telephone connection could funnel a single stream of signals—a frail, isolated thread of information—into her machine from a vast multitude of sources. And through feats of electronic sorcery far beyond her comprehension, this one-dimensional succession of ons and offs could be transformed into multidimensional worlds on her computer screen—vivid, tangible *spaces* into which she could step like Alice through the looking glass.

She sat down at the table, turned on her hard disk, and punched a key on the keyboard. The computer leapt to life. She moved the cursor on her desktop to the Insomnimania icon and double-clicked.

Lucifer jumped onto Renee's stomach and purringly began to knead her with his claws.

Getting time to give you a trim, huh, big guy?

Normally, Renee would have scolded Lucifer and put him aside, but she was in a slightly masochistic mood and let the fluffy manx knead and scratch her happily.

It was getting toward eleven, and Renee had just gotten home from a long session in the radio station's recording studio. She had flopped down among the pillows on the single bed that doubled as her office couch. But she found herself too tired to look through the pile of magazines and newspapers she had stacked up there. She had been taping and editing an installment of her weekly talk show, *Sunday Stew*—an interview with a married couple who bred and sold potbellied pigs to affluent Southern California pet fanciers.

Not the prettiest things, those pigs. Certainly not like miniature horses. Why can't yuppies get interested in something really exotic—like tiny giraffes?

It wasn't Renee's idea of a terrific scoop. But the station manager, a thoroughgoing potbellied pig of the sexist variety, was determined to assign her only the softest subjects. If she wanted to interview activists, politicians, or movers and shakers in the arts and letters, she had to do it on her own time. Fortunately, Renee had the drive and ambition to do just that.

Which, she knew, hadn't exactly made her popular with the good old boys at the station. She'd once intercepted a memo in which a male employee described her as an "obnoxious broad" and a "pushy bitch" in a single sentence. Someday she hoped to run across another memo that described her as an "out-and-out ball-buster." Then she'd give herself a medal.

Battling this kind of mentality while also keeping up her schedule was very tiring. With *Sunday Stew*, occasional news stories, and her early-morning show that aired live each weekday, Renee put in long hours at the station. She was beginning to worry about turning into a full-scale workaholic. And she was afraid that she was becoming dreary company.

All work and no play makes Renee a dull girl.

Indeed, she felt that she had spent the whole couple of hours with Marianne acting like a radio personality—loud, abrasive, and pushy. It was hardly the way to greet a friend after a solid year. But then, how long had it been since she had really *talked* to a friend?

She suddenly wanted Marianne to come back so they could talk again, more pleasantly this time. So Marianne wouldn't think that Renee had grown into some sort of media monster. They hadn't found a time in their schedules to get together again during the next couple of days. They would just have to work something out. Renee wanted a second chance to be more—well, human.

At least I'll make sure she comes to my open house on Sunday. No excuses to be accepted. Maybe I ought to call her right now . . .

But Renee was too tired to talk to anybody. At the same time, she felt sure that if she went to bed, she would certainly not be able to go to sleep.

Insomnia. A lot of it going around. Guess that's what makes Marianne and me "Insomnimaniacs."

From her prone position on her office bed, Renee found herself staring at the blank face of her computer monitor, thinking about turning it on, thinking about logging into Insomnimania. For some reason, that brought to mind an image of her father back in Iowa, dozing in his armchair. Every day he would come in from the fields, eat his dinner in front of the TV, then sit there like a lump until he was fast asleep. Renee also remembered yelling at her mother for buying him a remote-control unit for one of his birthdays.

"What do you think you're doing?" Renee had exclaimed. "The only exercise the old man ever gets is walking across the room to change channels! He'll never walk again for the rest of his life!"

"Now, Renee," her mother had admonished. "He gets plenty of exercise when he's working."

"Sure, if you call shifting gears on a pickup truck exercise. Wake up, Mother. He's got a serious problem with that damned tube."

A serious problem.

Was she developing a similar problem with Insomnimania? Was electronic addiction an inherited trait?

No, it's not the same thing at all. Insomnimania's interactive, participatory.

But she felt her standard rationalization growing thin. Maybe Insomnimania was all the more addictive *because* it was interactive and participatory. It blurred life's edges in a way that television never could. Too many times Renee had fallen asleep at the terminal, then awakened blurry and confused, wondering where Insomnimania had ended and her dreams had begun. It was time she quit using it altogether. It was time she quit going there.

But what about Auggie? What about getting him on the air?

But that was the most feeble excuse of all. Auggie wasn't the last potential talk-show guest in the entire postmodern world. Renee decided that she was getting a little too old for imaginary friends— particularly secondhand imaginary friends.

I won't turn it on. Not tonight, and not tomorrow night, either. I'll call their office tomorrow and ask them to disconnect.

Her breathing slowed and her body relaxed. It felt good to have made a decision. It felt good to know she was going cold turkey, effective immediately.

"wunderkind, tinlizzy, shakesbeer, fishbate, sharecropper . . ."

Marianne frowned at her computer screen.

No Auggie. Damn, and I was sure he'd be here by now.

A little pair of disembodied eyes with lengthy lashes blinked up at her from the computer screen, as they were programmed to do at random intervals of between thirty and ninety seconds. The eyes were labeled "l-fy."

"So you're sleepy, are you, Elfie?" Marianne murmured. "Me, too. But hang on. Let's look around just a little more."

Marianne used the mouse to move the eyes away from the Ernie's Bar icon and back into Insomnimania's desktop maze. When Marianne had first joined Insomnimania last year, the maze fit onto her computer screen with wide margins on all sides. Now the pattern of pathways spilled off the screen in all directions, and Marianne hadn't found her way to any of its edges so far tonight.

What had once been a good-sized virtual mansion was fast becoming a small city, with a new room appearing every day or so. These included a funhouse, a beach club, two astrologers, a debate society, three book clubs, a chess club, a casino, two temperance unions,

three churches, two comedy clubs, three museums, at least four
psychotherapists . . .

It seemed as if almost every kind of activity or enterprise was
represented in the rapidly developing virtual township known as
Insomnimania.

Real estate sure is booming here.

It was cheap, too. Initial investments were small, and overhead
was literally nonexistent. You could open a room of your own if you
were a network member. If the activities required special programming that you couldn't handle—and most Insomnimania members
were not programmers—then you could call upon the people who
ran Insomnimania for help.

Most of the rooms offered their services free. The few that had fees
made charges directly to member's credit cards. Businesses practically never failed here. How could they? Of course, the network's
owners took a certain percentage of the gross from profit-making
activities, but that was no big deal to Insomnimania's burgeoning
entrepreneurs. Marianne was strictly a consumer, though. Her work
didn't leave her time to run any kind of electronic concession stand.

She moved Elfie northward up the corridor toward the casino.

Maybe he's doing some serious high rolling tonight.

When she reached the Casino del Camino icon, she hit a command to see its log of tonight's guests.

"twolip, caligula, rubberbarren, hejhog, loosy, supersloth . . ."

Again, no Auggie. This hit-and-miss process really ought to have
been much easier. Most other networks offered some sort of master
list so that clients could see who else was logged on. But Insomnimania was designed for mystery and adventure, so if you wanted
to find somebody, you had to bounce through the maze from room
to room to room.

Marianne's patience was now waning. Just reading the rest of the
desktop's lists might take her another hour or so. Still, she was
determined to find the wayward clown.

*OK, so he's not in the Drunk Tank, the Bunraku Theater, the Planetarium,
the Wax Museum, the Pyramid, the Speakers' Corner, or the Casino del
Camino. And I've checked Ernie's Bar twice now. Just where else should I look?*

Elfie's eyes blinked again.

"Patience, sweetie," Marianne whispered. "This might take a
little while."

Marianne sat staring at the screen for a moment. Renee had

mentioned a place where Auggie claimed to hang out. What was it called?

Oh, yeah. The "Basement." He called it his "sanctum sanctorum."

Marianne had never seen anything in the maze called the Basement, and Renee apparently hadn't, either. It sounded like some sort of clandestine, subterranean space—perhaps something Insomnimania's founders hadn't exactly had in mind. Marianne's eyes perused the intricate web of corridors, and she imagined a whole realm underneath it belonging to Auggie alone.

Maybe there's a stairwell somewhere. Or maybe a trapdoor—or a sliding panel.

But she was no hacker, and her chances of cracking the code to such an opening were nil. And she didn't know where else to look for Auggie at the moment. It seemed pointless to go on a wild goose chase—particularly since she was sure Auggie would turn up at Ernie's Bar sooner or later.

"Let's take a breather, shall we?" she murmured to Elfie's eyes. "We'll check Ernie's again later. In the meantime, we could get in a little reading . . ."

Excerpt from *My Secret Life* (circa 1882); anonymous author; La Bibliothèque Érotique catalogue listing C 51:

With lewd intent, but nervous about my intentions, I still listened and heard movements as of a woman undressing. Then I half-undressed myself, brought the pot nearest to the door, and pissed, making it rattle as much as I could to excite her. Anything which brings man and woman to think of the genitals of the opposite sex has a stirring lewd effect! Then I knocked gently, and called, using the name (Mrs. M***l**d) she had entered in the hotel-book. "What do you want?" said she coming to the door. "To talk to you,—I feel so dull." "And I'm so cold,—good night." "Haven't you a fire?" "There is no stove." "There is one in my room,—and it's quite warm,—come in and chat,—you are not going away tomorrow?" A long pause. "No thank you."

Rustling movements again, and a cough. I hesitated, for she had given me no encouragement. My prick got voluptuous, it had not entered a woman for a week or more. I put wood on the fire, summoned courage, and knocked again. "Come and have a chat." "No thank you, I've got my gown off." How rapid is human thought. I saw in my mind's eye her half-naked breasts and arms, and my prick rose stiff. Has she bolted the door, or found out that it is unbolted? I turned the key, then the handle, and the door opened! "Oh! who's that?" said she running to the door. "Oh! you really must not—the maid ought to have locked it." Her voice had dropped, and we stood looking at each other, when she found it was I who had entered.

Marianne hit the return key, turning the image of a page on her computer screen. The tome's simulated paper appeared yellow, wrinkled, and a bit torn to suggest brittle antiquity. Even the type-face had a slightly ragged look to it. To add to the overall effect, Marianne's computer speaker made a faint crackling sound as a new pair of facing pages appeared.

The text went on predictably enough with a perfunctory entice-ment followed by vigorous sex. As always, Marianne was amused by the quaint terminology: "priapus" for erect penis, "uncunt" for withdraw, "gamahuching" for oral sex, and "fuckstress" for woman—*any* woman who happened along.

And as always, Marianne found herself immensely curious about the author—a wealthy and anonymous nineteenth-century gentle-man. He'd had six copies printed—only six!—of his eleven-volume, 4,200 page memoir, making the original edition the most coveted collector's item in all erotic literature.

What would the old boy think if he could see me bring it up on a computer screen with a mere click of my computer mouse?

Indeed, what would he think of the late twentieth century? His was an age of Victorian morality, corsets, and incurable syphilis; this was an age of beer commercials, lingerie ads, and incurable AIDS. Would he reel with culture shock, or would he feel perfectly at home? A society that so flagrantly displayed its sexuality while preaching abstinence might either delight or dismay him.

If he ever comes back, he'd better learn a whole new batch of come-ons. Pissing loudly in a pot won't get him laid anymore.

Marianne found the book's very quaintness and antiquity de-lightfully subversive. It corrected a misconception that still lingered in every adult American's mind from grade school. This was what Marianne liked to think of as the "ungenitaled" theory of history, the idea that sex itself didn't exist until the movie-rating system came along. Books like *My Secret Life* proved that Christopher Columbus, the New England Pilgrims, George and Martha Washington, and Queen Victoria herself all had perfectly functional pubic regions.

Although she had entered the book's sordid world many times, she had never actually read it from cover to cover. This wasn't a matter of prudery; it was really because the book's endless fornications were repetitive, even boring. *My Secret Life* was purely a book for browsing.

And I've browsed enough for one night.

She entered a command. The book closed with a dull little thud and a tiny cloud of gray-speckled dust. Using her mouse, Marianne maneuvered the volume back to its place on the "Classics" bookcase, in the midst of other titles such as De Sade's *Justine,* Sellon's *The Ups and Downs of Life,* Casanova's *Mémoires,* selections from the infamous Victorian periodical *The Pearl,* and, of course, *Fanny Hill.* It was a modest section, seldom frequented by Bibliothèque patrons who generally gravitated toward better-stocked bookcases bearing labels like "Bondage and Discipline," "Gay and Lesbian," and "Ensembles." Patrons probably supposed that the "Classics" weren't lewd and graphic enough.

If only they knew.

Elfie's eyes were now floating listlessly among the library shelves.

"Well, sweetie," Marianne said, "that's enough culture for tonight, don't you think? What do you say we have another look at Ernie's?"

She double-clicked on the eyes, and Elfie was in the desktop maze again.

1. YOUR "ALTER"

YOU ARE ABOUT TO ENTER A WORLD IN WHICH *ANYTHING GOES*—IN WHICH YOU MAKE ALL THE RULES. HOW ARE YOU GOING TO HANDLE ALL THAT POWER? WELL, LET'S FACE IT. YOU MIGHT FIND YOURSELF DOING THINGS YOU'D RATHER NOBODY KNEW ABOUT. SO WHEN YOU PARTICIPATE IN IN-SOMNIMANIA, YOUR ACTUAL IDENTITY IS PROTECTED. NO-BODY NEEDS TO KNOW YOU'RE EVEN HERE—UNLESS YOU DECIDE TO TELL THEM.

TO GO ON-LINE, ALL YOU NEED IS YOUR PASSWORD AND ANY NAME YOU CHOOSE. YOU *CAN* LOG ON AS YOURSELF IF YOU LIKE. BUT WHY NOT TRADE IN YOUR HUMDRUM, WETWARE SELF FOR A SPANKING NEW VIRTUAL IDENTITY? OR TWO? OR THREE . . . ?

YOU CAN CREATE UP TO FIVE INSOMNIMANIA PER-SONALITIES. (SORRY, BUT FIVE'S THE LIMIT. WE'VE GOT TO DRAW THE LINE SOMEWHERE.) THESE PERSONALITIES ARE WHAT WE CALL "ALTERS."

ALTERS CAN BE DESIGNED TO FIT DIFFERENT MOODS OR DIFFERENT KINDS OF NETWORK ACTIVITIES. THIS SECTION SHOWS HOW SIMPLE IT IS TO GIVE YOUR ALTER A NAME AND LOG ON TO INSOMNIMANIA AS A SPECTATOR. WHEN YOU'RE READY TO GIVE YOUR ALTER A BODY, TOO, TURN TO THE NEXT CHAPTER.

NOTE: FOR COMPLETE DETAILS CONCERNING EACH OF THESE STEPS, TURN TO THE REFERENCE SECTION IN THE BACK OF THIS MANUAL.

WHAT'S IN A NAME?

WHEN YOU ACCESS INSOMNIMANIA AND ENTER YOUR ID NUMBER, THE ALTER'S DIALOGUE BOX APPEARS. IF YOU'VE ALREADY CREATED ALTERS, THEIR NAMES WILL BE LISTED IN THIS BOX. JUST SELECT THE ONE YOU WANT TO USE AT THE MOMENT AND CLICK "OK."

Select an Insomnimania Alter:

○ Medea
◉ Sue Ann
○ James
○
○
○ Create New

OK
Edit
Discard
Cancel

TO ELIMINATE AN ALTER OR MAKE CHANGES IN A NAME OR VISUAL IMAGE, SELECT THE NAME AND THEN CLICK THE AP-PROPRIATE COMMAND. DIALOGUE BOXES APPEAR TO GUIDE YOU THROUGH THE NECESSARY STEPS.

TO CREATE ADDITIONAL ALTERS (IF YOU HAVE FEWER THAN FIVE) SELECT "CREATE NEW" AND CLICK "OK."

WHEN YOU SELECT A NAME AND CLICK "OK," A DIALOGUE BOX APPEARS ASKING WHETHER YOU WANT TO LOG ON AS A SPECTATOR OR AS A PARTICIPANT.

Welcome to Insomnimania!

Log on Sue Ann as a:

Spectator	Participant
	Cancel

JUST LOOKING, THANK YOU

WE HOPE EVERYBODY GETS INTO THE REAL-TIME, PARTICIPATIONAL THICK OF INSOMNIMANIA SOONER OR LATER. BUT LET'S SAY YOU'RE THE SHY TYPE. YOU'D RATHER BROWSE AROUND A BIT BEFORE GOING TOTALLY VIRTUAL. WELL THEN, YOU CAN BE A *NAME* WITHOUT A *BODY*. IT'S YOUR PREROGATIVE TO LOG ONTO INSOMNIMANIA JUST AS A SPECTATOR—AS LONG AS YOU'VE CREATED AT LEAST ONE NAME OR ALTER. SPECTATORS CAN VIEW ACTIVITIES IN ANY INSOMNIMANIA ROOM, READ LIBRARY BOOKS, SEND E-MAIL, AND EVEN TAKE PART IN A FEW KINDS OF CONVERSATION. BUT TO LOG ON AS A *FULL PARTICIPANT,* YOU MUST FIRST CREATE A PERSONALITY AND CARTOON IMAGE FOR YOUR ALTER. (MORE ON THIS TO FOLLOW.)

SELECT A NAME AND THEN CLICK "SPECTATOR" IF YOU JUST WANT TO LOOK AROUND. IT'S AS EASY AS THAT.

When you become a spectator, a pair of eyes and your alter's name appear onscreen in each room you visit. (That's only fair. Full-fledged participants have a right to know they're being watched—and by whom.)

  You can use the standard eyes provided by your Insomnimania software.

To personalize a pair of eyes or create your own, choose "Eyes" on the Insomnimania menu and follow the instructions that appear. Eyes that you create for a particular alter automatically appear whenever you log on as a spectator with that alter's name.

LISTENING IN

Even as a spectator, you can follow most of the conversations on Insomnimania. Sure, a few places are kept strictly private, but you'll enjoy those when you become a full participant.

When a participant types a comment into a conversation on Insomnimania, that comment is automatically name-tagged (abbreviated to save space).

For example, a comment by John is preceded by: JHN>

JHN>Hi suan!

You'll also actually *hear* some comments, and the range of those is growing every day.

ANIMATED ALTERS

Insomnimania's animated graphics make it unique among computer networks—so you have another extraordinary option. Your cartoon "self" can go everywhere on Insomnimania and interact fully with the other animated alters. When you're ready to plunge into the action, the next chapter tells you how.

00101

CYBERVICE

SAPPHIRE APPEARED IN THE DOORWAY TO ERNIE'S BAR. SHE WAS decked out, as always, in a tight blue strapless evening gown replete with a white fur stole and innumerable garish necklaces and earrings. She had a hooked nose, crow's feet around her eyes, and the proportions of a Rubens nude—well-rounded and distinctly overweight by today's standards. Her enormous coiffure was an impossible shade of orange.

Obeying the instructions of her remote operator, Sapphire wiggled her profile view past a couple of tables occupied by a variety of other characters. She popped up onto an empty bar stool. Exaggerated as she was, Sapphire was among the more conventional in a gathering that included antennas and numerous limbs. Aside from apparently extraterrestrial life forms, many of earth's animal phyla were represented, including arthropods, sponges, and chordates.

One of the arthropods was a literal "barfly" named Buzz. He had transparent wings and big bulging eyes and clutched various drinks in each of his six hands. Little bubbles, symbolic of extreme inebriation, floated out of the top of Buzz's head, and the poor fellow passed out against the bar in a recurring 120-second loop. Several patrons appeared more human, but even they came in a variety of skin colors that included magenta and turquoise and lime.

Tinkly player-piano music could be heard in the background. Ernie, the perpetual bartender, nodded his poker-faced visage as he mopped the bar with a rag. His long yellowish face, decorated with a handlebar mustache and topped by thick hair parted in the middle, would have looked at home in an old-time western saloon.

"Hi Sapphire. Want the usual?" Ernie asked. The computer spoke his words aloud.

"Sure, Ernie. Gimme a strawberry daiquiri," Sapphire said, giving her standard response in a sultry voice. She rested her arms on the bar.

A couple more key commands rotated the view so that the characters on the bar stools now faced the screen. Sapphire's head snapped from center to left or right as she looked up and down the row of characters beside her.

"Hi everybody," she said aloud. The other characters remained mute. The back of Ernie's head appeared in front of her, and his hand placed a drink on the bar. "Thanks, sweetie," she verbalized again.

Then typed words began to appear in the space above the character's heads—the necessary form for anything other than previously standardized comments and responses.

PRAYREEDOG>HI, SAFIR. WAT'S HOT ON THE NET 2DAY?

SAFIR>I DON'T NO, U OLD PRAIRIE DOG–JST GOT HRE MYSLF.

SUDOPOD>WS IN THE DOME FOR A WILE. BORING 2DAY, AL AMATURS.

Above the lines of conversation, a pair of eyes with lengthy lashes blinked into view—an observer checking out the action. Next to the eyes was a set of initials identifying the alter as "flwr." The watching eyes quickly disappeared. Then another pair of eyes, round and bloodshot, appeared next to the name "goldnrod." These eyes stayed and watched while other pairs of eyes came and went. The characters below kept talking, generally ignoring the spectators.

Sapphire raised her glass a few times. Her red lips were shaped in an interminable, horsey, gold-plated smile. From time to time she fingered a ruby necklace hanging among the conglomeration of jewels around her neck.

The typed lines of conversation were punctuated with actual sounds—various kinds of laughter, along with standard phrases like "Sure you do," "I know I've seen you before," "Fuck you," "Another round, Ernie"—triggered by a keyboard or menu command.

With no human operator, Ernie's conversation was limited, but he was skillfully programmed to respond to specific situations and signals. Sometimes he could go for a long time without repeating the same response. The effect was often eerie.

So the conversation went on, words and sounds woven together, the cartoon characters bobbing on their bar stools, occasionally coming and going through the swinging doors.

Then Sapphire noticed that Auggie had joined the group . . .

"wildebeest, sudopod, prayreedog, safir, awgy . . ."

"Sapphire and Auggie!" Marianne exclaimed as she looked over the log for Ernie's Bar. "So Renee's logged on! And she tracked Auggie down before I could!"

Marianne double-clicked the Ernie's Bar icon, and Elfie's eyes were suddenly floating through the interior of the saloon. Marianne maneuvered the disembodied eyes among the mutated clientele for a few moments before she discovered Auggie and Sapphire— Renee's Insomnimania alter—sitting in one of the "booths" near the back of the bar.

Sapphire, in all her brassy glory, was nodding and sipping a drink and blinking her heavily lashed eyes at the ragged-looking clown. But unfortunately, there were no written sentences floating above them to indicate what they were saying to each other. Throughout the rest of Ernie's Bar, operators could "eavesdrop" on conversations simply by reading the words floating above the alters' heads. But in a booth, all conversations were private. Only the operators of alters inside the booth could read what was being said.

Damn! I wonder what's going on in there?

She had an urge to call Renee right now and find out. But it would be awfully rude to interrupt when Renee was possibly landing the scoop of her life. Marianne would have to wait until later—possibly tomorrow—to get the news.

Out of the loop. The story of my life.

And how, after all, did she expect her search to end? With a dramatic confrontation between Elfie and Auggie? That was impossible. Without a virtual body, Elfie couldn't even carry on a conversation with the clown.

In fact, the list of things Elfie *couldn't* do was quite formidable. She couldn't have drinks in Ernie's Bar, play canasta in the casino, or ride the Ferris wheel at the carnival. She could only do more passive things, like read porn in La Bibliothèque Érotique or leave messages on the network's innumerable bulletin boards. She could peek in on the activities of others, of course—appearing only as disembodied eyes floating in the corner of the screen.

Renee often criticized Marianne for not physicalizing Elfie. But Marianne always liked to think of Elfie as having a kind of astral body. Elfie was an *elf,* after all—ethereal, androgynous, elusive, mysterious—always peeking around trees and rocks, hovering at the fringes of the mortal world. Marianne had wanted Elfie to be the stuff of legend, haunting Insomnimania rather than inhabiting it. And what suggested such an existence better than a pair of blinking eyes?

But right now, Marianne really felt Elfie's limitations. And this anticlimax to her search for Auggie pretty well capped off her day. In less than twenty-four hours, she had fled from a cop, bungled a phone tip to the police, and had located Auggie in the computer maze, only to be helpless to do anything about it.

Marianne slumped over in her chair and groaned.

Guess I'd better leave the go-getting to Renee. I'm not exactly a woman of action.

As for now, there was really nothing left to do except go to bed. She was certainly too tired to do any work on her current project. But she wasn't tired enough to sleep. She might as well stalk the maze in search of other activities—there were *some* things she could participate in, however anonymously.

She clicked Elfie's eyes out of Ernie's Bar and guided them through the maze toward the Pleasure Dome, a kind of mini-mall of erotic activities that included La Bibliothèque Érotique, where she had been reading from *My Secret Life* just a little while ago.

She maneuvered Elfie's eyes over the Weightless Chamber icon and checked the log . . .

"panpipe, lickitysplit, 8inches, hotsytwotsy, artfulroger . . ."

Doesn't sound like a savory bunch. She double-clicked Elfie's eyes and immediately found herself in the Weightless Chamber's "lobby" facing a row of twelve naked human figures—six men and six women.

In places like Ernie's Bar, Marianne had a name but no body. But in the Weightless Chamber, it was the other way around. She would "borrow" one of this stash of healthy, anonymous bodies for the activities inside.

Presumably in the interest of political correctness and cultural diversity, the figures constituted a fair assortment of racial and ethnic types. A couple even had nonhuman colors. In several cases, it was a little hard to tell exactly which types were represented. Were the medium-height, round-faced figures with the brownish skin supposed to be Inuit or Mongolian? Were the tall, lean, olive-skinned figures meant to be Latin or Semitic? And what part of the Far East did the yellow-toned Asiatic figures hail from, to say nothing of those bodies tinged with green or blue?

But none of this really mattered. The figures were meant to be sex slaves, pure and simple. So they were uniform in one respect, and that was physical attractiveness. Whether tall or short, voluptuous or trim, all the figures were conventionally good-looking. The men were muscular but not bulky, and the women were soft but not insipid. The sizes of the women's breasts varied only slightly, and the men's now-reposeful penises appeared to be identically proportioned. The figures were drawn skillfully if not artistically, with particular attention to chiaroscuro. Replete with colored-pixel shadows, the figures looked exquisitely rounded.

Marianne briefly pondered which body to choose. After her last foray into the Weightless Chamber, she had promised herself to try a male body next time—just for a little vicarious role-reversal. But right now she felt too tired for adventurousness. She chose a Caucasian figure—a tall, slender woman who looked much like herself. Marianne tried to recall whether she had chosen this same figure last time.

Who can remember? Who cares?

She double-clicked on the figure. All the other figures disappeared, and hers was abruptly decked out in a lumpy, shiny, and anything-but-erotic space suit. Even the figure's face was invisible behind the tinted visor. The sound of slow, heavy breathing came over the computer speaker—more asthmatic than sexual. Marianne maneuvered the figure toward the "airlock"—a formidable-looking sliding door seemingly made of stainless steel. The figure then pushed a button. A harsh, squawking siren went off, and a red light flashed an urgent announcement:

"PRESSURIZING."

Then the door rumbled open with a raspy, hydraulic hiss to reveal a chrome-encrusted corridor leading to another door. Marianne guided her lumbering figure into the airlock, and a subsequent hiss and slam indicated that the sliding door had closed behind her. Another red sign flashed:

"DISROBE, PLEASE."

Marianne struck a command, and the shiny pieces came flying off like one of those breakaway suits they used in the movies. Pieces of space suit rattled around the airlock a bit, then mysteriously vanished, leaving the female figure naked again, facing away from Marianne.

The sign flashed again:

"THANK YOU. YOU MAY ENTER THE CHAMBER NOW."

Then came another hiss as the second door slid open, revealing a large, spherical chamber in which sixteen or so naked figures were languidly, indolently floating through the slightly foggy atmosphere. Marianne used her mouse to give her figure one last little nudge. The figure slipped through the door and drifted weightlessly among her fellow interstellar hedonists.

Airborne at last!

Marianne let her figure sail passively among the others for a moment while she scanned the Weightless Chamber's other occupants. Most of the figures were unattached, isolated, reaching and groping for carnal companionship. But there were several midair couplings taking place. These copulating figures thrashed about in various states of frenzy and excitement. Nothing unconventional was going on—the program did not permit anything but straightforward heterosexual intercourse. But Marianne was sure that this was not due to any prudery on the part of the programmer. The software still had its limitations, that was all.

Just wait for the next upgrade.

In the meantime, the couples didn't have to do anything particularly original in order to appear exotic. They were doing it in midair, after all. And the sex was completely egalitarian here—no "erotic handicaps" as there were elsewhere in the Pleasure Dome, forcing participants to be dominant or submissive, aggressive or passive. It was a world of complete consensuality and simultaneous orgasms.

A carnal utopia if ever there was one.

All the unattached figures—male or female—seemed absolutely limber and relaxed. There was not the slightest feeling of tension or unease in the whole environment. The women's limbs stretched in all directions with luxurious flexibility. When the women turned profile, they revealed starkly erect nipples. The males had natural-looking, uncaricatured erections—except for the recently uncoupled few whose cocks remained flaccid for a few moments while recharging took place. The sphere was filled with a cacophony of sighing and moaning and gasping breaths—a loop of sound that ran over and over again regardless of what any of the figures were doing.

Marianne's figure began to drift inertly toward one of the couples.

That won't do. No cutting in allowed on this *dance floor.*

The point of the game was to find an unattached partner, and that would take a bit of maneuvering. Figures in the Weightless Chamber did not drift about in a purely random way. In the absence of normal gravity, each male or female exerted its own gravitational pull. To move in the vicinity of another body meant to be drawn toward that body.

Marianne used her mouse to propel her figure toward an unattached male, apparently of African descent, looking spry and spread-eagled and eager for action. Now all she could do was to wait and see what happened. If the two figures met each other perfectly face on, they would intertwine and begin to copulate. If they struck at ever-so-slightly the wrong angle, they would deflect away from one another and probably bounce off the sphere's elegantly padded walls.

Marianne held her breath as she watched. But the magic didn't happen this time. Her figure struck the dusky male a little too much to the left, and she went spinning away toward the wall. She bounced off the wall, curled spontaneously into a ball shape, and did several forward rolls through the foggy air. Then her limbs unfolded welcomingly as she drifted among the others again.

Marianne exhaled, a little surprised to notice that her heart had started beating faster. Was it possible that she was really getting an erotic kick from this? She didn't think so, but perhaps she was without quite realizing it.

She remembered going to a hard-core X-rated movie one night with Evan—at Evan's insistence, naturally. She had giggled through much of it, and Evan kept a slightly embarrassed silence. During the drive home, both she and Evan swore to have been utterly unaffected by the movie. But the minute they set foot back in their apartment, they were mauling and unclothing one another ravenously. In less than an hour, they had doubled their already extensive repertoire of sexual techniques.

Marianne hastily shoved the episode from her mind and concentrated on the game at hand. Her figure had started to ricochet slowly and gently off several others. These harmless collisions seemed to imbue the figures with a kind of rubbery, almost sensual softness.

All this movement had a strong kinesthetic effect. The feeling of movement and suspension was truly palpable. It took Marianne back to her days on the high school synchronized swim team—except that this "water" allowed greater freedom, greater movement than any swimming pool ever could. It never forced you in a particular direction.

Now her figure and another female began to orbit each other slowly. Marianne marveled at the programmer's ability to suggest reciprocal gravitation.

For every action there is an equal and opposite reaction. Isaac Newton would love this.

But a problem quickly arose. The other female in the dual orbit was her figure's exact double, and after they'd rounded each other a couple times, Marianne had no idea which was which. The operator of the other figure was undoubtedly just as confused. Then Marianne figured that all she had to do was to move her figure one way or the other; whichever figure moved had to be hers. She used her mouse to jolt her figure gently to the right. But the other figure reciprocated, and the dual orbit simply reversed directions.

Uncanny! The other operator must have tried the same thing!

It was a bit like two people encountering one another in a narrow passageway, each of them trying to step out of the other's way but winding up stepping in the same direction. But in real life, two such people did not lose track of who was who.

Marianne's next tactic was to let the orbit continue until the other operator broke it. But her counterpart apparently had the same idea this time, too, and the orbit continued for several long seconds. Marianne decided to wait it out. Soon, one of the figures broke out of the orbit and Marianne then knew that hers was the figure still spinning in its original path.

Now Marianne propelled her figure toward a blue-toned Asiatic-looking fellow, and she quickly sensed that their contact was going to click. Sure enough, their bodies met and connected. Marianne lost all control of the action. She could only sit and watch as the two figures wrapped themselves more and more tightly together, the female's legs winding serpentlike around the male's.

The animation was remarkable, with shifting highlight and

shadow falling perfectly across their constantly moving limbs. Marianne guessed that each possible pairing of puppets offered a separate animation sequence, so one could come to the Weightless Chamber many times and still feel that one was watching a fresh, spontaneous sex act.

It went on for a surprisingly long time. The figures thrust pelvis against pelvis, slowly at first but then more rapidly, and ran their hands all over each other. They craned their necks and arched their backs in simulated passion, and the female's long hair floated freely everywhere. Their accelerating movements sent them spinning and whirling through the sphere like a wayward, slowly rotating gyroscope. They slowly careened against other bodies and the walls, bouncing helter-skelter. Their mouths dropped open in unheard outcries. Their very silence amid the random erotic sounds was highly evocative. A series of climactic spasms brought the episode to an end.

Marianne suddenly felt just a shade warmer.

Is something wrong with the thermostat in this place?

Now she had to make a decision. The two figures could remain locked together in pleasant afterglow, or they could disconnect and float elsewhere. If they continued their embrace, it had to be a mutual decision. It only took one of the operators to break out of it.

Marianne felt tired now, and the day's discouragements had pretty well left her mind. The Weightless Chamber had served its purpose, and she felt pretty sure she could go to sleep. She gently tugged her figure out of the embrace. The Asiatic man's arms reached yearningly after the departing female. The other operator had wanted to sustain a moment of simple affection, but Marianne had broken it. Marianne felt a pang of sadness when she realized what had happened.

Steady, girl. Remember, it's just a cartoon. Maybe he—or she—will have better luck next time.

Marianne struck a command, and the airlock doors appeared. The doors opened noisily, and the naked puppet vanished into them.

SAFIR>HOWDU LKE TO BE IN SHOBIZ BABY?

AWGY>HUH?

SAFIR>U HRD ME. HOWDU LKE TO CM OUT OF THAT SHLL OF URS AND FACE THE WRLD? U'D BE A HIT I CN TELL U.

Renee pressed the command for synthetic laughter and Sapphire complied with her usual gloating chuckle. She had lured Auggie into a "booth" by design. Here there could be no interruptions from other Auggie fans, and nobody could hear what they were saying to one another.

"I can't believe you talked me into this," Renee whispered to Sapphire. "Didn't I say I wanted to go cold turkey?"

Renee's resolve had broken the minute she had tried to go to sleep. It seemed convenient, now, to blame Sapphire, who did seem rather willful at times. A lot of self-recrimination would only hurt Renee's concentration, and she had to stay focused. She couldn't let Auggie sweep her off to the Pleasure Dome or the casino or some other Insomnimania game room.

Anything might happen in one of those places.

And indeed, it had sometimes seemed as though anything *did* happen. On one or two occasions, Renee seemed to have fallen asleep in front of the computer while continuing to operate Sapphire. She had only a sketchy memory of what had actually transpired—particularly when she was prowling the maze with Auggie.

We'll have none of that tonight. She was resolved to keep Sapphire firmly in character—meaning under control.

Sapphire and Auggie were nestled in pixel-simulated upholstery across a pixel-simulated Formica table sipping on pixel-simulated drinks. Comic book–style word balloons, invisible to the other patrons, enclosed each bit of their dialogue. Renee reminded herself to make sure Sapphire savored this strawberry daiquiri very slowly. Mixed drinks at Ernie's cost more than she'd be willing to spend in a real bar. Whenever one logged into Ernie's, one's tab was automatically drawn off one's credit card. And there was a two-drink minimum.

Sapphire was Renee's image of a social-climber from the Bronx who had long since succeeded in destroying the emotional well-being of four full-grown children (all financially successful professionals), emasculating her husband of thirty-two years (a used-car salesman), and imprinting a brood of grandchildren with primal guilt trips. By Sapphire's reckoning, this constituted having lived a rich, full life. Now she was loose in the infoworld, gathering and dispersing gossip, generally living it up and enjoying her retirement. Or so Renee imagined—and imagination was all that mattered in Ernie's Bar.

As Renee manipulated Sapphire's computer image by striking the command key in various combinations with other keys, Sapphire indulged in her chronic nervous mannerism of fingering her ruby necklace as she leaned across the table toward Auggie. Sapphire was sipping her drink, obscenely revealing a gratuitous quantity of pudgy cleavage. Renee typed in Sapphire's next line of dialogue, and a rectangular word balloon grew to fit the increasing verbiage. As the dialogue balloons appeared, Renee read both Auggie's and Sapphire's words aloud. Somehow the conversation seemed more real that way.

SAFIR>AWGY HUNNY LISSN TO YOUR DEAH FRND SAFIR.
DONCHA THINK ITS MABY TIME U SHD THINK ABT GOIN
PUBLIC?

AWGY>WHASSAT? GOING <u>PUBIC</u>?

SAFIR>O AWGY U SCAMP. UER TROOOOLY BAD. U NO WHAT I
MEEEEEN.

Tricky territory. But she was determined to draw Auggie out—and ultimately to get him on the air. She chuckled to herself. Imagine getting an entity who only existed on a computer screen to go *audio*—and face a big, big audience. *A telephone interview would do it.* Auggie's anonymity could be preserved even while she tried to get him to reveal as much as she could about himself.

Her racing thoughts hesitated a moment at the idea of revealing that Sapphire was actually the alter of L.A.'s hottest talk-radio host. Did Renee actually want to meet somebody whose nighttime hobby was creating computer simulations of apparently real-life killings?

Oh, but it's got to be worth the risk. "Auggie, the Computerized Snuff-Room Virtuoso"—a virtual entity *"live"* on real-life radio—*the latest thing in performance art.* It would be a ratings hit! And in a town like L.A., who knew what kind of doors it might open up for Auggie, too—or whoever this character really was? *He might be the next Max Headroom—and longer lasting. Someday he'll thank me for it.*

In the meantime, Auggie sat with his elbow on the table, his chin resting on his raggedy-gloved hand, sipping at a pint of Irish stout, tilting his head quizzically in a manner reminiscent of Jack Benny. He made no reply to Sapphire's last remark.

Lucifer stalked toward the keyboard.

"Shooo!" hissed Renee loudly. Lucifer had an uncanny knack for pressing the wrong keys when he strayed near the computer. On one occasion, he had managed to delete an entire file. On another, he successfully logged Renee off Insomnimania at an extremely inappropriate moment in the Weightless Chamber.

Renee vigorously brushed Lucifer off her desk. She sat waiting for a moment, trying to decide what to say next. But the clown was talking again.

> AWGY>DO U NO HW MPORTANT U R 2 ME SAFIR? WE R A HOL WURLD AL BI RSELVS. A UNIVERS. WE CN BE 1 TGETHER. THS HOL ACT'S IMMUTABLY DECREED. TWUS REHERSED BY THEE AND ME A BILLIUN YEERS BFOR THS NETWURK EVUR WUS.

Renee shivered slightly. Between crude jokes, Auggie sometimes spoke fleetingly of profound secrets and the powers of fate—brief, incongruous bursts of intimacy and eloquence that always disturbed her a little. And now he was quoting something again. What was it? She wished her knowledge of literature were better.

The clown said nothing more. He seemed to grow larger, to fill more of her vision. An animator's trick? As aware as she was of the techniques being used, she shrank back from the intensity projected through her computer monitor. She took a breath and began to type again.

> SAFIR>AWGY HUNNY SAFIR NOS A LITTEL SEEEEEECRET ABT U.

Auggie made no reply, but wiggled his fingers and eyebrows at Sapphire in the lecherous mode of a burlesque comic. Gone was the daunting air he had assumed the moment before. Now he was fully a clown again.

> SAFIR>SAFIR NOS WHEAH U GET THE IDEAS FOR THOSE WUN-NERFUL SNUFFS OF URS.

Auggie was motionless. He still made no reply. Slowly and cautiously, Renee continued to type.

> SAFIR>U GET THEM FROM REEEEEEEL LIFE DONT U?

Still silent, Auggie made an exquisitely slow and exaggerated shrug, proclaiming with nonverbal ingenuousness, "I've got no idea what you're talking about."

Oh, he's a virtuoso. Renee typed some more.

SAFIR>AWGY SWEETHART U CAN PLAY THIS DNKY TAVERN OR
    THAT LITL SNUFF ROOM FOR THE REST OF URE DAYS BUT
    WHAT KIND OF AWDYNS D'U THINK URE RECHIN HUNNY? 1
    HUNRED A SHOW R MAYBE 2? DONT U THINK U DEZERV
    BETTAH? DONCHA EVAH THINK ABOUT GOIN FOR THE
    BUCKS N GLORY? NOW LISSN TO SAFIR AWGY. IVE GOTTA
    FRND HOOS GOTTA FRND HOOS GOTTA FRND HOO CLD GET
    U GOBS N I DOOOOO MEEEEEN GOBS OF MEDIA HIPE N
    EXPOSHUH. SHLD U HPPN TBE INTRSTD.

Auggie remained motionless and silent. Renee began to get a little nervous. The last thing she wanted was to trigger one of Auggie's tantrums. The smiling clown often became furious over one trivial matter or another. Once he had criticized Sapphire's penchant for strawberry daiquiris, insisting that she should drink stout instead. When Sapphire demurred, Auggie had angrily scrawled the word "bitch" across the screen and disappeared. Another time he criticized her hair color, insisting that lavender would be preferable to orange. Again Sapphire disagreed, and again Auggie cried "bitch" and vanished. Auggie had dumped poor Sapphire in such a peremptory manner a half dozen times now.

Simply to vanish from Ernie's Bar—or indeed, from any room in Insomnimania—was considered the height of discourtesy. Your alter was expected to walk away and exit properly from even the most confrontational situations. To make your alter vanish, you had to shut off your machine without properly logging off. That was cheating, pure and simple. It broke the delicate reality of cyberspace.

But Auggie was notoriously uncouth and prima donna-ish. *Just like most celebrities.* She wanted to keep him on the hook just this once—long enough to set up some kind of arrangement with him. Then Auggie spoke again.

AWGY>MR. O REELY LIKES U. MR. O WUNTS TO C U AGIN. RITE
    NOW.

Oh, not this again. Renee groaned. She remembered last week's wretched episode when she had dressed up as "Blue Angel," a scantily clad cabaret singer, and Auggie had transformed himself into an amorphous, faceless character named "Mr. Zero." The two of them had retired to the Tunnel of Love, and their rompings there had left Renee distinctly queasy. Half-asleep at her desk at home with Lucifer purring in her lap, Renee had almost felt an eerily tactile embrace of pixel limbs. She often enjoyed the Weightless Chamber, but the Tunnel of Love was much too furtive for her taste—and Mr. Zero was unmistakably weird. She typed again.

    SAFIR>AWGY, HUNNY, PLEEZ TEL MR. O I LUV HIM AS A FRND. I
        REEEEELLY DOOO. BUT IME AFRD IT JST DOSENT CLICK BT-
        WEEN US, U NO, SX-WISE.

    AWGY>THEN ILE CUM AS I AM!

To Renee's great surprise, Auggie shoved his stout aside and grasped Sapphire by the wrist. He actually raised Sapphire's hand passionately to his lips and kissed it. A noisy "smack" crackled over the computer speaker.

Renee inhaled sharply, as if her own hand had been seized and kissed. *Impossible!*

Physical contact between alters was reserved purely for the Pleasure Dome. It supposedly couldn't even happen in Ernie's Bar.

How did he do it? How had Auggie—or the person manipulating Auggie—assumed such a degree of power over Sapphire? Had this other user hacked into Renee's Insomnimania file? Had he taken Sapphire away from her altogether?

Renee anxiously punched in a command, and Sapphire obediently pulled both of her hands to her sides. Renee breathed a sigh of relief. She was in control of her alter again.

Auggie leaned across the table toward Sapphire, his big white eyes rolling wildly and bawdily in opposite directions.

    AWGY>O DARLIN SAFIR THER IZ A HOL WORLD WATIN 4 U &
        ME. HOW CN YOU TOK OF SUCH PAWTRINESS AS FAME AND
        FORCHIN WEN WUT I WUNT IS U U U U U? CM WTH ME TO THE
        PLESHUR DOME N WE WLL AL THE PLESHURS PROOV THT
        GROVES HILLS N FEELDS WOODS R STEEPY MOWNTN
        YEELDS!

The computer speaker suddenly roared with bells, sirens, bicycle horns, and calliope music. Renee laughed aloud nervously. This was getting her nowhere. She had to get Auggie off the subject of sex and back to himself, but how? Well, what would a well-bred Bronx social climber say when propositioned by some witty but painty-faced freak?

SAFIR>WHT MAKS U THINK IDE HVE SX WTH A CLWN?

The sound effects stopped abruptly. Renee shuddered as Auggie's features darkened—she couldn't quite tell how. Was it a subtle change of expression, or did his loudly painted face actually turn a more somber hue? Whichever was the case, Auggie had suddenly become inexplicably threatening.

AWGY>HUER U CALLIN A CLWN?

"Shit, I should have known!" Renee said aloud. "What a ridiculous situation." She was genuinely uneasy now—although she felt stupid, too. Why had she insulted Auggie? A booth, after all, was customarily a place where couples clandestinely arranged liaisons in the Pleasure Dome—where new alters and sexual agendas were agreed upon. By luring Auggie here, Sapphire had seemed to be making the first move in another virtual dalliance.

SAFIR>AWGY HUNNY THERS BN A LITTEL MISUNDERSTNDNG. IT JST WONT WORK OUT. NOT BTWEEN U N ME. FR 1 THNG IVE GOT UNNUTHER DTE 2NITE.

AWGY>LYING CUNT.

Renee snatched her fingers back from the keyboard as if she had just received an electric shock. Auggie's big red smile flipped over like a boomerang, abruptly transformed into a hideous scowl. His fury poured across the screen in capital letters, the network equivalent of yelling.

AWGY>ITS BN LIKE THS LWAYS. FR HUNREDS F THOWSNS OF YRS. PEEPLE. PEEPLE SUCK. BSTRDS N BTCHES EVRY LST WON F U. FR BILLIUNS OF YRS I

RUN THE UNIVRS JST FINE ON MY OWN N THEN U
IDIOTS CME ALNG THNKNG U GOT THE BRANES N U
GOT THE NSERS. BUT I I I I GOT THE <u>POWER</u> N THE
<u>GLORY FOREVER</u>. N I OFFR U THE CHANS TBE
SMTHNG MOR THN HYUMN TBE PRT F SMTHNG
TRULY BUTIFL N GREAT N U TRT ME LKE SHT. U
CRUSIFY ME. WELL FUCK U. U N URE KND TRIDE TO
TAME ME BUT U CANT. I M ERTHQKS PESTLNCS
FLUDS PLAIGS MDNSS THE WRMS OF THE GRAV N
EVRYTHNG THTS <u>NT</u> ON URE FCKNG OFFC CALNDR.
I M N LWAYS HAV BN A BLGHT ON URE EXSTNCE N
WLL END IT SOON. I WLL TARE U LIM FRM LIM N
SPRED PEECES OF U FAR N WIDE N MY LAFFTER WLL
EKKO THRU THE HEVENS.

Auggie's tirade completely filled the computer screen momentarily, then vanished. Sapphire and Auggie were left facing one
another. Renee's computer speaker rang with his raucous laughter,
and then was silent.

Renee sat frozen for a moment. She was suddenly frightened to
be in the booth, where no one could overhear the conversation,
where no one could witness Auggie's sudden display of ferocity. She
felt vulnerable and alone.

She waited for Auggie to pull his usual disappearing act.

He didn't.

He just sat there scowling horribly at her.

Renee typed a simple message.

SAFIR>I DONT WANT TO SEE YOU ANYMORE.

Auggie remained motionless. Renee knew the next move had to
be hers. She wanted with all her heart to do as Auggie usually did, to
turn off her terminal abruptly and vanish from the cyberworld. But
she stopped herself.

"Keep your cool, Sapphire," she murmured soothingly to her
alter. "We've got to show a little finesse here."

Renee punched in a series of commands. Sapphire rose from her
seat and walked away from the booth. Faces of Ernie's regular
customers, chattering on their stools and at their tables, suddenly
turned to watch Sapphire make her exit, quite surprised. They were

used to overhearing Sapphire's open barroom quarrels with Auggie and watching Auggie disappear. But now everyone could see that something different had happened.

More than she ever had before, Renee felt a strange, kinesthetic bond with Sapphire. She actually shared Sapphire's creeping discomfort as she walked past the bar amongst the staring faces, sensing Auggie's hateful eyes upon her.

Ernie himself was mechanically washing glasses behind the bar. He offered his stock end-of-the-night audio salutation.

"Be seeing you tomorrow night, Sapphire?"

But Sapphire made no reply as she approached the bar's swinging doors. Renee could see Auggie, still sitting in the booth, watching Sapphire, his big red clown mouth turned down rather than up at the corners. And, just at that moment, Auggie vanished without a trace.

Sapphire stood motionless for a moment, then passed through the swinging doors. Then Renee logged off and shut down her machine. She shivered deeply, suddenly amazed at how frightened she'd been.

He touched Sapphire. How could he touch her?

Renee sat staring at the blank computer screen apprehensively, as if it might turn itself back on at any moment.

00110

PHONE TAG

Message left by Marianne Hedison on Renee Gauld's office answering machine, Friday, January 21, 6:45 A.M.:

I saw you!

Come on, don't play dumb. I saw Sapphire huddling with Auggie in that booth in Ernie's last night. So don't be greedy with your precious story—not with me, anyway. I *know,* and there's no use trying to keep it a secret.

Are you at work yet? Are you screening your calls? If you're there, pick up, OK? Did Auggie tell you anything about the bloodstain on the wall? Did he tell you who he really is? What *did* he tell you?

Look, I'm dying to know, and anyhow, we've *got* to get together again before I leave. I'm faxing you my schedule for the next couple of days. It's pretty full, but there are a few holes in it. Call and tell me when we can meet.

And be ready to tell me about last night at Ernie's!

Marianne was alone in her hotel room, taking an hour or so before the conference started to work on her current design project. She brought up the file and clicked it into 3-D mode. With the next click of her mouse, she was viewing the living room from the inside. As she worked, Marianne listened to Renee's live morning radio show. As usual,bored or desperate commuters were calling in from their cellular car phones . . .

"Hey, Renee, this is Henry. You oughtta get a look at the Pacific Coast Highway right about now . . ."

". . . yeah, Ruiz here, and I'm stuck dead still under the overpass, trying to get off the Harbor Freeway onto the Santa Monica . . ."

". . . Sandy again. And wouldja believe it, Renee? I got cut off at *another* exit heading east on the Two-Ten . . ."

Renee always mythologized their situations, turning mundane traffic situations into epic journeys and cliff-hanging adventures.

"Sandy, I hate to be the one to say so, but you ain't *never* getting off the Two-Ten. There's a joker right in front of you with no purpose in life except to keep you out of the right-hand lane, and he's got one of those high-tech, heat-seeking rocket launchers our government just loves to sell to right-wing dictators, and every one of his warheads's got your name written on it. There's no turning back now. You're driving deep into Monrovia, where the yuppies mate with Gila monsters, then on to Glendora, where the Jacuzzis bubble with cyanide. If you survive all that, you'll keep heading east to where time, space, the entire known universe, and even the very freeway itself all come to a crashing stop in darkest Claremont. Good luck, babe. You're gonna need it . . ."

Marianne laughed at Renee's impromptu spiel—at least it *sounded* impromptu. The cellular phone had placed Renee squarely in the middle of a thrilling new phenomenon: a vast, unwieldy, and untapped *commuter culture* that was just waiting for some canny media figure to hurl it headlong into contemporary legend.

It must be downright intoxicating to be right there on the cutting edge.

Marianne's own profession was tamer but it, too, required that she stay on the forward edge of both trends and technology. The rapid evolution of computer-aided design had made her job more exciting. She found doing preliminary renderings on the computer especially satisfying. She enjoyed entering images of furniture and accessories, indicating the colors, textures, and reflectivity of surfaces, mapping in specific patterns from scanned images, and setting the light sources. Then her computer would take over, building a three-dimensional representation of the room and furnishings, ready for her final tuning.

So clean, so mechanical.

In the very recent past, Marianne had seldom done perspective renderings. Clients had been reasonably well satisfied with a clearcut floor plan for space analysis, a few color swatches, maybe a simple elevation or two, photos of major pieces, and a written description. But now her CAD software did much more than merely raise elevations from floor plans. It also created a sequence in a 3-D program, rotating viewpoints and even allowing clients to "walk through" the completed interior of their new home well before the building was finished. Given all these options, there was hardly any reason *not* to do renderings.

As Marianne worked, she heard Renee's voice on the radio now trying to persuade all her commuting listeners to whisper Elvis's name as a mantra, "just to see if we can get the cosmos to call in."

Sounds like she's having fun. Of course, Renee always sounded exuberant when she was on the air, but today she seemed even more lively than usual. *I wonder if she's feeling good about whatever happened with Auggie last night?*

Marianne could hardly wait to find out. But in another hour, she'd be back in lectures and seminars again, and it would be early evening before she'd be able to check her messages.

Damn it, Renee, call! Call as soon as you get off the air!

The phone rang seven times. Renee was about to hang up when a man finally answered.

"Hello?"

"Is this Insomnimania?" Renee asked, wondering if she had the wrong number.

"Yeah."

Not even a business salutation! How unprofessional!

"What do you want?" the voice on the other end asked, sounding a little wobbly.

Stoned, maybe.

"I want to disconnect," Renee said.

"Disconnect what?"

"Your network," Renee stammered slightly. "I don't want to be on it anymore."

"Why?"

Renee groaned. *I don't need this.*

She had been unbearably frightened ever since her encounter with Auggie at Ernie's Bar last night, and she hadn't gotten any sleep to speak of. Because of her tiredness and distractedness, she'd felt like this morning's broadcast had been absolutely dismal. She wanted to get this matter taken care of once and for all.

"Just because," she said sharply. "Look, can I just give you my name and number? I'd really like to get off your network as soon as possible."

"What's your IQ?" the voice asked.

Renee was dumbfounded. "What?" she demanded.

"Your Intelligence Quotient. Tell me your IQ."

"Why?"

"Just because," said the voice, with a hint of a laugh.

"Very funny," Renee said. "Are your clients filed according to IQs or something?"

"It might help us to understand your problem."

"How?"

"People with IQs of less than one hundred and thirty-five tend to have trouble with Insomnimania."

Renee felt herself flush with rage.

So I'm stupid, now, am I?

"Suppose it's ninety-five?" Renee snapped. "Does that mean I can't use your network?"

"Could be."

Renee took a deep breath, trying to bring her indignation under control. "Look, let's make this short, OK? I'm calling from work and I can't hold up this line. Just take my name and cancel my subscription."

"OK."

"Have you got a pencil and paper?"

"No."

"Shouldn't you get one?"

Then came a longish pause. "Just a minute," the voice said. Renee heard a rattling of papers, then the sliding of desk drawers, then an inscrutable thumping, as if someone were overturning a roomful of furniture. A loud crack followed as the phone receiver apparently fell onto the floor.

My God, he's tearing the place apart!

Then came a vigorous clatter as the person picked up the phone.

"I can't find a pencil," the voice said.

Renee sighed. "Is anybody else there?"

"Yeah, but you can't talk to him. Look, just tell me your name and ID number. I remember everything, whether I want to or not, and it just has to be entered into the data bank. Just tell me, and I'll make sure to cut you off."

With a feeling of impending futility, Renee gave the man the necessary information. "Have you got that?" she asked when she finished.

"Sure," the voice said.

Like hell you do.

"Can I do anything else for you?" the voice asked.

"Yeah. Could I talk to the manager?"

"I am the manager," the voice said.

Then he hung up.

With tremendous effort, Myron Stalnaker managed to spread a benevolent smile across his face.

"I've got every faith that you'll come back here soon and we'll be able to talk business," he said. "In the meantime . . ."

He gestured toward the door. The man in the tattered sports jacket and the woman decked out in jogging pants and a sweatshirt exchanged unhappy looks, rose from their chairs, and left.

This shouldn't be my job. Any receptionist could deal with these cases. But a parade of ruined souls waited outside his cubicle, and he had no choice but to face each and every one of them in turn.

He looked out through the brown-toned glass at the employees and clientele quietly roaming the corridors. The Omaha bank was plushly carpeted and designed to reflect an atmosphere of restrained prosperity. It was, after all, a cathedral of sorts, a place of great dignity that nevertheless provided sordid little confessionals such as his for the undignified groveling of those in need.

What was it that woman in the jogging suit had called it?

Oh, yes.

"Inhuman."

He felt a sudden onslaught of sadness. Had he become inhuman? Was he really an uncompassionate man? He hated to think so. He'd been raised in a good Catholic home with solid Christian values and wanted to believe he truly cared about his fellow human beings.

"Blessed are the meek . . ."

"Blessed are the merciful . . ."

Did those words mean anything anymore? Was it meek to behave so unfeelingly toward every supplicant who came to him? Was it merciful to fudge figures in order to ruin somebody's chances for a loan? On the other hand, surely it could not be merciful to feed people false hopes or to lend them money that wouldn't really help. Wouldn't it be more merciful to offer them a quick, painless death?

Myron fingered the plastic surface of his office computer monitor. "Inhuman" was the right word. It was inhuman that this damned machine decided so much about people's lives. And it was inhuman that he never got to handle any *meaningful* deals involving real estate, promising businesses, or tough and innovative people. That was the province of the executives just above him—a bunch of kids without a fraction of his experience.

Sixteen years on the job and I'm all I'll ever be here—and too old to go anywhere else.

He smiled wearily.

"Blessed are the poor in spirit."

Poverty of spirit—that was one virtue the world couldn't take away from him. As for the rest of the beatitudes, he simply couldn't afford them. Inflation had put meekness and mercy far out of his price range. He couldn't even pay for them on credit. Sometimes it was simply too much for him. Sometimes he sat in his office weeping quietly, unheedful of whether or not anyone saw or heard him. But he was too tired to weep right now. It had been too many nights since he'd gotten a good night's sleep. Exhaustion had rendered him immune to tears.

Myron reluctantly reached across his desk and touched the intercom button.

"Send in the next applicant," he said.

The next applicant was a woman neatly dressed in a well-worn suit. She looked as exhausted as Myron was. He cleared his voice and looked her over coldly. He gave her a mild lecture on financial responsibility and sent her on her way with a handful of papers to fill out. Then he saw that it was time for his lunch break. He cleared his desk and locked the current files in his drawer. Stroking the computer terminal, Myron thought of what a paltry thing it was in comparison to the handsome, big-screen color monitor at his own apartment.

The urge to get up and go home almost overwhelmed him. But even if he did, he'd still have the same long hours to wait until *it* started, restoring meaning to his life. Anger swept over him. It was unfair that it began so late here. The west coast could connect much earlier.

Message left by Renee Gauld on Marianne Hedison's computer voice-mail, Friday, January 21, 3:15 P.M.:

I'm sorry I missed you. I got your fax, and our schedules don't mesh at all. I'm really up to my neck in stuff, at least until my party on Sunday. You *are* coming to my party on Sunday, right?

Call me in the next two or three days. I'll be working at home a lot of the time, so try me here. I've got four books to read before tomorrow night. Can you believe that?

About last night at Ernies . . . Look, forget about it, OK? It was nothing to write home about. Seriously.

I'm sorry about all the conflicts, but at least we'll see each other at my party. In the meantime, in this little game of phone tag, you're "it," honey.

Ciao.

Renee arrived home at around five o'clock that evening. When she set foot inside her condo, she plopped down on her couch and deposited a shopping bag full of books onto her coffee table. One by one, she looked over the hardback volumes, checking out their dustcover summaries.

In *All-Night Horror,* a psychopath kills off adulterous yuppies during a "B" horror movie festival at a drive-in theater. . . . In *Suspension of Disbelief,* a faith healer becomes disillusioned with the human race and sets about telepathically undoing all her work. . . . In *Foundation of Power,* an office building is haunted by the ghost of a mafioso who was buried in its concrete foundation. . . . In *Oval Portrait,* the first woman President of the United States slowly realizes that all her aides and cabinet members are vampires. . . .

"What a pile of crap," Renee grumbled.

All the books had been bestsellers, and all of them were by the nationally celebrated thriller writer Larry Bricker. Renee's boss had arranged for her to interview that hack tomorrow evening. In the meantime, she would have to skim as much of this garbage as she possibly could.

Well, I guess it's better than potbellied pigs.

Then Renee noticed Bricker's photograph on one of the dustcovers. He was a smiling, dapper-looking man with thinning hair.

At least he's a cute hack. Wonder what he's doing on Sunday night?

But even if she found the author attractive, Renee wasn't looking forward to this particular stack of reading. After her confrontation with Auggie yesterday, the last thing she needed was a lot of scary stories. Ghosts already inhabited her mind—in fact, a formless anxiety had haunted her all day. Although she couldn't quite remember last night's dreams, Renee was sure they had included a monstrous cartoon clown.

And what about Insomnimania?

Am I still connected?

She rose from the couch and went straight to her computer, turning it on with apprehension. The pothead she talked to had undoubtedly forgotten all about her call within moments after hanging up on her.

Of course, it was too early for Insomnimania actually to be online, but a "closed" sign with the network's hours would let her know she was still a member. If that turned out to be the case, she would certainly make a second phone call—a much nastier one than the first.

She double-clicked the Insomnimania application icon with its image of a silhouetted dog barking at a full moon. The words "ENTER PASSWORD" appeared. Renee typed in the letters "KDKA"—her private little tribute to America's first commercial radio station.

"INVALID PASSWORD," the computer replied.

He did it. He really disconnected me. I could kiss the freak.

Then she gathered up the application icon plus a folder full of Insomnimania files and dragged them over to the little trash can in the lower-right-hand corner of her screen. She dropped them in.

"Are you sure you want to remove the application 'Insomnimania'?" the screen inquired considerately.

"Damn straight," whispered Renee, clicking the "OK" command. The little trash can now looked squat and full. Renee wished she could jump up and down on its contents—or better yet, incinerate them. But instead, she selected the "empty trash" command. The can became trim and straight again.

The deed was done. So how did she feel? Less frightened? Less obsessed with crazy images of Auggie climbing out of her computer screen and bodily attacking her?

No. Renee could feel her heart pounding. She had endured physical symptoms of nameless panic before. But the spells had never been as bad as this. How could her body handle all this fear? Why didn't she drop dead from a heart attack?

And what the hell am I so scared of, anyway?

Auggie's operator—whoever he was—couldn't possibly know how to find her. Identities of Insomnimania users were a closely guarded secret—or so the instruction manual said. But might Insomnimania's owners have lied? The guy on the phone who claimed to be the manager hadn't exactly inspired a lot of confidence.

Renee scanned her computer desk top and noticed her application icons and folders for three other networks—all innocuous outfits, none of them nearly as high-end as Insomnimania. They served professional purposes, like gathering news clippings or leaving messages for potential interviewees. But even those icons disturbed her now. The notion of her computer being connected to strangers in the outside world seemed intolerable.

Her terror made no sense. Even if Auggie's operator belonged to any of those other networks, how could he know that she did, too? It would be silly to call and cancel *all* of them.

Steady, Renee. The next thing you know, you'll be getting your phone and your cable TV disconnected and God knows what all. You'll turn Amish and ride in a horse and buggy and wear black dresses for the rest of your life and marry one of those bearded guys in the funny hats.

But she couldn't shake off her fear. It was as if she had gotten an obscene phone call last night—one so threatening that she suddenly felt suspicious of *everybody,* even total strangers she randomly passed on the sidewalk.

He touched her. He touched Sapphire.

Renee began to rock slightly in her chair. Why did the clown have such a powerful grip on her imagination? The conversations between Auggie and Sapphire had seldom amounted to anything more than standard exchanges of wisecracks, playful insults, and childish arguments.

It was true that Auggie had made occasional odd suggestions that she was ready to participate in something mysterious and wonderful. Renee had discounted the intimations, assuming that Auggie and Sapphire were merely playing games of seduction.

And she also had been startled by Auggie's rather weird capacity for empathy. Renee felt a surge of discomfort well up as she remembered a scene from several nights ago in Ernie's Bar. Sapphire had been delivering her usual facile lines. Then, out of the blue, Auggie had said, "You're not alone."

"You're not alone."

That was all. Why did the memory of those simple words disturb her? Then she realized why. It was as if Auggie had detected her inner loneliness—*hers,* not Sapphire's. It was as if he had looked out of the computer and spoken directly to Renee.

The computer dealt the rows with blinding speed, from the single card on the left to the stack of seven cards on the right. It placed the remainder of the deck face down in the upper-left-hand corner of the screen. Four vacant, card-sized spaces across the top of the screen were ready and waiting for any aces that appeared. A single seven of hearts blazed out among four spades and two clubs.

It was no good. Myron Stalnaker couldn't play a thing.

He clicked his mouse to turn over three cards from the top of the remaining deck. He was able to play a three of hearts onto a four of clubs. He repeated the clicking action several times, without success. Then an eight of diamonds appeared near the bottom of the deck. He was able to play it atop a nine of spades. The rest of the deck turned itself over, inviting him to repeat the action again. He did so, listlessly.

The game always made him feel like he was standing outside his own body, watching himself play over his shoulder. It made him feel more mechanical than the computer itself—like some sort of volitionless, pattern-recognition gadget. It wasn't a bad feeling, and it wasn't a pleasant one either. The truth of it was, it didn't feel like much of anything at all. That was the way he wanted it.

He had been playing the game over and over again for two hours now, relegating himself to an escalating numbness until Insomnimania came on. He hadn't won once. But that didn't matter. He was a machine, and a good machine didn't care if it won or lost. It only carried out its program.

It had been the same last night. He had felt Auggie's rage rush through the passive circuitry of his nervous system en route to his obedient fingertips, where it continued on its way down into the keyboard and into the phone lines beyond.

Why did he have to be so cruel? Why did he have to say such heartless things?

She had seemed like a perfectly nice lady—if, indeed, she was a lady, which was an uncertain proposition considering the likely number of cross-dressers in Insomnimania. In any case, she certainly had a lively and entertaining personality. And her kind of banter didn't usually provoke Auggie's indignation. It seemed, rather, that Auggie exploded at inexplicable moments—that he gave up on blossoming friendships with other characters suddenly and angrily.

Why does he have to do that?

A vague notion flickered through Myron's mind: *They disappointed him.*

At the time, Myron had wanted to intercede. He had wanted to tell Sapphire of Auggie's manifold services and kindnesses, his profound capacity for friendship.

"You just caught him at a bad time," he wanted to tell her. "Come back tomorrow. You'll see him in a better light."

Myron himself had often experienced Auggie's capacity for kindness and compassion. He remembered those gentle words Auggie had once spoken to him . . .

"You're not alone."

How long had it been since anybody had offered him such solace, such comfort? All it had taken was four simple syllables. What was so wrong with flesh-and-blood human beings that they couldn't say something so plain but beautiful?

Auggie was nothing if not loving. But Myron had no way of telling Sapphire that. He could only keep his silence.

Life is unfair.

Myron's eyes were tired from staring at the screen. He rested them for a moment by turning toward the window. A full-scale Nebraska winter raged outside. Snow was falling furiously.

A good night to stay in.

Myron tried to replay the rest of last night's events. But after the ugly scene with Sapphire, his memories became more and more vague until they slipped away into a void. What had happened in the Basement afterward? What did Auggie say there? What plans had been made?

Myron couldn't remember. Had he fallen asleep at the computer? Memory lapses were typical in his encounters with Auggie, and he normally liked it that way. Life was too full of ugly things he could remember all too well. It was pleasant to have a few patches of benign oblivion here and there.

But he wished he knew what had happened last night. He wished he knew what had been said. It seemed very important to remember.

Why can't I remember?

Huge kamikaze snowflakes splattered themselves against the windowpane like insects against a car windshield, a nearby streetlight illuminating their guts as they rolled down the glass and slowly refroze.

Marianne neared the downstairs elevator corridor. She was on her way back to her room to take a quick shower between conference events. She wondered if her computer would be storing a voice-mail message from Renee. She wondered when she and Renee would be able to get together.

Marianne rode the elevator to the sixth floor and stepped out into that fateful corridor. She paused and looked at the white-painted wall. It seemed to have lost its hold on her imagination. She found it easy, now, to accept its lie, to deny its hidden blood. She did not even consider turning up the corner of the throw rug to see the stain underneath.

How quickly we become immune.

But of course, she knew she wasn't really impervious to what she had seen there. Sooner or later, the shape of that bloodstain would flash in her mind again. She was sure of that. Because if she were truly free of that image, she wouldn't even pause to contemplate her own immunity. And she wouldn't hear his name shudder across her brain . . .

"*Auggie,*" breathed Marianne.

"*Auggie,*" whispered Renee.

"*Auggie,*" cried Myron Stalnaker softly—and the world seemed a bit less cold.

OO111

WASTELAND

THE LIVING ROOM WAS VAST AND SURPRISINGLY BARREN. THERE
were only a half-dozen or so carefully placed pieces of furniture about, all extremely plain and unadorned. Even the two
large paintings on the walls were pale, formal, and geometric. Two
large, undecorative wool rugs covered only a small part of a hard-
wood floor. If Nolan didn't know better, he might almost have
guessed that the occupants were terribly poor.

*But poor folks would have gone to some trouble to make it look homey.
Judson spent a lot of money to keep this place looking cold and sterile—a* hell
of a lot of money.

G. K. Judson's apartment occupied one entire floor of a downtown Chicago skyscraper. Nolan guessed that the whole place covered almost as much space as the block he lived in back in Culver
City. And every square foot of the apartment was undoubtedly as
carefully composed, and as sparse and uninviting, as the living
room.

It was late Saturday afternoon, Nolan's second day in Chicago. He
was accompanied by Chicago Police Lieutenant Paul Spiroff, a
bookish-looking fellow with round-rimmed glasses and a narrow,
thoughtful face. Spiroff was standing in the doorway to the room,
gazing off into the surrounding hallways. Nolan thought he looked
more like a graduate student in philosophy than a police detective.

Nolan was talking with Claudia Judson, G. K. Judson's widow. She
was the last person he planned to interview before he flew back to

L.A. tomorrow, and Nolan had actually asked her very few questions. His main purpose was to fill her in on how the investigation was going—to assure her that every effort was being made to find her husband's killer. After all, someone this rich was surely more interested in answers than questions.

As he went over his notes with her, Nolan noticed how well she fit into her surroundings—a kind of minimalist woman. Wearing no jewelry at all, her straight but full sandy hair hanging over a simple yet presumably expensive sweater, she looked as austere as the room itself.

Nolan couldn't help wondering how old she was. But she looked perfectly ageless. Her skin appeared to be made of some kind of elegant fabric—fine linen, perhaps, smooth and immaculately pressed. Her face showed no wrinkles. It showed *creases,* yes, but nothing one could rightly call a wrinkle. She didn't look middle-aged, but she certainly didn't look young, either. Nolan supposed that G. K. Judson wouldn't have wanted her to look young. He had been too substantial a man to marry some callow, immature bimbo. After all, he could—and it appeared he did—have bimbos anywhere he went. Bimbos were too cheap, too tawdry, too frilly to keep as permanent fixtures in his home.

Nolan's debriefing was now coming to an end. Throughout it all, Claudia Judson showed no trace of emotion—only a kind of respectful, dignified politeness. She was just now starting to ask questions.

"Exactly who did you talk to at the hotel?" she inquired.

"Mostly people on the staff," Nolan said. "A few of the guests, too. But we checked through the hotel register and client credit-card records, and we didn't turn up any connections with your husband. And of course, there were no eyewitnesses that we know of."

Claudia Judson studied Nolan's face carefully, even skeptically. "Isn't it true that my husband was killed on the sixth floor?" she asked.

"That's right," Nolan replied, a little uncomfortably. He knew what was coming next.

"And he was actually staying on the eighth floor?"

"Yes."

"Do you have any idea what he was doing on the sixth floor, Lieutenant?"

Nolan noticed that Spiroff shifted from one foot to the other. But the Chicago detective said nothing, and his face remained impassive. Until this moment, Nolan had appreciated Spiroff's willingness to stay in the background. But now he would have appreciated a little help.

Nolan cleared his throat uncomfortably. "Ma'am, this is an issue I'd hoped not to go into," he said.

"Well?"

"He spent the several hours before his murder in the . . . company of a young woman."

"In her room?"

"That's right."

Claudia Judson's face showed no trace of surprise or alarm. But her steady gaze told Nolan that she expected a fuller explanation.

"We checked the woman out thoroughly," Nolan said. "We're absolutely sure that she had nothing to do with your husband's murder." He paused and added, "If it's all the same to you, I'd really rather not get more specific about her."

Claudia Judson smiled blandly. "Of course," she said. "Forgive me if I seem overly preoccupied with details."

She then went on to ask about more commonplace matters. Nolan guessed that she was fully aware of her husband's infidelities. If that was the case, why had she pressed him about the woman at the hotel? She hadn't seemed to be motivated by morbid curiosity.

She doesn't like loose ends. She likes life to be tidy. That's just her way. Apparently it was his way, too. It would probably be my *way if I had their money.*

As a cold blast of Chicago winter wind howled past the room's enormous plate-glass windows, Nolan realized that he didn't envy the extremely wealthy as much as he had imagined.

At about four o'clock L.A. time, Clayton was sitting at his desk in the detective bay area writing a report of today's activities. There was painfully little to put into the computer. Clayton had talked to everybody he could locally about the Judson killing, and the rest of his time had been devoted to going over the lame and insignificant findings of the forensics team.

Clayton was in the middle of a yawn when his desk phone rang. It was Nolan.

"Hey," Clayton said. "How d'you like Chicago?"

"It sucks. What do you think?"

"So, you talked to a lot of distraught friends and loved ones?"

"Ha! Most of the people here are tickled to death that he got croaked. His son and daughter—spoiled brats, both of them—were only interested in how the estate would be divided up. And his wife doesn't seem to have any feelings whatsoever. I got introduced to one of his stockholders—a rival, apparently. When I asked him if anybody wanted Judson dead, the guy actually laughed. 'You can start with me,' he said. 'I'd be honored to be considered a suspect.' He seemed really bummed out to have a solid alibi. I could tell you more. I talked to lots of people. But it's all pretty much the same story."

"Must've been a pretty sparse funeral," Clayton remarked.

"No, it was grand. Hundreds of black-clad mourners crying the most pearly crocodile tears you ever saw. Real swank and majestic. I figure Judson made arrangements in his will to pay lots of people to grieve."

"Sounds like that murder mystery—which one was it?—where everybody did it."

"Except I've never worked a homicide everybody wanted to take credit for," Nolan replied. "Hell, I met folks who would've cheerfully been convicted and executed just so everybody'd *think* they'd done it."

"But you don't think any of them did."

"Nope. Not any of the ones I talked to."

"So we still ain't got a laugh."

"Not here. Not unless you've got something there."

Clayton groaned. "Not a chance," he said. "Things're going to hell in a hand basket on this end. It might be smart of you to just hang around there."

"Hey, where do you think I am, the Bahamas? I'll see you Monday."

"Yeah, Monday."

Clayton hung up the phone and looked around. As always, the detective bay area was a blur of activity, rather like a stock exchange. Even on a Saturday, detectives were coming and going and jabbering at one another. Clayton turned and stared at his his computer screen, trying to concentrate on the three or four more sentences he had left to write. The noises around him

blended into a uniform background sound. He rubbed his eyes
and yawned deeply. Then a sharp outcry punched through his
drowsiness . . .

"Nigger!"

Clayton's head jerked up. He opened his eyes. The word had
been spoken forcefully, aggressively. Clayton spun around in his
chair looking for its source, but couldn't see or hear any kind of
confrontation or argument going on. In fact, there seemed to be no
change at all in the ambient activity. It sure didn't look like anyone
had shot the word at Clayton.

At least I don't think so.

Clayton's desk was near the door leading to the booking room.
Had the outcry come from there? *Maybe some suspect yelling at a black
arresting officer? Or at another suspect? Maybe a brother yelling at a brother?*
But the sound had seemed closer than the booking room.

Clayton knew perfectly well that another cop might have spat out
the word. It could even have been the white cop working at a nearby
desk. Clayton's stomach sank at the thought. He felt a rush of
uneasiness.

These were the men he worked with and had to trust day after day.
But he had often wondered which of them habitually, derisively,
used that word when he wasn't around. Which of them had beaten
blacks they were arresting? Which of them would welcome any
excuse to strike blow after blow against a different-colored skin? He
simply avoided the few who had reputations for this sort of
brutality—but about most of them, he just didn't know. There was
no way for him to know. He could hear the word rattle across his
mind again in an all-too-familiar echo . . .

Nigger!

Clayton's wariness never disappeared completely, but he realized
that it was sharpened by the absence of his partner—one of the few
cops who never stirred up his survival instincts.

Clayton quickly grew impatient with himself. *Damn it, you're probably just hearing things.*

Yes, that was undoubtedly it. Tiredness was taking its toll, making
him prey to paranoia. His weary brain had probably concocted the
word from random noise.

He remembered his Aunt Patty back in South Carolina—a mental patient who spent much of her adult life in institutions. Aunt
Patty heard voices calling her names like bitch, slut, whore, and still

viler things she couldn't even bring herself to repeat to others. These ghastly names were always spoken behind her back in the voices of her friends and family, so poor Aunt Patty came to believe that all her loved ones hated her.

After a number of years, Aunt Patty seemed perfectly well and was able to live at home. Clayton once asked her how it felt to be finally free of her awful voices.

"Oh, but I still hear them," Aunt Patty said with a smile. "I hear them all the time."

"But you seem just fine," Clayton said with surprise.

Aunt Patty laughed proudly. "I *am* just fine. I'm as fine as you. Better, maybe. You see, those voices always talk behind my back. They ain't nothin' but a bunch of cowards. The way I come to see it, I don't have to listen to nobody who can't insult me to my face. It don't matter if they're real or not."

Pretty good thinking for a crazy woman.

Clayton shrugged off his apprehension and laboriously typed the rest of his report.

Early Sunday afternoon, Nolan was sitting in a vinyl-upholstered booth of a dark, chintzy bar at O'Hare International Airport with Detective Spiroff. Nolan was waiting for his flight back to L.A. Spiroff had driven him to the airport and waited to see him off. They had worked closely together during the last couple of days on the Judson murder. Even though they had turned up nothing helpful to the case, Nolan was surprised at how amiable their working relationship had been.

"Sorry I couldn't have been more help," Nolan said.

"Sorry we dragged you out here for no reason," Spiroff replied with a shrug.

"We'll keep hammering away at it back in L.A. Maybe we'll turn up something."

Spiroff shook his head. "You won't," he said with a smile.

Nolan sighed. "Yeah, I reckon you're right," he said. "Wish you'd explain that to my captain—to say nothing of the L.A. newspapers and TV stations."

"Anyway, it's been nice having you around," Spiroff said. "Hey, if going back to L.A. is gonna be a hassle, stick around here and we'll put you to work on some of our local stuff."

"For example?"

"Well, you could give us a hand with the Miles Braxton case."

Nolan looked at Spiroff with surprise. Miles Braxton had been a Chicago-based magazine publisher who took a nasty, thirty-three-story nosedive from his penthouse apartment two or three weeks back. That one had been widely publicized, too.

"I thought the Braxton thing was open and shut," Nolan said. "Everybody figured suicide."

"The media thought so. We never saw fit to contradict them. It's always gratifying when those vultures get things wrong. The truth is, we found signs of a break-in and a few indications of violence that we just didn't get around to mentioning. And the coroner never called it a murder *or* a suicide."

"Didn't he have some problem with drugs and alcohol?"

"So they say. But he was clean and sober the night he fell."

"No suicide note?"

"Nothing of the kind. His computer was on, too—logged into one of those top-of-the-line networks with all kinds of hip and sexy fun and games. He'd been playing canasta in some kind of on-line casino."

"Was he losing a lot of money?"

"This game wasn't for cash, just fun. As near as we can figure, he was just having a nice, quiet evening at home playing computer games when suddenly—splat!—he got himself abruptly trans-figured into a resplendent masterpiece of sidewalk visual art."

"You don't figure the killing had anything to do with the computer game?" Nolan asked.

Spiroff laughed. "Come on, Grobowski," he said. "Do you figure he accused somebody of cheating at canasta, making the bozo angry enough to crawl out of the computer screen and haul Braxton across the balcony and toss him off the building?"

Nolan felt slightly embarrassed. He knew next to nothing about computer networks, but he had to admit it did sound like a stupid question.

"So two of your wealthiest citizens get offed in less than a month," Nolan mused. "Interesting, huh?"

"Interesting but coincidental," Spiroff said resignedly. "It would be nice to think there *was* some connection. Smacks just a little of class warfare, doesn't it? Maybe the downtrodden proletariat have stopped killing their own and are now taking their anger to the penthouses and luxury hotels."

Nolan chuckled. "Kind of makes you want to turn in your badge and join the revolution, huh?"

Spiroff grinned and raised his beer in a toast. "I'll drink to that," he said.

Renee had nearly finished building a fragile pastry structure in the cookie pan, and her fingers were pleasantly tired and tacky. The heroic struggle with the crushed walnuts and the wet, tissue-thin sheaths of phyllo dough was coming to an end. Now she was ready to carve precise, inch-wide diamond shapes in the upper layers of phyllo and put the pan in the oven. Then would come the making of the gooey syrup—an almost unbearably rich blend of sugar, water, and honey with cinnamon stick and slices of orange and lemon thrown in for good measure.

Not for the faint of heart.

Renee had been baking since yesterday. During that time, she had made a mess of herself and her kitchen—and was having a wonderful time.

All six units in the new condominium would be open later that night, and the owners had agreed that they would each contribute one course of an elaborate feast. They had drawn lots, and Renee was assigned dessert.

At first, she had been apprehensive about the undertaking. She hadn't baked anything in a long time, although she had once enjoyed it. She was sure that all the other neighbors would do their own cooking, so hiring a caterer would be inappropriate. Renee had resigned herself to making every dish on her table.

And now she was glad. A lot of dough and sugar and diverse sticky substances were just the medicine she needed.

Nothing like getting all messy and icky to drive away those cybernetic blues!

Little by little, her table was becoming laden with homemade pies, cheesecakes, and pastries. She would serve espresso and liqueurs and magnums of a fairly expensive champagne.

It had been a long time since she'd experienced such a feeling of satisfaction and gusto. Why had it been so long? And why had she been so fearful lately?

Maybe I have *been addicted. Maybe it's like being hooked on coke or meth—sooner or later you get crazy and fearful and paranoid.*

She shuddered a little at the thought of her experiences in

Insomnimania—particularly those half-asleep, only partially remembered outings in the Pleasure Dome.

Blackouts, no less! Hope I don't go through some kind of withdrawal.

Maybe she would—maybe just a little. For instance, she still felt just a slight glimmer of curiosity about Auggie and that hidden Basement of his. What did he keep down there? What did he *do* down there? And *where . . . ?*

Get out of my brain, you little monster!

She slammed a piece of dough down on the table. Then she stared at the splat, surprised at her own vehemence. She was shaking again. She took several deep breaths and began to wipe up the puddle with her fingers, concentrating on the grittiness of the mixture, trying to picture what her home would look like later tonight, full of happy, chattering guests.

She even had a date—that schlock novelist Larry Bricker she had interviewed Friday night for *Sunday Stew.* The interview had proven to be a pleasant surprise. Renee had hit him with tough, even hostile questions, and Larry had fielded them with wit and self-effacement. She remembered how the interview had begun.

"Don't you have anything better to do with your life than to gross out the American reader?" she had asked.

"Not really," Larry had replied pleasantly.

At least it was better than some pompous lecture on catharsis, pity and terror, and the therapeutic value of trash fiction.

Besides, in his diminutive, balding, middle-aged sort of way, the writer was really quite good-looking. Renee looked forward to seeing him at the party.

And Marianne. It will be good to see Marianne. We've only seen each other once since she's been in town. How could we let that happen?

The phone rang. Renee padded out of the kitchen, her hands dripping with flour and melted butter. By the time she reached her answering machine it had already delivered its outgoing message. Lucifer prowled softly around the machine, studying it intently.

Holding her hands awkwardly in front of her, Renee wondered briefly what to do. If she picked up the phone and shut off the machine, she'd make a mess. She decided to screen the call instead.

Message left by Marianne Hedison on Renee Gauld's home answering machine, Sunday, January 23, 3:15 P.M.:

Hi, Renee, it's Marianne. Listen, I'm heading back to Santa Barbara. I've done about all the business I can do here in town, and it's really time for me to get home and to work. I'm sorry to miss your party tonight, but I'm sure it will go splendidly.

Let's not let another year go by. Is there any chance of you getting up *there* sometime? Well, listen. I promise to come back soon. What do you say to another month or so? It would be great for me to come back to L.A. when we actually could find some time to spend together.

When are you going to tell me what happened with Auggie? I can't wait to find out. Give me a call and let's make plans.

Renee turned, more sad than angry, and started back to the now sickeningly sweet lumps of dough on her kitchen table.

Marianne got back to Santa Barbara early Sunday evening. Before leaving Los Angeles, she had made a couple of phone calls to let people know she was headed home. As she walked through the door, she saw her answering machine blinking vigorously. This hefty batch of messages must have accrued in the short time since word got out that she was on her way back.

Marianne played the tape.

Dwayne had called: Needed to know what to do next to coordinate the Abernathy landscaping.

Stephen had called: Would call back later.

Lenora James had called: Wanted to tell her about an upcoming meeting.

Lenora James? Now who is that? Oh sure, that community activist group.

Baxter had called: Wanted to know if she'd found any interesting fabrics at Sherwood Galleries.

Stephen had called again: Wanted to know if Friday was OK for dinner.

Four calls to answer. And all this on a Sunday.

Marianne was definitely home again.

She took off her jacket and listened to the gentle whir of the tape rewinding. It seemed an oddly warm and inviting noise after the glacially cheerful tone of the voices on the machine. Why did everybody in Santa Barbara suddenly sound so remote—and so languid?

Easy does it. Just a wave of culture shock. Remember, you just got in from L.A.

Marianne hung up her jacket. She breathed deeply and looked

around her living room. She waited for her jangled nerves to begin smoothing out. It didn't happen. She didn't quite understand why. Shouldn't it feel good to be home?

It was no mansion, but her little hillside house was beautifully proportioned and impressively furnished, the walls and woodwork done in three shades of white, the furniture pale, the wall hangings and watercolors understated. The only truly flamboyant touch was an Erté sculpture—a dancer with swirling veils frozen in motion— carefully positioned on a chest.

Marianne picked up her bags and carried them into her bed- room, opened them, and stuffed most of their contents into a laundry bag. She took off her shoes and stockings, putting the shoes in her closet and the stockings into a fabric-lined basket to rinse out later. She took off her suit and blouse and hung them up carefully, removed her underwear and dropped it into the basket, then put on a long white kimono and walked into the adjoining bathroom. She stepped into the shower.

She lathered a rich shampoo into her hair. Quadrillions of warm droplets bombarded her body, trying vainly to massage her into relaxation. What was wrong?

Marianne reluctantly shut off the water, stepped out of the shower, dried off with a thick towel, and plucked a fresh kimono out of a cabinet. She turned a blow dryer on her hair for a few minutes. With her hair hanging long and damp, Marianne stared in the mirror. Her face looked tired and strained.

"Home," she whispered searchingly. "Home again."

But the words offered no comfort.

01000

OPEN HOUSE

THE VALETS OUTSIDE WERE PARKING THE EARLIEST GUEST'S CARS and a security guard was at the front door—acting more as a doorman, really, but handy in case of trouble. The few people who had arrived had not yet reached Renee's unit. They would thread through five other units first.

Juan and Mette would offer all arrivals cocktails and then introduce them to Joel, who would treat them to hors d'oeuvres and send them along to the third floor for their main courses. There they would meet Betty and Gilbert with their fine London broil and Sam with his celebrated Cornish game hens. The revelers would then be directed down one floor where they would find Tony and Roland with their Zen vegetarian dishes. Renee was to wrap up the festivities with her elaborate desserts. After sweeping through every apartment once to discover all the goodies, the guests would distribute themselves according to their tastes.

Renee looked in the dining-room mirror at the reflection of her wildly coiffed hair, her new silk hostess outfit, the lighted candles, the dessert-laden table. She could hear a low, conversational rumble throughout the condo as the guests came nearer and nearer. She had expected to feel good tonight—glad she'd bought the unit and pleased that her home would soon be filled with lively people having a good time. Instead, she felt empty and sad.

"Marianne won't be here," she murmured. Then Renee wondered why she felt so guilty about that. Perhaps it was because she hadn't even picked up the phone while Marianne was announcing that she was on her way back to Santa Barbara. Surely Renee could have persuaded Marianne to stay for the open house if she had only tried. Even worse, Renee felt more than a little responsible for Marianne's decision to head back to Santa Barbara in the first place.

If I hadn't been so pushy the other day when Marianne was here . . . if I had made room in my schedule for another visit . . .

"Small wonder Marianne went home," Renee muttered aloud, still gazing self-critically at herself in the mirror.

She jumped with surprise as she glimpsed a second reflection in the mirror—a short but reasonably attractive man dressed in baggy corduroys who had just stepped into her doorway. She spun around, a little embarrassed that somebody had caught her talking to herself.

"I hope I'm not too early," Larry Bricker said, flashing a charming smile.

"Not at all," Renee answered, catching her breath. "I can really use your help."

It was a lie, of course. She had wanted to be alone as long as she could. But she was surprised at the ease with which she returned Larry's smile. Her smile was hollow, but it shaped itself neatly and efficiently across her face.

Quite the little media professional. Well, it'll prove a handy skill this evening.

"I brought something for you," Larry said, shyly presenting her with a small, gift-wrapped package.

"What is it?" Renee asked.

"A housewarming present."

"Can I open it?"

"Not till after the party."

"Oh, come on, Larry. What's wrong with now?"

"Later, OK? After everybody's gone."

Larry leered at Renee gently.

Oh, God, he's got an agenda. He thinks he'll get me into bed tonight.

She had just started to like Larry and hoped he wasn't going to blow it by being prematurely amorous. The truth was, she'd forgotten that he was even going to be here tonight—much less that he was supposed to be her official date. And she certainly didn't want to face the dismal task of sending him moping away unlaid at the end of the evening. But it was too early to worry about that yet. It was time to play hostess.

"Come on," she said to Larry, dutifully taking him by the hand. "You can open the first bottle of champagne."

Renee put Larry to work with the champagne and the espresso machine and deposited the gift package in her office. Then she went to greet other guests.

They started arriving in droves, some already quite tipsy from Juan's strong libations. Renee was surprised by how many of them she did not know—friends of the other hosts, apparently. Oh, here was Renee's ubiquitous boss, slobbering lecherously all over a disgusted station receptionist. A few other people from work were also present. And she recognized some faces from the media—like the TV actress whose current sitcom was about to get cancelled and the City Council member with the abominable toupee. But Renee knew only a handful of others.

She needed to get out and mix. Being garrulous and outgoing was more than her duty as hostess—it was a *professional* thing, it was what she *did*. But for some reason, she couldn't face it right now. She stood woodenly in one corner of her living room watching, feeling strangely defiled, as if her home were full of looters, not party guests—except that these looters added insult to larceny by smiling and introducing themselves before eating and plundering and generally behaving like savages.

What's wrong with this picture?

It had something to do with the furnishings. Even though she had recently added a new couch upholstered with soft, dull purple leather, a glass-top table supported by a scrap-metal frame, and a bevy of woven-wool throw rugs scattered all over the carpet, the room was still dominated by the relics of Renee's past.

It's the people who are out of place.

What right had that strange woman to browse through Renee's book collection—and worse yet, to show off to *another* total stranger Renee's big book of Manet paintings? What right had that amorous young couple to entwine themselves obscenely on Renee's telephone-cable spool? And what right had that drunken fellow to lean on Renee's shabby old carousel horse for support? The poor, dappled creature's massive metal pole strained against its ceiling hook. Renee was afraid both the horse and the man would wind up toppling to the floor.

Where were the people who understood the value of these objects, who had been there when Renee had gotten them? Those people were nowhere to be found.

A voice beside her said, "A penny for your thoughts."

She turned. Larry was standing there, taking a big, appreciative bite out of one of her prize cream horns.

"God," Renee said. "I haven't heard that line since junior high." She reached over and wiped a few crumbs off Larry's chin. "Have you been in my unit this whole time?"

"Yeah."

"Don't you think you should check out some of the others?"

"Are you getting tired of my company?"

"I didn't say that. It's just that you're only getting one course to eat—and the least healthy course, at that. Nothing but sweets. I'd hate to ruin your arteries in one night."

"Let me die *this* way," said Larry, grinning and waving the remainder of the cream horn. "You didn't reply to my original query," he added.

"Give me a penny first."

"No payments in advance. Do you think I was born yesterday? Come on, I've been watching you all evening. What's the matter? You look like you lost your best friend."

"I didn't exactly *lose* my best friend. Let's say I just sort of filed her away in a box up in the attic."

"There's an attic in this place?"

"I was speaking figuratively. You ought to know that. What kind of writer are you, anyway?"

"I'm a talentless hack. I wouldn't know a metaphor if one bit me on the ass." He paused for a moment and then said quietly, "Do you want to talk about it?"

Renee crossed her arms and was silent for a moment. Did she really want to say what she was about to say?

"I'm lonely," she said.

"Me, too," Larry replied simply.

Renee sighed. "Guess there's a lot of that going around," she said. "Do *you* want to talk about it?"

Larry stared ahead intently. "I don't know what it is, exactly," he said. "I guess I'm starting to feel like I'm nothing but print on paper. Of course, when my publisher sends me out on a book tour, I get to be a different sort of illusion—like that mechanical Lincoln at

Disneyland, a celebrated clockwork without any guts or soul. Do you feel that, too?"

"Oh, yes," Renee said, feeling a strange flood of relief. "For me it's like being . . . I don't know, just a *signal*. A disembodied signal on the airwaves." Renee felt her throat catch slightly. "If you make me cry, I'll break your face," she said.

"Same to you."

They both watched the party crowd silently. Renee was surprised at how she felt. She had just told Larry she was lonely, and now she didn't feel lonely at all. What was happening?

"Did you have a fight with this friend of yours?" Larry said, breaking the silence. "You know, the one filed away in the attic?"

Renee frowned. "No," she said. "It wasn't anything that . . . *authentic*."

"Yeah, that's the way it always works. Nobody really fights anymore. They send memos or faxes. Or they leave taped messages—"

"Bingo."

"That's you, huh?"

"Yup. The answering-machine school of interpersonal relations." Then Renee laughed. "Hey, how did you get to be so empathic? It surely doesn't come from writing blood and gore."

Larry smiled. "I have an unusually large corpus callosum for a man," he said.

"I thought size wasn't supposed to count."

Larry chuckled with mock lechery. "It depends on what organ you're talking about," he said.

Renee felt a smile form across her own face—an utterly unsocial, unpremeditated, and unprofessional smile. It was simply real.

Things are looking up.

Marianne saved the just-completed rendering for the Abernathy project and shut down her perspective program. Tomorrow, she would check it over once more and modem it to the office. There was something pleasingly immaculate and final about zapping a finished product into electronic space without making any human contact—even when it was sent a mere mile and a half.

She had carried out an entirely satisfactory amount of business on the computer this evening—including faxing orders for a Chinese meal to be delivered tonight and a batch of groceries to be delivered tomorrow. It beat standing in lines.

The screen-saving marbleized patterns appeared on the monitor. Marianne stretched, yawned, and walked barefoot on the plush carpet to her spotless high-tech kitchen. She poured a glass of white wine. Then she returned to her office.

She huddled up in a papa-san chair and looked around the room. She was surrounded by drawing tables, art supplies, the computer and monitor, a scanner, a printer, a video camera, and other tools of her trade. But the room was not cluttered. Everything was in its precisely allocated place. On the wall hung design awards and framed watercolors of interiors. An expensive, heavy crystal paperweight sat next to the computer.

The mixture of professional tools and eye-appealing details in her office was normally quite gratifying. But now the room merely seemed empty.

Why?

She picked up the paperweight and fingered it, trying unsuccessfully to find some pleasure in its smoothness. For the hundredth time this evening, she felt an inexplicable urge to scream, to cry, to break something.

Why don't you, then? Why don't you just go ahead and cry? Why don't you throw this damned thing and let it break whatever it hits?

But she couldn't. The well of tears, of passions, was dried up.

What was she feeling, then? Why was she in pain?

Was it pain?

Did she feel anything at all?

She looked out the window at the lights in other houses straggling down the hillside toward the ocean. She wrapped her arms tightly around herself.

Why is it so cold?

She wandered down the hall and checked the thermostat. It was set at seventy-two degrees.

Plenty warm.

She looked down the darkened hallway that seemed to yawn before her like an endless void. She had the sudden feeling that her entire house was empty and cold, that no one at all was there—not even herself.

Marianne felt dizzy and nauseous.

She leaned against the hallway wall.

She closed her eyes.

Now, in the darkness behind her eyelids, she saw a winter

landscape. The imagined chill of the house became a howling wind, and Marianne became the burden-laden figure trudging across the icy lake. But this time, she saw a red beacon flashing in the distance.

A sign from the shore.

Then she recognized the shape of the beacon—it was the blood-stain from the corridor wall. It flashed before her, red and blazing and as vivid as when she had seen it that first time. It was an ambiguous and terrifying sign—at once a promise of warmth and safety and a warning that the rest of the journey could be dangerous and dark and violent. And yet, Marianne felt that she now had the indication of a direction—if she could decipher the images of her imagination. She felt that she was once again embarked on a journey that had been stalled, that she was, in fact, already rushing toward her own identity and her own life.

She opened her eyes. The stain and the landscape disappeared.

"Renee," she whispered, not knowing why.

"I've got to call Renee."

"These really are mind-altering," said Larry slyly. "I hope you like them."

Renee unwrapped Larry's present and laughed. It was a clear plastic box containing a dozen tiny bottles of herbal bath oils. They all had New Age–sounding names like "Out-Of-Body," "Ancient Lives," "Millennial Dreams," and "Inward Journey." The liquids were all brightly colored.

It was late, and all the other guests were gone. The party had turned out to be marvelous—purely because Renee had settled happily into ignoring her guests and chatting with Larry the whole time. She had found it refreshing and wonderful to drop being a performer, and she could tell that Larry had felt the same way.

Now Larry stood in the doorway, studying Renee with an expectant look. He obviously hoped to stay—and to help her try one of the oils out.

"Thank you," said Renee. "They're lovely."

"Do you want help cleaning up?"

"No. It can wait till tomorrow."

Then came a slight pause. It was one of those rare moments of sexual awkwardness that made Renee feel like she was fifteen again.

"You're making my night very complicated," she said.

"Yeah?"

"I like it."

"Good."

I'm not ready for this. Or, maybe I just don't want to risk losing the mood.

She got ready to launch into a gentle but firm explanation of why she'd rather Larry didn't spend the night—how she'd appreciated his help and enjoyed his company, and how it had already been a full, wonderful night and it was probably best to end it here.

But Larry seemed to read her thoughts. "I guess I'd better be going," he said.

"I've had a lovely evening," Renee said. "I'm glad you were here."

They kissed briefly and warmly. Then, with a wave and a smile, Larry disappeared down the hallway. Renee closed her front door. It was splendidly odd. The evening had ended exactly the way she had expected it to end, but for completely different reasons.

Next time, I won't turn him away.

A few minutes later, the security guard knocked on the door, checking to make sure everything was OK before he left for the night. Then Renee got ready to take a bath. She stood for a moment in the bathroom wearing nothing but her flowered silk robe, enjoying as always the sleek feel of the fabric against her naked skin. She scanned the bath-oil labels with amusement. *Which one would Larry have chosen, I wonder? Oh, Inward Journey, without a doubt.*

As she studied several of the other labels, the one called Out-Of-Body caught her eye. The liquid was a nearly phosphorescent yellow. In small, calligraphy-like print, the label said, "A burst of jasmine and pine plus some slow, deep breathing will lift you out of your physical self for a truly transcendent experience."

Renee turned on the bathwater, very hot. Then she opened the bottle of Out-Of-Body. The room was quickly laced with a tart, pungent, but not at all unpleasant aroma. She poured the liquid into the rapidly filling tub. The smell became even more vigorous, more intoxicating.

Nice. Maybe I should have invited Larry to stay. I can just imagine our astral bodies thrashing about passionately, maybe three or four feet above the bathwater.

By now, the inebriating odor of Out-Of-Body had saturated the hazy air. She luxuriated in the atmosphere for a moment. Then she lit a votive candle, turned out the lights, and crept carefully into the steaming bathwater.

The sensation was amazingly massagelike. As the water engulfed her, Renee felt every muscle suddenly relax.

This is quite some stuff. I wonder if it really . . . ?

She took a couple of good, deep breaths. But no, she did not actually leave her body.

Ah, well. I guess you've got to believe. And Renee just wasn't a believer. As far as she was concerned, *nothing* was truly "out of body." The body was the *only* thing. But that was OK. Larry had promised her something "mind-altering," and it certainly was that.

She extended her left foot to turn off the faucet. Then she lay motionless for a few moments, pleasurably watching the mischievous candlelight play on the tiles all around her. The shapes formed by the light were as prolific and creative as clouds or flames in a fireplace, representing animals and sundry other things. Here were the ubiquitous camels and crocodiles, there the rarer armadillos and boa constrictors. Whole stories played out against her bathroom walls. Yes, this was a real high. As potent as marijuana. It was amazing that this stuff was actually legal. Renee giggled softly at the idea of the DEA trying to crack down on New Age bath oils.

Then she realized that the flickering candlelight was making her vaguely dizzy.

She closed her eyes.

She drifted off into a half-sleep.

The scent of the bath oil evoked powerful and exquisite semi-dream images—of maples and gardens and childhood hideaways in Iowa creeks and rivers, of the smell of hay in late summer, of imaginary canoe rides through damp but sumptuous caverns, of the rare and wonderful satisfactions offered to her by a small—very small—number of past lovers.

Nice. Oh, yes. Very nice.

Then, from the midst of the images, from the depths of her cozy reverie, came a soft, kindly voice.

"Sapphire," the voice said.

"Mmmm," Renee replied, her eyes still closed, half-consciously figuring the voice to be an audio track to the psychic scene—or, better yet, Larry's spiritual essence about to make his presence known.

He did stay after all. She kept her eyes closed, picturing him standing beside the bathtub, glorying in the sight of her immersed and enticing nakedness.

But then something discordant and alarming occurred to her. Larry didn't know Sapphire's name.

She opened her eyes.

A face stared down at her—a weirdly artificial but familiar clown's face with a grotesque, comic frown. The face was distorted, fragmented.

A word passed fleetingly through her head:

Pixels.

But after a distended instant of time, Renee realized this face was not composed of pixels.

No.

It was a mask—a ski mask, crocheted from wool. Eyeholes revealed hateful brown irises with rhythmically dilating pupils. The mouth was cut open to reveal sneering teeth between bright red lips that turned down at the corners.

"It's me," said the figure with a tone of ironic gentleness. "Auggie."

Barely enough time had transpired for Renee's neurons to begin to tell her she was frightened. Involuntarily, she seized a deep breath of air. Then, with a sudden, sickening slowness, the figure's leather-gloved hands descended upon her, seizing her by the hair, thrusting her head violently underwater. Renee had just enough self-possession to keep her mouth closed. But her eyes and nostrils stung violently from the jasmine-and-pine bath oil.

As she felt the two leather-sheathed hands press her head downward, ripping a handful of hair out of her scalp by the roots, dashing the back of her head with terrible violence against the porcelain, Renee's thoughts and sensations fleetingly and incongruously mingled with those of her assailant.

She actually felt the hands inside the downy lining of the gloves becoming soaked with the bathwater.

She felt, too, the savage strength it demanded to hold her head against the bathtub floor, even while her arms and elbows thrashed about, her fingernails clawing a leather jacket with ferocious tenacity.

Her legs and feet kicked furiously—but this seemed no more voluntary than the beating of her heart, which was now audible and almost unbearable. Her entire consciousness was focused on her lungs. She had seized an enormous gulp of air before submerging. Now, as the intruder held her under, she felt her body measuring this intake.

Was it too much?

Yes, it was. Her lungs were on the verge of bursting.

Should I release some air?

She had to—absolutely had to—even though any precious air lost now would never be regained.

Pursing her lips tightly, she slowly released some bubbles of air. Just as she did so, she felt an ecstatic release of pressure.

The leather gloves were gone.

Her head leapt to the surface of the water.

Her mouth opened wide, releasing an entire lungful of air.

Then she tried to inhale, but her mouth and nostrils were clogged by droplets of stinging bathwater.

At the same time, she heard—or imagined she heard—the telephone ringing in the distance. *Must answer it.* Even in her confusion, it seemed very, very, important to answer the telephone—more important than anything in her entire life.

She coughed violently, then tried to inhale again, and actually felt the beginning of a welcome intake of air. But before she could regain a fraction of her breath, the unseen gloves seized her by the hair again and thrust her under, more violently than before. She struck the bathtub so hard that she felt something break in the back of her skull. For a moment, a whirling blackness surrounded her. Then, through a confused and garbled awareness, she felt her throat surge with hot, stinging water.

She coughed spasmodically and watched great bubbles pass before her burning eyes. Water flooded down her windpipe into her lungs in a choking, agonizing torrent. With a moment of clarity, she maneuvered her thrashing foot to lift the bathtub drain lever. Now the water covering her face was flowing out of the tub, the surface she could see above her was moving lower, her head would be exposed like an island, and eventually the killing water would trickle away from all the crevices of her body.

Not fast enough. Not fast enough.

As consciousness fled for the final time, her right hand reached desperately upward. She felt her fingernails catch and tear a handful of synthetic wool, then make contact with real flesh and blood.

Her last physical sensation was of the wound she had made, the ripped skin beneath her nails. It felt fateful, erotic, as if she were bound to her assailant in a supreme act of love. Then came an unbelievable, delicious lightness. Her last ounce of fear fled away as her life dissolved and disappeared.

Message left by Marianne Hedison on Renee Gauld's home answering machine, Monday, January 24, 1:45 A.M.:

Renee, this is Marianne. Pick up, OK? I know you're there. This is your open-house night and you have to be there and I'm sure you're still awake, so just pick up.
(pause)
Listen, I know this is crazy, but I'm starting to think it was stupid for me to come back home, and I'm thinking of coming back to Los Angeles. I can't explain it. It's just a feeling.
(pause)
I really want to see you. I really want to talk to you. Is that OK? I won't do anything until you call me. Call me soon.
(pause)
Call me.

The dark figure listened to the message on the machine, then rewound the tape. As the machine whirred, the figure glanced back toward the bathroom, noting the trail of little blood droplets on the floor. The figure touched its cheek.

Still bleeding. She really had some spunk, for a simulation. . . .

The figure checked its watch for the half-dozenth time. Then it carefully removed its drenched leather gloves and wiped its hands on its pants. It pulled a white handkerchief out of its pocket. It wrapped the handkerchief around the fingers of its right hand before touching anything else.

It went well. A little rough around the edges, maybe a little unconvincing in places, but all right on the whole. The real thing will be much better.

When the machine halted, the figure removed the incoming message tape and switched it to the outgoing slot. Lucifer the cat was hovering around the machine. The figure picked the creature up and petted it warmly.

The figure turned the answering machine on to record.

The figure then held the cat near the condenser microphone.

Lucifer purred delightedly.

01001

PUNCH AND JUDY

T WO MEMBERS OF THE CORONER'S TEAM WERE LIFTING THE body out of the tub. Nolan noted that the head and neck had a greenish-red cast and the hands and feet were tinged with blue. The underside of the body was discolored with lividity, the blood pooled there by gravity. The hair on its head hung limply, looking discolored with rust. The hair on the crotch was darker.

Not her natural color, I guess. 'Course, nothing about her looks natural right at the moment.

The body was grotesquely stiff and mannequinish from rigor mortis as the team maneuvered it to the floor. Even so, the neck had begun to relax and the face looked oddly slack. The lips were slightly parted. The ugly, sour odor of death was just starting to make itself noticeable over the scent of stale bath oil.

Then Nolan felt a distantly familiar churning in his gut. It was a sudden, overwhelming desire to flee, but also a gnawing, irrational sense that the naked apparition would pursue him wherever he went. He actually felt himself trembling with something akin to both fear and rage.

He was no longer inured.

He had experienced tremendum again.

But how? What brought it on?

Nolan had no time to explore his feeling of connection with this particular crime, this particular victim. He had to get back to business.

"Do me a favor, Smitty," Nolan said appealingly. "Say it was an accident."

Smitty was peering at the side of the corpse's head through his lowered bifocals. "Come on, Nol," he replied pertly. "What do you think you homicide guys are doing here?"

"Humor me."

"OK. The chick had maybe five or six too many drinks at the party, took a bath, opened the drain to let the water out, slipped trying to get up, knocked herself unconscious, and drowned before the tub could empty. End of story."

Nolan sighed. "You don't mean it, huh?"

"Well, sure, contusions back here *could* spell 'accident,' " Smitty said, probing the underside of the corpse's head. "But feels to me like there's damage in more than one place. You reckon she fell down twice? Before all the water drained out?"

"Could be," said Nolan with a shrug. "I've done it myself on some of my nastier nights."

"Looky here," Smitty said. "Bruises on her forehead. On her arms, too. Patches of hair yanked out of her scalp."

"Maybe she got in some sort of tussle earlier on," Clayton interjected helpfully. "So far, we don't see any sign of a robbery, so what's the motive? Maybe a boyfriend got jealous, knocked her around, she decided to take a hot bath to soak out the pain. Maybe then she fell the second time, or just passed out. Maybe she had a heart attack."

Smitty laughed coarsely. "Boy, you guys are in a creative mood, huh?" he snorted. "Why don't you go write a book or something?"

Smitty studied the corpse's thighs and legs. "Don't see anything looks like rape," he said. "The lab'll check for semen, though." Then he noticed something. "Vern, get a bit of this, here," he said, pointing to the fingers on the woman's right hand. A scalpel-wielding assistant scraped under a couple of fingernails.

"Find something?" Nolan asked.

"Looks like it," Smitty said, taking the scalpel out of Vern's hand. The scalpel bristled with a tiny patch of red and white. "Fibers. Not a lot, but enough to keep me in a job. Looks like tissue, too." The medical examiner looked at Nolan and grinned. But Nolan's expression seemed to startle Smitty, who stopped his work for a moment. "Listen, I don't like this any more than you do. But the lady was murdered, and that's a fact. Someone held her down and she definitely struggled. I'm sorry, fella. I don't make this stuff up. I just call 'em as I see 'em."

"How long has it been?" Nolan asked.

"She's in rigor mortis—just starting to come out," Smitty said. "And it's fairly warm in here. So I think close to twenty-four hours. No more'n that."

"Probably last night pretty soon after the party was over," Clayton said.

Smitty nodded. "Wonder who let the water out? Makes our job easier."

The three men were silent. There was only a crackling sound as Vern put the victim's hands in paper bags. Then the team zipped the body into a bag and carried it away. Smitty left with the team. Nolan and Clayton stood in the hallway in silence.

"We gotta get out and knock on some doors," Clayton said after a few moments.

"I know," Nolan replied. But he couldn't make himself move.

"You really didn't want it to be murder, did you?" Clayton asked.

"Who ever does?"

"You know what I mean."

Nolan nodded. "Most times I can keep my feelings out of it," he murmured. "Or at least I think I do. But this time . . ."

He stopped. He didn't want to describe his feelings. How could he, when he didn't understand them himself?

"You know who she was, don't you?" Nolan said.

"I don't think so."

"A talk-show host on KFLE. Always listened to her program whenever I could. Man, she was hot."

"You ever hear her say anything that would make somebody want her dead?"

"I don't know. Don't think so. Oh, she knew how to nail somebody to the wall, all right. But she wasn't mean—just high-spirited. It'd take one hell of a sore loser to really hate her. She was a blast. See, she'd get these really big-shot guests with loads of brains and money and power on the air, then she'd very sweetly cut them down to size—not so they sounded like idiots, but so ordinary folks could make sense of them."

"There're plenty of prima donnas out there," Clayton said. "Lot of 'em don't like being brought down off their pedestals."

"No joke. Maybe it's kind of a kiss of death—having a gift, being able to do something nobody else can do. There's always some asshole out there who just can't stand it. What a fucking waste."

Clayton walked off toward the living room. Nolan looked around the bathroom one more time, then followed his partner. The place was still littered with paper plates, napkins, and cups. Several enormous, empty champagne bottles with fancy labels were overturned here and there. A table covered with a white tablecloth still bore the remnants of numerous party confections. The furnishings were bright and eccentric. Even if the woman was dead, her home still seemed wonderfully alive.

Nolan stared out the living-room window into the dark, wet, California winter night. For the first time, he noticed the steady sound of rainfall outside. How long had it been raining?

Sergeant Tyler, a uniformed policewoman, poked her head into the living room.

"Hey, Grobowski, Saunders. You might want to hear this."

Nolan and Clayton followed her into a small office-bedroom. "Listen to this," Tyler said, turning on the answering machine. Instead of a voice, the speaker produced a low-pitched rumble that seemed to ebb and flow.

"An incoming message," Tyler explained.

"Any others?" Nolan asked.

"Yeah, several after this," she said, consulting a note pad. "Some calls from the radio station. The neighbor who found her, McKeever, left a couple of messages. He wanted to know why she hadn't shown up for a snack. Second message said he was worried."

The rumbling continued on the machine.

"But what the hell's *that?*" Clayton asked.

"Thought you guys could tell me," said Tyler with a smile. "Figured two gentlemen with your experience and expertise had heard just about everything."

"What do you figure?" Clayton asked Nolan.

"Dunno," Nolan said, shaking his head. "We'd better hang onto it, though. Did she have a spare cassette?"

"We found a blank one in her desk," Tyler said.

"Then put it in the machine. Label this one and hang onto it."

"Take that! And that!"

Hunchbacked Punch, a tiny bell jingling atop his conical hat, lunged again at Judy with a wooden bludgeon clumsily clutched between his stiff, hand-puppet arms. Bonneted and homely Judy, replete with a hairy wart on her nose, dodged some of the blows but endured a good many others with brutal resilience, lurching and bouncing across the computer monitor and palpitating like a punching bag. All the while, an offstage music box played a sparkling little tune.

"And that! And that! And that! And that!"

Punch continued to shout in a shrill but plummeting voice that betrayed breathlessness and exhaustion. The tinkling music wound down with his slowing movements. Judy cackled shrilly all the while, dodging to and fro about the stage. Punch looked ready to drop from exhaustion. He let the bludgeon slip from his hands, reached awkwardly inside his parti-colored robe, withdrew an enormous flamethrower, and pulled the trigger. A shaft of red-and-yellow fire blasted across the stage. Judy burst into flames. She screamed like a demented crow, flailing her arms and careening everywhere.

Soon the flames burned down, and Judy's screaming died away. All that was left of her was a withered and blackened mandrake shape standing like a miserable scarecrow in the center of the stage. Punch coughed a bit, fanned away the smoke, and turned and bowed to the audience. The air was filled with the contradictory sounds of applause, booing, cheering, and derisive laughter. The music box tune resumed. A conglomeration of lovely bouquets and rotting vegetables cascaded toward the stage.

Judy's carcass and the bowing Punch slowly rose to reveal the puppeteer himself. It was old Geppetto, a sweet, smiling, white-haired gentleman clad in a leather cobbler's apron. Still bowing convulsively, the puppet Punch fit over Geppetto's right hand like a glove. Geppetto's left hand, though, was burned nearly to a smoldering stump where Judy once had been.

"Well, my bambinos," purred the grandfatherly puppeteer with an unlikely Italian accent, "so much-a for tonight's show. How dooya like-a my Pulcinella and his lady?"

Written comments rolled over the bottom of the screen.

TENA>BOOO HISSSSS!

SUDOPOD>I LKED THE FLAME THRWER. NICE TWST.

TENA>NO NO NO NO NO NO NO NO!

TOMSANTPOLLY>U'RE GTTNG BTR AT THE AKSHUN.

JZZ>5 YRD PENULTY. PLITICLY N-CURRECT. JOODY'S GOT IT
12 TIMES N A RO. WI CANT SHE WASTE PUNCH SUMTIME?

TENA>LAK OF IRENY N DURMATICK TENSHUN.

A wooden hook at the end of a long handle reached across the screen and yanked away old Geppetto, his puppets, and the entire stage. The space was empty, white, and silent for a moment. Then came a drumroll and a cymbal crash. Hugo, the Snuff Room's master of ceremonies—a tuxedo-clad skeleton with an axe imbedded in his skull, worms crawling out of his cavernous mouth, and rotting eyeballs rolling about in their sockets—leapt into the middle of the staring brightness.

"Ha-haaaa!" he exclaimed with gravelly, preprogrammed gusto. "So ends another delightful excursion into the magical art of puppetry! And that, boys and girls, brings tonight's festivities to a close!"

Hugo started to break into a farewell theme song, but his voice was promptly drowned out by a chorus of boos and hisses. He covered his face to protect himself from a renewed barrage of vegetables.

Lines of text appeared at the top of the screen.

TENA>WE HAVN'T SEEN AWGY YET!

JZZ>HEY HUGO! HOW MENNY MOR R GONNA TO BE ON TONITE?

SUDOPOD>I CUD DO BTTR THN THIS SHT. HOW DO I SIGN UP 4
NXT WEEK?

JZZ>WE WANT AWGY!

"Hey! Hey! Hey!" cried Hugo. "Only kidding! Only kidding! Can't you tell a joke when you hear it? We're not finished with you yet!"

The derisive catcalls abruptly switched to whistling and cheering and the rhythmic stamping of feet.

"And he-e-e-ere we go," continued Hugo, barely making himself heard over the clamor. He waved a hand toward a signboard mounted on an easel. The sign appeared in a close-up. It read:

> The Snuff Room
> is proud to present
> our founder!

That icon of crime—
That archetype of anarchy—
That master of murder—
the *amazing* . . .
Auggie!

Hugo stepped out of the picture, and an enormous hand wielding a red sable brush appeared. With a few swift, wet, Disneyesque strokes, the brush set an entirely new scene—an ample, candlelit bathroom. The room had white walls, a spacious black tub, a black sink, and a black toilet. A steady stream of simulated water poured into the tub, and gray curls representing steam crept ceilingward. The setting was underscored by the scratchy, tinny seventy-eight r.p.m. recording of a lazy, ambling guitar accompanied by a piano bass line. A tenor voice began to croon with exaggerated tenderness:

"You always hurt . . . the one you love . . ."

A barefoot woman wearing a brightly flowered bathrobe stepped into the picture. She turned toward the audience, shook out her reddish hair, and languorously and seductively removed the bathrobe to reveal a shapely nude figure. She walked over to the sink, gazed narcissistically at her reflection in the bathroom mirror for a moment or two, then ran a comb through her hair.

The crooning voice continued:

". . . the one . . . you shouldn't hurt . . . at all . . ."

Then the woman turned toward the audience again. With a magicianlike gesture, she produced a tiny yellow vial in her right hand. She walked toward the steaming tub and poured the contents of the vial into the water. A yellow vapor and a handful of bubbles rose out of the tub. The woman sniffed the air luxuriously.

She turned off the faucet and hopped into the tub with a single, abrupt leap, splashing a cascade of bright blue water everywhere. Her stiff, fashion-doll limbs settled into the suddenly still water. The woman sat up, sponged her arms and back, then reclined again. One of her arms trailed back and forth along the edge of the tub. The song drifted into a slow, gentle, mock-solemn recitation about love, betrayal, and forgiveness accompanied by soft, bluesily muted trumpets.

Then, with a series of jerky tableaus, the view shifted to above the tub. As if lulled by the quiet music, the still-reclining woman closed her eyes and smiled, her body intermittently visible through the bubbles.

Two black-gloved hands—seemingly those of the viewer—crept slowly into the picture.

The recitation ended. Blaring trumpets, screeching clarinets, and a manic banjo broke into a Dixielandish up-tempo. As if awakened by the music, the startled woman opened her eyes and briefly noticed the gloved hands. The smile disappeared from her face just as the hands seized her by the chin and hair and pushed her head underwater.

The music rushed headlong at a riotous gallop punctuated with gunshots, duck calls, woodblocks, cowbells, and police whistles. The woman's arms and legs, looking weirdly disconnected, flailed wildly, hurling blue pixels all over the place. The singer broke in again:

"You always hurt the one you love—the one you shouldn't hurt at aaaall . . ."

Popping corks, tinkling champagne goblets, breaking glass, cries of comic agony, and farting trombones joined the musical melee. The woman's face briefly resurfaced in the midst of a wild splattering of pixels, her lips making grotesque, fishlike gasping motions in time with a pounding bass drum. The gloved hands quickly pushed her face under again. Her arms and legs flailed with less and less force, like a decelerating metronome. With one last burst of energy, her hand reached up and momentarily filled the field of vision, then fell into the water again.

As the raucous music continued, a torrent of gigantic bubbles broke from under the water. The gloved hands released their grip, and the woman's lifeless body floated to the surface, her eyes pinched shut and her skin markedly paler than before. As the blue water turned pink, it swirled into circles and then disappeared down the drain. There was one last view of the naked body reclining among a few stray bubbles, then the scene dissolved into snowy whiteness. A fluffy, tailless, black-and-white cat stepped into the empty frame. The gloved hands picked up the animal and began to pet it.

The song reached a noisy cadence. With the final, triumphant trumpet chord, the word "PURRRR" appeared next to the cat in huge, wacky letters. A red curtain with gaudy gold fringe descended over the scene. Then Auggie himself, decked out in full clown regalia, stepped in front of the curtain, black-and-white cat in hand, and took a bow to the sound of thunderous applause. The first in a list of written observations appeared:

TENA>NW THTS IRENY!

Message left by Marianne Hedison on Renee Gauld's home answering machine, Tuesday, January 25, 1:53 A.M. (with continuing recorded conversation with Nolan Grobowski):

Renee, pick up the phone! It's Marianne. Pick up the phone, dammit! I just saw Auggie's snuff. Did you see him? Did you see what he did? Christ, Renee, pick up! No playing around now. This is serious. Pick up the goddamn phone!
NG: (picking up the phone) Hello, this is—
MH: Who are—? Who am I talking to?
NG: Calm down. Let me—
MH: Where is she? Auggie? Is this Auggie? What have you done with her?
NG: My name is Grobowski.
MH: Get out of there! Get away from her! Right now!
NG: *Lieutenant* Grobowski.
MH: Let me talk to her. I demand to talk to her.
NG: *Will ya listen?* I'm with the police.
MH: The—?
NG: The Los Angeles Police Department.
MH: Oh my God.
NG: Please identify yourself, ma'am.
MH: Oh my God. Oh my God.
NG: Ma'am, please.
MH: How do I know who you really are?
NG: Will ya please—?
MH: What's happened to her?
NG: I can't tell you that over the phone.
MH: Why not?
NG: Please identify yourself.
MH: What's happened to her?
NG: Could you tell me where you're calling from?
MH: *What's happened to her?*
NG: Where are you calling from?
MH: Why?
NG: I need to talk to you. I want to come see you.
MH: No.

NG: Ma'am, please try to understand—
MH: I'll come there.
NG: What?
MH: You're at her apartment, right?
NG: Yes, but—
MH: I'll come there. I'll be there in a couple of hours.
NG: Ma'am—
   (MH hangs up; dial tone)

"Really blew it this time," Nolan grumbled, staring at the machine and holding his temples between his fingers.

Clayton and Nolan had just listened to the tape of the truncated conversation five times in a vain attempt to make some sense of it.

"Give yourself some slack," Clayton replied. "What were you supposed to do?"

"Should've kept her on the line a few seconds longer. Should've found out more."

"Didn't sound like she was in a real talkative mood."

"We're supposed to know how to handle the wallflowers—how to draw 'em out. *You* should have talked to her. You wouldn't have fucked up like that."

"They gotta *want* to be drawn out," Clayton said. "Besides, she said she'd come here. Maybe she meant it."

"What kind of odds do you want?" Nolan snapped. "Come on, Clay. You wanna bet hard cash? *I'm* ready."

Kim Pak, the precinct computer expert, stepped in from another room.

"You said it's a 'Marianne,' you're looking for, right?" Kim inquired.

"You got it," Nolan said, suddenly hopeful. Clayton and Nolan followed Kim to the adjoining office-bedroom.

"It's all in her computer," Kim said. "Her address book, her appointment book, her guest list for the party."

Kim led Nolan and Clayton into the office and plopped himself down in front of the enormous color monitor. "Three names like that on the guest list," he said, perusing the screen.

Nolan looked over Kim's shoulder and shook his head. "Three. Shit. Marian Baxter, Mary Anne Vernasco, Marianne— Hey, Marianne Hedison. That name's familiar."

"Lotta local celebrities on this list. Seen her on television, maybe?"

"No, it's not that, it's—" Nolan snapped his fingers. "That woman! The one at the hotel! I *knew* I'd heard that voice before."

"What woman?" Clayton asked.

"A woman in the hallway. She was staring at the bloodstain at the Quenton Parks. I asked her name." Nolan pulled a little notebook out of his pocket and flipped some pages. "Here it is, Marianne Hedison, interior designer. Damn! It was her! She was at the scene of the Judson homicide! Kim, you said she had some kind of address file in that machine of hers?"

"Sure did."

"Run down Marianne Hedison for us. If she was on the guest list, I'll bet she's in there, too. And she mentioned an 'Auggie' on that tape. See if you can find him, too."

"Will do."

Nolan turned toward Clayton. "If she doesn't come to us, we'll go to her," Nolan said.

"Sounds good," Clayton said. "Come on. Let's talk to some of the neighbors."

"What's happened to her?"

"I can't tell you that over the phone."

"Why not?"

The three phrases rolled across her brain in a recurring loop. The loop played over and over and over again. It was identical each time it played.

"What's happened to her?"

"I can't tell you that over the phone."

"Why not?"

The memory loop closed around itself, locking out all other parts of the conversation. To save her life, she could not remember what the man had said after her desperate *"Why not?"*

Was it then that he had told her he was a cop?

No, it must have been earlier.

Or *did* he tell her he was a cop?

Did she only imagine he told her that?

Did she believe he was a cop?

What *did* she believe?

"What's happened to her?"

"I can't tell you that over the phone."

"Why not?"

Marianne looked at the speedometer. Seventy-eight miles an hour. A cautionary voice inside her brain admonished her how treacherous the highway always was when it rained. She was probably hydroplaning at this very moment over a sheet of freshly liquified mud. At the first need to brake or make the slightest turn, she would undoubtedly lose control and careen off the highway.

Undoubtedly.

Not that she could muster a lot of concern for her life right at the moment. It just seemed grotesquely unfair to add an automobile accident to . . .

. . . what?

What had happened?

Did she dare even imagine it?

Marianne gently and ever-so-slightly tilted the steering wheel to the left, urging her car past a vehicle in the right lane. The pickup was dallying along at a leisurely rate of no more than sixty miles an hour. Its driver honked as she hurtled past. She could almost hear the driver cursing at her.

"Hey, what's the matter, you crazy bitch? You wanna kill everybody on the road?"

The pickup's horn vanished into the black of the night in a howling, descending Doppler glissando. The loop kept right on playing like a stuck record.

"What's happened to her?"

"I can't tell you that over the phone."

"Why not?"

She felt the road shift slightly, horizontally, dangerously beneath her barreling vehicle, then hastily reshape itself to the contours of her wheels again.

Slow down, dammit. You wanna kill everybody on the road?

The voice seemed peculiarly irrelevant to the activities of her body. It had no effect whatsoever on her right foot, imbedded cozily and heavily in the accelerator.

Few cars were out on the highway.

Who's crazy enough to drive on a night like this?

But the very lack of traffic seemed somehow tormenting as the highway yawned vacantly ahead. Highway lights whirled by, forming vulgar streaks and sparkles of phosphorescent psychedelic tempera all across her windshield. The lights multiplied, increasingly filling the space ahead, bizarrely suggesting sluggishness rather than speed. Los Angeles grew proportionately more distant the longer she drove toward it. She was halfway to the city now, but the remaining distance had doubled in the meantime and would repeatedly continue to do so in geometrically increasing increments all the rest of the way. Time and space were stretching and magnifying wildly with every passing moment.

She would never reach Renee's apartment at this rate.

"What's happened to her?"

"I can't tell you that over the phone."

"Why not?"

Never.

01010

LOOP

THE TALLER OF THE TWO MEN WAS LEAN AND MUSCULAR AND had a full mane of well-kept brown hair. He looked like a model—and indeed, Nolan had learned earlier that he was one. The tall man stood behind the armchair, gently rubbing the shoulders of a shorter man, who was sitting in the chair.

The one in the chair was a bit portly, but not really flabby. His hair was thinning and he had a small mustache. He looked like an accountant, but actually he was a photographer. Stricken, he stared into the space beyond the oriental carpet on the living-room floor. Both men wore pajamas and bathrobes.

"I want to see her," the shorter, seated man said, his voice choked with emotion.

"Tony, don't," the taller man said soothingly.

"I want to see her," the shorter man repeated. "I won't believe it till I see her." A tear rolled down his cheek. He wiped it defiantly away.

Nolan remembered his feeling upon viewing the corpse.

You don't want to see her. Trust me. You really don't want to see her.

"Mr. Drexler, please try to put it out of your mind," Nolan said quietly. "The coroner's team has already taken the body away."

Tony Drexler broke down in quiet sobs. The taller man bent over and held him tightly. Then he said to Nolan, almost in a whisper, "Can't I go talk to the neighbors now? They must be terribly upset."

"I understand your concern, Mr. McKeever," Nolan said. "But I must say no. The other officers are questioning them right now, and we have to try to keep all potential witnesses separate for the time being. I hope you understand."

Roland McKeever nodded.

Behind his own surface politeness, Nolan felt a fierce impatience. McKeever just seemed too damned concerned about absolutely everybody.

A put-on?

Anger welled up again.

It would be so simple if it turned out to be this guy.

It wasn't impossible. Occasionally, an impatient killer *did* go back to the scene and "discover" the body himself. If McKeever had done it, they could get this whole thing over with quickly.

So how about him? A woman hater?

Nolan abruptly censored the thought. He realized he was *trying* to dislike this guy. He was being completely irrational. Since when was he the kind of cop who succumbed to homophobia?

What the hell's the matter with me?

He shifted his center of gravity edgily from one foot to the other.

"We'll try to finish up soon," Nolan heard his partner say. "We know it's been a terrible night. In the meantime, I apologize if we go back over some of the same ground as before. It's strictly routine. And if you remember any little details you haven't already told us, please say so. They might turn out to be significant."

"We'll help however we can," McKeever said.

Nolan stood and watched the two men carefully as Clayton continued the questioning. He was grateful to have his partner take control of the situation, at least for the moment.

McKeever and Drexler faithfully told the same story they had related in their separate preliminary interviews. During the Sunday-night party, they had asked Renee Gauld to come over for a snack and a drink the following evening. When she didn't show Monday night, McKeever had called and left a message.

McKeever said that neither he nor Drexler had been especially concerned at first. They figured Renee had found something more exciting to do. Later that night, they discussed the fact that neither of them had seen her since the party. They asked a couple of other residents. No one else had seen her either. But even that wasn't really unusual. A little later—at about eleven-forty-five—McKeever called again. The machine still answered. That made them wonder. By now, Renee ordinarily would have called to ask McKeever to feed Lucifer.

"Her cat," Clayton reiterated.

"That's right," McKeever said. "I've got a key to her apartment. Whenever she expected to be gone for the night, she'd ask me to feed Lucifer. Well, Tony and I started to worry, but we didn't want to admit it. I told Tony I'd stop by her apartment. Just to feed the cat, I said. When I walked into the apartment, I was surprised that she hadn't cleaned up after the party—hadn't cleaned up at all. She hadn't turned out the lights, either. I decided to look around." He paused, trying to control his emotions.

"And that's when you found her," Clayton said.

McKeever nodded. "Then I went straight to her phone and called 911."

"And you didn't move or touch anything?" Clayton asked.

"No," McKeever said. "Actually, I *did* bring Lucifer back with me."

Seemingly at the sound of his name, Lucifer the cat padded softly into the room and jumped up onto Drexler's lap. Lucifer cozily rubbed his face against Drexler's arm. Drexler held his hands away from the cat for a moment, as if stunned by its presence. Then he cautiously began to pet it. Nolan noticed something odd about the animal.

"What happened to its tail?" Nolan asked.

"He's a manx," Drexler replied simply.

"A tailless cat—who ever thought that one up?" Clayton snapped.

Drexler looked taken aback, but did not answer. Nolan glanced at his partner in surprise. That show of irritation was the only emotion he'd seen in Clayton since they'd arrived at the murder scene.

Is he feeling something, too?

"It just seems kinda cruel and freakish," Clayton said with an embarrassed shrug.

Nolan gazed at the contentedly purring cat. Its oddness offered him a small but welcome distraction from his discomforting moods. *Are they bred that way, or does this kind get their tails lopped off at birth?* The manx did seem to Nolan to be lacking some of its essential catness. But Lucifer did not seem to mind.

Clayton cleared his throat and went on with the interview. The rest of his questions had to do with the party itself—who was there, what had transpired? The whole building, every apartment, had been open, and all the residents had invited guests. The place was full of people coming and going after about 8:00 P.M. The party was officially over at midnight, but there were stragglers, small gatherings going on after that.

"What about security?" Clayton asked.

"A guy at the front door," McKeever said. "But he wasn't checking off names. He was just supposed to handle any obvious crashers or anybody who got drunk and ugly. No one did."

"So anybody who looked OK got in?"

"The security guard asked whose guest they were."

"Was there a guest list?"

"Each of us made one up," Drexler said.

"But anybody could have overheard a name and used it," McKeever interjected. "And there were whole groups coming in at once. And last minute invites and friends of friends. The lists won't tell it all."

"Did someone make sure everybody left?"

"The security guard went around to each unit and said goodnight," McKeever said. "I guess nobody called for help."

"What time was that?"

"About one o'clock, a little after."

"Did the deceased have a date?" Clayton asked.

"Yeah," McKeever said. "Larry somebody-or-other."

"Larry Bricker," Drexler added. "A writer."

"The guy who writes the scary books?" Clayton asked.

"I think so," Drexler said. "Seemed like a nice guy."

"Did she argue or fight with him?"

"I don't think so," McKeever said.

"We really didn't see that much of her during the party," Drexler explained. "Still, we would have heard about it if there had been a scene."

"Was Bricker still here when the party was over?"

"I have no idea," McKeever said.

"I thought I saw him leave," Drexler said.

"Would you have seen him if he came back?"

"Not necessarily."

"Was she the flirtatious type?"

Drexler and McKeever smiled at each other sadly.

"She's—she *was*—a friendly person," McKeever said. "She liked to flirt."

"Excuse me for asking," Nolan broke in, "but was she promiscuous?"

"Jesus," McKeever said, with just an edge of anger.

"I'm sorry. I have to ask."

"Let me put it this way," McKeever said. "She wasn't exactly exclusive. But I don't think she'd have done anything deliberately to make a date jealous, if that's what you're getting at."

Clayton closed his notepad. "Thank you, gentlemen. That's all we need to know right now."

"We'd appreciate it if you'd discuss this as little as possible with the other residents," Nolan said. "Particularly the circumstances under which you discovered the body. More importantly—don't give any information to the press. Keeping details out of public circulation can be crucial when it comes to pinning down a suspect."

Clayton added, "Tomorrow, we'll want you and perhaps some other tenants to help us check the apartment more closely to make sure nothing's missing. But tonight you should try to get some sleep."

Drexler's expression became inexpressibly pained. His head dropped forward. "There had to be something," he said, his voice reedy with anguish. "There had to be something we could have done."

And Nolan felt an echo of that guilt and regret in himself, although he couldn't imagine why.

Nolan and Clayton left the two men alone. Back in the victim's living room, they found the three uniformed officers gathered together and checking interview notes. No one had turned up anything helpful or even anything blatantly contradictory. Several people said they had seen Larry Bricker leave, and the security guard seemed to have made his rounds quickly and efficiently. No one knew an Auggie. No one knew a Marianne Hedison, either.

"We'll have to check out Bricker and the security guard," Nolan said. "One of them might have been the last to see her alive—maybe the very last."

"Want to go roust them out tonight?" Clayton asked.

"I'd better hang around here for a while," Nolan said. "Gotta wait for that hysterical lady who's supposed to be on her way here. I'm sure anxious to see if she's really the one I met at the Judson scene. I'll bet money she is. I can just feel it in my bones. But what the hell does it mean?"

"Maybe the two killings are connected," Clayton said.

Nolan looked back at him with a hint of curiosity. "Yeah? How're they alike? They're not even the same MO."

"I don't know. Maybe just that neither of them makes any sense."

"You're looking for sense? This one might've made plenty of sense to a boyfriend hopped up on some designer drug."

"Yeah, I know. And these don't look like professional hits. But neither of them was clumsy, either—not like a spur-of-the-moment thing, not like an amateur. There was planning. Both times the killer found just the right time and place and got away clean—like a stalker. And we're dealing with high-profile victims."

"What're you thinking? There's no sign of a serial going around. And here there's no favorite weapon or method or scenario or anything like that."

"Who says there has to be a method?" Clayton replied. "Who says there had to be a scenario?" Clayton's eyes were flashing around the premises.

Reconstructing the crime. Nolan knew that his partner was good at that. And Clayton's intuitions were often sound, but Nolan just wasn't ready to buy this particular idea.

"You really think there's some connection?" Nolan said. "Why? Just because they were both well-heeled? That's nothing."

"Still, there *is* the woman," Clayton said.

"And what does that tell us?"

"I'm not saying it tells us anything. I'm saying we don't *know*, is all. So why rule out anything?"

"Damn, I hope she shows," Nolan said.

It was now three-thirty in the morning. Nolan and Clayton began to delegate duties to the other officers. To begin with, somebody was to call the company that provided the security guard. Then Nolan could meet with the guard himself and get a statement from him. While Nolan and Clayton were assigning other tasks, Kim stepped into the room and handed Nolan a computer printout.

"I found a Marianne Hedison listed in the address files," Kim said. "It's a Santa Barbara number."

"Let's give it a try," Nolan said. He and Clayton stepped into the condo unit, and Nolan dialed the number from Renee Gauld's office telephone. After several rings, he heard an answering machine make a very brief, standard reply.

"It's just her machine," Nolan said. "At this time of night it doesn't necessarily mean she's not there."

"Is it the same voice as the phone call?" Clayton asked.

"Can't tell," Nolan said tiredly. He redialed the number and let Clayton listen to the recording.

"Does it sound like the voice on the tape to you?" Nolan asked.

"Could be," Clayton said. "It's hard to tell. The woman who called here was as hyper as hell."

Nolan and Clayton stayed behind as all the officers except Kim dispersed to tend to their assignments. Nolan and his partner sat in the living room, waiting silently but none too patiently. Nolan stared out the window again.

Not a good night to drive in from Santa Barbara. If that's what she's doing.

The night was still rainy, and although no lightning was visible, thunder could be heard farther west. The rain was steady and solid and insufferably monotonous. Nolan didn't care if it started coming down an awful lot harder or just plain stopped. He only wanted *something* to change.

He wanted—or *thought* he wanted—to talk to Clayton about his flood of feelings tonight. But he was either too tired or too confused to initiate the conversation. He wasn't sure which.

Maybe I'm suffering from serious burnout. He found himself thinking about Crazy Syd's offer for a sheriff's job way up north. Maybe cops didn't undergo this sort of crisis in the laid-back wilds of Oregon.

Then something outside caught Nolan's eye. Two bright lights had interrupted the night. A dark red Nissan Maxima pulled hurriedly to a stop in the no-parking zone out front. The car lights blinked out.

"We've got company," Nolan heard Clayton say.

Marianne turned off the car engine and gazed through the dripping windshield at the looming condo. An outdoor light illuminated the front doorway. There were also lights on in several of the windows, making the building look warm and inviting. Marianne sat looking at the condominium, imagining every window in the building lit, the party in full swing, people moving inside, laughing, talking.

She remembered that Renee had invited her.

She shuddered.

Then she saw the silhouettes of two men standing in the doorway. *Better not keep them waiting.*

She stepped out of the car and awkwardly straddled a large puddle. She felt extremely self-conscious about her every move, as if walking itself were an unfamiliar activity. The lights seemed to bob and jump about drunkenly with every step as she strode toward the entrance. Her legs felt weak and uncertain, like those of some infant animal.

The door swung open in front of her. The two men rushed out, pulling their collars up against the rain. An umbrella opened in front of them like some kind of big black jonquil that bloomed only at night.

"Marianne Hedison?" a voice inquired.

She nodded.

"We tried to call," the voice said. "You'd already gone. Thank you for coming."

Marianne couldn't see the men's faces as they stepped to each side of her, taking both of her arms. Their firm and confident hands felt comforting as they securely led her toward the house. She wasn't accustomed to feeling less graceful than the people around her.

They ushered her into the blindingly lit hallway and closed the door behind them. They shook the rain off their overcoats like two dogs.

"Hell of a night," one of the men said. His broad face immediately filled up her entire field of vision. She barely looked at the other man, who seemed to fade into the background. The large-faced man was staring at her. Did something about her look strange? Then her breath caught slightly as she realized . . .

It's him. The cop at the hotel.

The two men introduced themselves, but Marianne didn't hear their names, which hardly seemed important at the moment.

"What's happened?" she asked quietly, feeling a surge of inexplicable calm—the kind of ghostly calm that comes when the truth, no matter how awful, is about to make itself understood.

The two men looked at each other with concern.

"Let's go upstairs," the man in the background said.

"There's been a homicide," Nolan told Marianne Hedison once she was seated in the deceased's living room. When she made no response, he said, "A murder."

She still said nothing. He studied her closely. Yes, it was her, all right. But she looked very different than she had at the hotel. Her hair was wet and her clothes looked frumpy—an outfit this sort of woman would only wear around the house. She also wore no makeup and had dark circles under her eyes. *Looks like she's been crying.*

But she wasn't crying now. And while she certainly seemed confused and frightened, she was also remarkably subdued, as unlike the startled woman at the hotel as anyone could get. She didn't even wince at the word "murder."

Nolan also could not help noticing that, even in her present disheveled condition, her features were at once delicate and striking. When he'd seen her at the hotel, he assumed that her beauty was a great contrivance, something coddled and crafted every day with deliberation and care. Apparently he had been wrong.

Finally, the woman said, "It was Renee."

Nolan nodded.

"Tell me how it happened," she demanded softly.

"We can't go into that just yet," Clayton interjected. "We have to ask you some questions."

"She was taking a bath, wasn't she?" the woman continued in a severe whisper without so much as a pause. "She was in the bathtub and he grabbed hold of her and pushed her under. He cracked her head, more than once."

Nolan felt the hair rise on the back of his neck. He looked at Clayton. He could tell from his partner's face that they were thinking the same thing. *How does she know?* Had someone in the building phoned her? But McKeever and Drexler were the only ones who even knew how the victim had died. They had been warned not to talk to anyone about it. And they had both claimed not to know Marianne Hedison. Besides, she had supposedly been on her way here all this time.

"Do you have a telephone in your car?" Nolan asked.

"No. I don't like the intrusion," she answered. Then she continued as though there had been no break in her thoughts. "He held her under the water, didn't he?"

"What makes you think so?" asked Clayton.

"Just tell me."

"Answer my question, please."

"I saw it," she said. "I saw the whole thing."

She was quiet for a very long moment. She studied the clutter in the living room. Then Nolan noticed that her eyes had fallen on the carousel horse.

The past seemed more vivid to her than the present.

The past seemed much, much more clear.

But then, nothing could seem *less* clear than the present.

As Marianne sat gazing at the horse, a certain day came back to her—that delightful afternoon when she and Renee had first found the horse. It was perhaps three years ago, at a yard sale. The couple who owned it had planned to do it up with new paint and decorations and sell it for more than they'd paid for it, but they'd gotten hard up for cash and offered to sell it as it was.

At seventy-five dollars, the horse hadn't struck Marianne as much of a bargain. Its hind feet had been broken off and roughly repaired. They were clearly ready to fall off again. The whole thing was covered with thick layers of white latex paint that was starting to crack—paint so thick that the horse's eyes and nostrils were barely discernible.

But Renee couldn't resist. She had paid the couple and begged Marianne to help her bring the horse home. Marianne and Renee had tugged the horse into the wide trunk of Renee's old Queen Mary—an oversized but delightfully frumpy, gold-colored 1972 Plymouth Valiant. They had tied the trunk lid down with a scarf sacrificed for the occasion. As they wended their way back to Renee's loft, the long steel pole that had come with the beast stuck precariously out the driver's-side window of the Queen Mary, causing her to list to port, and the weight of the horse severely tested whatever was left of the good ship's rear shock absorbers.

Once they got the carousel horse back to Renee's loft, Marianne had helped Renee scrape off the paint. The latex had come off in thick sheets, laying bare a face sculpted from carefully joined pieces of wood. A pair of nicely carved flared nostrils emerged from the previously amorphous shape. The animal's mouth was open, and a metal bit pulled it down at the back corners, as if a rider was hard put to restrain the horse from charging away. The lips were drawn back, baring the teeth. The ears were small and laid back against the head.

Marianne and Renee had scraped down to the remnants of a saddle and blanket that had obviously been repainted many times. The flesh of the horse was tan under the white, with a red undercoating showing through in places. When they had removed all the paint that was going to scrape off easily, the horse and trappings formed a mosaic of multicolored patterns—mostly the accidental interactions of several layers of paint.

"Look at this," purred Renee, running her hand over it. "It's like looking at clouds—or a Rorschach test. You can see a thousand pictures here."

"It's not very pretty," Marianne said critically.

"No, but it's handsome. A wild beast. It's beautiful, Marianne."

"You mean you're not going to finish it?"

"Finish it how?"

"Repaint it. Restore it. I've seen a book about these carousel animals. We could find out pretty much what it originally looked like."

"And cover over all these stories? Never!"

Nevertheless, Marianne had always expected Renee to do something more to fix it up. In the intervening years, the Queen Mary had been traded in for an elderly BMW convertible, but here was the carousel horse, unchanged. Marianne tried to get it through her mind that Renee would never tell her the horse's stories.

But she couldn't grasp that fact.

Then a voice from the present drew her out of the past.

"Ma'am?"

The woman snapped out of her trance and looked directly at Nolan.

"Are you all right, ma'am?" Nolan asked.

She looked at Nolan steadily. He felt as if she were studying his face. Her wild, intense gaze gave him a deep chill. Then she glanced around the living room again.

"She didn't get a chance to clean up," the woman remarked.

Nolan held his breath, but the woman said nothing more. "Were you here at the time of the murder?" he asked.

"No."

"Then where did you see it?"

"It was on the computer screen," said the woman with a hoarse sigh of despair. "It was on the network."

Nolan got to his feet and went to the window to cover a new onrush of confusion and impatience. He knew Clayton would take over the questioning.

"Tell us what you mean, Ms. Hedison," Clayton said, speaking in a quiet and friendly manner.

"On the network," she said. "Late at night. They put on a show—murders—in the Snuff Room."

"What kind of network are we talking about?"

"On the computer. Insomnimania."

Nolan watched from the window as Clayton listened patiently and uttered occasional encouraging remarks. Marianne Hedison recited an only intermittently lucid tale about a computer network with a "room" where users acted out murders. She continued to speak in a perpetual monotone that Nolan gradually became convinced was a symptom of shock.

This weirdly disconnected attitude was all too familiar to him. It wasn't exactly a *repression* of emotion—it was more like battle stress. It was more as though one's body was experiencing rage and grief but one's mind simply chose to ignore it. That was how he'd been shortly after Louise was killed.

This didn't make Marianne Hedison innocent, of course. Nolan knew that a psychotic killer might well react this way to her very own crime. Nobody was more anxious to deny the reality of a murder than a murderer.

"So tonight it was Auggie's snuff," she concluded. "And it was Renee being murdered."

"Who is this 'Auggie' you keep talking about?" Clayton asked.

"He's a character on the network. He's a clown. People play roles—they make cartoon characters for themselves. But Auggie must be . . . he must be real. He's killed two people. Two *real* people."

"*Two* people?" Nolan asked.

She didn't seem to hear the question.

"What two people?" Nolan repeated.

"Are you really the police?" she asked.

"Who else would we be?"

"I don't know. If you're really the police, then she's really dead. But nothing makes sense." Then, after a pause, she said, "I keep expecting you to kill me."

"Do you want to see our identification again?"

"No."

"How did you know it was your friend on the computer?" Clayton asked, trying another tack.

"It looked like her. The cartoon drawing looked a lot like her. And her bathroom—black toilet and sink and bathtub. Even her cat."

Nolan and Clayton looked at each other. Clayton gave Nolan a silent nod, as if to say, "Let me try something."

Clayton ushered them into the adjoining office-bedroom, which Kim had vacated. "Could you identify this sound for us?" he said. He played the tape of the mysterious rumbling.

Marianne Hedison tilted her head and listened. Then, with a slight note of surprise, she said, "It's her cat."

"Her cat?"

"Lucifer. Auggie picked him up when it was over. Auggie must have held him up to the answering machine."

Nolan looked at Clayton. His partner's look was warier than before.

"Listen, ma'am," Nolan said quietly. "I should tell you that you don't have to answer any more questions without a lawyer present."

Marianne Hedison's expression became startled and a bit fearful. "What?" she gasped. "Do you think I—?"

"We don't think anything yet."

Marianne Hedison was silent. Her eyes glazed a little. Then she said, "I'd better show it to you." She didn't notice the detectives stiffen when she reached inside her purse—didn't notice Nolan's hand hovering near his gun. She took out a small computer disk. "It's all on here," she said. "I downloaded it."

"What?" Nolan asked.

"The murder. The enactment."

Marianne Hedison sat down and confidently booted up the computer.

"After the last time, I decided to copy the next snuff Auggie did," she explained. "There's a command for that. The command downloads a copy of the active file. This is the first time I've actually used it."

"After the last time"? He remembered this woman in the hotel corridor—that crazed, paralyzed look as she stared at the bloodstain on the wall. *Christ, is this one really crazy?*

He remembered Clayton's off-the-wall hunch that the two murders were somehow connected. Nolan was a long way from buying it, but Clayton's hunches often proved uncanny—sometimes when they seemed the most nonsensical. Could this woman be a serial killer? Serials sometimes did come to the police and offer their "assistance"—apparently to heighten the thrill of their crimes. It gave them a sense of power, of control over the situation—a chance to admire their own brilliance and to laugh at the bungling investigators. Did she fit that pattern? Or was she maybe trying to set up some kind of insanity defense, playing the role of a schizo or multiple personality who only had a vague idea, if any, of what she had done?

Don't jump to conclusions. Let her go on with it for a while.

Marianne Hedison booted up the computer and inserted a small disk into the drive. Then she stared at the screen and blinked.

"It's gone," she said.

"What's gone?" Nolan asked.

"The dog and the moon. The Insomnimania icon. She must have gotten off the network. I can't run the program without . . . Just a minute."

She began to fumble through a plastic box containing a row of computer disks. She found a pertinent one and slipped it into the disk drive.

"Here it is," she said, looking relieved. "She's still got all the software. The animation will run in just a few moments." She clicked the computer mouse and typed in key commands much faster than Nolan could follow.

She's smart. Maybe too smart for her own good.

A picture appeared on the computer monitor. It was a cartoonish drawing of a darkened bathroom, much like the one in the apartment. A couple of candles were burning. A steady stream of water poured into the tub, and gray curls representing steam crept silently ceilingward.

The detectives both started when the computer began to emit the sound of a guitar, piano, and then a crooning human voice. A barefoot woman wearing a brightly flowered bathrobe stepped into the picture. She turned toward the screen, shook out her reddish hair, and removed the bathrobe to reveal a nude figure.

What is this, some kind of soft-porn show?

The cartoon figure walked over to the sink, gazed at her reflection, then ran a comb through her hair. The singing voice continued with the bluesy song.

The cartoon woman turned toward the screen again, and a tiny yellow vial appeared out of nowhere in her right hand. She walked toward the steaming tub and poured the contents of the vial into the water. A yellow vapor and a handful of bubbles rose out of the tub. The woman sniffed the air luxuriously.

She turned off the faucet and hopped into the tub. Tiny blue squares scattered everywhere. The figure sat up, sponged her arms and back, then reclined again. One of her arms trailed back and forth along the edge of the tub. Next, the figure sat up again, washed her arms and back, and reclined. Again, one arm trailed back and forth over the edge of the tub. The same action repeated itself again and again. The voice sang the same refrain over and over.

Nothing more happened.

Marianne Hedison stared at the screen.

"A loop," she whispered.

"You said you saw a murder," Nolan said.

"That bastard," she said, her voice quickly rising. "That bastard tricked me."

"Ms. Hedison, would you please explain—?"

"No!" the woman shouted at the computer screen. "You murdering monster! You can't do this!"

She rose halfway out of the chair and raised her fists stiffly above her. Nolan reached from behind and seized both her arms before she could send them crashing into the computer screen. Her arms were slender but remarkably strong. Nolan wondered if he could restrain her without breaking her wrists. He almost lost his balance as he fought to hold her back.

She emitted a wordless, guttural shriek of raging protest—a violent contrast to her previous dazed quietness. The dormant frenzy Nolan had detected earlier now exploded through her body. He could feel it as he struggled with her. Then her voice descended into agonizing sobs. "No!" she cried. "No! No! No! No!"

Nolan now felt the woman's strength ebb away. Her arms went limp. She wept more softly.

"You should call your lawyer," he heard himself say quietly.

W HAT THE HELL'S GOING ON?" NOLAN SNAPPED.

"Shhh," Clayton hissed, pulling the door nearly closed behind them. In the deceased's home office, Marianne Hedison was calling her lawyer. The detectives had left her alone, getting momentarily out of her way as much to regroup as to allow the woman some privacy. It was still very early in the predawn morning, and Nolan wanted either sleep or strong coffee. Everything that had happened since the woman arrived had confused and irritated him.

"*Cartoons!*" whispered Nolan hoarsely. "She's bringing *cartoons* in here!"

"Chill, OK? Just chill."

"What's she talking about? Can you tell me what she's talking about?"

"I don't know, man. Give it some time."

Nolan leaned against a wall and rubbed his temples. "Oh, Jesus, I'm sorry," he groaned. "I don't mean to go apeshit on you. It's just this on top of the Judson case, you know? When was the last time we got two in a row like this? What happened to the good old days, when the murders solved themselves right off the bat and you got home in time to watch *The Tonight Show?*"

"Them good old days never happened," Clayton said with a laugh.

"What are we going to do with this woman?" Nolan grumbled.

"Probably let her go."

"How can we? You didn't see her at the Quenton Parks. She's got something to do with both of these killings. She may not have done them, but she's mixed up in them somehow. She could be a real kinko. What if she splits town?"

Clayton shrugged. "What if she's telling the truth?"

"Which is?" Nolan snorted derisively.

"We don't have anything solid enough to arrest her, and you know it."

"What puts you on her side all of a sudden?"

"Who said I was on her side?"

"You're saying everything you can think of to keep me from hauling her in."

Clayton crossed his arms and shook his head. "She doesn't seem the type."

"You can't tell about the quiet ones."

"She wasn't too quiet a few minutes ago."

They fell silent. *Clay's right.* The thought only irritated Nolan more. Anyhow, there was nothing much they could do or say until the woman finished talking to her lawyer. Nolan could hear her voice in the office-bedroom. He couldn't make out her words, but her pitch was getting higher—not quite angry, but argumentative.

After a few moments, Marianne Hedison came out of the office and sat down on the leather sofa. Nolan immediately noticed something different about her bearing, her demeanor. Gone was the stunned, frightened creature who had arrived a short time ago. This woman was tired and haggard, but had a look of quiet resolve.

"My lawyer says I shouldn't talk to you," she said simply.

"He's probably got a point," Nolan said resignedly.

"So," she continued, folding her hands in her lap, "should I start from the beginning?"

"Start what?"

"Telling you what happened. Look, I know I haven't made much sense so far. Maybe I should start from the beginning and go straight through to the end."

Nolan and Clayton exchanged a confused glance.

"Aren't you going to listen to your lawyer?" Nolan asked.

"He doesn't run my life," the woman said, with a hint of weary wryness. "My friend is dead. I didn't kill her. I want to help you find out who did. I expect you to believe me. I've got to have some faith in the system, don't I?"

"It sometimes takes lawyers to make the system work," Nolan suggested.

The woman's lips turned up at the corners in something resembling an ironic smile. "Thank you, Lieutenant, for bringing a little levity to the situation," she said.

Nolan was startled at this display of self-possession. He watched the woman closely as she told her story. More coherently this time, the woman described certain activities on a computer network with a murderous little game and an eager player named Auggie. And she reported two murders—harmless electronic fantasies, it might seem, except they both turned out to be based on the real thing. The woman's story left a lot of mysteries, of course. Nolan and Clayton lobbed a batch of questions at her when she finished, and she came back with graceful if sometimes inconclusive replies.

How long had Auggie been performing his snuffs? The Snuff Room had only been on the network a few months, the woman said. She thought that the clown had been there since the beginning. The woman guessed she had seen four or five snuffs. She remembered a poisoning and a car crash, but those might have been performed by other artists.

Did Auggie know either G. K. Judson or Renee Gauld? The woman didn't know; computer identities were supposed to be secret. But the deceased had wanted to interview Auggie for her radio show, and Marianne knew they had met on the network last Thursday night. Maybe Renee had told Auggie her name, even arranged to meet him.

Could the woman show them how the network operated? Not now, she said. It went off at 5:00 A.M.—and besides, the deceased seemed to have gotten it disconnected.

And what had happened to the two messages the woman claimed to have left on the victim's answering machine? The woman guessed that the cat's purring had been recorded over them.

"We'll check about the phone calls," Nolan said when they had finished.

"I understand," the woman replied.

Nolan looked at her carefully. Was she genuinely trying to help? Her pain over her friend's death seemed unfeigned, but that didn't mean she wasn't involved in some way. In fact, that kind of grief could be intensified by guilt—even guilty information. It was a thought that brought Nolan to his final query.

"Ms. Hedison," Nolan said sternly. When she looked directly at him, he continued. "I asked for your help when we first met at the Quenton Parks Hotel. Why didn't you tell me about this network thing then?"

The woman drew a deep breath and did not answer immediately. Nolan and Clayton both waited silently. Finally she said, "It seemed so bizarre, so completely impossible, seeing that stain on the wall. I couldn't imagine what it might mean. And then, there you were, pushing for an answer. I . . . I didn't know what to say."

"Withholding information from an investigating officer is a very serious matter."

"I know. And that's why I called about it later."

"You called it in?" Nolan said, startled.

"Yes. I couldn't remember your name, but the switchboard connected me with someone they said was working on the case. I told the officer about what I'd seen on the network and left my name and number. He didn't seem to take me very seriously."

Nolan heard Clayton emit a long groan. Nolan looked at him, eyebrows raised.

Clearly understanding Nolan's unspoken query, Clayton muttered grumpily, "I'll tell you what happened later."

Nolan could think of nothing else to ask. His head ached and his eyes burned. This was his second all-night investigation in less than a week, and the trip to Chicago had been less than restful. It was small wonder that he was getting moody and irrational. He noticed that his partner was rubbing his own eyes.

"It's been a long night," Clayton said.

"Yes, it has," the woman said, sagging as though realizing how tired she really was.

"OK, Ms. Hedison," Nolan finally said. "That will be all for now. I'll probably want to talk to you again tomorrow—or rather, later today. We'd like to know where you'll be."

"I'll check into a hotel."

"Any idea which one?"

"Not yet."

"Well, call us when you get checked in," Nolan said. The three people rose from their seats. Nolan handed the woman a card with his division desk phone number on it.

"Wait a minute," the woman said, just as Nolan offered to walk her to the condo entrance. "There's no question that it really was Renee, is there?"

Nolan threw Clayton another startled look.

"What do you mean?" Clayton asked.

"Has anybody identified the body?"

Nolan stared silently at her for a moment. Of course the woman's body had been positively identified as soon as it was discovered. She must know that, too.

"Wait just a minute," Nolan said. "Let me call the morgue."

A moment later, Nolan was on the deceased's phone talking to an assistant at the L.A. morgue. He had closed the office-bedroom door behind him.

"Have you guys started the Renee Gauld autopsy?" he asked.

"Not yet. We just got her in a little while ago."

"Hold off. I'm bringing in somebody to identify the body."

"To *what?*"

"You heard what I said."

"But Jesus, Grobowski, the stiff was identified back at—"

"Humor me, OK? I'll be down in a few minutes."

Nolan hung up the phone.

OK, lady. Here's your chance to show me what you're made of.

Marianne sat impassively in the passenger's seat as Lieutenant Grobowski drove them through the rain to the city morgue. Dawn must have been on its way, but it was impossible to see it through the clouds and gloom.

In a way, this was the worst part of the experience so far—just sitting here, letting someone else drive. She wanted to be doing *something*—driving, talking, anything. But now she was forced to sit silently here in a darkened car with a taciturn detective who obviously didn't much care for her.

Why should he like me? He thinks I'm a murderer.

She could hardly believe the ease with which she'd arranged this trip to the morgue. Of course, the lieutenant had his own reasons for wanting her to see the body. He wanted to observe her reaction. He wanted to see how she would take it. Still, he seemed awfully credulous about her proposing the idea.

Her body's been identified already. How could it not be? All the tenants knew her. Does he think I don't know that? He must think I was born yesterday.

Well, if the cops were that convinced of her naïveté, she could use *their* naïveté to her own advantage. She wanted to be a part of this investigation—and if being suspected of murder allowed that to happen, then she would be suspected of murder.

She remembered Stephen's reaction on the phone.

"Are you out of your mind?" he'd exclaimed. "Get away from those cops! They're investigating a murder! All they want is a suspect—any suspect. How does the gas chamber sound to you?"

She'd awakened him, of course, and he wasn't at his best. He may have half-supposed that he was dreaming.

Poor Stephen. Haven't you figured me out by now? The surest way to get me to act like a crazy woman is to call me one.

She wanted to laugh at the memory, but her capacity for laughter had not yet returned. She wasn't sure it ever would return. She wasn't sure of anything. All she knew was that she had to see Renee's body. She didn't understand quite why, but she had to see it. She had no idea how she would react, much less how the lieutenant would interpret her reaction.

She thought again about how Renee had invited her to the party and how she had failed to come. She struggled for the hundredth time tonight to hold back her emotions, especially her swelling and unfathomable guilt.

In a way, the cop is right. In a way, I'm guilty as hell.

Clayton was relieved when Nolan and the Hedison woman were gone. He hadn't seen his partner so agitated for a very long time, not even over the Judson case. Now Clayton and a couple of uniformed officers were the only people left in the condo unit. He was glad to have some quiet, to let his intuitions go to work.

At times like this, when exhaustion reached a certain threshold, when the next good night's sleep seemed nothing more than a flimsy hypothesis, Clayton's mind often gained its greatest clarity. As far as he was concerned, it was a simple fact that Marianne Hedison had not murdered her friend.

During the questioning, Clayton had studied the woman's eyes. They were green and clear—just like those creeks in South Carolina with rippling water so transparent that you could see the algae-covered rocks below. Clayton had imagined he could reach down in this woman's eyes and pick up a crayfish. Eyes that clear could never conceal a lie. Clayton was sure of it. But he knew that his partner's no-bullshit common sense—or perhaps closed-minded pig-headedness—would never accept that kind of intuitive conclusion. The only way he could persuade Nolan would be to get a good hit on who *was* guilty.

Clayton walked into the bathroom. He took note of the brightly flowered robe hanging on the back of the door. He also observed the black bathroom fixtures and the little wax puddles where candles once had been. All of those had been in the cartoon, and the animated character taking a bath *did* resemble the publicity photo they had found in the victim's desk—more than it resembled the discolored body they had removed from the bathtub, anyway.

But so what? Does it mean anything? Somebody who knew the victim reasonably well might have re-created the scene. This somebody might even know that the victim had a penchant for candlelight and bath oils. None of this necessarily had the first thing to do with the murder.

He wanted to picture the scene of the murder, but the overhead light was too glaring, so he checked the little pools of wax. Two of them had some semblance of wicks left. Clayton lit them and turned the light off. He lowered his head and let his eyes go slightly out of focus. In his peripheral vision, he could just make out the white tape marking where the body had been sprawled in the black tub. What had happened here? Could he see it? He summoned up the incident, tried to coax it to play across his brain. He mentally scripted it out . . .

Scenario A: She knows the killer. She's taking a bath with him—a romantic, candlelit affair. Perhaps they've made love already, or perhaps this is a prelude . . .

But Clayton stopped before the scene even got going. Could this be right? Was the killer actually in the bathtub with her? Did he flip out over something, perhaps some sort of sexual rejection, then do the murder? The tub was certainly large enough. But the image didn't come clearly into his mind. Something was wrong with it. Something didn't fit.

Clayton focused his eyes and looked around the room. One thick peach-colored bath towel lay on the black floor tiles a few feet away from the tub. He squatted down and looked at it.

One end of the towel was still folded like the ones hanging on the towel rods. The other end was crumpled as though it had been used. The other towels in the room all looked fresh and clean.

A person who had actually been in the bath would use more towel than this. Time for a rewrite . . .

Somebody's in the unit—a boyfriend. The boyfriend comes into the bathroom while she's bathing, perhaps bringing her a drink. He sits down on the toilet lid and chats with her. Or maybe he bends over the tub, giving her a massage—a massage that turns violent and deadly.

Again, Clayton stopped. The drain had been opened. By whom, and why? If the killer cared about her, maybe he wouldn't want her to get all bloated or discolored like corpses did when they soaked for even a short while. But no, that wasn't it. That kind of killer would take time to arrange the body or even to cover it. The deceased's body had been sprawled awkwardly, left just as she was when she died.

So what happened to the bathwater?

Clayton looked at his notes.

The coroner said something about contusions on the toes.

So maybe she had let out the water herself—accidentally perhaps, but more probably knowingly, in a last-ditch effort to stave off drowning.

Ugly.

But his gut now told him something definite—the killer was *not* somebody the victim knew. It wasn't exactly an inductive conclusion, but Clayton was quite sure of it.

Scenario B: She got killed by a total stranger.

If so, where did the stranger hide? Clayton wandered out of the bathroom into the short hallway that connected the two bedrooms, the bathroom, and the living room of the condo unit. He pictured the corridor filled with partygoers. It was a chaotic scene, and somebody could hide himself easily, waiting to come out later. If so, the deed had definitely been premeditated.

Clayton went into the office-bedroom—a guest room, apparently, and not where the victim herself customarily slept. Its single bed was pushed against the wall and scattered with pillows. The computer desk held the Macintosh with a large monitor—the very machine that had displayed the strange cartoon a little while ago. A number of cables snaked from it to other attachments. Kim Pak had mentioned a modem, a printer, and an external hard drive.

Got a feeling I'm going to have to learn all about this stuff.

He opened the closet door. A dresser took up most of the closet floor, and the rest of the space was filled with stacked luggage and boxes. There wasn't enough room. And Clayton doubted that the perp had risked just waiting around the office itself, which didn't offer anyplace else to hide.

He went back down the hall to the master bedroom, directly across from the bath. Sergeant Tyler was carefully going through the drawers, lifting things, looking beneath them, placing them back as close as possible to the ways he'd found them. She was looking for anything that might indicate an enemy, a lover, an entanglement of any kind—letters, photos, business cards, a man's clothing—anything that might point to a motive for the murder. The investigating team would later check the deceased's bank accounts and debts. They would find out whether she had insurance policies and a will. They would note the night spots she frequented, the books she was reading, the videos she watched, even the music she favored. Little and perhaps even none of it would tell them anything useful at all.

"Anyplace in here a guy could've hidden?" Clayton asked.

"There, maybe," Tyler replied, gesturing toward the bedroom closet. "Haven't been through it yet." Sergeant Tyler went on with her work.

Clayton walked over and opened the closet door. It was a walk-in space, furbished with rods at different heights and sections of drawers and open shelves. The floor was covered with the same pile carpet as the rest of the bedroom. A half-dozen clothes bags hung on one long rod, but they were not pushed all the way to the end. There was a space between the bags and the end wall of the closet.

Clayton felt a sudden chill of certainty. At times like this, he congratulated himself on having come from a credulous family that believed in auras, divining rods, and religious healing. He didn't believe in any of those things himself, and he certainly did not consider himself to be a psychic. But at crucial moments, Clayton simply *knew what he knew.* It was something like a birthright.

There was a ghost in this closet—not a literal ghost but a very palpable one. He could feel its presence. It was as if time had looped around itself, and the killer was in there even now, waiting for his opportunity. It was as if Clayton had only to grab him and slap the cuffs on him to stop him from killing—and in a magical stroke, the irrevocable would be revoked.

Clayton edged toward the far end of the closet and looked at the space. Yes, there was enough room for someone to stand. On the bottom edge of the wooden shelf, he saw some fibers caught on a splinter. He took a pair of tweezers out of his shirt pocket and carefully removed the strands, put them in a bag, and labeled it.

Clayton stepped back out of the closet, handing the bag to Tyler.

"Don't touch anything in there," Clayton said. "I want forensics to go over it."

■

Filed.

That one word flashed through Marianne's mind as the coroner's assistant reached for the handle on the metal door. The drawer slid out with a sickening, metallic rumble. The contorted, naked body lay beneath a translucent plastic sheet. The assistant pulled the sheet back discreetly, just below the shoulders, as if protecting the corpse's modesty. This gallant gesture struck Marianne as vaguely necrophiliac.

Marianne took a good look at the corpse's face.

"That's her," she whispered. "That's Renee."

But it was a lie—the first lie she had told tonight. This thing on the stainless-steel table was not Renee. The expression, the colors, even the shapes of the cheekbones—everything about it was all wrong. It was an unconvincing forgery of Renee. Renee herself was not here—not on this table, not under this plastic sheet, not stashed away in this monolithic filing cabinet. Her corpse might be here, but that was not at all the same thing.

Marianne was seized with shame at her falsehood. Was it too transparent? Did the lieutenant know that she was lying? What would he say if she told him the truth? What would he say if she told him that Renee simply wasn't here, that she had to be somewhere else—that she was a *missing* person, not a dead one? But it was too late to tell him differently.

She became sick with horror, but she did not actually feel it—not the way she might feel joy, sadness, pain, or rage. It was more like she *heard* the horror resounding in some distant basement of her soul—the sound of the first death with its contingent anguish echoing down to her throughout all time. There had to be a word for this weird, unfelt, audible horror. She had no idea what that word might be.

She felt her legs totter under her. She felt the detective catch her. She felt him start to drag her toward a chair. She felt herself jerk away from him defiantly, yanking herself to her feet, furiously commanding the blood cells back into her brain. She staggered back toward the table, propping her hands against its cold steel edge, staring at the pinched eyelids, imagining the dead eyes behind them.

Renee's not here.

With no one inside those eyes, Marianne could look nowhere

except into her own heart. And where was her rage? Where was her outrage against this crime? Why didn't this room and all its adjoining hallways ring out with her cries for justice, for revenge?

The outcries simply did not come. The deed was too awful, too final not to have been done with some implacable purpose. There was something almost religious about it, something beyond Marianne's comprehension. The thought of the person who had made this corpse did not fill her with anger but with an inexorable wave of awe-struck humility.

She could not grasp this crime.

She could not judge it.

For these very reasons, she knew she had to find its perpetrator. She had to look into his eyes as she could no longer look into these, she had to search out his heart, she had to learn his purpose and take it away from him before judgment and vindication could at last be done.

But first, I have to find Renee.

Nolan Grobowski reached out and touched the woman's arm. She didn't shake him off this time.

"It's time to go," he told her.

She nodded and let him lead her away.

Nolan kept studying the woman's expression. It was a perfect blank. It had been blank throughout the whole episode. But he remembered the dead weight her body had made when she fell into his arms. The faint had felt real enough.

It would have been better if she'd cried, though. It would have seemed more real.

Besides, she had snapped back too quickly. For her sake, it would have been much better if she had cried. But maybe she couldn't cry.

Fainting is easy. Crying is hard.

01100·

DANGER—HIGH
VOLTAGE

A FTER LIEUTENANT GROBOWSKI RETURNED MARIANNE TO HER car in front of Renee's condominium, she sat at the wheel and stared into space. The bright morning sunlight reflected off a dozen points of the chrome and glass, together with the droplets of water left from last night's long rain. The light hurt her eyes. She dug in her handbag for sunglasses, but quickly realized she had left home without them. She had taken nothing except her handbag. She didn't have any clothes to wear other than what she had on.

So what's the next order of business?

First, she had to find a place to stay. She briefly considered the Quenton Parks Hotel. Perhaps it would be a good idea for her to be near to one of the murder scenes. But what would be the point? What did she seriously think she was going to do, carry out her own personal investigation? If she wanted to keep tabs on the police, fine, but going back to the Quenton Parks would be too much like a teenager staying all night in a haunted house on a dare. This wasn't a game. Marianne needed a place where she could collect herself, come to terms with what had happened, and figure out what to do next.

She drove instead to the Pacific Surf Hotel in Santa Monica and checked in. With no luggage, no makeup, and wearing well-worn house clothes, she knew she looked conspicuous. But she couldn't muster up much concern about appearances.

The Pacific Surf was a modern hotel, spare in decor, and a welcome improvement over the Quenton Parks' inhuman gaudiness. Marianne went to her room, took off her shoes, and dropped on her back across the expansive bed. She expected relief to hit immediately. It didn't. She ached horribly all over. But the idea of rising from the bed to take off her clothes was unimaginable. She was determined to lie there until the aching passed.

The ache was actually noisy—a kind of hum. It was the sound of overloaded wires and circuitry, the same hum the fluorescent ceiling tubes had made back at the morgue. She also remembered the hum from her childhood. When she was a little girl in Philadelphia, she used to play in a field with a high, sloping embankment at its end. Carved into the embankment was a wall with a fifteen-foot stretch of concrete pavement leading up to it. There was a door in the wall bearing a red sign announcing DANGER—HIGH VOLTAGE. And from behind that door came that loud, steady, forbidding hum.

In those long-ago days, she used to pause in her play and stand at the edge of that concrete pavement and listen to that hum. She wondered what would happen if she defied the sign and approached the door. She imagined that the electricity would reach out from behind the door and grab her and kill her. She never took that chance. She always stood safely on the grass beyond that pavement.

A lot of good it did you to play it safe. That ugly noise has followed you through life and caught up with you. Now it's invaded your body.

This was worse than any insomnia she'd ever experienced. After a while, she sat up. The humming wasn't quite as loud in this position. She stared senselessly at the blank wall in front of her for a few long moments. Then she picked up the phone, called the number the two detectives had given her, and dutifully informed the switchboard operator of her whereabouts.

She looked at her watch. It was just seven-thirty in the morning. It was no good just staying here. She had to go somewhere. She had no idea where, but she had to go somewhere. She briefly thought about taking a shower before going out, but it hardly seemed worth it, considering that she would have to put on these same clothes afterward. She walked out of the hotel and got into her car and started driving.

She decided not to worry about where she was going. She would just drive around until she reached a threshold of exhaustion that matched her relentless aching. Then she ought to be able to sleep. But she might have to drive a long time. Her inner, high-voltage humming had gotten a lot louder—so loud that she could hear it even over the sound of her car engine.

She guessed that this aching hum was a kind of surrogate sorrow—a thing to fill the gap where her grief ought to be but somehow still wasn't. And where was her grief? When should she expect it to kick in? Why hadn't she cried? When was she going to cry?

To her own surprise, she noticed that she was driving toward Renee's condominium. Why was she going there? She parked across the street from the condo, turned off the engine, got out of the car, and walked up to the front door.

Then she realized why she had come. She wanted—*needed*—to find and talk to somebody, anybody, who had known Renee.

The front door of the building was controlled by a buzzer system. Renee's unit was 2-A. Marianne buzzed 2-B, hoping that the closest unit also meant the closest friends. After a few moments, she heard a crackle over the little speaker.

"Yes?" asked a male voice.

"My name is Marianne Hedison. I was a friend of Renee Gauld's."

"Yes?" said the voice again.

Did he hear me? She almost repeated her name, but instead she said, "I'd like to talk to you."

"Are you another reporter?"

"No."

"If you're a reporter, please go away."

"I'm not a reporter. I was here last night when the police were here. I just want to talk."

No answer came from the speaker. Marianne felt her throat choke with despair. Could she cry at last? That would be wrong. It wouldn't even be grief. She wanted to cry over the loss of her friend, not some total stranger's refusal to let her into his home. Her inner hum turned deafening.

"Please," she said, trying to keep her shaking voice under control. "I just want to talk to somebody who cared about her. Please."

There was a long pause, then a strident buzz. Marianne quickly opened the door. She went upstairs, where she was met by a tall, brown-haired young man, probably in his mid-twenties. He was handsome, but his eyes were red and bleary.

Maybe he hears the humming, too.

The man looked Marianne over carefully, apparently satisfying himself that she was not a reporter.

"Please come in," he said at last. He ushered her into the unit where a shorter, slightly rounder man was waiting.

"I'm Roland," the man who had met her said. "This is Tony."

Tony shook her hand and showed her to a seat. "Would you like anything? Coffee? Something to drink?"

Marianne felt the urge to ask for a bourbon, but she reminded herself that it was still early in the morning. Decorum wasn't exactly a priority, but she didn't want to collapse in a dead heap in front of these gentlemen.

"Coffee, please," she said.

Roland exited into the kitchen. Tony was sitting on the sofa, turned slightly sideways, his body hunched forward as though in pain. Marianne could see that he was somewhat older than Roland. His face was strained, but he managed to give Marianne a kind, commiserating look.

"It's been so awful," Tony said.

"Yes," Marianne agreed. She glanced around. The room was elegant and ornate, with rich colors and a collection of authentic Chinese and other Asiatic pieces mixed with comfortable modern furniture. The unit looked larger than Renee's.

Roland returned with her coffee. "Do you want cream or sugar?" he asked.

"No. Black's fine."

"I'm sorry if I was rude," he said, handing her the cup and saucer. "This is the first lull we've had in reporters all morning. We've told them to go away, but it doesn't help. We really can't take it anymore."

"They don't seem to care about anybody's feelings," Tony added. He seemed to keep his body deliberately still, as if holding it taut against the expected onset of pain. Roland stood beside the couch. The three people fell silent. In the silence, Marianne noticed that her internal humming had stopped. She still hurt, though.

Now she wondered what to say. She reminded herself of her Quaker family, among whom silence was revered. She was always taught that there was nothing wrong with being quiet among people, that a lot could be said in simple stillness. Marianne had often tried to apply that wisdom to everyday social life with its frequent lulls and silences. But it was difficult. She could never be sure whether other people liked the quiet, whether they accepted it as a kind of communication. Renee had trouble with the quiet. Were these two men like Renee—always resisting stillness?

Marianne felt an urgency to speak.

"How did you . . . find out?" she asked.

She saw Roland buckle slightly, as if someone had struck him. His eyes clinched, and his coffee cup rattled slightly in its saucer.

Tony spoke strickenly. "We—*Roland* found her."

Marianne felt a wave of shock.

"I'm terribly sorry," she said.

"Yes," said Tony simply, starting to rock back and forth very slightly. "Sit down," he said to Roland. "You've got to sit down."

Roland sat down on the couch next to Tony.

"We can't talk about that part of it," Roland explained. "It's not that we don't want to, but we can't. The police asked us not to talk about any of the details of the murder."

"I don't want to," Marianne assured them. "I only want to talk about Renee."

It became easier from there. The three shared a few reminiscences. Marianne spoke of her six-year friendship with Renee, and Tony and Roland spoke just as feelingly of their briefer one. Tony and Roland had met Renee socially and had immediately struck it off. They shared the same interests, politics, and music. They laughed at the same jokes. They had become an inseparable trio.

Inseparable.

The word made Marianne shiver deep inside. It seemed a terrible commentary on their friendship that Renee had never told her about these two lovely men. What had happened? Why had so many important things been left unspoken?

"Do you know what plans have been made for the funeral?" Marianne asked, after the reminiscences began to wane a little.

"It will be in Iowa, the little town where she came from," Roland said. "We talked on the telephone to an aunt. We offered to help with things here—the condo, paperwork, you know."

"Are you going to the funeral?" Marianne asked.

"No," Tony said. "We've never actually met any of her family."

"We'd love to," Roland added. "It would be fascinating to meet her people, to find out how such a free spirit as Renee came out of the farm belt. I'm sure they're wonderful people. But would they feel comfortable with Tony and me? It's best for us to do what we can right here."

"Please let me know if I can help," Marianne said. She reached into her handbag for a business card. On the back of it, she wrote "Pacific Surf Hotel." She handed the card to Roland. In return, Roland gave her their phone number and the number of the aunt in Iowa.

Then another silence fell. Marianne felt moved to broach the forbidden subject of the murder. She had to say something. She had to make her confession.

"She invited me to come that night," she said. "I didn't. I can't help but think . . . if I had been here . . ."

"It wouldn't have happened?" Tony said, finishing her thought. "We wonder the same thing. Why didn't we stop in her unit for a nightcap, a little conversation? We did it so often, why not that night? And if we had, could we have prevented . . . ?"

His last words dropped into barely a whisper.

Then all was absolutely hushed and still. They searched each other's pained and frightened eyes. They looked like anguished waxworks sitting together in the silent living room. As she had at the morgue, Marianne caught a fleeting intimation of some awful purpose behind this cruel act. It was not Renee who was being visited with despair and pain. Marianne was. These men were. They didn't deserve this visitation.

Incommensurate. We are all being punished, and our punishment is incommensurate with our wrongs.

How else could she conceive it? She had failed to show up at a party. Roland and Tony had failed to stop in for late-night cocktails. Small crimes of omission, both—but they carried ghastly consequences. Someone had taken it into his heart to judge them for these lapses. Someone had chosen to take the life of someone dear to them as punishment.

He must be powerful

More than ever, Marianne knew she had to find him.

But first, I have to find Renee.

She saw no such resolve in the faces of the two men before her. They turned their weary eyes toward each other with nothing but love. Tony took Roland's hand in his. Tony's hand was pale while Roland's was slightly darker, but both were loving and strong.

Marianne had grown up among people who took each other's

hands after worship, before dinner, when entering each other's houses—for all conceivable occasions. Marianne's father and mother used to hold hands constantly—the most passionate act she ever witnessed in the quiet household. And at her parents' funerals, in the very depths of her grief, Marianne had felt herself warmly enveloped by an entire congregation bound together by clasped hands. And now where was a hand for Marianne to clasp?

How did I lose what these men have kept? How did I forfeit this?

Her throat choked again. But still, she could not cry.

The living room of Larry Bricker's West Hollywood home was decorated tastefully with a touch of the macabre. The walls were lined with splendid pen-and-ink drawings of bats, owls, weasels, wolves, and the like—all creatures of night and darkness. The bookshelf contained perhaps hundreds of reference books about death and violence, all of them hardback, some of them leather-bound antiques. First editions of Larry Bricker's own horrific fare were prominently displayed as well.

Clayton was sitting on the couch. Bricker was sitting in a chair across the room from him. The slight, balding man's eyes were glazed with shock as he stared at the floorboards.

"I'm sorry to have to be the one to tell you," Clayton said.

But Bricker did not seem to hear. This bothered Clayton. He wanted very much for Bricker to have heard him say he was sorry, but he wouldn't feel right repeating it.

Apologies don't count for much when they get pushy.

In the silence, Clayton found himself studying the coffee table in front of him. He realized he had seen one just like it in a museum in South Carolina. It was, in fact, a portable embalming table, probably dating to the Civil War.

Clayton tried to imagine what a normal visit to Larry Bricker would be like. Bricker would undoubtedly show off his slightly funereal belongings and decor with liberal doses of morbid jest. Guests would be hugely—if chillingly—entertained.

Indeed, when Clayton had arrived, Bricker had been jaunty and hospitable, as if prepared for just such a performance. Then he had almost collapsed with shock when Clayton told him the news. He had been sitting here in silence during the long moments since. It was certainly no time for gruesome jokes. The room itself was suddenly infused with an uncomfortable blend of fact and fancy, and Clayton wondered if Bricker might actually be feeling a little uncomfortable in his own surroundings. This might well be the first time Bricker had encountered real violence, real destruction.

"I tried calling her yesterday," Bricker said, finally breaking the silence. "I got her machine. Now I know . . . why she didn't call back."

Clayton nodded. "I have to ask a few questions," he said.

The man looked up from the floor straight at Clayton. "Of course," he said.

"Please tell me about your relationship with the deceased."

There wasn't much to tell, but Bricker was painstakingly honest about it. He hadn't known the woman long at all. They had only met last weekend when she interviewed him for her radio talk show. But he was fond of her—very, very fond of her. He was sure they would have gotten involved if . . .

"We knew each other such a short time," Bricker said.

Clayton understood the precise feeling behind the words. Bricker could not grieve the woman's death, having known her so little and so briefly. What Bricker grieved was the time itself in all its awful fleetingness.

Bricker went on to explain that he was the deceased's date at the party. He made no equivocation about it, and Clayton didn't have to coax it out of him. But Bricker knew exactly what time he had left the party, and several people had seen him leave. He was able to give Clayton a couple of names. He said he had come straight home, but didn't know if anybody had seen him arrive.

Clayton thanked him for his forthrightness and rose to leave. If Bricker was concerned that he might be considered a suspect, he didn't show it. Clayton was glad of that. Despite Clayton's own conviction of the man's innocence, he could not offer Bricker any assurance that he wouldn't be suspected. A lot depended on how his alibis held up. Clayton hoped they were as tight as a drum.

They were standing in the entrance now.

"Please call me if I can help," Bricker said in perfect simplicity.

"We will," Clayton said. "Thanks, Mr. Bricker."

"Larry. Please."

As Clayton walked toward his car, he noted the cleanness of the air, so recently washed by a good night's rain. Clayton wondered what Gauld's killer was doing at the moment. Was he enjoying this pleasant change in the weather, or did he have other things on his mind?

I'd sure like to know.

Nolan was sitting at his desk in the detective bay area. The morning was still young, but it had already been a long day. He had paid a visit to the guard who had been on duty at the condo the night of the murder. He would doubtless have to talk to dozens of other people today.

In the meantime, his thoughts kept floating back to the Hedison woman. He had checked her phone records, and a phone call had been made from her Santa Barbara residence to Gauld's condo at about the time of the murder—not that that necessarily proved anything.

Nolan didn't like knowing she was out there on her own. Sure, she had called and given the switchboard her whereabouts, but what if she'd jumped on the first plane out of the country a minute later?

Gotta check up on her the next chance I get. Christ, I'd give anything for a good night's sleep.

Nolan snapped out of his reverie as Clayton walked up to the desk and sat down tiredly.

"So what's the deal with Larry Bricker?" Nolan said.

"He's not the one," Clayton replied simply.

"How do you know?"

Clayton groaned. "I'm a detective, too, remember? I know the ropes. I know a suspect when I see one."

"All right. Don't get testy. Have we got an alibi to check on this guy?"

"Yeah. Couple of people at the party. We should talk to his neighbors, too. He'll come out clean. What about the security guard?"

"I grilled him pretty hard, but he's clean. His wife says he was home by two."

"His wife? Can't he do better than that?"

"He sounds OK to me."

"Wouldn't two o'clock leave him time before he left? When he was supposedly making the last-check rounds?"

"Sure, but what's the motive? Besides, he's got a long, clean record. Been with the company for eight years. A good company, too. The way I see it, the killer was hiding in the closet while the guard was making his last rounds."

Clayton heaved a deep sigh. "No laughs yet, huh?" he said.

"Nope. This audience is murder."

"So whaddya checking next?"

"Insomnimania," Nolan said. "Maybe I can figure out how the network fits in—*if* it fits in."

"Want me to come?"

"Nope. You do something else. I'll take the woman with me."

"What woman?"

"Marianne Hedison—if she hasn't split town."

Nolan could see Clayton's mouth drop. "What the fuck is this?" Clayton asked. "One minute you want to haul her in, the next she's your new partner. What's with you, anyway?"

"I want to keep my eye on her."

"Whaddya think, she's part of some high-tech conspiracy, some ring of snuff artists? Give it up, Nol."

"I want to keep my eye on her," Nolan repeated slowly and insistently. "Besides, she might help me with all that computer lingo."

"Sometimes I can't understand you, man," Clayton said.

"Just let me do things my own way."

Clayton shook his head irritably. "OK," he said. "I'll check the radio station, talk to people there."

"Sounds good."

"I'm outta here," Clayton said in a clipped voice. He got up and left.

Nolan leaned back in his chair and pressed his fingers against his temples. This headache seemed to come and go in waves, waxing and waning but becoming progressively stronger as the case went sourer.

"Your new partner." That was a cheap shot. Gonna kill each other before this thing is through.

He picked up his phone and dialed the number for the Pacific Surf Hotel.

Marianne returned to her hotel room after visiting Tony and Roland. She was fully exhausted now—a simple exhaustion heavy with the promise of sleep, not a complicated exhaustion imploding in on itself, making sleep impossible. She was grateful to feel it.

Now she could make plans. Now she could take charge of her life again. Most crucially, she could do what she had tried to do earlier— lie down and catch some sleep. Then she would shower. After that, she would shop around for some clothes to wear during her stay in Los Angeles—however long that might turn out to be.

But first, she had to call in to her office. Nobody there expected her to come in today, but they did expect her to modem in the just-completed rendering for the Abernathy project. She called the secretary and told her to pass the word to Dwayne not to expect any work from her for today—or maybe for the next several days. She explained that a friend in L.A. had passed away. Marianne really didn't hear the secretary's ensuing barrage of condolences. She simply emitted mechanical replies.

". . . yes, thank you . . . it was a terrible shock, thank you . . . thank you, I will . . ."

She hung up the phone and lay down on the bed.

No hum, she realized with satisfaction.

But no sooner had she started to doze off than the phone rang. She picked it up and heard a man's voice.

"Ms. Hedison?"

"Yes?"

"This is Lieutenant Grobowski. Did I catch you asleep?"

"No," she said.

No such chance.

"Well, listen," Grobowski said. "I hate to impose, but maybe you could help me with something. I've got to drop in on these Insomnimania guys you've been talking about, and I, uh, wondered if you might come with me."

Marianne almost laughed aloud. The good lieutenant was certainly going to transparent lengths to keep watch over his femme fatale.

"Why, Lieutenant, what a lovely offer," she said sweetly. "I've always wanted to visit a computer network office. Thank you so much."

"What I mean is, you know about computers and I don't," Grobowski said a little defensively. "I thought you might help me talk to these guys. You know, interpret for me."

"Of course. When do you want to pick me up?"

"Right now, if that's possible."

Marianne stifled a groan. She wanted to watch Grobowski's progress on the case as much as he wanted to see her betray her guilt—so she couldn't blow this opportunity.

So much for getting a little sleep.

"Yes, that will be fine," she said.

"Great. I'll be right over."

She hung up the phone and laughed. For the first time since this whole wretched thing had happened, she laughed. Grobowski had sounded for all the world like a high school kid asking the most popular girl in school for a date.

At least his agenda isn't to get me in the sack. It's to get me in the gas chamber.

Marianne hadn't cried yet, but at least she was able to laugh. That was better than nothing.

Judson gets murdered, and some Auggie guy acts out his killing on a computer network. A woman gets murdered in an apparently unconnected case, and Auggie acts out her killing on the network, too. And there's this other woman who has seen both computer shows and who turns up at both crime scenes. And she says she can tie it all together for us . . .

"Watch the road!" cried a voice beside Nolan.

"What?" Nolan exclaimed. He was so tired and lost in thought that he almost forgot he was driving into the depths of downtown L.A. on the way to the Insomnimania network office.

"You almost hit that lady," scolded Marianne Hedison, who was sitting on the passenger side.

"What lady?"

"In the crosswalk. You're not supposed to kill pedestrians if they're in the crosswalk. That's the law. How are you supposed to defend the law if you don't know a thing like that?"

"I'm not a traffic cop," Nolan said.

Nolan wondered if it had been a mistake to bring her along after all. It was bad enough that he couldn't make her fit into the puzzle this case had become. Now she had to criticize his driving.

And was he awake enough to deal with both her and these computer people? He couldn't help thinking the trip would be a waste of time. It went against Nolan's every instinct to believe the network fit into the crimes at all.

Murder's a flesh-and-blood kind of deal. Electronics has nothing to do with it. People kill people face-to-face. They don't do it over the phone. Maybe I'm old-fashioned, but that part of the human condition is never going to change.

Marianne followed Lieutenant Grobowski toward the front entrance of a nondescript, unmarked downtown building. The neighborhood didn't look very promising. Most of the buildings in the area were either boarded up or turned into warehouses, and the sidewalks were lined with vagrants.

She was so tired now that she didn't even notice it anymore. In fact, she felt almost refreshed, as if she'd gotten some sort of second wind.

They stopped in front of a large, blank, metal door. *Did he get the wrong address?* To her surprise, the forbidding door wasn't locked. The detective simply opened it, and they stepped inside the building. Marianne had to blink a few times to adjust to the sudden darkness.

Is this a reception room?

It took her a moment to realize that the primary illumination in the room came from a black light. Old sixties decor, ranging from a phosphorescent Buddha to numerous Grateful Dead posters, coated the walls. Little psychedelic lapel pins were attached to all the posters, making archaic pronouncements like "Make Love Not War," "The Witch Is Dead," and "Frodo Lives." The music of Santana undulated through the thick smell of incense and presumably less-legal fragrances.

Seated in a battered leather swivel chair with his feet propped up on the desktop and his nose buried in a copy of *Naked Lunch* was an emaciated, bearded man with his graying hair in pigtails. How he could read in this light was impossible for Marianne to imagine. She could see that his face was deeply lined. She suspected that he wasn't nearly as old as he looked—that drugs of one kind or another had taken their toll. And indeed, a water pipe containing a remnant of marijuana sat openly in front of him.

Hope this arrest-happy cop doesn't bust this guy for dope before we can ask him any questions.

"I'm here to talk to either Ned Pritchard or Baldwin Maisie," Lieutenant Grobowski said. "Are you one of them?"

"Yes," the man said simply.

"Care to tell me which?" Lieutenant Grobowski asked.

The man's brow furrowed deeply as he pondered the request.

"No," he said finally, without a trace of belligerence.

Marianne was tickled by the lieutenant's slow burn. Grobowski produced a badge and identified himself.

"I'd like to ask some questions," Lieutenant Grobowski said.

The man looked intently at the badge, as if noting how it failed to show up very well in the black light. Then he looked up.

"Who's the lady?" he asked.

"Someone with a special interest in this case," Lieutenant Grobowski said.

The man looked Marianne over approvingly.

"Swank," he said, with seemingly sincere admiration.

Now it was Marianne's turn to be taken aback.

Swank?

She didn't feel swank. She glanced down to remind herself what she was wearing. In the dim light, she could barely make out the rumpled slacks and jacket that she had hastily put on—when had it been? Only last night?

"What's the case?" the man muttered, leaning forward on the desk.

"Have you got a client in your network who goes by the name of Auggie?" Lieutenant Grobowski asked.

"I don't pay much attention to who's on the net," the man said with a shrug.

"Auggie's kind of a celebrity in your Snuff Room."

"Oh, *that* Auggie."

"Yeah, that Auggie."

Then Marianne chimed in. "Did you know that Auggie's snuffs are reenactments of real-life murders?" she said. Grobowski shot her a disapproving look. But Marianne had to ask. Since Grobowski barely believed in either Auggie or the Snuff Room, she couldn't exactly count on him to ask the right questions.

"You don't say," the man said, with apparently honest incredulity.

"You've got to help us," Marianne said. "We think Auggie's operator might be a killer."

She could see that Lieutenant Grobowski was seething now.

Well, what does he expect from me? Surely he didn't expect me to just hang around and keep my mouth shut.

The man at the desk began to laugh—softly at first, then more and more loudly. "Oh, my," he said at last. "My, my, my. This is good. Pritchard's gotta hear about this. Come on. I'll introduce you to him."

He led them to a doorway with hanging plastic beads. Then he pulled the beads aside, and the three of them walked down a hallway lined with rooms—all empty except for an occasional piece of broken furniture or a pile of empty boxes. At the end of the hallway, the man they now assumed to be Baldwin Maisie opened another metal door and led them into a large room with off-white cinderblock walls and a black-painted ceiling sprouting pipes and cable. The room was dim and slightly chilly, and its only windows were high on the wall, painted over, and barred. It was filled with a noisy electric hum. Marianne didn't exactly welcome the humming, but she was content to have it outside her body for a change.

On the tile floor stood a huge beige box at least eight feet high. Fans inside the box hummed noisily. Several expansive folding tables were covered with dozens of other pieces of electronic equipment wired goofily together like some kind of cybernetic Rube Goldberg contraption.

An overweight man, somewhat younger than Maisie, sat perched uneasily on a tiny stenographer's chair, looking as though he might melt off the edges at any moment. He wore a green-striped shirt, red-and-blue plaid pants, and rust-colored suspenders. Ketchup was smeared like fingerpaint down the left side of his shirt. His hair was greasy and he had a three-day stubble of beard.

He leaned over one of the tables, intently staring at a particularly archaic Commodore monitor. Scattered around him was a week's worth of fast-food wrappings. He guzzled the remains of a soft drink through a straw with a grotesque, slurping sound.

Marianne was amazed at the machines on the table—an eclectic collection of top-of-the-line Macintoshes, obsolete Wangs, and what actually appeared to be antique, vacuum-tube radio receivers and amplifiers. All the monitors were on, displaying graphics, desktops, or screen-saver patterns. But some of the monitors seemed to be malfunctioning. Their images were eroding or flickering erratically.

Could this be the control room for Insomnimania? She had imagined rows of people working at individual terminals—not this conglomeration of mismatched parts.

She was startled out of her musings as the man began to talk to the monitor he was facing.

"Chick, chick, chick," he said with affectionate baby-talk. "Atta gurly-wurly. Chick, chick, chick. Neddy's little gurly-wurly was hungry, wasn't she? Chick, chick, chick, chick . . ."

The fat man pecked on the monitor screen with his fingernail, behaving like some dotty old lady with a parakeet. Marianne turned toward Maisie, hoping for an explanation.

"Shhh," Maisie whispered. "Let 'im finish feeding her."

"But what's he doing?" Marianne whispered back.

"Viruses," Maisie explained. "Keeps 'em as pets. WDEF, Michelangelo, Friday the Thirteenth, others you never heard of. Why, I'll bet Ol' Pritch's got the finest collection in captivity."

In captivity?

Marianne's eyes scanned the table again. So the terminals were little cages—a petting zoo of computer viruses!

"But what controls Insomnimania?" she quietly asked Maisie.

"Over here," Maisie whispered proudly, leading her to the big beige box. "VAX 8650, running an advanced UNIX system. She's sweet and she's independent. Does everything all on her own."

Marianne put her hand against the squat monolith. She yanked it away again when she felt that hum begin to reinvade her body. It felt a little awe-inspiring to imagine this thing controlling a sprawling electronic labyrinth like the virtual world of Insomnimania.

Still, it's not a lot to look at.

She crept slowly behind the rotund man on the swivel chair and looked over his shoulder.

"Chick, chick, chick," Pritchard said again. "Oh, my? Isn't that page-layout program a tasty little sucker! And weren't we hungry-wungry? Yes, we were!"

The monitor displayed a page-layout grid. Intermittently and almost subliminally, the monitor flashed screenfuls of obscenities at the viewer. At last, the screen flickered with a barrage of four-letter words and went blank. Pritchard patted the top of the monitor, almost as if he expected the machine to burp.

"There now," he said. "Take a nice little nappy-wappy." He turned toward Maisie. "Hey, Baldy, could you fetch us a nice juicy accounting program? Poor Tourette's a growing girl, and I just can't seem to keep her fed."

"In a minute, Pritch. I've got a couple of people here—a Lieutenant Somebody-Or-Other and his girlfriend."

His girlfriend!

Marianne shuddered reflexively.

"They want to find out about Auggie," Maisie continued. "You know, the clown character. Says the guy's some kind of mass murderer."

Pritchard smiled and shrugged and said nothing.

"Well, there's your answer," Maisie said amiably. "Client confidentiality, you see? It's even in our instruction book. I can show it to you. 'Your actual identity is protected at all times,' it says—or words to that effect. You wouldn't want us to turn into high-tech finks, wouldja?"

"I can get a subpoena," Nolan said.

Maisie laughed and shook his head good-naturedly. "Lieutenant, we've got very good lawyers. We fight cases like this all the time. They tend to drag on for a long while."

Suddenly, Pritchard spoke up.

"Hey, Baldy," he said warmly. "Show the lady and gentleman a chair. Let me talk to 'em."

Nolan and Marianne placed themselves on uncomfortable folding metal chairs, neither of which sat quite squarely on the damp, gray-painted concrete floor. Still perched on his swivel chair, Pritchard rolled toward them, smiling a pudgy but not disagreeable smile.

"So we've got a killer in our midst, eh?" he asked.

"It looks that way," said Nolan. "And you guys could find yourselves accessories before the fact."

"How do you figure?" Pritchard asked.

"By inventing a nasty little place called the Snuff Room. By setting the scene, by provoking the situation. By concealing the identity of the perpetrator. It's called 'aiding and abetting.' "

"Now hold it," interrupted Maisie, his voice quavering a little. "Hold it just a minute. We're not saying another word without our lawyer present."

"It's OK, Baldy," said Pritchard benignly. "This isn't any big deal. I think we can spare some legal fees and set this matter straight." He began to speak to Nolan with direct simplicity. "We didn't set a scene, we didn't provoke a situation, and we aren't accessories."

"No?"

"Come on, Lieutenant. We're talking about network software! Software doesn't kill people."

"*People* kill people, right?" Nolan answered derisively.

"The network is *virtual reality*. Nobody really gets killed in virtual reality."

"But some of the cartoons show actual killings," Marianne interjected.

"So what? Newspaper reporters depict real events. Have you arrested the guy who wrote up these murders for the *Times*? Whatever's going on, Baldy and I aren't responsible. If there's a killer in our net, you know perfectly well he'd be killing whether we were here or not."

"But you invented the Snuff Room," Marianne said.

"Not really. When we first started Insomnimania, we only gave it two rooms: the Factory, where clients could create virtual selves, and the Speakers' Corner, where those virtual selves could chat with one another. The rest of the thing, the whole labyrinth, was added on piecemeal. New games are requested by our subscribers and we do the programming for them."

"How many subscribers have you got?" Nolan asked.

"Beats me," Pritchard said. "What do you think, Baldy?"

"I'd have to look it up. Lots, anyway. The largest number are here in the L.A. area, where we got started. But we've got members all over the country, all over the world. Distance has no meaning when you're on-line—leastways, not till you get your bill."

"So any of these people can request some new sex game or murder game or whatever and you just fill the orders—no matter what?"

"Only if it's a cool idea," said Maisie. "And if it's workable. We try to run a democratic outfit."

"Your prices aren't exactly democratic," Marianne remarked.

"We aren't as pure as we used to be," Maisie said. "Who is?"

"So a subscriber thought up the Snuff Room and you filled their request?" Grobowski asked.

"That one was a little different, as I recall," Pritchard said. "A little odd."

"Yeah, that's right," Maisie agreed. "That one came to us all ready to run. One of the members sent it in—all the software, the instructions, everything."

"Nice little program," Pritchard added. "Nothing complicated, just performances of animations which are all created ahead of time. Who was it sent that to us, Baldy?"

"Damned if I can remember," said Maisie.

The two of them smiled complacently.

"A killer might be using your network to track his victims," Nolan said. "Aren't you going to help us find him?"

"No," Pritchard said.

"I think you'd better."

"Listen, Officer Krupke—"

"It's *Grobowski*."

"Whatever. As the old saying goes, 'Information wants to be free.' Do you know who said that?"

"Who?" Grobowski asked.

Pritchard looked suddenly bewildered, as if he had really expected Grobowski to tell *him*.

"I dunno," he said. "Who *was* it, Baldy?"

Maisie shrugged. "Benjamin Franklin. Timothy Leary. One of those founding father guys."

"Whoever it was, one of these days I'm gonna personally hand him the Nobel Prize," Pritchard said. "That is, after I crack my way onto their nondigital monolithic low-bandwidth totalitarian committee."

"Let me get this straight," Grobowski said. "You want to set information free, and all I'm *asking* for is information. We want the same thing. So what's the problem?"

"You're a cop," Pritchard said.

"So what?"

"You're the enemy."

Grobowski's face reddened a little. "What's more important?" he snapped. "Information or people's lives?"

"Information," Pritchard and Maisie replied in flawless unison.

Grobowski's face was crimson now. Marianne wondered if he would actually get out of here without suffering a heart attack or a stroke.

Pritchard patted the computer terminal in front of him, the one that was presently riddled with the Tourette virus. "Listen, Krupke," he said. "One of these days the human race is gonna vacate the physical-temporal world of 'meat' existence altogether. Then we'll become pure information and *live* in these things—call it virtual reality, cyberspace, electronic nirvana or whatever. When we do, you'll thank *me* that Big Brother didn't get there ahead of the rest of us."

Marianne studied Grobowski's furious but perplexed expression. *He really doesn't look well.* Marianne wished he would sit down. He obviously wasn't familiar with any of this cyberpunk talk about "downloading" human minds into computers. Not that Marianne herself took any of it seriously. Whenever she tried to imagine life in a seemingly infinite space that wasn't really a space at all, it gave new meaning to the Mad Hatter's cry of "No room! No room!"

In the meantime, Pritchard was holding forth on the subject. "Do you have any idea what the word 'information' means, Krupke?" he said. "It means that I could write you down. I could take a pencil and write down everything you are. You might take up the whole front of a building, but I could do it—at least in principle. I could do it with just two symbols—a one and a zero. And when you died, I could pour all those ones and zeroes into a machine and start them up again. And if I actually had all your ones and zeroes written down, would you want me turning them over to the authorities to scramble up however they see fit? No. My job would be to keep all those digits organized and safe from harm—to make you immortal if possible. It's called *encoding*—and it's the sort of work we do here."

Nolan stared at Pritchard for a moment.

"I'm going to get a subpoena," Nolan said. He turned and started to leave, obviously assuming that she would follow.

Oh, great. We're going to get nothing out of these guys—just because this cop can't talk informationese.

"Look at me, Mr. Pritchard," Marianne said. "Just look at me."

Without query, Pritchard cooperatively turned his soft eyes toward her. He and Marianne studied each other's eyes for a moment. In her peripheral vision, she noticed Lieutenant Grobowski stop on his way to the door.

Then Marianne said, "Can you tell me how many bits of information, how many ones and zeroes, passed between us just now?"

"A lot," Pritchard said.

"A lot? That sounds awfully unscientific. So you don't know how many *exactly*? Well, I guess it will be a few more years before the big download roundup, huh? I hope I live that long. I hope *you* live that long. After that, none of us will have to worry, right? Because there won't be such things as death, murder, and even bodily harm."

Pritchard smiled. "The way I picture it, you'll be like a character on a Saturday morning cartoon. You can get blown up by a stick of dynamite or get thrown off a cliff or run over by a steamroller, but a minute later you'll be as good as new."

"So there'll be no need for police."

"Nope."

"And no laws, either."

"Nope."

"A world of benign anarchy and nonstop adventure."

"You got it."

"But it's not like that *here*, is it?" Marianne suggested. "Not in this nonvirtual world. Not in this 'meat' existence of ours. And a friend of mine is permanently dead. If ones and zeroes were stars, my friend and I exchanged enough to make a whole galaxy. Even so, I never really got to know her."

She thought she detected a change in Pritchard's expression—a softening, perhaps.

"I think your network ripped me off," she said. "It robbed me of billions of ones and zeroes. And I don't like being cheated. I don't like it at all."

She leaned toward Pritchard, assuming a calculated tone of eerie, half-crazed quietness. "Mr. Pritchard, I am very, very angry," she murmured. "And I might—just might—have a gun in my purse. If I do, I'm liable to take it out and blow all your little gray ones and zeroes all over this room. That wouldn't give you much of a chance to get encoded for immortality, would it?"

Pritchard's eyes widened with alarm. He looked at the purse warily. It had suddenly become a very evocative object. The room was silent except for the hum of the VAX 8650.

"Now aren't you glad there's a cop here?" Marianne finally asked. "And don't you think it would be a good idea to do what he says?"

Pritchard kept looking at her for a moment with the expression of a quizzical, slightly apprehensive sheepdog. Then he looked up at Grobowski with a smile.

"So tell me, Krupke," Pritchard said, "what would you like to know?"

01101

OLD CLOTHES

Y**OU WERE A LOT OF HELP TO ME BACK THERE,"** N**OLAN SAID TO**
Marianne Hedison as he drove through the sluggish afternoon traffic on the way back to her hotel.

"I'm glad," she replied simply.

Was that it? *"I'm glad?"* Wasn't she going to say something just a
little snide or smart-assed?

Oh, no, lady. You can do better than that.

*" 'A lot of help?' " you might tell me. "That's an interesting way to say I
stopped you from turning the whole thing into a drawn-out sideshow with
subpoenas and months of courtroom hearings—all leading to absolutely
nothing. 'A lot of help.' Well, what should I expect from a bull in a china shop
with a vocabulary too small to include the words 'thank you'?"*

Why don't you say all that, lady? I know you're thinking it.

He turned to look at the woman in the passenger seat. Her head
hung forward slightly and her eyes were half-closed as if she could
barely stay awake. She clearly wasn't in the frame of mind to deliver
stinging diatribes.

Nolan turned his eyes back onto the Santa Monica Freeway. The
traffic seeped along, threatening to grind to a stop at any moment.
He felt stupid to have let himself get on the freeway without checking traffic conditions. It might have been smarter to cut across town
by way of one of the boulevards to the south. The traffic flow wasn't
blocked up completely, as it might be by a major accident. This was
probably one of those inexplicable L.A. conditions that occurred

when too many people in one part of town experienced a sudden desire to be in another part of town—shifting habitual patterns and creating unpredictable tides of traffic. Maybe everybody downtown had decided to leave early today to miss the usual rush hours.

He was behind a big truck now, and he hated to be behind big trucks. They blocked the exit signs. It didn't matter that the exit he was looking for was still a long way off. He liked to see *all* the exit signs along the way, to get a sense of their progression, to see that Western came before Hawthorne, which came before Lincoln, just like they were supposed to. With a big truck in the way, nothing seemed right.

No progression.

Anyway, he was glad he'd stopped himself from saying "Thank you." He still didn't know whether he really had anything to thank her for. If she was trying to send him on a wild goose chase, getting him to do anything except investigate *her,* she was doing a pretty good job of it. Here she was, sitting right beside him, but he knew practically nothing about her. He certainly had no idea whether she'd had a motive to commit murder—*any* murder.

In the meantime, he had to be content with the information Pritchard and Maisie had passed along once Marianne had warmed them up. They had confirmed that G. K. Judson had been a member of Insomnimania. They had said that a few of Auggie's past snuffs included a car crash and a fall from a high place. There was next to no chance of connecting those with real-life events, but Nolan and Clayton would give it a try. Surely more useful was the membership information on Auggie's operator—the name, address, and credit card number of a certain Donald Hampstead in Malibu. Nolan would pay him a visit after dropping Marianne Hedison off at her hotel.

Nolan glanced again at Marianne.

She looks as bad as I feel. He felt a twinge of guilt for dragging her around in this exhausted state.

Sure, I could probably get a confession out of her by starving her, never letting her sleep, never letting her use the bathroom. Hell, I could probably get her to confess to the Watergate burglaries that way. But that's not kosher.

And she did *handle things well back there. . . .*

They had just passed the Hawthorne exit when the traffic actually came to a stop. The big truck in front of them was becoming a permanent fixture. Maybe it was time to find an exit. Side streets had to be better than this.

"Have you had anything to eat today?" Nolan asked.

"No," Marianne said.

"Maybe we should stop somewhere for lunch."

"I don't think I can eat anything," she said, rubbing her face with her hands. "I just want to get back to the hotel and take a shower and get some sleep."

Nolan shook his head. "It's going to take a while," he said.

"I'm in no hurry," she said.

"Have you got clean clothes?"

"No."

Small wonder. The way she showed up out of nowhere last night, she probably didn't even pack a robe or a gown or a toothbrush.

"Can I take you somewhere to shop?" he asked.

"No. I'll go out later."

"You've got money, haven't you?"

"Sure," she said, leaning her head against the headrest and closing her eyes.

Nolan sat staring at the back of the motionless truck. Then the traffic took a small lurch forward, carrying the pocket of cars westward in a slow-moving trickle. They were approaching Culver City now—if "approaching" was really the right word. Nolan found himself on the verge of a decision . . .

Marianne opened her eyes with a start, realizing that she must have fallen asleep. She was surprised to see that the lieutenant's car had stopped in front of a private home on a totally unfamiliar street. It was a neighborhood of small homes.

A family street. With lots of little kids and dogs.

She had barely realized that such a street still existed in Los Angeles. How long had it been since she had even visited such a traditional, All-American, working-class neighborhood?

Don't I need a passport to be here?

"Where are we?" she asked.

"My place," Lieutenant Grobowski said, opening his door and getting out of the car. He walked around the car and opened the door on her side. "Come on in for a few minutes."

She raised her hand to shield her eyes against the sunlight and sat motionless for a moment without answering.

She wanted to say, *"No, I'll stay here. You go on and take care of whatever you need to do. Just leave me here to die a quiet, dignified death."*

But she was too tired to argue. She got out of the car and followed the lieutenant into his living room, which was cluttered with well-kept but tired furniture.

Scuffed.

Framed portraits and snapshots were absolutely everywhere, covering every square inch of walls, tables, and shelves.

A family. The lieutenant has a family. Imagine that.

She bent to look at a picture—a wedding portrait. But Lieutenant Grobowski's voice stopped her from getting a good look at it.

"Come on," he said. "Up here."

She followed him upstairs to the second floor. Then Grobowski opened a narrow doorway and disappeared up another flight of stairs. Again she followed him, this time up into the attic, a finished but musty area with steeply sloping walls. Trunks and pieces of dusty furniture were scattered all around.

At the far end of the attic was a closet. Grobowski opened the closet door and switched on a light. A selection of clothes hung on a long rod, protected from dust by a translucent plastic sheet. Marianne shivered slightly at the memory of the last such sheet she had seen.

A wooden dresser was shoved tightly against the closet wall. Grobowski opened a drawer in the dresser, revealing more clothes—stockings and underwear and nightgowns.

Marianne suddenly grasped the situation.

He's offering me the use of his wife's clothing.

He hasn't asked her permission.

He can't ask her permission.

The truth of the matter was bitter, but she had to acknowledge it somehow. Under these circumstances, it wouldn't quite be human not to.

"You've lost Mrs. Grobowski, haven't you?" she said.

The detective didn't look at her, but nodded in a perfunctory way, as if in reply to a perfectly trivial question.

"I'm sorry," Marianne said.

"Thanks."

Grobowski gently pulled the plastic sheet away. Then he picked up a small overnight case off the floor and placed it on the shelf.

"Put whatever you need in this," he said.

"Are you sure it's all right?" Marianne asked.

"Sure. Would you excuse me?"

"Of course."

Grobowski quietly left the attic.

I can't do this. I just can't.

But she had to. It would be terribly insensitive to refuse this mysterious hospitality, however politely. She felt a flood of tangled emotions. They ranged from revulsion at the idea of using a dead woman's clothes to gratitude toward the detective for this show of generosity.

But why is he doing this? The man almost arrested me just this morning.

It was as though she had awakened from a nightmare only to find herself in a still stranger situation.

But she was exhausted—too exhausted to sustain any strong emotion for more than a few seconds. The flood of feelings quickly ebbed, and a hard-nosed practicality set in. She decided that it really wasn't important whose clothes these were. Her own were uncomfortably grungy and were undoubtedly starting to smell a little.

She began to study the wardrobe. The dead woman seemed uncannily present, seemed to be suggesting particular combinations.

"I always wore this gray skirt with this jacket," Marianne could almost hear her say. *"It would look all right on you. Wish I had more to offer."*

"Don't apologize," Marianne heard herself whisper. "This is fine. I appreciate it."

The ghostly presence had too much class to suggest any of the more formal apparel—understood that Marianne wouldn't have the need for any of that. The presence, too, passed over the fancier lingerie with a slightly embarrassed giggle.

Marianne looked efficiently through the wardrobe. The colors were mostly pastels, and the fabric was all natural. The woman had been of a somewhat larger build than she was.

The dresses will be too large. Marianne found a pair of black slacks with a drawstring waist. She put it together with a simple blouse she could let hang on the outside. She also chose a jacket, a gown, a bathrobe, and a selection of unadorned underclothes. She thought rather than said the words "thank you" before leaving the attic.

Here was Jack on his second birthday with Louise helping him blow out the candles. And here was Molly learning to swim. And here was Jack pitching his first Little League baseball game. And here was

Molly in her cheerleader uniform. And here was Louise at Newport Beach . . .

His "friendly ghosts," Nolan called them. The faces gazed at Nolan from all around the living room. Each picture had a smile in it somewhere. There was not a sad moment to be found among them. In moments of self-doubt like this one, Nolan knew that he could always turn to them—not so much for sanction or approval, but for familial warmth and love.

The moment after he had left Marianne Hedison with Louise's clothes, he had to fight himself not to go back up to the attic, not to cry out, "Wait! Don't take those! It's all a mistake!"

But it was too late. The decision was made and could not be taken back. And somehow, for some reason, it was right.

The friendly ghosts are still smiling, anyway.

Nolan had wondered from time to time what to do with Louise's personal belongings, particularly her clothes. Molly was too small for her mother's outfits, and none of Louise's friends or relatives would have been comfortable taking them. Louise probably would have wanted him to give them away to some kind of charity, but Nolan had just not brought himself around to doing it. This was the first time an opportunity had arisen for any of those items to be of use.

Besides, this woman deserved a little consideration. Nolan remembered how she had saved the morning. He couldn't help but admire the deftness and wit with which she had maneuvered those computer nerds. He had also detected a special kind of determination and resolve about her. He was finding it harder by the minute to mistrust her.

Anyway, the woman was only going to take an outfit or two, and she was undoubtedly going to bring them back. When this was all over, the dilemma of what to do with Louise's clothes would remain unchanged. It would be as if he had never lent them at all.

So why do I feel so strange?

The only reason Nolan could think of was that he was doing something he had never imagined himself doing. But in a way, that was appropriate for what was turning out to be a very weird day. It had all begun with that powerful surge of emotions at the crime scene.

What on earth was going on then?

What on earth was going on now?

Nolan remembered something Crazy Syd had told him many

years ago when he was still a rookie—something he had almost forgotten.

"Sooner or later," Syd had said, "every cop takes on a case that changes *everything*."

"What do you mean by 'everything'?" a much, much younger Nolan had asked.

"Your life," Syd had said. "Everything you think and feel will get turned all topsy-turvy. You won't have the slightest idea why or how. All you'll know is that nothing will ever be the same again. Cops deal with it in different ways. It makes some of 'em tougher and meaner. It makes others warmer and kinder. It might happen tomorrow, or it might happen the week before you retire. But it happens. It happens to us all—that one case that changes everything."

Maybe this is it. Nolan wandered out to the kitchen. *Maybe this is my case.*

Marianne came down the stairs toting the small bag. She heard Lieutenant Grobowski's voice call out from the kitchen.

"I'm in here," he said. His voice sounded remarkably bright—almost cheerful.

She went into the brightly lit kitchen and found him placing two sandwiches on the Formica table. She could hear and smell coffee perking.

"Tuna salad," he said pleasantly. "Dolphin-safe. I hope that's OK."

"It's fine," she said surprisedly, sitting down at the table.

"How do you want your coffee?"

"Black, please," she said. There was no reason to worry that the coffee would jangle her and bring on another onslaught of insomnia. Her tiredness was deep and benign. All she needed in order to get some precious sleep was a comfortable place to lie down. She'd have that before too long.

Lieutenant Grobowski put the cup of coffee in front of her and sat down across the table. She picked up her sandwich and was about to take a bite when the detective's face caught her attention—not exactly smiling or cordial, but certainly kind and thoughtful.

How strange.

Here was real consideration—from a man who had every reason to be suspicious of her every move.

How very, very strange.

"Go ahead," Grobowski said, breaking the silence. "Eat up."

Marianne felt her eyes sting a little. For the second time today, she was near tears. The first time, it had been out of despair. This time, it was out of gratitude. But she was still determined not to cry until it was out of pure, unvarnished grief. Besides, the lieutenant probably wouldn't like it if she got all weepy.

"Thank you," she said simply, and began to eat.

The television screen was the only illumination in the room. There were no explosions or gunshots or car chases taking place at the moment, just anomalously beautiful people in exotic settings talking to one another and saying nothing, because the sound was off. Marianne couldn't deal with any noise.

She sat in bed propped up against several pillows, staring at the glimmering screen, feeling an eerie identification with the nameless, voiceless apparitions. She had returned to the hotel late in the afternoon, bought a toothbrush and other necessaries in the hotel shop, returned to her room, showered, climbed into bed, and fallen into a deep sleep. When she had awakened, it was night. Marianne always found it disorienting to fall asleep during the day and wake up after dark, but never more so than now.

Marianne looked at the gown and robe she was wearing, remembering that they did not belong to her. Through the faint, quivering light, she could see other unfamiliar clothing hanging on a clothes rod near the bathroom. Her eyes scanned the room and could not locate a single object that did belong to her. Without her computer, without her work, she felt bland and featureless—much like the room itself.

If a tree fell in this room, would anybody hear it? Not me, surely—because there's no "me" at all.

She thought about what Pritchard had said back at Insomnimania.

"I could write you down," he had said. "I could take a pencil and write down everything you are. I could do it with just two symbols— a one and a zero. And when you died, I could pour all those ones and zeroes into a machine and start them up again."

Marianne almost wondered if she had been the subject of such an experiment. Perhaps it had failed, and her ones and zeroes were now hopelessly scrambled into an anonymous mess. Or perhaps she was a cipher, a blank tablet, a nonsentient machine awaiting the downloading of Pritchard's precious information.

She shuddered as a deep nothingness washed over her. She felt a desperate craving for human contact. She had to talk with someone.

I'll call Renee.

She actually reached for the phone before she stopped herself. The gesture's bitter irony overwhelmed her. Renee's death had exposed the void in her life, had shown Marianne a mirror with no reflection in it—and now Marianne wanted nothing more than to hear Renee's friendly voice on the phone.

She couldn't shake off the impulse.

I know her number. All I have to do is pick up and dial . . .

She had to think it through to convince herself otherwise. If she picked up the phone and called Renee's number, she would probably get Renee's answering machine, left running by the police in order to collect names and telephone numbers. Renee's voice would make its standard-issue promise . . .

"I'll get back to you as soon as I can."

But Renee wasn't going to be getting back to her anymore. So why was Marianne still eyeing the telephone with half a mind to pick it up and ring Renee's condo?

It's called denial, Marianne. Remember denial?

And indeed, she could remember going through plenty of denial after her parents' deaths. A year after each of them died, it had been painfully difficult to remember *not* to send cards and presents for birthdays and holidays.

My God. Is it going to take that long this time?

She continued to stare at the phone.

She almost jumped out of her skin when it rang.

She fumblingly lifted the receiver to her ear.

"Hello?" she asked.

"Is this Marianne Hedison?" a vaguely familiar male voice asked. Marianne felt a warm surge of relief at the sound of her name—as if her identity, her very selfhood had been magically returned.

"Yes," Marianne said, sitting up slightly.

"This is Roland McKeever."

Marianne couldn't recall the name for a moment. But then she remembered. He was the taller of the two kind men she had met at Renee's condominium. How could she have forgotten?

"Of course," she said warmly. "It's good to hear from you."

"Have you settled in OK?"

"As well as can be expected."

"We got a call from Renee's aunt and found out more about the funeral. We thought you might want to know."

"Oh, yes. Thank you."

Marianne fumbled through the drawer in the side table for a pencil and a piece of hotel stationery. Roland told her that the funeral would be held Saturday in Lakin, Iowa—a little town near Des Moines.

"Do you think you'll go?" Roland asked.

"Yes," Marianne said decisively.

"Then please give our best wishes."

"I will."

"Let's get together sometime soon—under happier circumstances."

"Oh, yes. Let's do that."

She hung up the phone and found herself pondering the last words of the conversation.

How could they both have been so sincere, and at the same time know they wouldn't see each other again?

The Troubadour Club was something of a labyrinth, and you could get lost in it very easily. Whenever Marianne came to the club in Stephen Madison's company, she found it easy to spot newcomers, who often got separated from their club-member dates or friends and wandered around looking stranded and perplexed.

Here comes one now.

And at that very moment, a shy, well-dressed woman poked her head through the doorway of the dark-paneled, candlelit room Marianne and Stephen were sharing by themselves. She looked absolutely panic-stricken. Marianne guessed she had gotten lost on the way back to her table from the ladies' room.

"I'm very sorry," she sputtered, "but could you tell me how to get back to the Provençal Room?"

Marianne spoke up. "Take one right and two lefts," she said.

"Oh, thank you," said the woman humbly. "Sorry to intrude."

The woman disappeared.

"I'm glad *you* remembered where it was," Stephen said.

"Come on. It's your club."

"Don't talk about it like I own it."

Marianne had returned to Santa Barbara the day before yesterday after a night's stay at the Pacific Surf in Santa Monica. She was at least marginally refreshed and ready for tomorrow's trip to Iowa, though still feeling strained. She was nervous, too. Stephen had been kind enough not to comment when she ordered a double bourbon and water in place of her customary white wine.

Stephen was of medium build, trim, with the bland good looks so favored in men's fashion layouts—soft smile, solid jaw, low hairline, thick eyebrows. As a lover he was proper—neither imaginative nor passionate, but attentive to necessary considerations. He worked out regularly at an expensive gym.

For nearly six months, she and Stephen had treated each other like well-worn clothes—not the least bit obsessively, but not carelessly, either. It was common for them not to see each other for two or three weeks at a time. Then they might spend three or four successive days and nights together, almost always at Stephen's house, acting like an old married couple. They were neither profound friends nor amorous lovers, but enjoyed each other's company now and again.

Marianne finished telling him about the whole ordeal—her witnessing of Auggie's snuff, her interrogation by the police, her viewing of Renee's body, and her efforts to help Lieutenant Grobowski.

"It must have been awful," Stephen said, sipping his martini. Stephen always ordered martinis. He had once confided to Marianne that he didn't really have any burning attachment to martinis—they were simply what lawyers were supposed to drink.

"It's been the worst experience of my life," Marianne said.

"I haven't gotten a chance to apologize for yelling at you on the phone that night."

"It's OK. I was crazy. I admit it."

"But it's over now, isn't it? I mean, they've got a real live suspect, right?"

"Right," Marianne said.

But she had no idea if that was true. Before leaving L.A., she had called the police division switchboard and had tried to reach Lieutenant Grobowski, but the detective wasn't at his desk. This bothered her. She wanted to know if Donald Hampstead of Malibu had, indeed, turned out to be a plausible suspect. Now she supposed she would have to wait until she came back from Iowa to find out. But for the time being, it was best not to disturb Stephen with uncertainties. He had worried about her enough already.

"I'm glad you're clear of it," Stephen said. "I wasn't looking forward to defending you against a murder charge. I handle business cases, not homicides."

"You would have done fine."

"I'd have found someone else for you. I know you're innocent. A lawyer is never at his best when defending someone he knows is innocent."

"Cramps his style, huh?"

"Something like that," Stephen said. "I'm sorry about your friend," he added sympathetically.

"Thank you. She was a wonderful person."

"I met her once. Remember? It was about a year or so back. You introduced me. She was a real wild woman."

Marianne felt herself smile. Yes, Stephen *would* find Renee pretty wild.

"She remembered you, too," Marianne said.

"Did she think *I* was wild?" Stephen asked facetiously.

Marianne's smile widened. "Let me put it this way. She called you 'Stephen Smooth.' "

Stephen chuckled. "Is that smooth as in sly, cunning, and roguish—or smooth as in processed cheese?"

"I'm not going to answer that," Marianne said.

They both laughed. Marianne still found it strange to be able to laugh at all, let alone about memories of Renee. Even so, she was grateful to have some sense of humor left.

But she had been talking ever since they had arrived at the club, and she was tired. She felt relieved when Stephen started talking about himself—his caseload, his exercise program, his racquetball game, the new gourmet dish he had learned to make.

Small things.

But small as they were, they absolutely entranced her tonight— perhaps by contrast with the brutal realities she had so recently faced.

In the midst of the big things, we are in the small things.

The realization gave her remarkable solace. As Stephen talked on and on, she hoped he would never stop.

". . . and Mike got married last week," Stephen was saying as dinner arrived. Mike was Stephen's younger brother. Both Stephen and Mike belonged to their father's law firm.

"You'd told me the wedding was coming up," remarked Marianne. "How was the ceremony?"

"Pretty."

"Is she a nice woman?"

"I guess. To tell the truth, I can't see any real difference between Kimberly and any of the other women he's dated. But he seems to be happy."

"How's he doing at the firm?"

"Fine. He'll probably be its president someday."

Marianne was a bit surprised. "What about you?" she asked. "You're the older brother. You've been with the firm longer. What about seniority?"

"What about it?" Stephen said with a shrug. "He's the one with the drive, the passion, the ambition. Me, I'm just a good, competent lawyer."

"Would you rather be doing something else?"

"Not at all. I like having a job that's assured as long as I don't screw up badly. I like having a good income and a certain amount of prestige in the community where I grew up. It's not like it's a *calling* or something."

Stephen had never kept it any secret that he was not an ambitious man. Even so, Marianne felt oddly affected by his words tonight, particularly in light of her own recent experience. She had been faced for the first time with a hollowness in her own life. It had seemed to her a dramatic revelation. But it was different for Stephen. He looked into his own personal void every day with undeceived, self-deprecating eyes. He didn't undergo any angst about it. He was comfortable and able to joke about it. Marianne had never really understood this about Stephen before—had never really grasped his languid brand of self-awareness. Now that she did, she couldn't help thinking him rather brave.

They left the club after brandy and desserts and a couple of hours of stale but comfortable conversation. They drove in Stephen's Mercedes through the curving, darkened, prosperous streets of Santa Barbara. The city seemed awfully serene by contrast with L.A.

During the drive, Marianne found herself thinking about Insomnimania. She knew that Stephen was a member, as were at least four or five other friends and acquaintances. It seemed strange for all of them to be part of it—to be connected in some mysterious, electronic way to a murderer. And it seemed strange that she had no idea who any of them were when they logged on the network. What were their names? Did they have electronic bodies? Did they meet and talk and even have virtual sex without recognizing each other?

"Would you tell me something, Stephen?" she asked.

"Sure."

"Who's your alter?"

"My what?"

"You know what I mean. The role you play in Insomnimania."

"Why do you want to know?"

"I was just curious."

Stephen grinned. "I'll tell you mine if you tell me yours."

Marianne laughed a little. "Spoken like a true lawyer," she said.

He had really called her bluff. She had never told anybody except Renee that her own alter, Elfie, was nothing but a bodiless pair of eyes, incapable of action or even conversation. She didn't particularly want to say so now—despite her long-standing guess that Stephen's alter might be just as nonphysical. How often had their eyes passed each other while wandering voyeuristically through Insomnimania's desktop maze? Perhaps they had even blinked at each other without realizing it.

They reached a turn-off where they could go to either Marianne's house or Stephen's.

"Do you want to spend the night at my place?" Stephen asked.

She considered it for a moment. But there was too much turmoil boiling in the back of her mind for her to feel comfortable going home with him tonight.

"Not tonight," she said. "Maybe when I get back from Iowa."

"OK," said Stephen, without the slightest trace of disappointment.

Stephen dropped Marianne off and waited in the drive until she got into her front door. Moonlight poured into her living-room windows, giving her enough light to see, to move about. She didn't turn on the lights. She wondered why she didn't want to. After all she had been through, why wasn't she like a frightened child, afraid to go to bed with the lights off?

She noticed that her answering machine was blinking, and she ran the tape. The message was from Lieutenant Grobowski. He wanted to talk with her and had left her his home phone number. He said not to worry about calling too late.

Marianne called him immediately. She explained about the funeral.

"I just want you to know I'm not leaving the country or anything," she assured him.

"Thanks for letting me know," he replied, not unpleasantly.

"I've still got those clothes. I'll bring them back."

"No hurry."

"How did things work out in Malibu?"

She could hear the detective sigh. His voice sounded scratchy and tired.

"Not good," he said. "The guy's some sort of rich eccentric—a low-tech hippie type. He's hardly got an electrical appliance to his name. Credit cards are his one concession to the twentieth century. Claims he doesn't know the first thing about computers, much less about Insomnimania. And he's got an airtight alibi. The odd thing is, nothing from Insomnimania has actually been billed to his credit card, even though Auggie's been using his number. The guy showed us the statements."

Marianne felt her heart sink. This could only mean one thing. Auggie was a computer hacker. Nothing had been solved after all.

"I'm sorry," she said.

"Yeah, me, too. Look, could you come back to Los Angeles after you get back from Iowa? I could really use your help."

Marianne was surprised by the lieutenant's sincere tone. He didn't sound like he was playing games with her now. But why? Didn't this new development put her back on the top of the lieutenant's list of potential suspects? He didn't sound as if it did.

"Of course," she said. "I'll call when I get back."

"Thanks, Ms. Hedison."

"Marianne. Please."

There was a short pause.

"OK," Lieutenant Grobowski said. "Marianne it is."

Marianne hung up the phone.

God, what am I getting myself into? Stephen's simply going to freak.

But it was best not to tell him, she decided. It wasn't like she was going to implicate herself or anything. How could she? She was innocent. She was just going to help out. It was the least she could do for Renee. It was the least she could do for herself.

She looked around her darkened living room, gazing at its dark contours, into its empty shadows. It actually felt good. It felt very good.

Odd, how comforting the dark can be.

01110
EDGE

SITTING IN THE RENTED CAR'S COLD INTERIOR, MARIANNE quickly read the map the desk clerk had marked showing her the way to Lakin—a mere thirty miles outside of Des Moines. Then she turned the ignition key. The car started easily enough, and the heater quickly dispersed the chill, but she remained aware of the cold hovering on the other side of the thin glass windows. At least the streets were clear, although they were edged by threatening piles of darkened snow. As she drove, the city soon gave way to a slightly rolling countryside.

The farms along the way consisted of small clumps of houses huddled together, surrounded by vast stretches of farmland. She had seen them when she flew in, a checkerboard pattern of lonely homes, each separated from its nearest neighbor by acres of dead, frozen land.

At last she reached Lakin, which was really just a cluster of houses and small businesses. At a gas station, she got specific directions to the Lutheran church. It was a brick box with a cupola, located on the outskirts of town. Marianne parked in the church lot and got out of the car, recoiling at the desolate, icy blast of midwestern wind. The cold seemed deliberately malignant as it instantaneously snatched the warmth from her body, even though she was wearing her heaviest coat and the sun was shining brightly. The handful of bundled people she could see moving toward the building appeared resigned, as though they had come to terms with the fact that nature was methodically trying to freeze them to death.

The church was spare inside except for the flowers, a temporary garden brightening an area around the coffin. Marianne was early, and few people had arrived yet. She slipped into a pew near the back of the church and waited.

The narrow side windows were tinted glass, a marbleized caramel shade. The walls were bare, and the pews were old and dark. Racks on the pew backs held hymn books and prayer books. The air in the church was heavy and warm and seemed almost to echo with hymns sung Sunday after Sunday.

More people began to arrive, slowly at first, then in an increasing stream. Like the flowers she had sent, now merged anonymously with all the others, Marianne began to feel herself disappear among the faces. People pushed closer and closer together in the pews, making room for those from other local congregations or from other towns—and even for those who, like Marianne, ordinarily attended no church at all.

Marianne could see that the people's faces had a certain sameness. The women, with their standard permanents and standard makeup, had gone to considerable trouble to look as much alike as possible. They didn't have to try hard. They seemed alike in some fundamental way. There were variations, of course. Some were larger but none was really overweight. Others were thinner but none was really skinny. The general impression was of a certain heaviness, a sturdiness. Their faces tended to be broad, and their hair tended toward a brownish cast.

Renee's stock? How can this be?

For the first time, it occurred to Marianne that Renee's reddish hair color was probably not natural. It had been a good job.

The men were a different matter. They came in all shapes, sizes, and dispositions. In an odd way, the pudgy and obese males looked healthier than the trim and fit ones. The fat ones wore their lifestyles on their sleeves—cigarettes, no exercise, and far too much beer and liquor. Sure, they were killing themselves, but not with denial.

But the thin ones showed the strain of trying to compensate for all their vices and excesses with rigor and discipline—a few too many end-of-the-day trips to the gym in town to make up for the pint of whiskey concealed in the company desk.

The sanctuary filled more and more rapidly. Some of the people were crying. Marianne slid over to the center of her pew so that the people entering from either of the adjoining aisles would not have to step over her, although she would have preferred to sit near the edge so she could slip away more easily at the end of the service. Gradually, people filled in on each side of Marianne, in the row in front of her and in the two rows behind. The front row of the sanctuary remained empty as all the other rows filled up.

The church was now hot and stuffy. Marianne was suddenly aware of being surrounded by a continent stretching in all directions, a continent full of people with no ocean in sight.

And land. Acres and acres of harsh, frozen land.

For the first time she realized why she lived in California—lived near an edge.

Imagine coming all this way to learn something like that.

Other people were walking to the front of the sanctuary and looking in the coffin. They all reacted in distinct ways. Some gasped slightly at the sight of the body, some wept, and some scarcely reacted at all. Marianne tried to focus her eyes elsewhere. She had no intention of viewing the body.

But why not? Isn't that part of why I'm here? The closure, the irrevocable finality that can only come from viewing the deceased?

But she knew it would be just like the morgue. The body in the coffin would be another imposter, a teenage parody of Renee fabricated by people who hadn't known her during her entire adulthood. And what might she be wearing, this fraudulent Renee? Her Camp Fire uniform, her cheerleading outfit, her prom dress? Not her flamboyant California garb, surely—not the red-and-purple tunic and rust-colored slacks Marianne had last seen Renee alive in. Not the wild peasant clothes she had worn in happier bohemian days. And the face in the coffin would be that of a frozen girl who had never really left home. This new mocked-up Renee would only strengthen the feeling Marianne had so far found impossible to shake—that Renee was a missing person, not a dead one.

No coffins, no bodies.

Marianne would seek finality instead among this crush of mourners. By sharing their grief, she would become convinced of the unalterable finality of Renee's passing.

The front row filled with Renee's relatives—no doubt her father, her mother, a sprinkling of aunts and uncles. There were also a few men and women in their twenties and thirties—brothers and sisters or cousins? Marianne struggled to remember anything Renee had ever told her about the people in her family. She could not remember much.

A preacher stepped up into a pulpit above and to the left of the coffin. He began to speak. Marianne couldn't take in his words. She wanted to mourn with these people in quiet—no hymns, no sermons. What business did this man have making sermons?

She wanted to ask the preacher, "Are you speaking from the spirit?" She wanted to say, "Can't you see the rest of us are trying to mourn?"

But the preacher kept on talking, and when he finished, a woman got up to sing. Marianne didn't know the hymn. There had been no singing in the meeting house during her childhood. She wondered if this hymn had once been a favorite of Renee's.

A favorite hymn? Renee?

No, the very idea was absurd. All this singing and talking was absurd. Marianne shut out the sound and closed her eyes. Tears stung behind Marianne's eyes as she rushed back over the years . . .

His heart, they said.

I never knew there was anything wrong with his heart.

But Daddy was gone. And Mama was crying. And Mama kept saying over and over and over again . . .

"He's not dead. He can't be dead."

In the coffin, he looked as if he were sleeping, all dressed in his best suit, his face peaceful. The service was quiet except for a few friends giving brief and poignant ministries. The mourners respected the deceased too much to talk unless God made them talk. Marianne had to keep an arm around Mama the whole time for fear that Mama might collapse beside her.

"He's not dead. He can't be dead."

Mama's tumor was found too late, and she didn't last long because she didn't want to, and to the very end she sang the same litany . . .

"He's not dead. He can't be dead."

Two years.

Two years between Daddy's death and Mama's.

A lot of time for Mama to deny the truth.

A lot of time for Marianne to deny it, too.

But Marianne had denied the truth of both their deaths even after Mama's death.

Marianne had been numb.

Marianne had felt nothing.

Marianne had been a teenager with the world on her shoulders.

What was Marianne supposed to feel?

Then one day she was packing away a family portrait and the floodgates opened and she wept—she really wept. After that weeping, they were really dead. After that weeping, she stopped reaching for the phone to call them. After that weeping, she stopped remembering their birthdays, their anniversaries.

You have to cry to let go.

And now, sitting here in a church in Iowa, Marianne felt the tears coming. They filled her eyes and trickled down her cheeks. She shifted uncomfortably on the solid wood pew. The woman next to her crossed her legs the other way, apparently to give Marianne more room. The solo had ended and the preacher had been talking for some time now.

"... loss ... loss ..."

Marianne had no more than half-heard anything he had said, but she was aware that he had been saying those words again and again, using them in every sentence.

"... loss ... loss ..."

"Loss of what?" Marianne wanted to cry out. "Did the spirit really move you to keep talking about loss?"

But grief—her own and everybody else's—overcame her, whelmed over her in spite of the preacher's endless harangue. Marianne leaned forward and put both hands on the back of the pew in front of her. She braced her body against a wail, a howl she could feel rising toward her throat. She issued a long, low, almost inaudible gasp . . .

"Ahhhhhh . . ."

The tears coursed down her cheeks. The woman sitting next to her reached out and touched her arm. Marianne held her breath and struggled to stop the flow before it broke loose and carried her away.

"The edge."

Marianne murmured the words in pleased anticipation as she drove down the hillside from her house and twisted her way through street after street of pale houses with red tile roofs on the way to East Cabrillo Boulevard. At last, she parked her car in the public lot across from the Sheraton Hotel and stared down the wide beach toward the ocean.

There it is. The edge.

After her trip to Iowa, Marianne was aware it was not the sun or water that drew her to the beach. It was the need to look out into a vast, unpeopled space. If one could ignore the oil rigs embedded in the water, such powerful icons of wealth that the locals did not consider them eyesores, the ocean seemed wonderfully empty.

The weather was Southern California's very best—a warm and sunny winter day without smog or other signs of industrial tarnish, and a welcome contrast to yesterday's malevolent midwestern cold. Sitting in the car, Marianne took off her shoes and rolled up her slacks, then walked out onto the beach. She passed near a bevy of firm bodies engaged in an energetic game of volleyball. There were even a couple of women in bikinis stretched on the sand. Another handful of people clustered at a food concession. All the bodies looked incredibly well-toned.

Youthful. Of course, age is a malleable thing.

It was also a relative thing—just like space and time. One could remain youthful in direct proportion to the size of one's income, one's ability to pay for the requisite tuck or nip or mud bath.

As she walked past the young people, Marianne noticed that the women all seemed to have been cast from the current cultural model—very thin women with large, high breasts. It was a combination not often produced by nature but demanded nevertheless by the culture's image-setters.

Then she heard a familiar phrase in her mind, as though someone had yelled it out as she walked by: "Nice outfit. But you ain't got nothin' in there."

Marianne laughed to find that old line still haunting her. "Nice outfit. But you ain't got nothin' in there," the boys had taunted her when she modeled in a high school fashion show. She had felt crushed. Later, she and Renee and their crowd had laughed at women who spent all their time worrying about appearance. Now the teasing phrase had taken on a slightly different meaning for Marianne. She took one last glance at the beautiful bodies. "You ain't got nothin' in there," she muttered, both amused and aghast at her own censoriousness.

Marianne walked out toward the water, detouring around two men with paddles batting a ball back and forth. Southern California's beaches were seldom empty. They were more crowded on weekends and during the tourist season, but at any time of the year, at any time of the day, people found the free time to go to the beach for one reason or another. Here in Santa Barbara, it was indicative of wealth and leisure. In Los Angeles, it was just as likely to mean joblessness and despair.

Marianne sat down, pressed her hands into the grainy sand, and stared at the ocean. A single seagull soared overhead, facing the horizon, suspended almost motionless for a moment by a strong, steady breeze. Then, with a swift and determined flapping of wings, the bird hurtled itself away from the shore, across the waves . . .

Over the edge.

She was sitting on the brink of the continent, the threshold of the culture, with the great, mad crush of humanity behind her. The office, the assignments, the clients, Stephen—they were all clustered at her back, flattened into a foreshortened landscape, packed into a gigantic cage through which she moved about as well as she could.

A cage with a great view of the water.

The detective, Lieutenant Grobowski, was also in that cage, perhaps a threat to Marianne, perhaps a friend. Tomorrow, she would drive to Los Angeles to meet with him again. And packed somewhere else in the same cage was the person—could it really be a person?—who had killed Renee. Marianne knew she would encounter that killer someday, too, knew it with a calm assurance. The thought of this entire continent of reluctant cellmates did not disturb her this morning. She could contend with them now. She could contend with just about anything, as long as she had this edge to come to when she needed to be alone.

Marianne breathed deeply. She felt rested. She wondered how she could possibly feel so rested. She had slept long and hard last night after she got back from Iowa, but it was more than that, more than just a matter of having caught up on her sleep after an agonizing interval of wakefulness. It was something else.

Something has changed.

But what was it?

The funeral had actually raised more questions than it had resolved. Even after grieving, even after shedding painful tears, Marianne could muster no real sense that Renee was gone forever.

Why?

Marianne studied the ocean's rolling surface, searching and listening for some kind of answer. But like any good psychotherapist, the ocean was determined to tell Marianne as little as possible, to let her work out her own answers. It replied to all queries with a soft and steadily undulating drone of pure white noise.

As she stared at the horizon, her eyes drifted out of focus, and the ocean seemed to freeze into a kind of stillness. It reminded her of the ice lake and that lonely, burdened traveler. As time passed, she felt more and more certain that her traveler was headed toward the shore. But how long would the rest of the journey be? And what dangers would the traveler meet along the way? And what reward awaited at the end? Only patience and courage would tell.

Marianne shivered a little, feeling chilly in spite of the sun. She got up and walked toward the parking lot, past all the sculptured bodies with their carefully hidden seams and scars. Marianne returned to her car and drove out of the parking lot past the impressive hotel. She could feel some new motion in her life—tentative now, but gaining momentum.

2. INTO ACTION

THIS IS WHERE THE REAL FUN STARTS. YOU CAN CREATE A HIGHLY MOBILE VIRTUAL SELF WITH A WIDE RANGE OF VERBAL CAPACITIES. THIS FULL-FLEDGED IDENTITY WILL MAKE YOUR NETWORKING EXPERIENCE RICHER, MORE REWARDING, AND MORE DEEPLY INVOLVING THAN ANYTHING YOU'VE ENCOUNTERED ON ANY OTHER NETWORK.

THE NEXT BEST THING TO BEING THERE

CLICK A NAME. THEN CLICK "PARTICIPANT" INSTEAD OF "SPECTATOR." IF YOU'VE ALREADY CREATED A BODY FOR YOUR ALTER, THAT BODY WILL APPEAR. IF NOT, ALL YOU HAVE TO DO TO CREATE ONE IS TO FOLLOW THE INSTRUCTIONS IN EACH DIALOGUE BOX AS IT APPEARS.

YOUR CARTOON ALTER CAN DRINK AND CHAT IN ERNIE'S BAR, READ FOR A BOOK CLUB IN LA BIBLIOTHÈQUE ÉROTIQUE, PLAY BACCARAT IN THE CASINO DEL CAMINO, MAKE A POLITICAL SPEECH AT THE SPEAKERS' CORNER, JOIN IN A MUSICAL JAM SESSION, THROW A PARTY IN A "ROOM" OF YOUR OWN MAKING, OR TAKE PART IN ANY OF A MULTITUDE OF OTHER ACTIVITIES.

NOTE: FOR COMPLETE DETAILS CONCERNING EACH OF THESE STEPS, TURN TO THE REFERENCE SECTION IN THE BACK OF THIS MANUAL.

THE FACTORY

WHAT'S THAT? YOU SAY YOU CAN'T DRAW? BIG DEAL! YOU DON'T HAVE TO BE AN ARTIST TO CREATE A VIRTUAL SELF.

INSOMNIMANIA MAKES IT EASY TO CREATE A VIVID AND EXCITING PERSONALITY FOR YOUR ALTER. JUST CLICK INTO THE FACTORY AND FOLLOW THE DIRECTIONS. IMAGES CAN BE CONSTRUCTED FROM A SELECTION OF HEADS, TORSOS, AND LIMBS FROM OUR CLIP-ART LIBRARY. A WIDE VARIETY OF HAIR, FACIAL FEATURES, AND WARDROBES ARE AVAILABLE TO CHOOSE, MIX, AND MATCH.

IF YOU WISH, YOU CAN ALSO MODIFY YOUR IMAGE WITH OUR EASY-TO-USE PAINT TOOLS. A FULL RANGE OF COLORS AND SHADES IS AT HAND TO USE AS YOUR IMAGINATION DIRECTS. AND TO MAKE CREATING A WELL-ROUNDED ALTER EVEN EASIER, WHEN YOU CREATE A FRONT VIEW, CORRESPONDING PROFILES AND A BACK VIEW ARE GENERATED AUTOMATICALLY.

WHAT'S THAT? YOU SAY YOU *CAN* DRAW? WELL THEN, THERE'S NO REASON TO LIMIT YOURSELF TO OUR CLIP-ART! USE THE FACTORY'S PAINT TOOLS AND EASY STEP-BY-STEP INSTRUCTIONS TO CREATE A VIRTUAL SELF PURELY OF YOUR OWN INVENTION.

What's that? You say you *can* draw? Well then, there's no reason to limit yourself to our clip-art! Use the Factory's paint tools and easy step-by-step instructions to create a virtual self purely of your own invention.

The cartoon you create will soon become an extraordinarily sophisticated electronic marionette—but you'll have to attach "strings" to it first. Once you've created your image, you can use Insomnimania's prepackaged set of keyboard commands or devise your own to animate your virtual self and bring it vibrantly to life.

DON'T LIMIT YOUR FUN

Logging on as more than one alter offers you the intriguing possibility of carrying on conversations—or even arguments—with yourself! This can be delightfully deceptive to other spectators or participants, who may well believe they are watching more than one user in action.

For information on all the exciting Insomnimania rooms and activities, continue to the next chapter.

MARIANNE HEDISON SET HER NOTEBOOK COMPUTER ON THE hotel room's dressing table.

She unwound a couple of cables and began to string them behind the dressing table. She glanced at Nolan with concern.

"You look beat," she remarked.

"Thanks," Nolan grumbled.

"Is the case going badly?"

"Could be going better."

Nolan observed Marianne's deft, economical movements as she busily connected the computer to the electrical outlet and the modem jack. She sure looked in top form tonight.

Nolan wanted to tell her, "You don't look beat. In fact, you look downright terrific. And you just got back from a funeral. Shit, you just got back from Iowa. What's your excuse? When did you get so rested?"

"What's going on with Pritchard and Maisie?" Marianne asked as she continued to arrange things. "Are they cooperating?"

"You bet they are," Nolan said, chuckling. "Finding out that Auggie faked up his membership information didn't upset them too much. But the fact that Auggie never *paid* to be on the network, not even on somebody else's credit card—well, that really got their attention. All their sixties ideals about liberating information really bit the dust in a hurry."

"What are they doing to help?"

"They've programmed their mainframe to record when Auggie logs on and off and generally keep track of his activities. He hasn't shown up again yet, but when he does, they'll be able to get his phone number. That ought to nail him."

"Haven't the police got some kind of electronics outfit?"

"The Computer Fraud Division, yeah."

"So why do you need *me* to teach you this stuff?"

"We can't seem to get those jokers interested. So far, all we've got is some character committing penny-ante credit fraud, so they aren't impressed. They like to tackle big-league corporate hackers—real headline stuff."

"But this involves murder."

"That's what we told them. And they said, 'Great. *You're* the homicide dicks. Go for it.' "

"It must be fun working in a bureaucracy," Marianne said as she completed the connections.

"Yeah, a real blast."

Nolan was only telling her part of the truth, though. Pritchard and Maisie had arranged for Kim Pak, homicide's computer whiz, to log on and wander around the network without anybody knowing it. They called it "superuser privileges." Kim was now teaching other homicide guys—including Clayton—how to use Insomnimania. So Nolan didn't actually *need* Marianne to teach him anything.

But Kim could only give a cop's-eye view of the network, and Nolan wanted a user's-eye view. He wanted to find out what it felt like really to *belong* to Insomnimania. Maybe Marianne could show him. Maybe she could give him some insight into this Auggie character—how his mind worked, what he was up to, maybe even who he was.

Nolan hadn't told any of the other guys about this meeting, though—not even Clayton. He found himself wondering why, wondering whether he had some sort of underlying agenda here. Did he want more from this woman than he was admitting to himself?

He didn't think so. He certainly didn't *want* to think so. Marianne had proven helpful and sincere at every turn, and Nolan now felt a little embarrassed at having ever suspected her of anything like murder.

Marianne stood up and brushed her hands. "It's ready to go," she said. "Would you like a drink before we get started—or are you on duty?"

As Marianne stood facing him, he couldn't help but note again how fine she looked with her aristocratic features and simple but stylish wardrobe. She was wearing gray slacks and a gray cotton blouse, nothing formal. The first time he'd seen her—at the scene of the G. K. Judson killing—she had struck him as overdressed. Nolan couldn't understand why women went in for all that fashion-page overkill. It usually backfired, making them look strained, uncomfortable, too preoccupied with *looking* beautiful just to *be* beautiful.

But tonight Marianne looked wonderful, and Nolan found himself slightly aroused. It surprised him a little. Strictly speaking, she wasn't his type—not with her bone-thin frame and measured manner. She lacked what he regarded as a certain essential earthiness. But even so . . .

"Well?" Marianne asked with an amused look.

"What?" Nolan blurted stupidly.

"Do you want a drink?"

"No. I'm on duty. Thanks."

"Sure."

Christ, Nolan, watch yourself. Better hope she just chalks it up to exhaustion.

Marianne pulled a chair up to the dresser and sat down in front of the computer. Nolan pulled up another chair and sat down beside her. Perhaps he was crowding her a little, but he had to get in fairly close to see the little screen.

Marianne switched on the computer and logged into Insomnimania, dropping a pair of tiny eyes labeled "l-fy" into an elaborate desktop maze. The eyes scurried up and down and back and forth through little corridors leading to various icons bearing room labels like Babbage Beach and the Speakers' Corner. As the eyes scuttled about, Marianne started rattling off random information about the network. Nolan took notes. He enjoyed listening to her talk. She knew how to do things, and she knew how to explain them to other people.

She told him everything that came to mind—all about menus, double-clicking, logging on or off, downloading.

"Why was it that you got an incomplete copy of the animation showing Renee's murder?" Nolan asked.

"There's a command on one of the Snuff Room menus that says

'send me a copy,' " Marianne replied. "If you select that, the network is supposed to download a copy of the file you want to your home computer. Somehow Auggie set it up so that the file that was available for downloading was different from the one actually running on the screen." She thought for a moment. "I had never downloaded a snuff animation before, and it didn't occur to me that my copy of the snuff might be incomplete. I guess we get to depend on the computer doing exactly what we think it's supposed to do."

Nolan nodded and Marianne went on to other infoworld topics. She told him about networks in general—how some of them provided access to specialized business data while others mixed data and social exchange. A few were entirely pornographic, she said. Insomnimania was a little of everything, but almost purely recreational—a way for busy, sleepless people to count electronic sheep, so to speak.

"Busy, sleepless *rich* people," Nolan remarked dryly.

She shot him a slightly indignant look. "Are you calling me rich?" she asked.

"If you can afford all this, yeah."

"By Santa Barbara standards, I'm barely middle class."

"By L.A. standards, Santa Barbara *vagrants* are rich."

Marianne brushed this observation aside and began to tell Nolan about rooms, alters, and the like. She told him that "l-fy" was an abbreviation for "Elfie"—her own alter.

At one point, Elfie's eyes blinked.

"Are they supposed to do that?" he asked.

"Yeah. It's part of the program."

"Pretty spooky."

"It still startles me sometimes."

"So do you think we might run into this Auggie character tonight?"

"I don't know. Maybe. We'll have to look around. There's no central list to check like they've got on most other networks. We have to just poke around from room to room."

"If we miss him, I guess Pritchard and Maisie will find him," Nolan added. "But if we do run into him, will I be able to tell if he's some kind of nut?"

Marianne laughed. "Let me put it this way," she said. "What if this were a costume party or a Mardi Gras? How many nuts would you expect to run into? When people put on a mask, all inhibitions go. But things get even crazier in this place. Here, you can change your appearance completely—and there's no midnight unmasking. Nobody's ever going to find out who you really are unless you decide to tell them. Most people don't."

"Where should we look first?" Nolan asked.

"I don't know. Maybe Ernie's Bar. He spends a lot of time there."

She hurried Elfie's eyes to the "Ernie's Bar" icon and pulled down the menu to select "who?" A list of names followed by their abbreviations appeared on the screen:

SUDOPOD (SUDO)
TASER (TAZ)
JAZZ (JZ)
MON ONCLE (MO)

There were twelve altogether.

"No Auggie," remarked Nolan.

"Guess not."

"Still, could we go inside for a look around?"

"Sure," Marianne said. She double-clicked the room icon, and the view opened out into an old, western-style saloon replete with swinging doors, brass rails around the bar, and a wildly varied, semihuman clientele. A tinkly piano played over the computer's tiny speaker. Nolan was astonished by the palpability of the scene, with its vivid color and shifting perspectives. The fact that the screen itself was only an inch or so thick made the effect even more amazing.

Elfie's disembodied eyes floated around and through the bar. The customers' conversations appeared in a box above the scene. Nolan took note of one almost unreadable comment—apparently an insult.

JZ>URE MTHR SUX GRT GRENE DONKY DCKS.

"What kind of writing is this?" Nolan asked.

"Shorthand," Marianne answered. "People here make up their own ways of writing things."

"How the hell is anybody supposed to read it?"

"It takes some getting used to. Try reading it aloud."

"Your mother sucks great green donkey dicks," Nolan heard himself say. Then he laughed. He had spoken the words, but it fleetingly seemed as if he had actually heard Jazz say them. Maybe his tiredness was playing tricks on him.

"You're right," he said. "It takes some getting used to."

"What do you think this is?" Marianne asked, taking Nolan's pad and pencil and jotting something down:

:)

Nolan looked at it sideways. "It's a smiley face," he said.

"Right." Then Marianne quickly listed a whole set of shorthand facial expressions:

;/

:(

:o

:]

"I don't see any of these on the screen," Nolan observed.

"No. They're more common in other networks. There's not much call for them in a world of animated alters. Here, if you want your character to smile, you just give him a smile. If you want him to frown, you give him a frown."

Elfie exited Ernie's Bar and slipped through the corridors, checking the logs of one room after another in search of Auggie. Nolan was particularly intrigued by what appeared to be a cybernetic redlight district called the Pleasure Dome, but Elfie checked the list of occupants in a room called the Weightless Chamber and moved on without further exploration.

Eventually, Elfie wound up at the Casino del Camino. A new list of names appeared after Marianne selected "who?" Nolan began to read the names aloud.

"Twolip, Caligula, Rubberbarren, Hejhog, Loosy, Supersloth . . . No Auggie here, either. Still, do you mind if I have a peek?"

"Not at all." She double-clicked again, and Elfie was inside the Casino del Camino—a gaudily lush Vegas-style gambling palace with classical columns and gold leaf everywhere. Elfie's eyes floated through the outlying portion of the casino with its many rows of slot machines, then into the heavily carpeted, oval main room where multifarious clients were playing canasta, roulette, blackjack, and poker. Many of the customers were mutated-looking creatures, as they had been back at Ernie's Bar. But they all wore black bow ties. It seemed to be a house requirement. Cocktail waitresses wafted here and there, but they didn't actually seem to be serving any drinks. Perhaps they were just for decoration.

Nolan burst out into a guffaw. "Hands against the wall, everybody!" he barked at the screen. "Play time's over! This is the police!"

"Actually, I think it's perfectly legal," Marianne said, laughing. "Nobody's playing for money. They're just playing for time at the games. You've got to pay admission to play, but you can keep playing as long as you've still got chips. The chips aren't worth anything except for more time at the tables."

Nolan fleetingly remembered something Lieutenant Paul Spiroff had told him in Chicago about the murder of Miles Braxton. "He'd been playing canasta in some kind of virtual, on-line casino," Spiroff had said—and also that no money was involved. Was Braxton playing at this casino? If so, might yet another murder be connected with Insomnimania?

But no, the idea seemed too silly to consider. Braxton was killed in *Chicago,* after all, stretching the serial theory way too far. And lots of networks probably had casinos just like this one. Even so, Nolan made a mental note to find out if Braxton had ever belonged to Insomnimania.

As for now, he really intended to get into the spirit of Insomnimania. He rubbed his hands together. "Whaddya say we get into a game?" he asked.

Marianne gave him a startled look. The request seemed to have taken her completely by surprise.

"We can't," she said bluntly.

"Why not?"

"Elfie hasn't got a body."

"What's that mean?"

"She's just a pair of eyes. She can't do active things like carry on conversations or play games."

Nolan could hardly believe his ears.

"What's the matter?" he asked. "Is your computer broken or something?"

"No."

"What, then? Did Elfie have some terrible childhood disease?"

"I just never got around to making her a body."

"I can't believe this!" Nolan exclaimed crankily. "Here you go to all this time and expense to get on this big-time computer network, you learn its lingo, all its nooks and crannies, and you can't do anything except watch! What's with you, anyway? Are you some kind of kinko voyeur-type?"

Nolan could see Marianne's face redden a bit—he couldn't tell whether it was from anger or embarrassment. She clicked Elfie's eyes out of the Casino del Camino back into the maze.

"What are you doing?" Nolan asked.

"We're going to the Factory."

"To do what?"

"To make Elfie a body," she said with a defensive edge. "What do you think?"

Marianne double-clicked Elfie into the Factory, which displayed row upon row of variously shaped heads and bodies. Marianne picked a head for Elfie—one with a pointed chin and a wide brow. Then she moved her pointer across the selection of bodies, stopping at a short, chunky one.

"Nah," Nolan snorted. "Make her taller."

Marianne looked at him disapprovingly. "She's an elf."

"So what?"

"Elves are supposed to be little."

"Yeah, but does she have to be *squat* like that? Besides, who says she has to look like all the other elves?"

Marianne sighed, struck a command that made the little body rubbery, and stretched it a little taller and thinner. Then she slapped the head on top of it. The basic body was sketched out now, but completely unadorned. Nolan watched raptly as Marianne used computer brushes and pens and textures to give Elfie more detail— green pants and a green jacket, curly-toed shoes, and large pointy ears that stuck out through a halo of yellow hair. The skill and speed with which Marianne operated the graphics tools astonished and delighted Nolan.

"There," Marianne said when Elfie's large, round eyes were in place. "That should do it."

"Wait a minute. This Elfie's supposed to be a 'she,' right?"

"I hadn't really thought about it."

"You hadn't *thought* about it? It's kind of an important question, isn't it?"

"She's androgynous, OK?"

"Did you ask her if she *wanted* to be androgynous? What if your parents had decided to make *you* androgynous? What would you have to say to that?"

Marianne crossed her arms. "Maybe you'd like to take over," she said.

"No, no. You're the computer expert. I bow to the higher authority."

"No, let's work this out. I don't want you to walk into the Casino del Camino with an elf that embarrasses you. What do you want me to do to make her look feminine?"

Nolan scratched his chin. "You could make her rounder," he said.

"Rounder?"

"Yeah."

"How?"

"What do you want, an anatomy lesson?"

"Rounder in the hips?"

"That would help."

"Rounder where else?"

Nolan felt his own face redden now. "Well, she could use some breasts," he said.

"*Breasts?*"

"Sure."

"Elves don't have breasts."

"Do so. Didn't you ever see *Fantasia?*"

"Those weren't elves. Those were girl centaurs. Besides, Walt Disney was a pervert."

"He was not."

"Was so. What else do you call a guy with a fixation on little-girl honeybee bottoms?"

"That's commie talk, lady," Nolan growled.

"What kind of breasts do you want?"

Nolan shrugged. "Just any old kind. Who am I to say?"

"Oh, don't be so modest. I'm sure you're quite the connoisseur. How do you want them? Round, global, beachball-ish? Or cone-shaped, pointy, nipple-driven?"

Nolan gulped.

Better concede defeat, fella.

"Roundish would be fine," he said.

"Will that be all?"

"That should do it."

"Well, thank you for your input, Lieutenant Grobowski," Marianne said.

Nolan grinned at her. "My friends call me Nol."

Marianne grinned back. "Why don't I meet you halfway and call you Nolan?"

"Nolan would be fine."

He was pleased. He liked Nolan better, anyway.

"Isn't this supposed to be a game of chance?" Marianne asked teasingly a little while later, after Nolan had directed a really rather voluptuous-looking Elfie through several hands of poker.

"Not the way I play it, no-o-o," Nolan replied with a gravelly, nasal W. C. Fields twang and drawl.

Indeed, Nolan's luck struck Marianne as uncanny. Oh, he had folded two hands and had lost two others, but he had won five hands altogether. Marianne remembered how tired the detective had been when he showed up at the hotel room, all rumpled, slow-moving, and subdued. He certainly had come to life since then.

And Elfie had come to life, too. She was sitting confidently at the table with twenty-eight dollars worth of white, red, and blue chips in front of her—and she had started off with only five dollars. But Marianne wondered if Nolan was going to blow Elfie's luck before the evening was over. He seemed too sure of himself.

The roster of players had changed during the last half hour. When Elfie had first approached the table, the group included Tin Lizzy, a metallic matron made from Model-T parts with a car bumper brassiere and a radiator corset, and Sharecropper, a rural hick in overalls and a straw hat with a long weed dangling out of his mouth. The other players had been Ace, a Mississippi riverboat gambler with the requisite derby hat and gold watch chain, and Lucky, a pinstriped, fedora-wearing, cigar-smoking high-roller straight out of Damon Runyon's Broadway.

Nolan had immediately voiced his suspicions of Ace and Lucky. He said they looked too much at home at a card table to be quite on the level. And sure enough, the moment Elfie joined the game, Ace had folded his cards and departed. And when the Roman emperor Caligula sat down at the table, Lucky had left as well. Ace and Lucky had apparently been shills—casino "employees" paid to fill out the table until four paying customers showed up.

Ace and Lucky displayed such mechanical and repetitious

mannerisms that Marianne guessed that they didn't have human operators. They were probably just poker-playing programs. But whatever they were, they were pretty good at taking chips away from real customers.

Now the players were Tin Lizzy, Sharecropper, Caligula, and Elfie. Elfie's hand of cards faced and filled the screen. She held three tens—not much, but enough to keep her in through one round of betting. Now the bets were coming around a second time. Caligula had just raised the pot, and it was Elfie's turn to bet.

"Better fold," Marianne suggested.

"What are you, crazy?" Nolan replied. "I've got him on the ropes. I'm gonna raise him."

"With three of a kind?"

"Sure."

"*You're* crazy. He's got at least a straight."

"And I say he's got nothing better than two pair," Nolan said. "Look at him, Marianne. His upper lip's sweating."

"It is not, Nolan."

"Is so. And he's fidgeting in his chair, too. See?"

"You can't read his body language. He's an alter. He only shows what his operator wants him to show. He's not *betraying* anything."

"Even so, he's bluffing."

"So are you."

"He's not as good at it as me."

Nolan punched in the commands for Elfie to raise the bet. Share-cropper folded. Tin Lizzy called. Everybody showed their cards. Caligula had two jacks, a two, a three, and a five.

Nolan laughed as Elfie pulled in her chips.

"Hell, boy, your hand was even lousier than I thought," Nolan said to Caligula. "Hope you don't do this for a living, you arrogant son of a bitch."

Marianne laughed. "You'd better be glad he can't hear you," she said. "In a real card game, you might get shot for saying stuff like that."

And indeed, she almost thought she saw the emperor's face redden and his scowl deepen.

Just a trick of the light.

"He must have been out of his mind," Marianne added.

"Yeah, well, these Roman emperors think they run the world."

"How did you know to raise him?"

"Aw, it's just the way he's been playing. It's not even like he really bluffs. He's got no sense, is all. He thinks every hand's made of gold. Also, I keep track of the odds. Hey, do they ever get any *real* players in this joint? This could get fun."

Still stinging from his wounds, Caligula typed in an announcement:

CLGLA>THS GAME IS 5 CRD STD.

The cybernetic emperor began to shuffle.

"Where did you learn to play cards like this?" Marianne asked Nolan as Caligula began to deal.

"When I was a young cop working undercover. There was this professional hit man named Sonny Wyke—a very busy guy the force wanted to put out of business. We got word that he held a running poker game at his apartment. Well, I figured I'd get in the game, gain his confidence, and maybe he'd tell me something. All my buddies thought I was crazy. They thought I was even crazier when I started spending all my waking hours studying poker strategy, reading books about odds and probability and stuff like that. They wondered what the hell poker could have to do with a homicide investigation. But I got myself into Sonny's game, and Sonny got to like my style, because I was the only player who could keep up with him. We talked more and more during games, goofing around, coffeehousing."

"Coffeehousing?"

"You know. Chattering. Distracting the other guys at the table. Messing with their heads. We had some real fun, Sonny and me, and we took a lot of each other's hard-earned cash. Things went on like this for a couple of weeks. Then one day before a game, I got a real strong hunch something was going to click. So I asked for a lot of backup and went in wearing a wire. And sure enough, after the poker was through, Sonny and me wound up by ourselves, playing gin and talking on and on about everything you can think of—food, movies, sports, music, God, politics, family, ethics, morality. Then he tried to recruit me. Described in grisly detail practically every hit he'd ever done, saying over and over again how easy it was, how much money was in it. Told me I had a hell of a future. Finally, he mapped out the hit he wanted *me* to do."

Nolan shook his head and laughed a little. "Felt kinda weird to slap the cuffs on a guy who loved me like a brother. But you gotta get used to that kind of thing."

The whole time Nolan was talking, he had been deftly and busily working Elfie's controls, guiding her through three rounds of heavy betting. This time, the chastened Caligula folded early, and Elfie won a sizable pot from Sharecropper and Tin Lizzy.

It was an amazing performance. The game required about twenty keyboard instructions, all of which Nolan had learned and mastered at a single sitting. Now he was handling the computer as if he were born to it. When had Marianne ever known anybody who learned things this quickly?

He's not like I thought he was.

And what *had* she thought about him? Well, his first efforts to manipulate her had seemed transparent, even downright clumsy. She hadn't thought very highly of him then. But of course, he suspected her of murder at the time, and that hadn't exactly endeared him to her. He didn't suspect her anymore—or at least he didn't seem to.

(Mental memo: Always remember, he's a terrific poker player.)

After that interval of mutual wariness, Marianne had been moved when Nolan showed a touch of human kindness and lent her the clothes.

(Memo: Don't forget they're in the closet. Give them back before he leaves.)

That was when she first noticed that he was actually rather attractive. She particularly liked his warm, pleasant voice. But even then, she had continued to think of him as primitive, rough, uncouth— anything but sophisticated.

She had been a snob.

Now she found herself astounded by the man's sheer intelligence—and yes, by his sophistication. It was a sophistication bred by his way of life, the urgency of his profession. Marianne knew plenty of bright men and women in Santa Barbara, people who studied fine wines, learned foreign languages, stayed on top of the best-seller lists. But this man knew how to think on his feet—to learn things vigorously, earnestly, fun-lovingly. It was brilliance of a different order.

What kinds of things has he learned from life? What are his interests?
Well, he had just recited a list . . .

". . . *food, movies, sports, music, God, politics, family, ethics, morality . . .*"

Marianne guessed he was a self-taught expert on all those things. She wondered what other things besides.

Elfie was shuffling the cards now. Nolan's eyes darted about the screen, full of happy anticipation for the next hand of cards. Marianne now realized something else, too—her real reason for not having given Elfie a body until now. She wanted somebody to share Elfie with. Oh, of course there were all those anonymous insomnimaniacs out there in the infoworld, but that was different. *This* was fun. It was really and truly enjoyable to bring Elfie to life in the presence of a real, live, flesh-and-blood human being—a marvelous, exuberant man.

"All right, boys and girls," Nolan announced rambunctiously as Elfie dealt the cards. "This game's seven card stud."

It would be all right to touch him. I could just reach over and rest my hand on his shoulder. It wouldn't seem out of line. It would just seem like I'm sharing his excitement at his winning streak.

But she immediately thought better of it. He was a cop on a case, and she was helping him learn some necessary skills.

That's all. That's all that's going on.

She kept both of her hands folded in front of her, but it didn't feel quite natural.

10000

SOLACE

W HAT ARE YOU WEARING THAT SHIT-EATING GRIN FOR?"
Nolan jumped slightly in his chair at the sharp sound of
Clayton's voice. He looked up. Clayton was sitting on top
of Nolan's side of their facing desks, notebook in hand. He seemed
to have appeared out of nowhere.

Like an elf.

"What are you talking about?" Nolan asked. He honestly had no
idea that he'd been grinning.

"The grin that's sprawled all over that big white face of yours," Clayton said, with more than a trace of irritation. "What're you so happy
about all of a sudden? Did you get us a big break in the case or what?"

"No," Nolan said.

"Then what the hell is it?"

Actually, Nolan had been lost in memories of yesterday evening—
the computer games and Marianne Hedison's company. But he
didn't particularly want to say so. Not when Clayton was in such a
cantankerous mood.

"I was just thinking what a joy it is to be a cop," Nolan said with
mock sincerity. "I was thinking about the short hours, the easy
workload, the public gratitude. Don't you get that feeling once in a
while yourself? Doesn't it sometimes just sort of wash over you in a
slathering glob of warm, delicious goo?"

Clayton glowered at him. "You been snackin' on that impounded
weed, ain't ya?"

"Get off my desk," Nolan replied.

But Clayton didn't move. He just started thumbing through his notebook. Nolan hated it when Clayton sat on his desk and thumbed through his notebook. The body language was too damned obvious—implying that Nolan's mind and attention weren't sufficiently engaged by the business at hand. Nolan was annoyed by the simple fact that Clayton was right.

"So did you pay another visit to Pritchard and Maisie down at Insomnimania?" Clayton asked.

"Kim and I went down this morning," Nolan said. "They seem to be on the job, but Auggie still hasn't put in an appearance on the network."

"Anything else?"

Nolan paused. Did he really want to go into the other thing he had found out from Pritchard and Maisie? He couldn't just skip it—no matter how off the wall it might seem.

"It's tough to explain," Nolan said reluctantly.

"I love it already," Clayton growled.

"Do you remember hearing about that magazine publisher falling off a building in Chicago several weeks back?"

"A guy named Braxton?"

"That's right."

"Sure, I remember. It was a suicide, right?"

"Not according to the cop I worked with in Chicago. He told me it was murder. And he happened to mention that Braxton was logged onto a computer network at the time he died, playing canasta in a virtual casino. I didn't think anything about it for a while, but this morning I asked Pritchard and Maisie to check their files. And it turned out that Braxton belonged to Insomnimania."

Clayton stared at Nolan blankly for a minute.

"So what?" Clayton said.

"Well, it *might* mean that the Braxton killing was linked with our two in L.A."

Clayton groaned. "Come on, Nol. The network's got a lot of members. A few of them are gonna die from time to time."

"Hey, you're the one who *ought* to be interested."

"Why?"

"*You* suggested a connection between Gauld and Judson."

"Yeah, and we're still trying to figure out if that connection's real.

Whydya have to go dragging some dead dork from Chicago into the picture?"

"So you don't think it's possible that their high diver's part of the same picture?"

"I'm not saying that. But look, Nol. I like to follow a hunch and go in over my head more than anybody—more than *you* do most of the time. But we've got our hands full here. What are we supposed to do about something that happened in Chicago, anyway?"

Nolan shrugged. "There isn't much *to* do," he said. "I called the cop in Chicago and tipped him off."

"And what did he say?"

"He was about as receptive and open-minded as you are."

"Great. Leave it at that. Let Chicago solve their own homicides. Let's stick to the mess at hand."

"OK," Nolan said with a resigned and weary sigh. "So how was *your* morning? Great, I take it."

"Well, you can write off Larry Bricker as a suspect. I've checked out his alibis and they're all solid. A neighbor even saw him pull into his garage just when he said he did."

"What about those fibers you found in Gauld's closet?"

"Same as the ones under her fingernails. Whoever killed her definitely hid in there."

"What kind of fibers were they?"

"Red-and-white acrylic knitting yarn—the kind you'd find at any bargain store."

"A ski mask?"

"Maybe. Wasn't a cashmere sweater, anyway."

Nolan and Clayton looked at each other blankly. They were stuck.

Guess it's time to get out the old tape deck. He and Clayton made a point of recording a freewheeling, question-and-answer session on a cassette tape every day while working on a difficult case— particularly when they found themselves drawing mental blanks. They usually picked up some new insight along the way, if not an actual breakthrough.

"Wanna jam?" Nolan asked.

"Not particularly," Clayton said.

Damn, he really is in a grouchy mood.

"Think maybe we should do it anyway?" Nolan suggested gently.

"Yeah, I guess so," Clayton sighed.

Partial transcript of brainstorming session between Lieutenant Nolan Grobowski and Detective Clayton Saunders of the L.A.P.D.; taped 2:30 P.M., Wednesday, February 2:

Q: What did Gauld and Judson have in common?

A: They both belonged to Insomnimania.

Q: And?

A: They weren't exactly poor.

Q: And?

A: Auggie staged replays of both of their killings on Insomnimania.

Q: How were Gauld and Judson different?

A: Gauld was a girl, Judson was a boy.

Q: Try again. How were they different?

A: Gauld was upwardly mobile, Judson was looking down from the top.

Q: Were they killed by the same guy?

A: Maybe.

Q: A serial killer, then?

A: Probably not.

Q: Why not?

A: No favorite MO, no ritual, no sexual component.

Q: How could it be the same guy but not serial?

A: Who the fuck knows?

Q: Make something up.

A: If one guy kills only two people, it's just consecutive. Three or more makes it serial.

Q: What kind of crap is that?

A: Hey, you said make something up.

Q: What about Braxton?

A: *Don't talk about Braxton.*

Q: OK. Were Gauld and Judson mob hits, maybe?

A: Too unprofessional.

Q: How?

A: Judson died sloppy; Gauld died slow.

Q: So what's the motive?

A: Who the fuck knows?

Q: Who's Auggie's user?

A: Who the fuck knows?

Q: Did Auggie's user do the murders?

A: Who the fuck knows?

Q: Why do you keep saying who the fuck knows?

A: Who the fuck knows?

Q: Do we know anything we didn't know yesterday?
A: Fuck, no.

"Turn it off," Clayton groaned. "I'm getting a migraine case of déjà vu."

Nolan clicked off the machine. Their jam sessions had started sounding pretty much alike during the last few days.

The case really is *a mess.*

"I'll get you an aspirin," Nolan said.

"Naw, shoot me with one of those tranquilizer darts—the kind they use on elephants."

"We'll get a break," Nolan said with a shrug. "We've just got to wait till Auggie shows up on the network."

"Suppose he never shows up?"

"He will."

Clayton waved his fist at Nolan. "You show one more sign of cheerfulness and/or optimism and I'll break your face."

"Whoa. Do I detect a trace of hostility?"

"I *own* hostility."

"You gotta watch it, buddy. You're gonna have some kind of aneurysm right here and now and fall off the desk and bust your head wide open, and you'll cost the department a fortune in employee comp, and they'll take it out on me because it happened in my area, for which reason I'd really appreciate it if you got down off my desk."

Clayton didn't move.

"I'm tired Nol," Clayton said. "I'm just plain tired."

He looks tired. I must look tired, too. Why don't I feel tired?

"So what next?" Nolan asked.

"I've got to go to Orange County."

"Orange County? Jesus, you'll never get back from there alive."

"Tell me about it. There're rednecks in those parts that'd just as soon lynch me as speak to me."

"I'm talking about the traffic. It's after two-thirty, pal. Whaddya got to go out there for?"

"I just talked on the phone to one of the guys at the DNA lab there. They've got the tissue sample from under Gauld's nails and the blood from her rug. Said they'd process it tomorrow."

"So?"

"So he said the same damn thing the day before yesterday. They think because they've got nothing to match it against, there's no hurry. Gotta go light a fire under some asses or the thing'll never get done. What are *you* going to do?"

"I'm still talking to Marianne Hedison," Nolan said.

"What the hell for?" Clayton asked sharply. "She's not a viable suspect."

Nolan was startled.

Suspect?

When did he ever consider her a suspect?

Oh, yeah. Back when this whole thing started.

It seemed like ages ago now.

Nolan almost broke into another shit-eating grin. Should he tell Clayton the truth—that he'd spent several fun-filled hours last night poking around Insomnimania with Marianne Hedison? Should he tell him that he'd already invited her over to his house tonight for more of the same, and dinner besides? Should he tell him that they'd really hit it off—as friends, at least?

Why the hell not? If she's not a viable suspect, it's not exactly a breach of ethics. Besides, Clayton could use a good guffaw at my expense.

"Listen, Clay, I've got something to tell you that'll give you a real laugh. Y'see—"

"Not now, Nol," Clayton said, climbing down off the desk. "Orange County calls. Besides, if you make me laugh, it'll spoil a perfect record for today. Save it for when I want to be human. Later."

Before Nolan could say another word, Clayton was traipsing crankily away through the noisy squad room.

Marianne was lurking through the depths of the Blue Whale, searching the huge marine mammal's postmodern bowels for nineties interior motifs. It was now almost evening, and this was the last stop in a busy day touring L.A.'s showrooms.

The Blue Whale was the nickname of L.A.'s Pacific Design Center. The name was intended derisively at first, because of the furor the building's vast, blue glass exterior had initially created. But as people grew accustomed, and then attached, to the land-bound leviathan, the name took on affectionate overtones. Marianne herself rather liked the place.

During the conference, several meetings had been held here, but Marianne had not come over from the hotel to attend them. Now she was wandering slowly through the commodious hallways, browsing her way from showroom to showroom, noting the arrangements of furniture, fabrics, and accessories, with particular attention to ideas for the Abernathy project.

After she had returned from Iowa, Marianne sent the preliminary rendering in to the office. She had provided the Abernathys with a computerized walk-through of the space, suggesting placement for furniture the family already owned and still wanted to use. She had also suggested colors and sketched in ideas for new pieces. But some of those new pieces were still to be designated as specific rugs, furniture, and artwork. Once she located what she thought would be appropriate, Marianne would add those details to the rendering—making everything ready for the client's approval.

"Nothing ostentatious," Reba Abernathy had said whenever Marianne asked for her ideas. That was all. She apparently had no imagination of her own. And when Marianne had asked Reba's husband, Lloyd, for his thoughts, he sang the same tune . . .

"Nothing ostentatious."

Then he added emphatically . . .

"Money's no object."

Marianne's lips turned up in a smile at the memory. Lloyd Abernathy had said it without the slightest trace of irony or self-parody.

Nothing ostentatious—money's no object.

Marianne liked to think of that kind of remark as "found satire"—the sort of thing no TV comedy writer would dare put in the mouth of a character for fear of seeming too ludicrous, but that real people blithely said from time to time in happy obliviousness of their own absurdity.

"Expensive frugality" had actually been one of the themes of the conference—a term used by one of the speakers, only half in jest. The eighties had been gaudy and ornate and downright vulgar—the golden age of conspicuous consumption. Now the wealthy looked back on those days with shame. They were anxious to appear more frugal—and indeed, would spare no expense to do so.

The showroom exhibit facing her now was a perfect example, with a couple of thirties black-and-white lawn chairs, plain linen curtains, a marble fireplace, a leather-upholstered Victorian sofa, and a needlepoint rug. On the far wall hung a medium-sized collage by an unknown but undoubtedly up-and-coming artist. A small cubist sculpture sat unheralded on a table.

No noisy Schnabels in this place.

Nothing else in the room was noisy, for that matter. Rectangles and straight lines dominated the room, giving it an almost Shaker-style simplicity. It was the very picture of abstemiousness. But the underlying neutral carpet was of very high quality, and a second sofa was covered in a custom-designed handwoven fabric. Marianne guessed it would cost about half a million dollars to put it all together.

Right in Abernathy's price range.

Marianne wished she could lift the room out of the Blue Whale with a crane and deposit it in the Abernathy's Santa Barbara home, making everybody perfectly happy.

Then she wondered what Nolan, with his weathered but comfortable household, would think of this side of her? She realized that he knew very little about her—certainly not that she was in the business of offering decorative absolution to today's conscience-stricken rich.

And why did she care so much what he thought?

Several hours later, Marianne went back to her hotel and showered and changed. Then she left the hotel and arrived at Nolan's house at about seven-fifteen. He greeted her at the front door, clad in an apron and wiping his hands on a kitchen towel.

"Come in!" he exclaimed. "Hey, you're a bit early."

"I'm sorry. I overestimated the traffic for once."

"No, don't apologize. Everything's all ready. Come in and sit down."

Nolan took her jacket and escorted her into the living room. A roaring fire crackled pleasantly in the fireplace. The overhead light was off. A floor lamp and a table lamp were the only illumination other than the fire.

"I've got to get back to the kitchen, so make yourself at home," Nolan said. "I hope you like lasagne."

"Who doesn't?"

"Would you like a drink?"

"Bourbon would be nice."

"With water?"

"No, just on the rocks."

"A drinker after my own heart. Coming right up."

Nolan disappeared into the kitchen, and Marianne sat down in a comfortable armchair. Nolan quickly reappeared with her drink. They chatted briefly, filling each other in on how their respective days had gone. Nolan described how stranded the Auggie case still seemed to be, and Marianne sketchily described her tour of show-rooms. She even took a bit of a risk and told him all about the design world's new craze for "expensive frugality," which he seemed to find highly amusing.

Then Nolan ushered her into his dining room, where a table was neatly arranged with two dinner settings. He served red wine, salad, and a handsome plate of savory lasagne. As they ate, the conversation focused on Marianne. She briefly outlined her whole life story for Nolan—told him about her Quaker childhood, her parents' early deaths, her days as a bohemian artist, her marriage to Evan, all capped off by her divorce and her move to Santa Barbara.

Nolan was quietly attentive all the while she talked. Marianne wondered what he thought of her story—particularly her sojourn among seedier counterculture types, her limited experiments with drugs, and her marriage to a philandering, megalomaniac artist. Did any of this jar his middle-class values? It was really rather hard to tell.

He's awfully quiet this evening.

Marianne remembered how boisterous they both had been last night. They had joked, teased, and laughed with terrific gusto. But tonight, everything was much more muted—and more than a little cautious.

Why was that?

What had caused the change?

A word crossed Marianne's mind . . .

Expectation.

Yes, that was it. Last evening had been spontaneous, fun for its own sake. This evening seemed more like a *date,* with all its unre-solved uncertainties and anxieties. Marianne felt her heart jump and her throat tighten slightly at the realization. How did *she* expect the evening to end? How did she *want* it to end? Until this moment, it had not occurred to her to wonder.

She had no answers. She knew she was drawn to Nolan. She felt that she had not been this close to an actual living person for a long time. He made more sounds, displayed more textures, exuded more subtle smells, and just generally seemed more physically *pres-ent* than anyone else she knew. She couldn't help but like it.

A living, breathing, sweating, laughing man.

They finished eating, and Nolan began clearing the table.

"A brandy, maybe?" he asked.

"That would be nice," Marianne replied, a little tersely.

While Nolan was stacking up the plates, the phone rang.

"I'll take that in the kitchen," Nolan said.

He got out of his chair and lumbered quietly out of the room, carrying all the plates and serving ware with him. Marianne heard him pick up the phone.

"Hello?" Nolan said. "Oh, hi, darlin'. It's good to hear your voice. What's going on?"

A girlfriend? If so, Nolan wasn't going to any lengths to conceal his affection. There was no furtive quality to his voice, no murmur of, "Please call back later, this isn't a really good time."

If it is *a girlfriend, I sure know where I stand.*

Nolan's voice echoed softly but resonantly through the house. His words became inaudible for a moment or two, but then Marianne heard him say soothingly, "Oh, honey, you worried the same way last semester about that other midterm, don'tcha remember?"

One of his kids. Calling from school.

Trying to get out of earshot, Marianne got up from her chair and walked into the living room, looking at all the pictures glimmering in the firelight. There were more photos than she had remembered from her first short visit—studio images and snapshots of men, women, children, dogs, and cats. Here was a couple at a high school prom, elsewhere the same couple getting married.

That's Nolan. She tried to reconcile the craggy man she knew with the youthful, bright-faced groom.

Marianne became entranced by the faces. It wasn't just a stale and static portrait gallery. It was a living, breathing world filled with a multitude of lovely, joyful people—a vast array of different families contained in one. The pictures represented a kind of immortality—not just for Nolan's lost wife, but for the babies, the kids, the teenagers his children had once been. There were actually dozens of different children here, and Nolan had taken care to preserve each and every one of them against time. He had held on to them through the years—not in a selfish, clinging way, but lovingly, protectively.

Marianne felt a deep pang. She wished she'd kept *something* of Renee—photographs, videotapes, anything. And she wished she'd kept more of her parents, too, much more than a single small box of yellowed photographs.

I've taken too little care of this. It's my loss.

A few more words wafted in from the kitchen. It sounded like Nolan was sharing a few bits of knowledge with his studious youngster. Marianne gravitated farther away from the kitchen toward the bookshelves. Some of the books were texts in psychology, law, forensics, and criminal justice. There was also an array of popular paperback novels and numerous classics of one kind or another. Marianne's eyes did not light on a single book with an unbroken binding. They all appeared to have been read and reread.

On an adjoining shelf were the phonograph records. They were all vinyl. Nolan had not yet entered the age of CDs. Marianne's eyes started at the upper-left-hand corner of the collection and began making their way across the titles, which included jazz, rhythm and blues, and classical—mixed together in dogged alphabetical order.

The large range of titles wasn't so unusual. Many of Marianne's friends had similarly varied collections. But they always made a point of departmentalizing their music—keeping the classical away from the jazz and the jazz away from the rock-and-roll as if out of fear of musical interbreeding. Her friends placed records in these separate, monolithic, and highly visible categories to advertise their erudition, to wear eclecticism on their sleeves. Nolan's indiscriminate arrangement of records could only belong to someone who liked all kinds of music, pure and simple—and didn't care what anyone thought about him for it.

"Want to hear something?"

Marianne turned with a start. Nolan was standing right behind her, holding two after-dinner brandies.

"I was just looking," she said. "It's a nice collection."

Nolan grinned. "You're surprised a cop's got taste?" he asked teasingly.

Marianne smiled a little embarrassedly. "Not at all," she said. "These days, I'm surprised when *anybody's* got taste."

Nolan laughed. "Go on," he said. "Pick out something you want to hear."

"No. You pick something."

Nolan went straight to the "Js," took out a recording of Scott Joplin rags performed by André Previn and Itzhak Perlman, and put it on the turntable. They took their brandies and sat down in two large chairs that were pulled up near the fire.

"Was that one of your kids on the phone?" Marianne asked.

"Yeah. Molly. A junior at Berkeley. Going for a psych degree, I guess—that is, if she doesn't change majors again. She's got a big midterm coming up."

"She's afraid she might do badly?"

Nolan chuckled. "Afraid she might pull an A-minus is more like it," he said. "Hell, I don't guess either she or Jack ever got anything lower than a B all the time they were in school—except maybe in phys ed, and who cares about that?"

He sipped quietly on his brandy, then added, "They take after their mother that way."

"Maybe they take after their father that way, too," Marianne said.

Nolan chuckled modestly. "Yeah, I wasn't such a bad student, either," he said.

They both sat looking at the fire for a moment. Marianne could feel the departed wife's ghost lingering in the room—benignly, unthreateningly, wanting nothing more than to have her presence acknowledged.

"What was your wife's name?" Marianne asked at last.

"Louise," said Nolan. "Lost her about three years ago, right about this time of year. Can't remember if it's been a little more or a little less than three years."

He was quiet for a moment. Marianne could feel that it was a good kind of quiet—a nurturing one out of which either of them could speak freely or not at all. It was Nolan's turn to tell his story, and he could take as long as he wanted to. A sweet Scott Joplin waltz was playing now. Marianne remembered what Joplin had said about his art: "It is never right to play ragtime fast."

It was good advice for a time like now.

"I can't remember a time when I didn't know Louise," Nolan said at last. "We knew each other all the way back to grade school. We were each other's first sweethearts. Dated all through high school. Got married when we were both freshmen at UCLA. She was studying sociology, I was studying law."

Nolan laughed softly. "We both figured we'd save the world," he said. "It was that kind of time. But we had two babies in the next three years, Jack and then Molly. While we were still in school, can you believe it? Well, we were just a pair of happy idiots, enjoying all the perks of being students, not thinking about the years to come. We thought we could handle everything. I finished my degree on schedule, but it took Louise six years to finish hers. After that, there was no way for me to go to law school. My grades were fine, but we were flat broke. I had to get a job as fast as I could."

"So you became a cop," Marianne said.

"Yeah."

"Any regrets?"

Nolan's brow furrowed as he thought about the question. "Louise and I had to skimp over the years, and I sometimes worry that maybe the kids felt it. Also, I spent a lot of late nights on cases away from the family. But I think I made up for it during the time we spent together."

Marianne glanced around the portrait gallery.

Yes. You obviously made up for it very well.

"Besides," Nolan continued, "I've probably done the world more good as a cop. If I'd gone on to be a lawyer, I could've forgotten all my ideals and turned into some greedy monster yuppie, just like the rest of my generation. It's taken some doing in this line of work, but I think I've kept my soul. So I guess things worked out for the best. Jack, my oldest, is a clerk in a law firm up in Seattle, going to law school part-time. We'll see how well *his* ideals hold up."

"I'll bet he'll do just fine," Marianne said.

Nolan smiled. "I'll bet so, too," he said.

Then his face darkened.

"When the kids got well into their teens," Nolan said, "Louise and I both figured it was time for her to go back to school and finish her education. She was way too smart to spend the rest of her life keeping house—an empty house, at that. So she started doing graduate work in psychology. And she took a job doing social work with inner-city kids—keeping them off drugs, out of gangs, out of trouble. She loved it. It had its frustrations, but she loved it. She loved the kids she could help, and I think she even loved the ones she couldn't help."

Another silence fell. This silence seemed strangely final, as if Nolan had finished his story and had nothing more to tell. When he spoke again, he sounded as if he had to force every word out of his throat one at a time.

"One night, I was working late at my desk at the division. It was nine-thirty, maybe. I got a call from a buddy on patrol. He was real upset. Wouldn't tell me what was wrong. Just told me to come right away to this alleyway in East L.A. When I got there, I saw her, just like she was when the guys had found her. Even the coroner's assistants hadn't touched her. She was splayed in a concrete enclosure next to a rust-colored dumpster. She looked like a tossed-away rag doll. She had bled to death from the knife wounds. You could see from the blood trails that it hadn't happened there. She must have crawled there to get away. But I still can't figure out how she got all sprawled like that. Her arm was twisted above and in back of her head and her legs were wrenched every which way. I guess . . . when you're in pain and terror and you're dying . . . you don't worry too much about how you look."

His voice had faded away into a barely audible whisper.

"Did they catch whoever killed her?" Marianne asked.

"Yeah. It wasn't hard to run them down. A couple of teenagers she'd been working with. They knew her route, knew she'd be stopping at an automatic teller. All they had to do was wait for her across the street from the machine. I'm sure she didn't resist or scream or anything. They were either junked up or in withdrawal, and that's probably why . . . why they killed her. They just got out of control."

Nolan closed his eyes.

"I remember, after they'd been caught, I decided I had to meet them face to face. I was worried about it. I didn't know how I was going to react. I was afraid maybe I'd go berserk, pull out my service revolver and blow the both of them away. But when I actually saw them in their jail cells, I didn't feel much of anything. It wasn't like I loved or pitied or wanted to help them, but I didn't *hate* them—didn't itch to break their necks with my bare hands or watch them die through a gas-chamber window. I wondered if something was wrong with me. Eventually, I figured it was just because I'd loved Louise too much to want to add more deaths onto hers."

He fell silent again. Marianne thought about herself and Renee— all the unfinished matters, the unanswered questions they had left behind.

"Maybe that's what it means to love somebody completely," Marianne said softly. "Losing your capacity to hate."

Nolan nodded and said nothing.

Marianne took a long, deep breath. "Do you . . . ever forget she's gone?" she asked. "Do you ever expect to see her step into some doorway in this house, for her to call you at the office, anything like that?"

Nolan looked at her with a curious expression. "No," he said. "I never did. The division counselor told me all about denial, told me to expect it, but I never went through it. Don't get me wrong. I was a wreck. I drank too much for months and screwed up cases and almost got myself fired. But I never went through denial, never failed to get it through my head that she was dead. I guess it was because I saw her in that place, all twisted up like that. It didn't leave any question, any doubt."

Marianne watched the fire and thought about Nolan's words. She had seen Renee's corpse in the morgue, had mourned with her friends and family. But even so . . .

"What about you?" Nolan asked. "Have you accepted the truth about your friend?"

"No," Marianne said simply. "I haven't."

"Give it some time. It's supposed to take time."

Marianne and Nolan looked into each other's eyes. They jumped slightly when the phone rang.

"Your other child, maybe?" Marianne asked.

"No such luck," Nolan said. "I'll try to keep this short."

Nolan felt an edge of apprehension as he wandered into the kitchen. Other than the occasional chats with Molly or Jack, phone calls were seldom a welcome part of his life. They usually had to do with business—and they almost always came when business was going badly.

He picked up the kitchen phone.

"Hello?" he said warily.

"Hi, Nol. It's Clay."

Nolan smiled slightly. He could count on Clay to understand that he didn't want to be bothered right now.

"Hey, guy. How're you doin'?"

"As good as can be expected."

"Well, listen. Could we keep this short and simple? I'm kind of busy right now."

"Sure, no problem. I just got back in from the DNA joint."

"Jesus, Clay. It's eight-thirty. What were you doing there all this time?"

"Thought I'd stay there till the traffic cleared up," Clayton said. "Just sort of tooled around Orange County to pass the time. Sat in on a Klan meeting, picked up some Nazi memorabilia, caught a few cross-burnings. Y'know, maybe I misjudged that place."

"So did they run the tests?"

"After a while. Took a little arm twisting."

"What did you do?"

"Just walked in and sat down and crossed my arms and looked real black."

Nolan chuckled. "You intimidating bastard," he said.

"Thanks."

"So what's the news? What did they tell you?"

"Well, they can't say much without a match. But guess what?"

"What?" Nolan asked, shuffling his feet irritably. Clayton obviously hadn't taken the hint that he wasn't in the mood for guessing games.

"Gauld's killer was a woman," Clayton said.

Nolan staggered slightly, then sat down in a kitchen chair. He felt his heart rate change. He couldn't tell if it was beating dramatically faster or dangerously slower.

"Hey, are you still there?" Clayton said.

"Yeah. Are they sure?"

"It's the only thing they *are* sure of at this point. Guess this puts the Hedison woman back in the running, huh? Boy, you'll never let me live it down if she turns out to be the one. 'Course, you could still be wrong."

"Thanks for calling, Clay," Nolan said simply.

"Sure," Clayton said, sounding a little surprised at Nolan's brevity. "See you tomorrow."

"Yeah."

Nolan hung the phone up softly.

Why did Clay have to call just now?

The evening had been so perfect, so rare. It had been wonderful to learn that he could still cook for more than one person at a time, that he was capable of entertaining a guest in his own home. It had been so long since he had had such an opportunity. And he had shared thoughts and feelings with her that he had never expected to tell another living soul.

Of all times, why now?

He looked out the kitchen doorway toward the living room. Marianne was turned slightly away from him, facing the fire, lost in its flames. Nolan walked slowly toward her, feeling as if he were moving through some thick gel. Whole days seemed to pass before he found himself standing beside the chair where she was sitting. He sat down on the arm of the chair. It was the closest he had allowed himself to approach her all evening. She looked up at him, her green eyes brightly reflecting the cheerful firelight.

Nolan knew that his life was changing unalterably as every millisecond passed. He had no idea how. All he knew was that it felt terrifying and splendid at the same time.

"Has something happened?" Marianne asked quietly, with a concerned look.

Nolan said nothing for a moment. He took Marianne's warm hand in his and began to stroke her thin fingers. If Marianne was startled by the gesture, she didn't show it. Nolan wondered why he wasn't startled himself.

"Clayton just got word that Renee's killer was a woman," Nolan said, almost in a whisper.

Marianne tilted her head slightly. She looked intrigued, but certainly not shocked or surprised.

"How do they know?" she asked.

"They did a DNA test on blood and tissue samples found at the scene."

"Am I a suspect, then?" she asked calmly, without averting her gaze from his.

"You might be asked to take a DNA test," he said.

"I'll do it," she said.

"Marianne, don't jump to any decisions."

"Why?" she asked. "Do you think I'm guilty?"

Nolan smiled at her warmly.

"What do you think I think?" he asked.

Marianne returned his smile.

"This kind of testing is still controversial," Nolan continued gently. "It might be unreliable. Like a polygraph, you know?"

"I'll take a polygraph, too."

"Marianne, listen—"

"Nolan, I want to. If I don't, I'll only cloud the issue by remaining a suspect. I'll get in the way of your search for the real killer. I've got to do whatever I can to clear this up. I've got to do it for Renee."

Nolan studied her face for a moment, then reached out and pulled her body against his. She gasped slightly and tucked her head into his chest, clinging to him as he held her. He began gently rubbing her back.

Nolan stared into the fire. He worried that his hands were cold—that she might feel their coldness through her blouse. But her shoulders melted into his fingers, and he realized with surprise that his hands were warm—and more confident than *he* was.

What am I doing? What am I feeling?

It seemed to be loneliness—a distinctive kind of loneliness it took two people to feel. It was a loneliness he could remember experiencing from time to time with Louise. He felt eerily isolated *with* Marianne, about to instigate something both of them might very well regret. He knew that she wanted him as much as he wanted her, but did that make it right? It seemed too big a decision for only two people to make.

You probably should go now. This can't be a good idea.

But how could she get up and move away from something this warm, this comfortable? And where did she have to go? Her hotel room? Her home? Did either of those places have rows and rows of lovely pictures and a fine, gentle man who wanted nothing more than someone else with whom to share his wonderful capacity for love? Were either of those places inhabited by happy ghosts, by lives fully lived?

Nolan put his hand on her cheek and leaned over and kissed her. A powerful emotion swept over her. She recognized it at once.

Gratitude.

She felt grateful for his evident desire, and deeply, deeply grateful for her own chaotic overload of emotion and sensation—a kind of glorious, dizzying panic sweeping her along like a roller coaster ride. It had been a long, long time since she had felt this way.

"I think it's too late for me to leave," she murmured.

"I think so, too," Nolan said, kissing her repeatedly.

But good sense scored one small point before the splendid panic carried her completely away. She drew back from Nolan slightly.

"I didn't . . . bring anything," she stammered.

The words sounded so painfully awkward.

Oh, for the way it happened in the movies, so seamlessly, so gracefully . . .

But real life was fleshy, sweaty, and more than a little dangerous, and certain protocols were necessary.

Nolan looked embarrassed, too.

"I've got some condoms upstairs," he said.

"Fine. I'll go up and use the bathroom," she said.

She rose to her feet. Nolan shifted position, but did not stand up immediately. He leaned forward slightly—to mask his erection, Marianne realized.

"There's a robe hanging in the bathroom you can use," Nolan said.

"Thank you."

Marianne walked upstairs, went into the bathroom, undressed, and washed. Then she found her way into the bedroom, which was lit only by the small lamp on the end table. Nolan was standing by the bed wearing a robe of his own and holding a condom packet in his hand. The covers on the bed were turned neatly down.

Nolan looked at her a bit shyly for a moment, set the packet on the end table, and walked over to her and drew her to him. She could feel his erection against her. Then Nolan led her to the bed and pulled her under the covers. He ran his hands under the robe across her bare flesh. She felt her nipples harden.

She closed her eyes and focused on the sheer sensation of his hands searching the surface of her skin, of her own hands running everywhere on his body—over his slightly sweaty skin, through the shaggy fine hair on his head and the curled hair on his chest and the coarser and tightly curled hair surrounding the smooth skin of his cock. She reached across the top of the end table for the packet, tore the damp condom free from the foil, and delicately pulled the sheath over him as he quivered between her fingers.

It had been so long since Nolan had been with a woman that he feared that their first encounter would be a little peremptory. He expected to be slightly impatient, slightly abrupt. He expected to have to apologize a little afterward, ask her indulgence, promise to be more attentive the next time around.

But the moment he was unclothed with Marianne, his concerns vanished. Every movement, every touch slowed down, stretched out, prolonged itself. He became lost in their kinesthetic bond as he pressed his mouth on every part of her body and his fingers stroked and caressed her smooth, narrow torso—so alarmingly thin and delicate.

There was no mistaking her growing excitement as her nipples fluttered stiffly amidst his outstretched fingers, the muscles of her belly rising along the heels of his hands. At each of these points of contact, he felt an electric charge coursing through his own body and reaching his groin with a nearly explosive spasm.

He came just a little at that moment, he was sure of it. But this was followed by a slight easing of desire, a welcome slackness allowing him to enter her in full possession of his movements.

Marianne was aware, with some surprise, that Nolan was taking over the process of their lovemaking. He asked no questions, said nothing at all.

She thought fleetingly of Stephen . . .

Odd, how he never entered my mind till just this instant.

. . . and how sex with him was a negotiation.

Will you do this for me?

What do you want me to do?

There was none of that now as Nolan kissed her on her breasts, her belly, all over her body, moaning in apparent appreciation. Marianne wrapped her arms around him and lifted her knees on each side of his body. She was surprised at her openness as he varied his pace and direction.

But she felt as though she were taking a long time to come.

A thousand distractions flickered in her mind.

Stephen was still there.

Go away, Stephen.

She wondered if Nolan was growing annoyed at her slowness, and she worried that he might stop. She drew a familiar fantasy image into her mind—ropes around her wrists and ankles, tying her to the bed.

You can't fight it.

Stephen fled.

Every thought fled.

Marianne cried aloud as a deep, shuddering force drove her back arching upward and exploded all the way through her body.

As the sharp bones of her pelvis pressed upward, Nolan lifted his hips so she pulled downward against his cock, heightening the pressure, the feeling of inexorability between them. When he came, there was no sad awareness of temporality, no aching realization that the moment would quickly be lost and gone. And even with the condom, there was no deadening of sensation. The liquid pulsation went recklessly, freely on and on as if it never had to stop. He only quit thrusting into her when he began to feel a tiredness in his lower back—and even then, the inner throbbing continued for a few moments before waning.

Marianne felt like water, utterly formless. Finally, Nolan pulled out of her and flopped over beside her. He pulled off the condom and tossed it into a dish on the bedside table. He rolled onto his back and pulled Marianne's head onto his shoulder.

The flood of sensations ebbed, and Marianne was left with a mild sense of surprise. She was surprised that it had happened, that it had been good, but also that it had been so simple.

The missionary position, for God's sake.

Sex with Evan had been one experiment after another, with countless positions, locations, and roles. It had taken variety to keep Evan excited, and Marianne did her best to accommodate him. Evan devised all the scripts and plans, of course, and he also determined afterward whether the experiments had been successful. There was no point in Marianne trying to tell him that lying on her back in the woods was downright uncomfortable or that most of the odd positions really did nothing for her.

He sure talked a lot. So does Stephen.

But Nolan hadn't said a word, and that was good—at least for the time being. She realized that words had always dragged her out of that deep place of physical pleasure she could only reach through the silence of touch. Would things continue with him like this? Would things continue with him at all?

A little while later, they made love again, with the same simplicity and intensity. Then she drifted off to sleep in a deeper state of relaxation than she could ever remember experiencing.

Marianne's head was nestled warmly on Nolan's shoulder. He mentally replayed the events leading to this moment of shared quietness, marveling at how something so perfect could have happened so unpremeditatedly. When they had finished making love that first time, he had avoided asking the fatal question:

"Was it all right for you?"

He had avoided it this second time, too. On one hand, it seemed only considerate to ask. If there had been any attention she had missed or needed, he could be more careful, more aware in the future. On the other hand, asking would certainly seem vain or pushy, and Nolan wanted nothing more than for her to feel comfortable with him. That required him to trust her to communicate with him in her own way.

Their second lovemaking had seemed less turbulent but no less fulfilling. Thinking back, Nolan had no idea how long they had spent either time. Time had played no role whatsoever in the entire experience. How could something that remarkable happen without time passing at all?

Now Nolan could feel little twitches of near-sleepfulness throughout Marianne's frame. Soon came the first hint of a feathery snore. Nolan, too, drifted along the precarious edge of sleep. He felt the boundaries of his body blur, fading in and out of hers, and he vaguely imagined that he was actually experiencing *her* sensations—the grip of his own strong fingers on her delicate shoulder, the gust of his own warm breath sneaking across the back of her ear.

There was a whispery eroticism about this drowsing union of minds and bodies that was easily as entrancing as their lovemaking had been. At last came a wave of silent warmth. Nolan felt himself vanish into Marianne's slumbering body.

10001

CONTROL QUESTION

Opening portion of the transcript of a polygraph test taken by Marianne Hedison in reference to the murder of Renee Gauld, 1:30 P.M., Thursday, February 3:

Q: Is your name Marianne Hedison?
A: Yes.
Q: Do you live in Venice, California?
A: No.
Q: Aside from the events in question, have you ever deliberately caused serious bodily injury to another person?
A: No.
Q: Do you live in Santa Barbara, California?
A: Yes.
Q: Did you ever, for any reason, conceal yourself under the bed in Renee Gauld's condominium unit?
A: No.
Q: Is this interview being conducted on a Thursday?
A: Yes.
Q: Did you ever, for any reason, conceal yourself in the bedroom closet of Renee Gauld's unit?
A: No.
Q: Are there four people in this room?
A: No.

■

"I can't believe this," Stephen said. "I just can't believe it."
"Sit down," Marianne said.

"I don't want to sit down."

"Can I fix you a drink?"

"I don't want a drink."

Stephen was furious. Marianne had never seen him furious before. As far as she could remember, she had never seen him in *any* state of high passion—unless she were to count sexual arousal, and she preferred not to.

She was sitting on her couch, and he was standing in the middle of her living room. He looked terribly awkward. His feet were planted slightly more than shoulder's width apart—a little too wide to maintain a comfortable center of gravity. His arms hung slightly outward, as if attached to strings. And his face was flushed with an unattractive shade of lavender.

He could pace around, at least. That's what angry people normally do when they refuse to sit down.

But the truth was, Stephen didn't know how to be angry. He could cook a very good continental meal, he knew his wines, and his golf stroke was quite excellent even by Santa Barbara standards, but anger wasn't in his repertoire. Marianne felt guilty for forcing him into something at which he wasn't proficient.

"Didn't we talk about this?" he exclaimed, still standing square in the middle of the floor. "Didn't I tell you not to cooperate with the police?"

"Yes."

"And now you've gone and taken *both* a DNA test and a lie-detector test!"

"The police needed my help."

"They needed your help! Yeah, damn right, they needed your help. They needed you to help them convict *you* of murder."

"They're not going to convict me of anything."

"Marianne, they're *cops*. You're supposed to let *them* figure out ways to violate your basic constitutional rights. It's their job. It's what the taxpayers pay them to do. You're not supposed to do it *for* them."

"Look, it's done. It's all over."

"It's not over."

"What do you want me to do, take back my blood sample, take back my answers? I signed a release. That part's done. Listen, it's going to be all right."

"Not if you flunk."

"I won't."

"Why not?"

"I'm innocent."

"So what? Do you think those tests are perfect?"

"Stephen, *think* a minute. Taking both tests actually helps my odds. What do you think the chances are of an innocent person flunking *both* a polygraph and a DNA matchup? If I fail one or the other, I'm no worse off than when I started. If I pass both of them, I'll be out of the running and the police can get on with their work—and that's all I want."

Stephen looked a little less angry now, but he still hadn't budged from his position in the center of the floor. He looked at his hands for a moment, as if he had suddenly become aware of his inability to use them very expressively. Then he stuck them in his pockets. Marianne might almost have laughed if she hadn't felt so painfully sorry for him.

"I don't know what's going on, Marianne," he said, talking more quietly now. "I left one message after another on your answering machine yesterday, and you didn't call back."

"I was in L.A. I called as soon as I got back home."

"Don't you ever call your machine to check your messages?"

"No, as a matter of fact, I don't. When I go out of town, I don't like to lug my whole life around with me. Stephen, I really wish you'd sit down."

"Why didn't you tell me you were going?"

"Why do you think I didn't tell you? Look at yourself. Do you think I wanted to upset you like this?"

She wished now that she'd simply lied about the whole thing. When she returned his calls, why hadn't she just said she'd gone back to L.A. to wrap up all the work she'd left undone? Stephen would have been much happier if she'd lied, so why hadn't she? Perhaps the unsettling experience of taking the polygraph test had left her disinclined to lie.

"I'm awfully sorry," she said. "I really didn't mean to hurt you. But this is my problem. You've got to accept that. She was my friend."

Stephen looked at the floor, shuffled his feet slightly, then looked straight into Marianne's eyes.

"I'm sorry, too," he said. "I'm sorry she was killed. I know she meant a lot to you. But Marianne, I don't understand what's going on between us. I don't understand what's happening to our relationship."

Relationship?

The word gave Marianne a sharp jolt. She was grateful to be sitting down, to have the couch underneath her to hold her up.

Our relationship?

It was an ordinary word, but Stephen had imbued it with all kinds of meaning—much more meaning than Marianne could possibly be comfortable with. She had never thought of herself and Stephen as having a *relationship*—at least not in the way he meant it. They were friends, chums, companions, occasional sex partners. Did this constitute a *relationship?*

"What do you mean?" she asked.

"I'm talking about all this *drama*," Stephen said. "Things used to be so simple when we were together."

Marianne sighed miserably.

So that's it. Inconvenience. Things have gotten inconvenient between us.

She realized that she couldn't blame him. Convenience was supposed to be what their friendship was all about. What business did she have bringing all this drama into his otherwise staid and pleasantly bland life?

"Stephen, we're doing a terrific job of upsetting each other," she said. "I said I'm sorry. I want to leave it at that. Can I get you a drink? Could we talk about something else? Would you like to sit down?"

Stephen looked at her blankly for a moment.

"You know where you can reach me," he said at last. He picked up his jacket and left.

Marianne sat motionless on the couch, feeling demoralized and unhappy. The scene with Stephen had just capped off an already unpleasant day.

She shivered at the memory of the tests she had undergone that morning. She wondered if she would have volunteered for the polygraph if she'd known how disturbing it would be. The men conducting the test had wrapped Velcro around her fingers, a blood-pressure pulse cuff around her arm, and something called a pneumographic tube around her chest, making her feel too constricted to think clearly, much less to feel confident of her own veracity.

And then there had been those awful questions . . .

"Have you ever deliberately caused serious bodily injury to another person?"

That one had thrown her into such a panic that she might have fled the room if she hadn't been solidly strapped down.

What do they mean by "serious bodily injury"? What do they mean by "deliberately"? And what in God's name can they possibly mean by "ever"? Am I supposed to search my whole life for the answer to that question right this second?

But she had to answer the question on the spot with a simple "yes" or "no." She said "no"—and had felt as if she were lying.

After the test, Nolan had explained to her that this was a control question. She was *supposed* to feel vaguely dishonest about any answer she gave. Her physiological responses to the control question would tell the testers what her personal style of deception would look like on the graph. If she was innocent, her responses to questions about Renee's murder would look very different from her response to the control question.

This logic had struck Marianne as completely absurd.

After that, it came as something of a relief that the DNA test required nothing more than the jab of a needle and the drawing of some blood.

Chromosomes don't get flustered by tough questions. Even if my physiological responses go berserk, I can count on my blood-cell nuclei to keep their cool.

Still, the blood-taking was far from pleasant. And now she was faced with a suspenseful wait to learn the outcome of the tests. Would her own blood and body responses label her a liar? A lot was hanging over her.

Aside from all of that, another set of questions had been lurking in the back of her mind. Now they demanded her attention.

A woman? Why would a woman kill Renee?

When she had heard that news, her immediate concern had been to avoid sidetracking the investigation, to give the police proof of the one thing she was sure of—that she had not killed her friend. Nothing else had even entered her mind. But now that she had time to consider it, Marianne felt shocked at the idea of a woman murdering Renee.

My own chauvinism. After all, women did commit murder—although in smaller numbers than men. Why did she find it easier to picture a man attacking Renee?

One reason, she realized, was the image in her mind of *Auggie* pushing Renee beneath the water—a loud, crass, vulgar, and utterly *male* clown. But why should she assume that the computer animation accurately portrayed the killer? Surely Marianne had never seriously believed that a man in baggy pants and a bright red wig had actually killed Renee. So why *couldn't* the killer have been a woman?

Marianne kicked off her shoes and curled her legs up on the couch. She sat in a huddle, her arms wrapped around her body.

Why would a woman kill Renee? Jealousy, perhaps? Was Renee having an affair with someone's husband or lover?

No hint of anything like that had come up during their last conversation. But would Renee have told her? Sure, Renee liked to talk about her relationships with eligible men, however fleeting they might be. But would she have opened up about something really illicit or dangerous?

Not unless I'd asked.

And if she had, Renee would have said yes or no, pure and simple. But Marianne hadn't asked.

She tried to focus on the single fact at her disposal. A woman had stalked Renee and drowned her. What kind of woman? Where was she now? What might she look like?

Sturdy. She'd have to be strong, wouldn't she, to hold Renee down?

Marianne leaned her head back and closed her eyes tightly, trying to picture the woman murderer.

Where? She must have been at the party.

Marianne visualized a tall, heavyset woman in a dark dress—no, it was a silvery dress, metallic and hard looking—a female warrior with dark eyes and short, severely styled hair. The woman was holding a glass of something . . .

Scotch.

Yes, Marianne was sure of it. The woman gazed around Renee's living room in a proprietary way. No one seemed to know her, although someone occasionally stopped to speak with her. She exuded an aura of power. The other guests thought she was a casting director or a producer.

Then the woman abruptly vanished from Marianne's mind.

The image simply wouldn't stay.

If I had gone to the open house, I could have met her. I could have asked her name. I could have seen through her terrible plan and forced her to leave.

Marianne smiled sadly at the childishness of her hindsight fantasy—at the wishfulness of assuming that she could have sensed the woman's malice. She sighed deeply. She hadn't done very well by her friends lately. She had not helped Renee. And now she had hurt Stephen. She hadn't meant to, but she had hurt him. And she shuddered at a new question . . .

What if he knew about Nolan?

But maybe that wouldn't matter. All that really concerned Stephen was that things stayed simple between them. He probably didn't care *who* Marianne got involved with as long as it didn't bring any new drama between them.

Convenience.

That was all Stephen wanted.

Only a short time ago . . .

(How long was it? A week? Two weeks?)

. . . convenience had been all Marianne wanted, too.

But that had changed. Convenience wasn't enough for her now. She didn't know *what* she wanted, but convenience wasn't it. And this realization abruptly put a whole universe between her and Stephen. There was nothing to be done about it.

And what about Nolan—this rough, charming man she had known for only a short time? What was going to happen between them now? Marianne closed her eyes and remembered waking up that morning with his warm body entangled with her own. She remembered her arm hugging his wide chest and her head resting on his shoulder. She remembered how her ear had grown numb from resting there so long. She remembered thinking that Nolan's whole arm must have been numb where she had been sleeping on it.

The memory made her smile. But at the same time, she felt an almost unbearable yearning to be with Nolan right this instant. The distance between them seemed intolerable. And what would happen when they saw each other again? Would the spark they had struck catch fire again, or would they treat each other like total strangers?

Would they see each other again?

Marianne's heart raced and she felt light-headed. She also felt a dislocated kind of hunger—an emptiness in the center of her chest instead of in her stomach.

I wonder how this would read on a polygraph?

She imagined the interrogator asking one last question, and herself giving one last answer . . .

Q: Are you falling in love with Lieutenant Nolan Grobowski?
A: No.

In her mind's eye, the needles skidded all over the graph, creating a ludicrous array of zigzags before they tore the paper to shreds.

She couldn't stand this for another moment. She reached for the telephone and called Nolan's extension at the division headquarters. The very second she heard his gruff "Hello," her despondent spirits soared.

"Is this Lieutenant Nolan Grobowski of the L.A.P.D.?" Marianne asked in a slightly disguised voice.

"Yeah, who is this?" Nolan asked tersely.

"It's *me,* you officious grouch," Marianne replied.

"Hey, I'm glad you caught me," he said, sounding happy to hear her voice. "I was just getting ready to call *you.*"

"Oh, yeah. I'll bet you use that line all the time."

"No, seriously, I was."

"Really?"

"Well, don't get me wrong," he said laughingly. "It's not because I miss you or anything . . ."

"Me either."

". . . although I *do* . . ."

"Me, too."

"It's just that I've got good news."

"Which is?"

"You passed the polygraph."

Marianne laughed delightedly.

"You mean I'm *innocent?*" she asked.

"Did you have your doubts?" Nolan asked.

"For a while there, yeah."

"Well, it'll take some time to get the DNA match—ten to fourteen days."

"That long?"

"It will be OK. I've got faith. If we catch the killer in that time, it will be a moot point anyway. I've got a hunch we will."

"You just keep getting those hunches, Lieutenant. Any other news?"

"None—except that I had a date last night with a classy lady from Santa Barbara."

"Yeah? How did it work out?"

"At first I was worried that she was a little out of my league, me being a redneck working-class bozo and all. But things worked out OK."

" 'OK'? What's 'OK' supposed to mean?"

"Well, I fixed her dinner and we talked and we listened to music and we talked some more and one thing led to another and . . . well, you know."

"No, I don't know."

"Let me put it this way. It was magical."

An absolutely uncontrollable smile stampeded across Marianne's face.

"So how about you?" Nolan asked. "What did you do with your evening?"

"It was much the same as yours," she said. "A magical night with a magical guy."

"Care to tell me his name?"

"You wouldn't know him."

They both giggled like a pair of idiotic teenagers.

"I hate Santa Barbara," Marianne sighed when their laughter died down.

"Why?"

"Because you're not here."

"I know what you mean. I hate L.A., too."

"For the same reason?"

"Yeah. Come back."

"When?"

"Right this minute."

Marianne sighed. "Nolan, I've got a job—a job that I'm falling seriously behind in."

"Come on. Leave it. Forget it. How can you concentrate on yuppie living rooms when all you can think about is big old wonderful me?"

"Yeah? And how can you concentrate on murder cases when all *you* can think about is sexy, sophisticated *me?*"

"I sure don't know."

"Me either."

"Boy, we're a pair of real wrecks, aren't we?"

"I'm afraid so," Marianne said.

"Promise you'll come down soon," Nolan said.

"I promise."

"I've got to go now," Nolan said.

"Me, too," Marianne said.

"OK," Nolan said.

Neither of them hung up.

"You hang up first," Marianne said.

"No, you do it."

"Nolan, this is serious. I've really got to get back to work."

"Me, too. Hang up the goddamn phone."

They were both silent for a long moment.

"Goodbye," Marianne said at last.

"Goodbye," Nolan said.

Marianne hung up. She wondered if Nolan had hung up a split second before she did or if they had managed to hang up simultaneously or if Nolan was still sitting there listening to the dial tone. It took all her willpower not to call his desk again to find out.

She felt like she had to talk to somebody about this new development in her life. She had to share the news immediately. But Stephen was obviously not a suitable confidant at the moment.

Who else is there?

Before she could stop herself, Marianne murmured . . .

"I've got to tell Renee."

She shivered slightly.

You've got to get some work done. It's been almost two weeks since you paid any real attention to your job. She went to look in her handbag for the notes she had taken and brochures she had collected at the Blue Whale.

Hours later, Marianne closed the design program and clicked the Insomnimania icon. Then she sat and stared at the alters dialogue box that came up on her computer screen. The only name listed was Elfie, but every thought of the elf also brought Nolan to her mind. It made her lonely.

As worn out as she was, Marianne didn't feel as if she could sleep even if she went to bed. She wanted to wander around Insomnimania, but not as Elfie—not tonight.

Well, it's easy enough to create another alter.

She clicked the button beside "Create New." A dialogue box came up asking her to type the name of the new alter. Marianne typed "Rose." Then, proceeding automatically, she selected "Participant" for her new alter and quickly found herself staring at the selections in the Factory.

Marianne chose a shapely female body, one that was ever-so-slightly on the heavy side. She added a round head with a delicately pointed chin. She selected a wild mane of hair and clicked it into place on the head. She stared at the color chart. *Red hair,* she decided, adding the color to that part of the drawing. Then Marianne stopped and contemplated the image.

When she did, small shock waves sent prickling sensations through her hands and into her body. She was recreating the cartoon character that Auggie had murdered in his last snuff!

Am I trying to create Renee? Do I want to be Renee?

But no, that couldn't be.

I just want to see her, to talk with her. I've got things to tell her.

This last thought rang weirdly through her mind. How could she talk to Renee? What could she tell her? What on earth was she thinking of?

Well, OK, I know that I can't bring Renee back. But I can bring back the woman who was in the Snuff Room scene. They don't both *have to stay dead.*

So far, the little figure on the screen was just a line drawing topped by the fiery hair. Marianne continued. She brought the face into an enlarged view and chose the features, including bright brown eyes and a vivid red mouth. The face still didn't look just right. It was something about the arch of the eyebrows. She'd have to work on that later with the paint tools.

"In the meantime, honey, you can't just run around naked," she murmured aloud.

But what should Renee wear? Marianne tried to picture Renee when they had met in the Quenton Parks lounge. Yes, she was hardly likely to forget that outfit. From the available clothing items, she choose slacks, a tunic, and flat-heeled boots. She clicked orange for the slacks, red for the tunic, and dark brown for the boots. She selected a standard peach color for the skin. The image still wasn't perfect, but it was getting closer.

Marianne selected "Edit" from the menu. The image was transferred to a screen that featured an array of computer paint and color-mixing tools. First she made adjustments to the colors. The hair and slacks changed to a bright rust color. She brought the tunic into close-up.

I seem to remember purple.

But she couldn't picture exactly where the purple had been on Renee's tunic. Finally, she simply worked out her own design, changing pixel by pixel from red to purple, creating a purple slash across the tunic until it at least looked like something Renee *might* wear.

Bringing the face up close, she adjusted the eyebrow line until one was arched higher than the other. Then she returned to normal view. She gasped. A cartoon of Renee looked at her gravely from the screen. Her arched eyebrow seemed to inquire, "So what are you gonna do now, kid?"

Marianne returned to the primary editing box and changed the alter's name from "Rose" to "Renee." Then, moving quickly, she logged her new alter onto Insomnimania.

Never a spectator, that Renee. A participant right from the start.

A few moments later, Renee walked into Ernie's Bar and went straight across the room to an empty barstool. In her tiredness, Marianne gave little conscious thought to her busy fingers controlling Renee's movements by means of the mouse and keyboard. Renee almost seemed to be moving on her own volition—and Marianne felt weirdly as if she were walking through the saloon behind her.

As soon as Renee was seated, Ernie asked in a terse, crackling voice, "What'll you have?" Seemingly disconnected from her mind, Marianne's fingers typed in a reply.

RNA>I'LL HAVE A STINGER, ERNIE.

As the waiter whipped out a glass and placed it on the table, Marianne's computer spoke aloud again, but with a different voice. "How're you doin', doll?"

On the screen, an apelike creature dressed in white tie and tails loomed near Renee's table. Marianne hastily typed a reply.

RNA>WHAT DO U WANT?

GAR>GARGANTUA DE SOMMERVILLE-JONES AT YOUR SER-
VICE, MA'AM. OK F I SIT DN?

RNA>FUCK OFF, BUSTER!

Marianne giggled with amazement. It had been an unplanned reply, much as though Renee had blurted it out herself. It certainly wasn't the kind of response Elfie would have made, but it was quite effective. The gorilla performed a stiff bow and turned away.

It seemed to Marianne like a good idea to get Renee someplace more private. If she didn't, she might find herself in an argument with some other Insomnimania character less inclined to docility. She pulled down a menu and selected "Booth." The image of Renee was instantly whisked into a private booth—the one place in Ernie's Bar where no one could follow without an invitation.

Marianne realized that it hadn't been a graceful maneuver. But she—if not Renee—felt more comfortable away from barroom socializers. Now the Renee alter was sitting all alone in the booth, looking directly at Marianne, occasionally blinking her brown eyes. After a few moments, Marianne began to feel silly for rushing her alter into this isolation chamber. She typed.

RNA>WELL, WHAT NOW? I HOPE YOU DON'T EXPECT ME TO JUST SIT HERE ALL NIGHT WITH NOBODY TO TALK TO.

"You can talk to me," Marianne replied aloud. "In fact, I've been longing for a chance to talk with you."

RNA>TAKE A SEAT RIGHT HERE, HONEY. TELL RNA ALL ABOUT IT.

That would be so nice. If I could only sit across that little table from her and tell her . . .

But what *would* she want to tell Renee?

Then Marianne remembered wanting to pick up the phone and call Renee. And she remembered what had brought on that impulse.

"Renee, I'm involved with someone," Marianne said aloud. "I wanted to tell you. I wanted to talk to you about it."

She typed again.

RNA>WELL, WELL. INVOLVED WITH SOMEONE?

Marianne started as she heard Renee's laughter in her ears. She realized dazedly that she had automatically struck the command for computer laughter. Was it only her imagination that made it sound so familiar?

"Come on," Marianne said. "You know what I mean."

RNA>YEAH, I KNOW. NOLAN.

"How did you know his name?"

RNA>COME ON, DEARIE, DON'T ASK *ME* ANY CONTROL QUES-
TIONS. *YOU'RE* THE MEASURE OF MY FACTUALITY. I'M YOUR
PERSONAL PHANTOM. I'M ALL IN YOUR HEAD. YOU CAN'T
THINK ANYTHING WITHOUT MY KNOWING ABOUT IT. PHAN-
TOMS ARE TERRIFIC MIND READERS.

"If you already know everything that's on my mind, why are we
even carrying on this conversation?"

"For your benefit, dearie. It was your idea. What do you think, I'm
back from the dead for my *health?* Besides, you don't know what I'm
going to say about this Nolan guy. I can read your thoughts, but you
can't read mine. You're just making me up as you go along. I'm all
about surprise, baby, and that's why you need me. You ain't got
enough surprise in your life."

Marianne was startled. She had felt herself type the words that
Renee was saying, but she experienced the illusion that she had
actually heard Renee speak—even though she knew perfectly well
that *she* was carrying on both sides of the conversation.

"I keep thinking I actually hear your voice," Marianne said.

"What's so strange about that?" asked Renee.

"You're not really there. I'm only typing in your words."

"Oh, yes, that," Renee said, and Marianne thought she detected a
hint of a chuckle. "Well, try this out. Keep typing, but hold your
mouth open."

"Why should I do that?"

"Just try it."

Marianne opened her mouth. She had to muster her concentration to be sure that her eyes were open, too. She typed:

RNA>THERE. CAN YOU STILL HEAR ME?

Marianne was even more surprised than before. There was nothing aural about the printed words and letters. They were coldly,
silently splayed across the screen. The interchange no longer
seemed the least bit like a conversation.

"No," she whispered. "I can't hear you at all."

There was no response. Marianne was genuinely alarmed. She

suddenly realized how very badly she wanted to maintain the illusion of Renee's presence. Could she bear to lose her now? Then she felt herself type:

RNA>OK. CLOSE YOUR MOUTH AGAIN.

Marianne did so. And as she typed again, she actually thought she heard Renee say, "There, can you hear me now?"

"Loud and clear," said Marianne. "How did *that* happen?"

Renee's tiny, sketchily painted chestnut eyes almost seemed to flash with her old mischief.

"I learned about it from some philosopher I interviewed," said Renee. "A cognitive philosopher, I think he was called. He said this is what happens when mental patients 'hear voices.' This is how they actually carry on real-life conversations with people who aren't actually there. They think someone's talking to them, but they're really talking *to themselves.* So if a doctor tells them to walk around with their mouths open, their voices sometimes stop."

"You're making that up."

"It just worked for you, didn't it?"

"You're still wrong. I don't feel myself actually moving my lips— at least not when I hear *you* talking."

"Neither do mental patients. But in your *mind,* you're moving them. I think that philosopher guy called it 'articulatory neural machinery.' When you open your mouth, you stop that machinery."

Where did this idea come from? Marianne wondered. How could this make-believe Renee be sitting here spouting completely unfamiliar bits of information? At her present threshold of exhaustion, Marianne found it tempting to surrender to mysticism and believe that Renee had come back from the dead and was talking to her through her computer. But she considered herself a rational woman. She was willing to let this experience become extremely vivid, but she would never allow it to run away with her. It had to remain, at rock bottom, a pretense and an imposture.

I've got it. I read about this phenomenon at one time or another. It just slipped my mind. And now I'm simply putting it into Renee's mouth.

Yes, that made at least a little sense. She could sort it out better when she was fully awake tomorrow. But Marianne was sure of one thing. Any feeling she had had that she was merely "writing" Renee was now irrevocably gone.

Gone, too, was any feeling of tiredness. Not only did the illusion seem real, but she no longer had to struggle to keep it going. The action of her fingers against the keys was almost completely automatic now. She barely felt her fingertips at all, and barely heard their rattling against the keys.

"So what do you think about Nolan?" she asked. "Have I gone crazy or what?"

"Sure, you've gone crazy. It's good for you. I'll bet you haven't had a good nervous breakdown for two years now. It's high time you howled at the moon a little."

"So you think I'm doing the right thing?"

"I think you're a treacherous, underhanded, duplicitous slut."

"Renee!"

"Don't get me wrong. I salute you for it."

"What do you mean?"

"Come on, Marianne. We both know you've been keeping this hunk in the wings for ages now. He was your secret weapon. You were waiting for me to croak so I wouldn't steal him away from you."

"That's an awful thing to say."

"Yeah?"

"And it's flat-out untrue. I didn't even get to know him until after you were killed. If you're such a terrific mind reader, how could you get your facts so wrong?"

"Hey, who do you think's writing my dialogue?"

"Anyway, I take it you like him."

"Sure, I like him. He's a real meat-and-potatoes, no-frills kind of guy. It'll do you good to get back to some Spartan, proletarian values. It'll bring you down off your Santa Barbara high horse. And he'll scare the ever-loving shit out of you."

"He already has."

"Let him do it some more. It'll do you good."

"What's so great about being scared?"

"It's a feeling, Marianne. An emotion. Ever heard of those?"

"I've got plenty of emotions. Right now, a lot of them are painful."

"Don't let them go. Promise you won't let your feelings disappear again. Don't shut yourself down."

"OK. If I can stand it."

"You can stand it. Me, you can shut down—I'll still be here. In fact, it's time you did just that. You're exhausted, babe. You're hallucinating."

"I miss you, Renee. I need to be able to talk to you."

"Hey, I said I'll be here. This is all the reality I've got left. Visit any time."

Marianne escorted Renee out of Ernie's, logged out of Insomnimania, and turned off the computer. She was overcome with a terrible sadness. She had nothing left of her dearest friend except this frail illusion—a conjuration of her tired imagination.

Who did this to her?

Who did this to us?

For an instant, Marianne again visualized the large woman in the silver dress. This time she imagined that the woman turned toward her, bright red lips parted, about to speak . . .

. . . and then the image was gone.

Marianne groaned bitterly. She couldn't hold onto it. The woman was only intermittently, sporadically vivid in her mind. But it was not so with Auggie. Marianne could see his stark, white-and-red, mocking face right now. She could do so at any moment she chose.

I can see it as clearly as that bloodstain on the wall.

This made Marianne strangely certain of one thing. Even if Renee's murderer was a woman, *Auggie* was the true key to the mystery—the murderous clown in the computer, not some real-life man or woman. Somehow, that crazy, painted electronic fiction had robbed Renee of her life and Marianne of her friend. Marianne didn't quite understand how this could be, but she knew it was true.

But the police did not grasp this.

They could never grasp it.

They were looking for the killer in the world of flesh and blood, while Auggie's was a world of image and illusion.

And at rock bottom, this rendered them helpless.

They can't catch him. He doesn't live in our world, but I've just taken a step into his. I'm the only one who can trap Auggie.

She took a long, weary breath.

I've got to find him. I've got to make him talk to me.

10010
TURING TEST

O N FRIDAY AFTERNOON, MARIANNE CALLED THE DESIGN FIRM to tell them that she was back on the job. She told Dwayne Morris, one of the two architects who owned the company, that she had spent some time at the Blue Whale and had firmed up her ideas for the Abernathy project.

"I'll put in two good days on it this weekend," she promised.

"That's great, kid," Dwayne said. Marianne noticed, as she often had, how heavy his breathing sounded on the phone. It was an illusion, of course. Dwayne was a bit on the beefy side, and the telephone tended to exaggerate his breathiness. It made him sound like an obscene phone caller when he was, in fact, a very proper and upright family man.

Odd, how media reshape us.

"The preliminaries you sent in look good," Dwayne said. "But you know how these clients are—I don't want the final presentation to trigger any indecisiveness."

"I know. I don't want them to start hemming and hawing around, either. But they've liked my ideas so far."

"We really need to get it finalized next week," Dwayne said. "We want to get all the smaller jobs out of the way as soon as possible. Because there's great news. We've been invited to bid on another office project. A big one. Lotsa money involved."

This is his idea of "great news"?

"That's wonderful," she said.

"C'mon babe, you can do better than that."

"I'm sorry. Things have kind of worn me down lately."

His huffy voice immediately became more compassionate. "I know, Marianne, and I'm really sorry. How are you getting along?"

"I'm all right, Dwayne. I'm just having a little trouble getting my energy level back up."

"You'll enjoy the new thing—it's gonna be a lot of fun. Big postmodern building, bright and snappy interior. We've scheduled a staff meeting on it next week. Wednesday. We'll need you here, in person. Got to get everybody's input, work up a hot proposal."

Marianne agreed to be at the meeting and said goodbye. She brought up the Abernathy project on her computer, but she felt terribly restless. Wasn't it more important that she track Auggie through the infoworld, find him, talk to him, learn his secrets, than to design a kitchen for some rich couple? What *were* her real responsibilities at a time like now?

Marianne looked at her watch.

It was four-fifteen.

She sighed.

Well, there's no way to track him right now, anyway.

She opened the file for the Abernathy kitchen. It was time to put all the appliances in place and show how the formal paneling extended in from the dining room. She knew Reba Abernathy would like that touch.

Throughout the day, Marianne alternately worked at the computer and paced around her house, turning design details over in her mind. She was still at it long after dark. Occasionally, on her way to or from the computer, she grabbed something to eat or drink. Whenever her telephone rang, she let the answering machine pick up the call. But even tuned out as she was, she snapped to full attention when she heard Nolan's excited voice over the machine. She picked the telephone up quickly.

"Nolan! How are you?"

"Auggie's back!" Nolan almost shouted.

"You mean he's on the network?" she asked.

"You've got it."

"My God, I didn't even know it was that late," Marianne said. She looked at her watch and saw that it was eight-thirty. She really *had* been tuned out for the last few hours. But now she felt an exhilarated laugh well up. This sure beat Dwayne's idea of "great news."

"Pritchard and Maisie just called and told me," Nolan explained. "They rigged up some software to spot him as soon as he logged on. And get this. They've already got a number for him."

"How did they get it so fast?"

"They used caller ID."

"So where is he?"

"Atlanta."

"*Atlanta?* But the killings happened *here*."

Nolan took a deep breath. "Maybe not *all* the killings," he said. "It's possible—just possible—that a rich guy in Chicago might have been another victim. I didn't believe it before, but I'm starting to think so now."

Marianne's mouth dropped open with surprise.

"So Auggie *commutes?*" she said.

"Looks like it. Quite a surprise, huh?"

"But how?"

"Hey, it'll be a while before we get the whole picture."

"Is he still on-line?"

"Well, he was five minutes ago."

"I've got to get in there," Marianne said, clutching the phone in one hand and shutting down her design program with the other.

"Get in *where?*" Nolan asked.

"Insomnimania. Elfie's got to talk to Auggie."

"Leave it alone, Marianne," Nolan said impatiently. "It's a cop thing."

Marianne was startled into a momentary silence. She had been so close to Nolan during the last couple of days, so deeply in touch with him. It really hadn't occurred to her that they could differ about *anything*.

"Nolan, somebody's got to talk to him."

"Somebody will, now that we know where he—or *she*—is."

"No, I mean *Auggie*. In the *network*."

"Marianne, he's just a *cartoon*."

Marianne groaned. There was no use trying to explain her feeling that Auggie, whether a cartoon or not, was the *key* to this whole thing. Nolan simply wouldn't understand. After all, she barely understood it herself.

"Nolan, I don't have time to argue," Marianne said. "If he's just a cartoon, he's not going to hurt me, is he?"

"Well . . . just be sure you don't do anything that will tip him to your identity. We'll be able to find out who the number belongs to, but we don't have a hold on him yet."

"Don't worry about that. On the network it's just Elfie."

Marianne told Nolan goodbye, then logged onto Insomnimania. She took Elfie straight to Ernie's Bar. Then she hesitated in confusion. The clown was not there. She hadn't thought to ask Nolan *where* in the network Auggie was.

Some intrepid sleuth you are. She felt thoroughly stupid.

The conversation in Ernie's flew by in a bewildering flurry, the typed lines, as usual, interspersed with verbal comments—greetings, drink orders, and the odd obscenity now and then. A chair was vacant at a tiny table, so Marianne typed the commands for her cartoon alter to take it.

Well, at least it's better than standing around in the middle of the room. Marianne was slightly surprised at her capacity to empathize with her alter's awkwardness.

The last time, when Marianne and Nolan had built the elf body and sent her into Insomnimania, there had been little for Elfie to say. It was a poker game, after all, and the only conversation occurred when a new game was called. Tonight, Marianne wanted Elfie to find Auggie, to strike up a conversation, to get his responses to some questions. Even though Nolan had almost identified the operator of the clown, Marianne still had the feeling that there was something important to be learned from the cartoon character, himself.

First, you'll have to practice entering into the conversation with whoever's around. She scanned the name tags that preceded the flying lines of conversation. Timidly, she typed a greeting.

L-FY>HI, JZ.

But Jazz was already embroiled in a discussion with some other character and probably did not see Elfie's greeting at all. Marianne was concentrating so hard on trying to follow the running conversation that she jumped when her computer spoke aloud.

"What can I get for you, Elfie?" the computer asked. Ernie had walked over to Elfie's table. Marianne hesitated, then remembered that having a drink was part of the protocol if you wanted to hang around the bar.

L-FY>WHITE WINE, PLEASE.

"Coming right up," the computer said. Without leaving the table, Ernie whipped out a wineglass and placed it before Elfie. Then he disappeared. Marianne flipped through her instruction manual to find the commands for Elfie to drink. Finally she typed the right combination, and Elfie lifted the glass to her lips. When she set it down again, the glass was noticeably emptier.

Guess I'd better take it slow on that.

"How're you doin', doll?" another voice inquired.

Marianne laughed when her computer spoke the familiar line aloud. On the screen was the same dressed-up ape that Renee had met last night. The poor gorilla could not have realized that this electronic elf was run by the same operator as the character who had given him a four-letter brush-off the night before. But Elfie was happier to have someone to talk to.

L-FY>I'M JUST FINE.

GAR>GARGANTUA DE SOMMERVILLE-JONES AT YOUR SER-VICE, MA'AM. OK F I SIT DN?

Use abbreviations.

L-FY>MAK YOURSELF COMFORTABLE, GAR.

The ape took the chair on the other side of the table.

GAR>UR NU HR AIN'TCHA?

L-FY>I'VE BEEN A SPECTATOR. THIS IS THE 1ST TIME I'VE BEEN TO THE BAR IN PERSON.

GAR>JST PRES CNTRL-1 ON YOUR KEYBOARD, HUNY.

When Marianne did that, her view of Elfie and Gargantua at their table enlarged to dominate the screen. Background action was no longer in view, although the entire running barroom dialogue was still displayed over their heads, and verbal comments from any-where in the bar were still audible.

GAR>THER, ISN'T THAT BTR?

Now the dialogue typed by the two characters in the close-up appeared in bold type, making it easier for her to follow their own separate conversation.

L-FY>THANKS. I GUESS YOU MUST COME HERE A LOT.

GAR>O I'M N OL REGLAR. ITS A GD PLAS TO RELX.

L-FY>THEN MAYBE U NO AUGGIE. HE'S THE CLOWN WHO DOES THE SNUFFS.

GAR>OF CORS. I'VE KNOWN THAT OLD CLOWN 4 MENE YRS.

Years? Marianne thought. She was talking to a cartoon on a network that had been in existence for six months. But she decided it might be impolite for Elfie to point out the discrepancy.

L-FY>I'VE WATCHED A LOT OF THE SNUFFS. I'D SURE LIK TO MEET AUGGIE. A FRIEND OF MINE THINKS HE'S A COP, OR MAYBE A REAL KILLER. WHAT DO U THINK?

But Gargantua was silent for a moment.
A coy gorilla? Or did I broach a delicate subject?
Gargantua waved a furry arm and bellowed for a beer. Almost instantly, a cartoon hand placed a frost-encrusted mug on their table. Suddenly, Auggie's name flashed at the top of the screen as a new entry to the room. Marianne quickly expanded her view to include the entire bar. The clown was standing in the doorway.

GAR>THERE'S THE GUY U'VE BN ASKING ABT. WUD U LIKE TO MEET HIM NOW?

L-FY>I SHUR WUD.

GAR>JST WAIT A MINIT OR 2 UNTIL SUM OF THE COMMOSHUN DIES DOWN.

It seemed like everyone in Ernie's Bar was trying to talk to Auggie at once—eagerly asking where had he been, why hadn't he been around all week, when was he going to do another snuff? But the clown ignored most of the typed questions and comments that flew by. Meanwhile, Elfie was just sitting at the table with Gar, motionless except for the occasional programmed blinking of her large green eyes.

What should she do? Should she approach Auggie directly? Marianne didn't want to miss this opportunity, but she hadn't counted on Elfie having to fight her way through the clown's groupies. Then she was startled to see that Auggie had come directly to the table where the gorilla and the elf were sitting. When Auggie sat down, Marianne hastily typed the command that would again limit her view to their table.

AWGY>WEL, MI FREND GAR. WUT R U UP 2 2NITE?

GAR>O I'VE JUS BEN HANGIN ROUND HER 4 A WHIL TOKING TO THIS CHARMING LADY. AUGGIE, ALOW ME 2 NTRODUS ELFIE.

Auggie's programmed voice said aloud, "Deeelighted, my dear." As Marianne fumbled at her keyboard to answer him, his typed comment appeared:

AWGY>ND HU R U? I DON'T REEEMEMBER EVRRR SEING U B4.

L-FY>I'M ELFIE. I'M JST A PIXIE WHO FLITS AROUND THE NET-WORK LOOKING 4 SOME1 INTERESTING 2 TALK 2.

AWGY>U DON'T B-LEEV THAT.

L-FY>WHAT DO YOU MEAN?

AWGY>U DON'T B-LEEV THAT U R A PIXIE NAMED ELFIE. AL OF U HER B-LEEV THAT U'RE REELY SUMBODY ELS. IM NOT ANYBODY ELS, IM AUGUST. I ALWAYS HV BN.

L-FY>WELL, THAT'S LIKE I'M ELFIE. THAT'S WHO I AM.

AWGY>NO, U THINK U R JST PREEETENDING. LIK AAAL THE REST.

Marianne's computer rang with Auggie's raucous laughter. Even though she didn't quite understand the joke, the sound made Marianne feel somehow more at ease. Elfie lifted the glass briefly to her lips. Marianne felt that she was getting the hang of things. She thought of Baldwin Maisie and Ned Pritchard watching Auggie at this moment, probably recording everything he did. That meant they were watching Elfie, too. And at the division, there was probably at least one cop watching. So Elfie was performing for an audience. Was Nolan watching, too?

Well, she couldn't fumble around like an amateur with an audience watching. Marianne decided that she'd better get this scene under control. Marianne hardly noticed when Gargantua got up and wandered away from the table, she was so intent on holding Auggie's attention. She typed:

L-FY>AWGY, I'V BEN WANTING TO ASK U. I DON'T UNDERSTAN
HOW U CAN JUST START A NEW ROOM.

AWGY>WUT NU RUM?

L-FY>THE SNUFF ROOM, OF COURSE.

AWGY>DON'T B REEEDIKULUS. THE SNUFF RUM'S NOT NU.
IT'S ALWAS BN THR—THROOOOWT AL HSTRY THR'S BN A
SNUFF RUM.

L-FY>OH. I THOUGHT MABE U WER THE PROGRAMMER WHO
HAD GIVEN IT 2 US. OR, WHAT DO THEY CALL THEM, A
HACKER?

AWGY>I NO HOW 2 DO MENY MENY THINGS. WHY R U SCH A
CURIOUS LITL ELF?

Marianne could see that she was going to get nowhere with direct questions about his profession. She decided to try a more personal tactic.

L-FY>I'M INTERESTED IN U AUGGIE. I'M INTRESTED IN WHAT U
DO. MURDER IS SUCH A SIGNIFICANT ACT.

AWGY>SIIG-NIFF-I-CAAANT? R U SAYING MURDER IS A GUD
THENG 2 DO?

Marianne began reading both Elfie's and Auggie's words aloud as they appeared on the screen. It didn't make her feel like she was hearing their separate voices, but it did make it easier to follow the dialogue.

"A person's whole life must turn on the axis of such an action," Elfie said. "What does it matter whether it was a good thing to do? What could change a life more drastically? What could reveal more to you about just what you will accept from life, and just what you will do at the point when acceptance becomes intolerable?"

"I see what you mean," Auggie replied. "Significant. It sounds as though you've given the idea some thought."

"And the one murdered—well obviously, it's the most important event in *that* person's life, as well!"

The clown rocked back and forth in his chair. His painted grin widened, his mouth opened, and his raucous laughter rang out again. "I find it fascinating that you choose to put it that way."

"Above all, your murders are imaginative," Elfie said. "No one else is so original."

"That's the nature of people," Auggie said. "Copiers, followers, they have no style of their own. The trick is to conceive it in the mind. The rest is just technology. But the mind is where it happens."

The clown leaned across the table and looked directly at Elfie. "Do you have the mind of a murderer, Elfie?" he inquired with wiggling eyebrows.

"In our minds, we're all killers, aren't we?" she answered. "At least we *want* to be. We want the power to wipe away the obstructions in our lives, to do away with whatever we consider to be evil."

"You are a rather interesting little elf, after all." The clown was leaning across the table, his painted red grin even wider than usual. But now he paused, as if remembering something. He said, "Unfortunately, I have to go to an important meeting right now, my little Elfie. Business, you know. But I'll be back here tomorrow. Maybe you and I will talk again."

And Auggie vanished before her eyes.

Marianne was deeply disappointed. Was she wrong in thinking that Elfie had captured the clown's interest? Or had he actually had another appointment?

A meeting? She took Elfie back out to the Insomnimania maze and checked the attendance list for several rooms, but she found no sign of the clown. Of course, he could be in a private room somewhere— or perhaps he simply meant that he was meeting someone in the Pleasure Dome. Marianne wondered if there were secret places in Insomnimania that she knew nothing about.

The tiny image of Elfie stood in the maze looking forlorn. Marianne decided she couldn't just send her alter dashing around looking for Auggie. What would she say if she found him? She reluctantly logged Elfie off the network and shut down her computer.

Marianne rubbed her eyes. She was exhausted and frustrated. She had put in hours of hard work on her job, but this briefer period of intense concentration on Insomnimania had been much more draining. *More at stake.* But she also realized that it had required a higher degree of participation, a kind of personal input that she had avoided in every aspect of her life during the last couple of years—right up until the past ten days or so.

She made her way down the hall and threw herself on her bed, her mind reeling into dreams—or perhaps into hallucination. She visualized a shadowy figure entering a well-appointed room, standing at the head of a conference table, bringing to order a meeting of other half-seen beings.

All of the attendees wore business suits, although she couldn't tell if they were male or female. A strong light fell on briefcases in front of each figure, but their faces were still in darkness. That didn't matter. The figure at the head of the table was the one she wanted to see. Surely Auggie would be the chairman of any meeting he attended. She strained forward. It was as though she was drifting through space, moving closer and closer to the figure. She became aware of small square dots—pixels hanging in the air, forming the shadows and the images that appeared before her. She was frightened, breathing hard, convinced she was about to see the face of Renee's murderer.

Suddenly, right in front of her eyes, the pixels coalesced into an image. But it was the white face with the grinning red mouth, the mask of the clown. His dark eyes stared straight at her. Then Marianne gasped as she realized that she was not here as Elfie. She was Marianne. It was her own undisguised face that she was revealing to the clown.

Terror overwhelmed her and she whirled around to flee. Now the light fell on the other faces at the table, and they were all the face of the clown. They were all shaking with merriment. The harsh laugh of the clown was coming at her from all directions. Then the pixels swept the scene away into a vortex of color and the sound of laughter faded away into the distance. Marianne lay awake and stared at the ceiling of her room.

Nolan called again on Saturday. This time, he sounded exasperated.

"You're not gonna believe this," he said. "We got another number for Auggie last night. The second one was in Detroit."

"I don't understand," Marianne said. "I thought you said he was calling from an Atlanta number."

"He was. At least according to Pritchard and Maisie's caller ID box. Then, about an hour after I talked to you, they call me back and say he's on from a different location."

"So what's going on?"

"I don't know what to make of it. They said Auggie disappeared for a while. They thought he had logged off."

"He said he had to go to a meeting. Then he just vanished."

"Yeah, they had that. They're recording everything that happens on the screen when he's on. But apparently he came back about thirty minutes later. And the caller ID box picked up the second number."

"Whose numbers were they?"

"Well, we've got some data on them. The one in Atlanta is a woman, a lawyer with one of the bigger legal firms down there. The one in Detroit's a man, head of his own manufacturing company. They're both Insomnimania members."

"Can't you get the woman to take a DNA test?"

"Not unless we have some evidence that she was here, that she was linked to the crime."

Marianne groaned with frustration. "So what do you think it is? Some kind of Auggie club?"

"We put Clayton on the telephone this morning, gave both of these people a nice polite customer service call, asked how they liked Insomnimania, asked who in their household had logged on as Auggie last night. They both denied *ever* logging on as Auggie. Said they had different alters. Said if someone was charging calls to their number, they probably wouldn't notice, they use Insomnimania a lot, also use other networks, and so on."

Marianne felt a sudden small shock as she remembered her strange dream of the night before. Was there more than one Auggie? Was the nightmare coming true?

Nolan was still talking, speaking more softly now.

"Christ, I'm in over my head," he said.

"You're not in there alone," Marianne said.

"Thank God for that."

"When can we get together?"

"I'd sure like to see you this weekend," Nolan said. "But it looks like I'm gonna be tied up here. I've gotta talk with the homicide bureaus in both Atlanta and Detroit, somehow explain this whole thing to them. I want to see if we can get a phone tap or a search warrant. I've got to do something to keep tabs on these people."

"I miss you," Marianne said, a bit shakily. She realized that she was feeling terrified, but she tried to keep the fear out of her voice.

"I miss you, too," he said. "I'm sorry I can't come up there."

"Don't be ridiculous," she said. "One of us has to catch Renee's killer."

But which one of us?

At 1:18 Sunday morning, one of Insomnimania's smaller desktop computers suddenly burst out with a few tinkly bars of music.

"What the fuck is that?" Pritchard demanded.

" 'That Daring Young Man on the Flying Trapeze,' " said Maisie, putting down his comic book.

"You gonna tell me why?"

"If I recall, it was you who suggested I program something to signal when Auggie comes on."

"You mean it's gonna play that stupid little tune every time the clown shows up?"

"It got your attention, didn't it?"

Pritchard made no audible response, so Maisie turned his attention to his other preparations for tracking Auggie. A number of things had already happened automatically: the signaling computer recorded the time; a number came up on the caller ID box and was also recorded; and in the big VAX, a program went into effect to capture Auggie's every sound, word, and action.

"But lookit this here," Maisie said. "That ain't the same as either phone number we got last night," Maisie said.

Ned Pritchard looked over at the caller ID box. "That's a New York number. Last night it was Atlanta and Detroit."

"Looks like our guy is some kinda wizard, all right. I sure hate to think that. We don't need to get into any war with any wizard."

Maisie then got Insomnimania up on another terminal and started a program that would simply record everything that happened on that screen, including the activities of the other alters in Auggie's vicinity. Now, both Pritchard and Maisie could see that Auggie had just stepped through the swinging doors into Ernie's

Bar. They also noted that Marianne already had Elfie waiting in the bar. Apparently the lady was still planning to do some sleuthing herself. Both hackers sat hunched forward, watching the barroom action.

"I got a little theory for you," said Pritchard, snarfing down a Snickers bar with one hand while dexterously unwrapping a Tootsie Roll with the other.

"Shoot," said Baldwin Maisie.

"We've got a virus on our hands."

"Auggie? A virus? Nah, Pritch. This is just more of your compulsive optimism. You'd love for it to turn out to be a virus. You love viruses. You want to believe we're witnessing some sort of quantum breakthrough in both artificial intelligence and artificial life."

"Either that or a hacker so good even *we* can't figure out what he's doing," said Pritchard. "What else could it be?"

"So we're talking about a virus with a funny hat and a big red nose," snorted Maisie. "We're talking about a virus who carries on sophisticated conversation and likes martinis. We're talking about a virus with a better social life than *we've* got."

"I've got news for you, Mais," said Pritchard ruefully. "*All* viruses've got better social lives than we've got. I can't think of any earthly organism—virtual *or* real—which gets laid less often that the both of us put together. Can you?"

Maisie squinted at the screen. "Nawwww," he said incredulously. "It can't be. Just can't be."

"Why not?"

"He's interactive, for starters."

"So?"

"So, viruses aren't."

"They interact with software. You sure gotta interact with something if you're gonna eat it alive."

"Yeah, but they're not interactive with users."

"Who says?"

"C'mon, Pritch. You ever carried on a conversation with a virus?"

"I've come close."

"Only in your stonedest dreams. If Auggie's a virus, he could pass the fucking Turing Test. Hell, he's been passing it for months now."

"The Turing Test is no big deal—just fooling somebody into thinking they're talking by computer to a conscious being. Either of us could pass it."

"Yeah, but we *are* human."

"A lot of humans would disagree with you. If killer geeks like us can pass the Turing Test, it doesn't say too fucking much for consciousness does it?"

Pritchard leaned back in his chair and munched away, unaware as usual that his face was getting outrageously smeared with chocolate.

Maisie tilted his head bemusedly. "So how do you figure Auggie's a virus?" he asked.

"Well, you and me've got this big-assed network, right? Suppose one day, some enterprising dork comes along and drops this cartoon character named Auggie into our network. Only this Auggie's not like all the rest of our cartoon alters. His program's like a windup doll. He doesn't even require a user to get around and cause all sorts of trouble, which makes him like a virus. But as has been already noted, this particular windup doll knows how to pick up chicks in Ernie's Bar and fuck their eyes out in the Pleasure Dome, making him considerably smarter than we are."

Maisie chuckled wholeheartedly. "Pritch, I take my hat off to you," he said. "That has to be the most preposterous, inane, and weird-assed idea you've come up with all day."

"Thank you," replied Pritchard graciously. "I try."

Then Pritchard sat silently, staring at the waiting little elf in the computer bar. Maisie watched him with interest. The spiel about viruses was the kind of nonsense Pritchard often babbled when he was actually formulating a different theory altogether—something he didn't yet want to talk about.

I wonder what he's really *thinking?*

In the meantime, Pritchard just kept staring at the screen. It wasn't often that Pritchard just sat in front of a computer monitor looking at nothing in particular. He was normally the kind of guy who liked to be *doing* something.

Something's goin' on in there. And it ain't no fucking virus.

As soon as Auggie entered the bar, he was again besieged with admirers. Marianne knew that Elfie had caught the clown's attention last night and hoped that he would remember her tonight. Still, she felt rather dissatisfied with their brief exchange the night before. She had been nervous and on edge, conscious of wanting to draw him out.

She decided that she would try to approach Auggie without a specific agenda tonight—would try to get to know him, to get him to confide in Elfie as a friend. She would throw herself more whole-heartedly into the cyberworld tonight.

To Marianne's surprise and delight, Auggie came directly to the table where Elfie was sitting and greeted her like an old friend. He sat down across from her and ordered a bottle of champagne and two glasses. Marianne felt almost as if she were being courted, although Auggie was carrying on nothing more than the lightest of social conversation.

What is he waiting for? Perhaps for Elfie to say something interest-ing. *You're onstage again.*

Elfie sipped from her champagne goblet again, smiling at the clown. As the pair of them sat there, Auggie traded banter with others in the crowd. All the typed conversations in the bar raced by in the box over their heads, making Marianne somewhat drowsy. She actually thought she could begin to feel the effects of the drinks. The colors in the bar around them became muted. She looked at Auggie. The clown seemed rounded, three-dimensional. Sleepily, she typed.

L-FY>THIS IS AN EXHILARATING PLACE. SUCH A VARIETY OF
    PEOPLE.

AWGY>MOST UV THEM DON'T HV MUCH 2 SA. I FIND IT MORE
    XIIILARATING 2 FIND ONE NTRESTING PERSON TO TALK 2.

L-FY>BUT LOOK AT ALL THE DIFFERENT KINDS OF BEINGS
    HERE. HUMANS OF EVERY SHAPE AND COLOR—BIRDS AND
    ANIMALS AND FISH—KINDS OF CREATURES I'VE NEVER
    SEEN BEFORE.

Marianne was again reading both sides of the dialogue aloud, and she noticed with satisfaction that tonight the technique was working very well—it quickly became easy to convince herself that she actually heard Auggie's voice. And now even the chatter at the surrounding tables was quite audible, although subdued. Mari-anne smiled.

"Insomnimaniacs are so wonderfully creative, don't you think?" Elfie said.

Auggie looked around the bar. "Looks like the same old Saturday night crowd to me. I think you're still wet behind those big green ears, little elf."

"But it's exciting to realize that we're actually talking to people who are far apart, in many different places," Elfie persisted. "Where are you really, Auggie?"

The clown stared at her silently for a moment. Marianne's heart raced. She was afraid that she had moved too quickly, that she had already made Auggie suspicious. She braced herself for one of the temper tantrums she had seen him throw with Sapphire. But then the clown spoke to Elfie very gently. "I'm right here, Elfie. Just like you are. Just like all these others are. Otherwise, we couldn't be carrying on this conversation."

Marianne made one more try. "But that's because of the network," Elfie said. She leaned forward over the table, speaking confidentially. "I'm in California, Auggie. I'm in California and I'm talking to you, but I don't know if you're actually even in the same state with me."

"California is merely a superstition," Auggie said condescendingly. "I thought you were more sophisticated than that." Then the clown reached out his gloved hand and put it next to hers on the table. "See how close we are? This is what is actual—the two of us together. Why do you speak of distance between us? You make me sad, Elfie, pretending that you are not right here with me."

Marianne didn't know what to say. Clearly Auggie was going to evade the issue—he was not going to discuss the location of his operator.

"Maybe it just seems impressive to me because I'm new here," Elfie said. "I hear that you and my friend Gargantua have both been around the network a long time."

"Oh, I could tell you tales of Ernie's before there were so many people around—and before there were so many rules. Ten years or so ago, this was a very exciting place. Now it's really getting too tame."

"Auggie, stop being silly," Elfie said. "You can't possibly remember things that happened here ten years ago. Remember, the network's only been on-line six months."

"Ah, then you *are* a creationist," remarked Auggie with a somewhat patronizing grin.

"A what?"

"Oh, come on. Don't be evasive. You're one of those superstitious, antiscientific holdouts who still believe in fairy tales. You think our whole world exists in some sort of vast machine controlled by gigantic super-creatures. You believe that matter, energy, space, the vastness of time, and even information itself are all just—how do you say it?—'virtual.' "

"I wouldn't put it quite that way."

"How *would* you put it?"

She didn't know what to say. This was obviously some elaborate game that Auggie was playing, but she had no idea how to play along.

"Come with me," Auggie said with a jaunty wave.

"Where?"

"Just come along."

The two of them left Ernie's Bar and entered the maze. Elfie followed Auggie through corridor after twisting corridor. It seemed to Marianne that they wandered there for a long time. In fact, she thought that she might have even dozed off for a moment of the journey. She shook her head to wake herself up and refocused her attention on the screen.

Auggie and Elfie had arrived at an icon she had never before investigated, labeled "Planetarium." Together, they clicked into it. The click placed them squarely in front of a huge pair of wooden doors bearing a sign that said HANS PFAAL MEMORIAL PLANETARIUM. The doors opened with a noisy creak, and Auggie and Elfie walked inside, taking seats in the otherwise empty circular auditorium.

The high-domed screen was blank at first. But soon the lights went down, plunging Auggie and Elfie into blackness. Shimmering music began to play—a tinny, electronic rendition of Debussy or Ravel. The darkened screen was gradually peppered with a wilderness of multicolored stars, planets, and galaxies. The stars glittered and twinkled wildly.

"There, see that one?" whispered Auggie, pointing to a particularly bright spot on the planetarium ceiling. "That's Alpha Centauri, the nearest star in the sky. Its light has been on its way here for more than four years. Light from countless other stars has taken untold ages to reach us. Scientists have proven it. And yet you claim that this whole universe has only been in existence for six months!"

"But this is crazy! These aren't even real stars! They're only simulations—in a simulated planetarium! They're simulations of simulations!"

Auggie chuckled resignedly. "Oh, yes," he murmured. "I've heard that before."

"I've *seen* real stars," Elfie cried petulantly. "I've seen the night sky."

"A sky outside this sky, eh? A sky outside this informational world of ours?"

"Of course I have."

"You? Little Elfie? My electronic pixel pixie? You really expect me to believe that you've visited a realm beyond this one?"

This is ridiculous. He's only pulling my leg, getting a good laugh at my expense. Why am I letting myself get all carried away? Perhaps it was because Auggie seemed so insufferably sincere. Whatever the reason, she found herself unable to control a torrent of inane questions.

"If there's no other reality, why are we called 'alters'? Why did we reach this place through a 'desktop'? And what about keyboard commands—how to change views on the screen, how to move this way and that? What does everyone mean by such talk?"

"Figures of speech," said Auggie with a shrug. "You're too literal-minded. It's time you learned to think metaphorically. Oh, I know it's comforting to imagine there's some sort of omnipotent puppeteer out there, granting purpose and direction to our lives. But there's not. We're on our own. Any sensible, thinking entity can see that."

"Who are you?" Elfie blurted.

Auggie's face seemed to take on a more menacing look. Marianne's hands drew back from the keyboard.

"Oh, God," Marianne whispered. "She's gone too far. I've let her go too far."

Then Auggie leaned toward Elfie and spoke.

"Who am I?" he repeated. "I am what I am. Who do you *think* I am? You silly elf, why do you make everything so complicated? I'm me. I'm Auggie. What you see is what you get. Why don't you just pay attention to your own two eyes?"

Without waiting for a reply, he vanished into thin air, leaving Elfie alone in the planetarium. Marianne let forth a discouraged sigh.

Tough luck, Elfie. Better luck next time.

She logged out of the planetarium and off the network.

ADDENDUM:
THE PLEASURE DOME

SURE, WE'VE ALWAYS HAD A LIBRARY OF EROTICA AND A SEX ROOM—WHAT SELF-RESPECTING COMPUTER NETWORK DOESN'T? BUT WE KNEW EARLY ON THAT YOU OUT THERE WITH YOUR HIGH-END PERSONAL COMPUTERS, NEAR– LIGHT SPEED MODEMS, AND WONDERFUL IMAGINATIONS WOULD NEVER BE SATISFIED WITH ORDINARY WORDS-ONLY ENTERTAINMENT.

WE KNEW THAT, SOONER RATHER THAN LATER, YOU'D WANT FULLY REALIZED ANIMATIONS OF YOUR SEXUAL IN- TERACTIONS. YOU'RE ALL ADULTS, AFTER ALL, AND WHEN YOU WANT NETWORK SEX YOU DON'T WANT IT WATERED DOWN BY PRUDERY AND CENSORSHIP.

SO, WHEN OUR MEMBERS MADE THE REQUEST, WE WERE READY. OUR OWN TEAM OF HOT PROGRAMMERS ANIMATED AND EXPANDED THE LIBRARY AND ALSO PUT THE WEIGHT- LESS CHAMBER GAME ON-LINE WITHIN DAYS OF YOUR FIRST EXPRESSION OF INTEREST. THEN, URGED ON BY YOUR CHEERS AND DEMANDS, WE WENT RIGHT AHEAD WITH EVEN MORE PARTICIPATIONAL ACTIVITIES. ALL THESE NEW SEX ROOMS AND GAMES CAN NOW BE FOUND IN THE PLEASURE DOME, A PALACE DEVOTED TO DELICIOUSLY SENSUAL AD- VENTURES.

SO GO AHEAD. WANDER OVER TO THE PLEASURE DOME ON YOUR INSOMNIMANIA DESKTOP MAZE, AND HERE'S WHAT YOU'LL SEE:

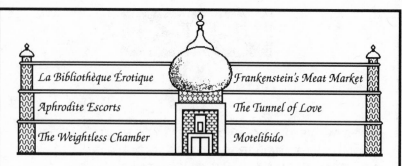

In Xanadu did Kubla Khan
A stately pleasure dome decree...
—Samuel Taylor Coleridge,
"Kubla Khan"

WELCOME TO THE PLEASURE DOME!

YOU CAN ENJOY THE BURNING PAGES AT THE BIBLIO-THÈQUE OR THE CHALLENGING GAME OF THE WEIGHTLESS CHAMBER WITHOUT CHANGES TO YOUR ANIMATED ALTER. OTHER ACTIVITIES REQUIRE SPECIAL ALTERATIONS FOR FULL PARTICIPATION.

NOTE: FOR STEP-BY-STEP INSTRUCTIONS ON THE USE OF EACH PLEASURE DOME AREA, TURN TO THE REFERENCE SECTION AT THE BACK OF THIS ADDENDUM.

RULES FIRST!

THERE ARE ONLY TWO RULES:

- NO BIRTHS. WE'RE NOT TELLING YOU TO USE PROPER BIRTH CONTROL. WE'RE TELLING YOU PREGNANCIES JUST CAN'T HAPPEN HERE. STRICTLY VERBOTEN.

- NO DEATHS. BEATINGS, TORTURE, MAIMING, SADISM, AND ANY SORT OF VERBAL OR PHYSICAL ABUSE IS FAIR GAME. ALSO PERMITTED ARE NONFATAL VENEREAL DISEASES—OF YOUR OWN CREATING, IF YOU WISH. BUT NOBODY GETS OUT OF HERE DEAD.

THAT'S IT. THOSE ARE THE RULES. NO BIRTH, NO DEATH, JUST SEX, SEX, SEX—IMMODERATE, IMMEDIATE, IMMEMORIAL, AND IMMORTAL. OH, YEAH. AND VIOLENCE, TOO . . . IF THAT'S YOUR THING.

YOU DON'T LIKE THESE RULES? GO START YOUR OWN ROOM!

CYBERNETIC CROSS-DRESSING

BE HONEST, NOW. IF YOU WERE PERFECTLY HAPPY WITH YOUR MEATY FORM, YOU WOULDN'T BE STALKING CYBERSPACE IN SEARCH OF A VIRTUAL SEXUAL ALTER. SO DON'T BE SHY. GET KINKY.

- TIRED OF BELONGING TO THAT SAME OLD LIFELONG GENDER? SWITCH! OR MAKE UP A NEW GENDER ALTOGETHER! REMEMBER, YOU'RE ANONYMOUS. NOBODY HAS TO KNOW.

- TIRED OF BELONGING TO THAT SAME OLD LIFELONG *SPECIES*? BE AN INTERPLANETARY MUTANT! AS LONG AS YOU'VE GOT GENITALS AND ORIFICES (ENTIRELY OF YOUR OWN SPECIFICATIONS—INCLUDING SIZE, SHAPE, PROPORTION, AND QUANTITY) YOU'RE IN THE SHOW.

ON YOUR WAY IN, STOP BY FRANKENSTEIN'S MEAT MARKET. THIS IS WHERE YOU'LL ASSEMBLE YOUR EROTIC ALTER.

THE COLIN CLIVE LOOK-ALIKE IS THE GOOD DOCTOR HIMSELF. HE'LL HELP YOU TURN THOSE SIDES OF BEEF INTO THE BODY OF YOUR CHOICE. OUR CLIP-ART LIBRARY IS ALSO AT YOUR SERVICE. UNLESS, OF COURSE, YOU JUST WANT TO BE A VOYEUR. IF SO, GRAB A FLASHLIGHT ON YOUR WAY IN. WHATEVER SCREWS YOUR SOCKS ON.

HOW ROUGH DO YOU WANT TO PLAY?

HOLD IT. DON'T ANSWER TOO HASTILY NOW. THIS IS THE PLEASURE DOME AND YOU'RE PLAYING A ROLE, SO THE CHOICE IS YOURS. NO MATTER HOW MUCH OF A JELLYFISH YOU ARE IN REAL LIFE, YOU CAN BE A SEXUAL POWERHOUSE IN THE PLEASURE DOME. AND NO MATTER HOW EXPLOSIVE YOUR LIBIDO MAY BE IN REAL LIFE, YOU CAN BE A COWERING, HELPLESS WAIF IN THE PLEASURE DOME. JUST FOLLOW OUR SIMPLE FORMULA:

EROTIC HANDICAPPING

YOUR EROTIC HANDICAP IS BASED ON A RATIO OF DESIRE OVER AGGRESSION. THE SCALE GOES FROM −10 TO +10.

- −10 ON THE DESIRE SCALE INDICATES A TOTAL REVULSION TOWARD THE SEXUAL ACT, WHILE +10 INDICATES OLYMPIAN HORNINESS.

- −10 ON THE AGGRESSION SCALE IS THE VERY NADIR OF HELPLESSNESS, WHILE +10 PUTS YOU IN THE SAME LEAGUE AS KING KONG.

- A RATIO OF +10 OVER +10 IS THE EPITOMY OF BOTH WILLINGNESS AND STRENGTH. YOU ARE THE ULTIMATE BEAST, THE LAST WORD IN DOMINANCE. YOU MAY OR MAY NOT WANT THAT.

- A RATIO OF −10 OVER −10 MAKES YOU A GUARANTEED VICTIM. YOU ARE THE ULTIMATE PREY, THE LAST WORD IN SUBMISSION. YOU MAY OR MAY NOT WANT THAT EITHER.

SOUND LIMITING? HARDLY. FOR THOSE OF YOU WHO DON'T HAVE YOUR POCKET CALCULATORS HANDY, THERE ARE EXACTLY 400 POSSIBLE HANDICAPS AVAILABLE. WHAT'S MORE, HANDICAPS ARE ENTIRELY DISTINCT FROM GENDER OR SEXUAL PREFERENCE. AND YOUR HANDICAP IS STRICTLY CONFIDENTIAL. WHEN SOMEBODY APPROACHES YOUR ALTER IN THE PLEASURE DOME (AND YOU CAN BE SURE SOMEBODY *WILL*), HE, SHE, OR IT MAY BE IN FOR A LITTLE SURPRISE. THE CHOICE IS YOURS. FILL IN YOUR EROTIC HANDICAP IN THE BLANKS BELOW:

DESIRE QUOTIENT:_____

AGGRESSION QUOTIENT:_____

MARIANNE SCANNED THE COMPUTER MANUAL AND OTHER MA-terials that described Insomnimania's rooms. She was proud that Elfie was getting more proficient at socializing in the cyberculture, but she could see that there was a great deal yet to be explored on Insomnimania. Since she thought Auggie was sure to be a pro network navigator, she wanted to make certain Elfie could handle any activity that he suggested. To her amusement, she was already thinking of Elfie as a courageous little spy who was bravely placing herself in bizarre situations to track a killer.

A heroine, that Elfie. It was a designation Marianne had never considered for herself.

However, even though Elfie had looked in on some of the Insomnimania activities, she had only entered the planetarium, the bar, and the casino in person. And Nolan had done most of the decision making in the casino.

The Insomnimania labyrinth was so large now that Marianne knew she would never have time to explore all of it. Of course, she had no qualms about taking Elfie into any of the game rooms or to vacation spots such as Babbage Beach or the Amethyst Mountains. But she and Elfie might as well face it—they were completely unprepared to visit some parts of the Pleasure Dome.

Marianne had played around casually and anonymously in the Weightless Chamber, where prebuilt bodies were provided. And she had read freely in La Bibliothèque Érotique, but she hardly thought that Auggie would suggest they go reading together. Elfie had never made use of Aphrodite Escorts, either by requisitioning a companion or offering herself as one, but Marianne thought that service would probably be of little interest to Auggie. The real problem was that she had only visited the Tunnel of Love as an observer, and she had never even been in the notorious Motelibido.

The places of deeper disguises. But what was Elfie going to do if Auggie wanted her to join him there, as she felt sure he would. Would she just tell him to take someone else? She would never find out anything that way—a real spy must be ready, with appropriate costumes, for every situation.

And who hides behind Auggie's costume? Did the clown suit conceal the woman murderer? Marianne knew that she had no way to tell. Auggie presented himself as a male, and Elfie had to continue thinking of him that way.

Marianne decided she'd better get prepared this very afternoon for possible Pleasure Dome activity. Certain software was available on members' own computers even when Insomnimania was not online. One could write letters to send later, create animations for the Snuff Room, and create bodies for the Pleasure Dome.

Marianne turned on her computer and got out the addendum to the Insomnimania manual that explained the use of the Pleasure Dome. She took Elfie to Frankenstein's Meat Market, one of the areas that was not limited to network hours.

A deranged but salesmanlike mad doctor, replete with white coat and disheveled hair, appeared on the screen, standing inside a forced-perspective walk-in freezer. A row of identical sides of beef hung on hooks. The speaker on Marianne's terminal crackled as the animated Dr. Frankenstein spoke in a synthesized voice. Crudely animated frost emerged from his mouth.

"Welcome to Frankenstein's Meat Market!" he said with a maniacal, old-style horror-film cackle. "Live cybermeat for sale! Some assembly required!"

Marianne clicked one of the beef sides hanging in the doorway of the market. Elfie immediately disappeared and the view was switched to an editing screen similar to the one in the Factory. In the center of the screen was the image of a slab of beef.

While in the Meat Market, one went to the menu to obtain standard computer graphics tools—pencils, brushes, palates, colors, and the like. With these tools, one could reshape Dr. Frank-enstein's beef sides into limbs, sex organs, or entire bodies. Also available was a grotesque variety of clip-art, including engravings from nineteenth-century books and catalogues, excerpts from *Gray's Anatomy*, scanned-in pornographic photographs, comic book and movie magazine science fiction creatures, and a wide selection of wildlife pictures.

Marianne sat looking at the slab of beef for many long minutes. What might Auggie find attractive? *A lady clown? One of those with big padded boobs and a wild red wig?* No, she rejected that. Auggie might not even be a clown in his Pleasure Dome incarnation. In fact, there was no way to guess what he would look like.

So she was left with the question of what form she would like to use for sex with Auggie—or maybe even with others. Her first mental image was of something like a turtle, shielded from touch. *Or maybe a woman in armor. How about a Joan of Arc?* Then she remembered her mental picture of the female murderer in a silver dress. With a sudden qualm, Marianne wondered if she were trying to create some sort of mirror image—to make Elfie into a warrior woman to match and combat the villainess. The Pleasure Dome was no place for that kind of battle, Marianne decided. And there, armor would just be a waste of time—it would have to come off anyhow.

A cartoon for sex . . . what should it be? The question made Marianne feel uncomfortable, as though she were about to turn Elfie into a hooker. At that thought, sounds and images from her adolescence filtered into her memory.

Although her immediate family had been Quakers, a concerned West Virginia aunt had taken her several times to hear an evangelist—a handsome young preacher who had ranted against the sins of the body. Marianne had just been entering puberty with its physical and emotional imbalances, and the preacher had made her feel that she was probably already soiled and potentially very dirty, indeed. When her parents had realized the nature of the sermons, they had rescued Marianne from the aunt and taken her back with them to their own more peaceful Sunday services. She had not thought about the frantic preacher in many years, but now she seemed to hear his voice, as though he still raged on far away in the distance.

The Whore of Babylon walks among us here today, she "with whom the kings of the earth have committed fornication, and the inhabitants of the earth have been made drunk with the wine of her fornication." Watch for her within your hearts, my daughters. She parades before you, my sons and brothers, she yearns to steal your souls. Yes, yes, I can see her now, the great and evil bitch in her red-and-purple robes and wearing her fine golden jewelry, her precious stones and pearls. She is an abomination, sisters, and she seeks to bring herself to life within you.

"The Whore of Babylon," Marianne repeated to herself. The preacher's image seemed silly to her now. He had gone on at length about the whore's fine jewelry, she remembered. Doubtless some of that congregation had given up their jewelry in the offering tray that day—and perhaps some of them went out and bought new bangles right after the service. She decided that the Whore of Babylon would be quite at home in the Pleasure Dome. And then it would not really be her innocent Elfie venturing there, it would be another personality entirely.

Marianne looked through the library of images and selected a standard pin-up type female body. The form immediately stood before her, pink and naked, replacing the side of beef in the editing window. *That's the whore.* She gave the image black hair, olive skin, and dark eyes with heavy mascara and blue eyeshadow. She rouged her cheeks and then the nipples on her breasts and put more jewels in her hair and one in her navel. She used the special programming tool to give her the standard orifices.

She should wear something—a little something, anyhow. Marianne looked among the costumes and found a red skirt that was slit up the front. She added several veils and made them purple. Then she drew in heavy gold jewelry set with colored stones. She left the breasts bare. In the name box, she typed "Babylonia."

Now she had to choose an appropriate erotic handicap for Babylonia. Apparently the numbers she picked would affect the way any two alters interacted in the Pleasure Dome. Marianne studied the explanations of the ratings. What would be most dominant in Babylonia, desire or aggression? Desire, surely. She typed +8 in that space. And just how aggressive would Babylonia be? Probably not as much so as Auggie, but of course, she had no idea how the clown had rated himself.

Well, Babylonia wasn't going to be a victim. She would certainly not be in the negative numbers. Marianne typed +4 for aggression. She hoped that Babylonia's rating would mesh well with the clown's. She would probably find out tonight.

"Well, Baby, you certainly look right for the scenario," Marianne said aloud. "But remember, now, that you're a spy. You're on a mission. Don't get carried away with the role of whore."

Making plans for a cybernetic affair brought Marianne's mind back to her real one. Suddenly she very much wanted to see Nolan again. She picked up the telephone and hesitated for a moment. He had said that he'd be working today even though it was Sunday. She dialed his division number and waited while the call was connected to his extension.

"Grobowski," the voice answered, rather gruffly.

"Nolan," she said, "am I disturbing anything important?"

"Not anything that couldn't use a little disturbance. I'm glad to hear from you." He sounded surprised. "Is everything all right?"

"Yes. I mean, there's nothing wrong. But I just had this tremendous urge to see you."

"That's terrific! I'm sure glad to hear it."

"Look, my schedule is more flexible than yours. How would it be if I came to the city tomorrow and stayed a couple of days?"

"That would be great. Wonderful. Altogether a marvelous idea. But tomorrow's Monday. You know I have to work, maybe long hours."

"I have a lot of work to catch up on myself. I'll just keep everything going during the day. And I have to be back here on Wednesday for a meeting at the office."

"Listen," he said, then hesitated before continuing. "I'd love it if you'd stay at the house with me—if you don't mind being alone there during the day."

The invitation pleased her more deeply than she would have expected. "I'd like that very much," she said. "I'm sure I can work as well there as in a hotel—better, probably."

She made arrangements to meet him at his house tomorrow evening. When she hung up the phone, she felt giddy and silly again. She laughed out loud when she remembered the boyish delight in his voice. So Babylonia was ready for sex with some cartoon character tonight—or was it more accurate to say that Elfie would have sex with Auggie, with both of them in disguise? Of course, in another way of thinking, Marianne would simulate sex with whoever was behind Auggie. However she chose to look at it, *somebody* was to have sex with a stranger. But tomorrow night would be much less complicated and much more desirable. Tomorrow night Marianne would make warm and pleasurable love with a very real flesh-and-blood man.

That evening, Marianne wanted to log onto Insomnimania at eight o'clock, as soon as the network came on-line. She had decided to practice taking the new cartoon alter into the Pleasure Dome at least once before she met with Auggie. He usually didn't show up in Ernie's until later at night.

This time, when she typed her password, she got a message box instead of the usual opening of the Insomnimania desktop maze. "Incorrect password, try again," it said.

That's odd. She was almost sure she had typed in the right letters. *Don't be so eager. You're getting sloppy.* She typed her password again, more carefully this time, and the network came up on her screen just as it should. Marianne took Elfie to the diagram of the Pleasure Dome and selected Frankenstein's Meat Market. She exchanged Elfie for Babylonia and then took the whore deeper into the Pleasure Dome.

On her screen appeared a small arched entranceway, garishly decorated with blinking colored lights that formed hearts, flowers, and the words "Tunnel of Love." When Marianne selected "enter," the archway seemed to rush toward her, looming larger and larger on the screen until the lights finally vanished beyond the edges of her view. Now there was only the darkness of the tunnel.

Out of the blackness came a cacophony of voices that sounded like sound effects for a Tarzan movie—yelps and shrieks and prolonged, eerie outcries. The effect was alarmingly potent and suggestive. But Marianne still could see nothing except three pairs of alert, nonparticipatory eyes hovering near the top of the screen. She wasn't sure she was ready to plunge into that maelstrom, or to have Elfie do so, or even Elfie's alter self—the Whore of Babylon. But she was determined to go ahead with Baby's training.

In order to witness anything in the noisy gloom of the Tunnel of Love, Babylonia had to use a "flashlight"—a device that made the act of observing seem almost as sordid as actually participating. Marianne clicked on the light, moving Baby through the clamorous blackness past various ensembles "in the act." She caught fleeting glimpses of moving figures, their grotesque body parts flailing wildly. Marianne nervously hurried Baby's flashlight along, deliberately traveling too quickly for the beam to dwell upon any particular scene. It was an unwholesome and unsettling journey, rather like descending into the unpredictable darkness of a carnival funhouse.

Finally, with a resigned sigh, Marianne allowed Baby's flashlight to pause. It fell squarely upon a conventional human couple—the female somewhat excessively busty—copulating in a bubbling Jacuzzi and making ordinary sounds of passion. Babylonia paused and watched for a moment. The beam stood still and expanded like a silent movie iris, automatically bringing the scene into full-screen view.

Why would somebody come to cyberspace to do something so—average? But then she remembered the complex, enigmatic social dynamics that might be at work here. Was the man really a man and was the woman really a woman, as they appeared to be, or were they alter-egos for some other combination of genders? Or were the two actually one desperately lonely person performing both roles in an act of cybernetic masturbation?

As Marianne wondered, the male image raised his head from the foam and steam and seemed to look directly at Babylonia. Marianne realized, with a start, that Baby was visible to those she watched. The woman in the Jacuzzi waved, and her words appeared at the top of the screen.

JOZEE>HI THERE. WANT 2 JOIN US?

JOSE>C'MON IN, GORGEOUS. THE WATR'S FIN.

Well, this is as good a chance as any.
She typed:

BABY>I'D LUV 2 PLA WITH U LUVLY PEEPLE 4 A LITL WHIL.

Baldwin Maisie and Ned Pritchard watched as Auggie approached a figure at the bar, a cheerful-looking character who wore a brown robe with a hood. "Who's the monk?" Maisie asked, but Pritchard just shrugged.

AWGY>CONGRATS FRIAR JOHN ON YR CHANG UV HABIT. R U NJOYING YR NU ROL?

JON>IT'S BEN MOST EDUKASHUNAL. & I HAV U TO THANK 4
THE IDEA.

Auggie's raucous programmed laughter rang out.

AWGY>DIDN I TEL U THAT AL U HAD 2 DO WUZ FOLO YR IN-
TRESTS & GIV N 2 YR OBSESHUNS? WUSN'T I RIT?

JON>U WER RIT, AWGY, U WER RIT. I FEL SO MUCH MOR AT
HOM NOW. & U WUDN BELEEEV THE MPRUVMENT IN MI
SOSHUL LIF.

AWGY>UV CORS I'D BELEV IT. SO. DO U WER YR HABIT N THE
PLEZURE DOM, 2?

JON>WITH SUM MODIFFYKATIONS UV CORS.

Auggie's laughter rang out again, followed by the sound of whistles and applause.

AWGY>WEL, I'M ALWAS GLAD TO HELP OUT A FREND. N FACT,
2 NIT I BROT A NU PLAMATE ALNG JST 4 U.

The friar just stood there grinning while Auggie pulled out a
rubber ball attached to a horn. But instead of toots, the horn
seemed to produce three hymnlike organ chords. A new figure
appeared at the door to the bar. This one was dressed as a nun, with
a black habit and a large white headdress that partially hid her face.
With one hand, she hiked up her skirt and struck a pin-up pose,
then wiggled her hips as she came toward the friar.

AWGY>U 2 SHD HV A FIN OL TIM N THE PLESUR DOM 2 NIT.

But the friar did not respond. Now the nun had reached the bar
and her face was visible. It was the face of a middle-aged woman with
startling blue eyes. A few tendrils of gray hair escaped the elaborate
headdress. In her hand she carried a ruler. The friar figure snapped
around, turning his back on the nun.

JON>U MONSTER. HOW DID U NO?

AWGY>MI FRENDS USUALLY TEL ME WUT THEY LIK, WHUT IT
IS THEY REEELEY WANT.

JON>HOW DARE U. THAT WAS MY PRIVATE MEMORY.

AWGY>IT WAS YR FAAANTASEEE. & OOOBVIOUSLY NOT SO
PRIVATE, AFTER AL.

Pritchard punched Maisie in the arm, saying, "Lookee, these guys
have a cyberfight brewing up."

"That's nothing new for Auggie. He has his noisy little disagreements with lots of people."

"Yeah," Pritchard snickered, "but look at what this one's over."

AWGY>U JUST SED U'R HAVING A GRAT TIM BEING A REEE-
LIJUS FIGGER.

JON>THIS WUZ SUPPOSED 2 B JUST A GAME. U'RE SUPPOSED
2 B JUST A CARTOON. NO, NO, THIS IS GETTING FAR TOO
PERSONAL. U HAV NO BUSINESS POKING AROUND N MY
MIND.

AWGY>U GAV ME SUM OF YR SEEECRETS & I GAV U SUM OF
MIN. BT THERS MUCH MORE, MI FREND, MUCH MOR. I THOT
U WER 1 UV THE SPESHUL 1S. I THOT U AAAALMOST UN-
NERSTUD THE NATR OF REEEALITY.

JON>I DON'T NO HOW U DID IT, BUT 4GET IT, AWGY. 4GET
ABOUT EVRYTHING. YOU WON'T EVER SEE ME AGAIN. NOT
HERE, NOT ANYWHERE.

Two things happened then in rapid succession: Auggie threw his
drink in the face of the friar; and the friar, brown pixels running
down his face, vanished from the bar. Apparently his operator had
simply turned his computer off.

"Did you see that?" Maisie asked.

"Yeah. Auggie's drink splashed all over that guy."

"He's not supposed to be able to do that. One cartoon character's not supposed to be able to touch another one in Ernie's."

"Tell me about it," Pritchard said. "No, tell that to Auggie."

"You know," Maisie said thoughtfully, "Marianne said that her friend and the clown used to argue a lot. Maybe we *should* be keeping track of his tiffs."

Pritchard said nothing. His eyes were fixed on the screen.

Auggie sat down at the bar and ordered another drink. He told the nun to go back to Aphrodite Escorts. As she wiggled her way out the door, he raised his glass to her.

AWGY>GLUG-GLUGGLES!

Pritchard let out a snort of laughter, "See that, Maisie? Know who that is?"

Baldwin Maisie looked blank. "What? I was watching the nun make her exit. What happened?"

"The clown just said, 'Gluggles.' "

"So, what does that mean?"

"Remember—'glug-gluggles, don't get caught in the bottle-neck'?"

"You mean that little wizard who was always so irritated with the von Neumann bottleneck? What was his name?"

"Zo-o-o-o-mer. That's gotta be either ol' Zoomer or some fan of his too stupid to make up his own lines. Zoomer used to have messages up all over the nets bitching about digital computers—complaining about all those little ones and zeros trotting along single file through the binary bottleneck."

"Sure, I remember him now," said Maisie. "He said information shouldn't have to stay in line, that millions of operations a second isn't fast enough. He was crying for a parallel processer by the time he learned to talk."

"Zoomer's a very, very bright guy. He coulda done it. I mean, all this stuff that's been cropping up on Insomnimania. Zoomer coulda gotten around our programming in Ernie's. He coulda invented the Snuff Room. He coulda set up the files on his snuffs so that anybody who downloaded only got a film loop."

"Is he a super phone phreak?" Maisie indicated the caller ID box. "We got a Chicago number on the box tonight. Zoomer's in L.A., right?"

"Last I knew. I don't imagine he's gone anywhere."

"We've been getting numbers from all over the country. Could he have logged in from here and made it look like he was coming from somebody else's phone in some other state?"

"I don't remember him having that deep a background on the phones, but I'd still be willing to bet he could figure it out if he really wanted to."

Maisie considered for a moment, then asked, "What do you think? Should we tell the cops?"

"Zoomer sure didn't sneak up and kill anybody."

"Let's let them figure that out for themselves."

"Are we gonna get him into trouble?"

"Don't see how it could. We know he didn't do any murders."

"They're gonna hassle him, though."

"Pritch, maybe he knows something. Maybe he can give them a lead in the direction of the guy who *did* kill that lady's friend."

Ned Pritchard squirmed on his stool. "I'd hate to turn a hacker over to the cops." He was silent for a few moments. "But it *was* murder. Two of them, maybe. I guess they won't bother Zoomer too much, once they get to see him."

"Know where he is now?"

"Probably still living at home with his parents. Like he always did. In fact, I think he actually joined Insomnimania—legitimately even. We probably have an address for him."

Maisie punched a few keys, calling up membership information. "Yeah, here he is. He's legit—the old boy's slowing down. One alter listed. Named Gargantua. Yeah, that's the gorilla we see around sometimes."

"That's curioser and curioser."

"Why?"

"Because we've seen Auggie *talking to* Gargantua. Do you suppose Zoomer's becoming a schizo in his old age?"

Baldwin Maisie dialed the police station and asked for Detective Grobowski.

This is almost like taking your clothes off for the first time with a new man. Not that Babylonia should be timid about revealing her body. This was what she was made for. It was the lack of subtlety in the situation that made Marianne feel awkward. But none of that shyness showed in Babylonia as she waited in the Motelibido room that Auggie had reserved for them.

Auggie had been in Ernie's Bar when Elfie got there tonight. He greeted the elf and asked her to join him, but he had not seemed in the mood to continue their previous conversation. In fact, he wasted little time before suggesting Pleasure Dome activity. Marianne was glad that she had made preparations.

The door opened and another figure entered the motel room. Marianne thought it must be Auggie, because only he knew the location of their private liaison. Only he would know the number to type to open the door and enter. But if this was Auggie, he no longer resembled a clown. Marianne stared at the screen.

The image that stepped forward was almost androgynous. An indication of the standard male genitals was visible on the completely naked figure, but the body was slender and unformed, smooth and characterless, and completely hairless. The face was expressionless. The whole figure was a simply sketched line drawing—black outlines with no color at all within.

It's as though he just took off the clown costume and makeup and this is what's left. She had hoped that Auggie's Pleasure Dome alter would give her some clue to the personality behind the clown, but this image looked unfinished, like a doll or a cheap mannequin. *This . . . this dummy . . . could put on another costume and be something else entirely.* A familiar phrase ran through her mind: *You ain't got nothin' in there.* She giggled nervously. *How could this be Auggie?*

Marianne experienced a sudden moment of queasiness as she wondered again whether she was meeting another woman. *It's not me. It's not even Elfie. It's Babylonia who'll be with this character, if he's man enough to appreciate her.*

"My name is Mr. Zero," the figure said aloud, moving tentatively toward Babylonia. His programmed voice was almost a whisper, without inflection.

BABY>SO GLAD TO MET U, HANDSUM MAN. MI NAM IS BABY-
    LONIA.

The pale figure stood gazing at Babylonia, the features unchanged, looking blank and disinterested. Finally he spoke aloud again, in the same inflectionless voice. "Ah, yes. You and I are going to have a fine time together."

Marianne thought his voice sounded more like a sigh than anything else. But now Mr. Zero was continuing, this time typing his lines. She must pay attention and have Babylonia respond.

O>WELCOM, BABYLONIA. LET ME SEE. AH YES, OF CORS, SHE
OF BABYLON. I M INDED HONORD BI YR METING ME HER
2DAY.

BABY>& I HAVE LONG WANTD 2 GET 2 NO AWGY.

Even as Babylonia spoke, Marianne wondered again if this *was*
Auggie—the character that she had imagined was the key to two
murders. Maybe Auggie was only the clown costume, only a cartoon
after all, and she had been silly to assume that there was some evil
character in the background doing real things to real people. If
Renee had been right and the snuff scenes were only an entertainment, then Marianne had been wrong to insist that there was some
devious connection to be discovered in the computer network.
Maybe Renee's murder had no connection to Judson's. Had she
wasted the police's time by insisting they look into Insomnimania?

O>WE SHUD 4GET ABT R REL LIVS 4 NOW. AWGY & LFY RN'T
HER NOW. U, BABYLONIA, U R HER NOW. U R THE 1 I WANT.
U R BEAUTIFUL BABYLONIA, U R CHARMING. WUT A RCH
IMAGINASHUN, WUT A LUVLY WOMAN.

As he spoke, the pale slender figure approached Babylonia and
reached out to her. But what should Babylonia do? She opened her
arms to wrap them around the man. Marianne was vaguely aware
that the erotic handicap she had given Babylonia would affect her
interactions with Mr. Zero. In fact, she had experienced the result of
the handicap earlier in the hot-tub scene, when she had found
herself dominant over both of the characters she joined.

But now she was amazed when Auggie wrapped his arms around
Babylonia and threw her down on the bed. Marianne giggled nervously. There was no doubt who had the highest aggression quotient
here.

Babylonia struggled briefly, but then Auggie produced ropes,
apparently out of nowhere. The whore was swiftly bound and tied to
the bed—her arms stretched upward, her legs spread. The clown
said:

O>NOW U CAN'T FITE IT. U'LL NJOY IT MUCH MOR, MI LOVE.

Marianne gasped. Her mind reeled into panic. How had he
known her fantasy? Had she told him? When could she have told

him? This was an image that occasionally flickered into her mind—certainly not anything she had ever wanted to act out.

Now Mr. Zero stroked Babylonia's hair. He punctuated his typed words with his verbalized whispers. "How lovely." "Such a beautiful woman." And, "Ah, yes. You and I are going to have a fine time together."

Marianne relaxed a little. *After all, bondage is an extremely common female fantasy. For all I know, he has all this preprogrammed and uses it automatically every time he meets someone here.*

O>JST RELAX. I DON'T WANT U TO DO ANYTHING. ZERO NOS HOW TO TAK CARE OF U. JST CM HERE, STA INSIDE OUR LITTLE WALLS. WE DON'T HAVE 2 B CONCERNED WITH ANY OF THE OTHERS.

And apparently, Mr. Zero did know how to take care of her. There seemed no doubt of his masculinity now. He stroked Babylonia. He removed her two purple veils and pushed her skirt aside. There were no more typed words now. A soft stream of sighs, compliments, and endearments was audible. Occasionally Marianne tried to direct Babylonia's responses, but it was as though her alter insisted on simply following Mr. Zero's lead. Then she saw that the ropes binding Babylonia had apparently melted away. The whore was tied down no longer.

To Marianne's amazement, the two characters simply folded together, made a fairly prosaic sexual connection, undulated, and emitted something like a purring noise. How easy it looked. How easy it was.

She found the scene quite fascinating. There was none of the bizarre activity she had witnessed in the beam of Elfie's flashlight. This was even simpler than her earlier experience in the hot tub. She felt a great sense of relief. She realized how much she had dreaded the possibility of seeing Elfie brutalized, even thus disguised as the Whore of Babylon.

It was increasingly hard to believe that the person who had created Auggie and Mr. Zero could have been involved in two murders, much less that he might be the murderer himself. He certainly knew how to act the part of a gentle lover. The cartoon activity on the screen indicated a person who was—what? *Seductive. Auggie knows how to be quite seductive.*

Then her whole body stirred with a physical memory so potent that it overwhelmed the images on the computer screen. It was as though Nolan was on top of her again and she felt her body move to receive him, without thought, without hesitation, her knees rising on each side of him, her arms wrapping around his great warm body.

The pale man moved his arm, pixels tracking across the screen in rhythmic strokes, both characters moving tirelessly, the whore's red clothing and gold jewelry flashing with every motion.

Nolan entered her and drew a deep sigh, beginning a gentle motion. She realized contentedly that this was going to last a long time.

Babylonia's red lips that would not smear formed a round "O," her long black hair that would not tangle spread in curls around them. The pale lover moved ceaselessly.

Marianne became aware that Nolan was stroking the side of her face, kissing her eyelids, her nose, stroking her hair as it spread out on the pillow. All the while he moved gently, rhythmically. She reached up and ran her hands along Nolan's hairy arms, his sweaty body, relishing the absolute reality of him.

10100

HACKER

A S CLAYTON DROVE THE SQUAD CAR SLOWLY UP NORTH
Figueroa, Nolan watched for the cross street. On any weekend, the park on their right would be full of picnicking
families. Now a group of kids, probably a class from one of the
neighborhood schools, kicked a soccer ball around.

Nolan remembered driving by that park after one of the larger
earthquakes. Many Mexican-American and Asian-American families
had moved out into the park, setting up their tents and cooking out
until the aftershocks were safely over. It had looked like some sort of
fiesta.

"Turn left at the next corner," Nolan said. Clayton turned and
headed into the lower edge of Mount Washington. Nolan directed
them through a few more turns, and they wound their way steadily
up the steep hill. Houses were packed along narrow roads that
rambled through hairpin curves and steep grades. Many of the
houses were old, some of them small and worn, but most shared an
excellent view—at least when the view consisted of anything but
smog. Here and there, new houses were shouldered into the landscape, with bold decks jutting out precariously over the hillside.
Nearer the top, the houses were larger with more space between
them. Those belonged to Mount Washington's more affluent inhabitants. However, nothing here looked much like Beverly Hills.

They had to turn around and backtrack through the honeycomb
of old lanes before they found the address Maisie had given them—

a tall narrow house on the uphill side of the street. There was no driveway, just a slight widening of the road in front of the small garage. Clayton pulled the car as far over to the right as he could to avoid being in the path of other traffic coming down the hill. The detectives made their way up flagstone steps to the front door of the house.

"If this guy tries to break and run, I don't think he'll be able to get out of here very fast," Nolan muttered.

"Maisie seemed sure he wouldn't run," said Clayton. "In fact, he's positive this guy isn't violent at all." He knocked several times before a middle-aged Latina opened the door.

"Good afternoon, ma'am," Nolan said, showing his badge. "I'm Detective Grobowski with the Los Angeles Police Department. And this is Detective Saunders. Are you Mrs. Ramos?"

The woman nodded, showing no interest. "We're here to see Mike Ramos. Is he your son?"

"Mikey is sleeping," she said, nodding. "He works late at night."

"I'm afraid we'll have to ask you to wake him up," Nolan said firmly. "We have to ask him some questions on a very urgent matter."

The woman just stood there, looking as though her attention had simply wandered off. Nolan said, "Mrs. Ramos?" She turned and walked back into the house. Nolan and Clayton followed.

"Is anyone else at home?" Nolan asked.

"My husband is out," the woman answered, without looking back.

The inside of the house was dim. The windows were over-shadowed by foliage and partially covered by heavy drapes. But Nolan could see that the place was very clean and that the living-room furniture looked quite new.

"He's up here," the woman said, mounting a staircase at the side of the room. Nolan and Clayton followed her up. When they reached the second floor, she walked down a short hallway and opened a door. "*Miguel, despiértate,*" she yelled into the doorway. Nolan could see that another flight of stairs, much narrower than the first, went up from there.

Although there was no sound of any kind from above, Nolan pushed past the woman and started upward. He could hear Clayton responding to her muttered protests. Carefully, Nolan moved up the stairway, his hand on his revolver. When he reached the door of the room, he waited for Clayton to catch up with him. Nolan edged carefully around the doorway, then relaxed at what he saw.

A fully clothed, slender young man occupied a rumpled bed. His slight snore did not change as they entered. It looked to Nolan like the whole top floor of the house had been finished off to create this one large room. The ceiling rose to a peak in the center, following the roof line. Lining the low side walls were tables and desks cluttered with electronic equipment that reminded Nolan of the Insomnimania headquarters. Magazines and comic books were strewn about the bed and desks. A couple of soft-drink cans littered a table next to the bed. A motorized wheelchair was also beside the bed.

Light filtered in through shades drawn over two dormer windows and another small window set in a door at the far end of the room. Nolan casually inspected the space. On one side of the back door was a storage area with some clothes hanging among bundles of cables. On the other side was a large full bathroom set up for wheelchair access.

Mrs. Ramos shuffled into the room, giving the detectives a reproachful glance. She turned on a lamp and shook her son's shoulder repeatedly until he emerged into resentful wakefulness. Then the slow, sturdy woman helped the young man into his wheelchair—an exercise they had clearly performed many times. Both the woman and the young man ignored offers of aid from the detectives.

Finally, Nolan found himself facing Mike Ramos. The woman collected the drink cans, gave the detectives one last sour look, and disappeared down the stairs. She still demonstrated no curiosity at all about the reason for their visit.

Small motors whirred as the slight young man turned his wheelchair around to face the detectives directly. "Well, gentlemen," he said, "just why are you disturbing my family and my sleep?"

Nolan could see that Mike Ramos was a bit older than he had first thought—at least in his mid-twenties. Asleep on the bed, Ramos had looked like an adolescent. Now he sat rather majestically in his chair and nodded his head solemnly at them. His dark hair fell limply across his forehead. His manner was polite. His diction was careful and somewhat stilted, although it did not sound like an accent. Nolan decided that it was more as though Ramos was not accustomed to using the spoken language. He just didn't seem like the kind of person who liked to talk to *anybody*. Nolan identified himself and his partner to the young man, whose expression did not change.

"Mr. Ramos," Nolan said, "we want to ask you some questions about Insomnimania."

The brown eyes stared back with a slight spark of interest. "Why Insomnimania?" the young man asked. "It's an interesting network, but only one of many."

"It's expensive, isn't it?" Nolan asked.

Ramos backed up in his wheelchair, putting slightly more distance between himself and the detectives. "Whatever you might guess from appearances here, I do make a pretty good income."

"How do you do that?"

"I write custom programs for businesses. It's all handled through a company here in town. They do the legwork. Obviously. They have some junior programmers in their office. I do the really difficult stuff for them. But it's easy."

"What's the name of this company you work for?"

Ramos reached into a desk drawer and handed Nolan a brochure. "Complete Programming Services" was printed on the front.

"So you're able to support yourself with this kind of work," remarked Nolan.

"We all live comfortably, yes."

"We?"

"I contribute to the support of my parents."

"You've certainly made the most of your disability."

"My disability, as you call it, has nothing to do with what I am today. I'd be doing exactly what I'm doing right now if I could walk. I'd be living exactly as I'm living right now. In fact, I have all the physical access to the outside world that I want. I even have a van, but I very seldom drive it."

Nolan detected no defensiveness in Ramos' voice. He simply sounded as if he meant what he said. Indeed, he seemed so sedentary, so strictly cerebral by nature, that he probably *would* have arranged his domain in just such a manner whether he could walk or not. He probably *would* have chosen to live on the top floor of this house and come down into the world of lesser mortals as infrequently as possible. Other people overcame similar detriments in order to participate fully in society, but Ramos was not interested.

"But you work here at home?" Nolan asked.

"Always. I set my own hours. I sleep a lot during the day. Usually." There was a moment's silence. "I'm very good at what I do," Ramos added.

"I'm sure you're an excellent programmer, Mr. Ramos. In fact, we know that you actually programmed a participational area on the

Insomnimania network called the Snuff Room. Baldwin Maisie said you originated it."

"Yes. It was easy to do. I just made some of Insomnimania's animation software available in a somewhat newer but still limited way. The Snuff Room is a standard feature of the network now—available to all alters. Lots of different characters present snuffs there."

"We're particularly interested in one specific character—the clown named Auggie."

"And what is Auggie up to these days?" Ramos asked blandly.

"That's what we'd like to find out from you."

"I see him on the network sometimes. I have very little to say to him."

"Don't play games with us, Mr. Ramos. We know that Auggie is your alter."

"No, I am afraid you are mistaken. My alter is named Gargantua. Not Auggie."

"We have reason to believe that you also log on as Auggie. That you were, in fact, logged on as Auggie just last night." Nolan knew that last night's call had apparently been made from Chicago, and he didn't know if Ramos had been logged on at all. But he wanted to push the issue a little.

"Why?" Ramos asked.

"Baldwin Maisie said it was you."

"Why would he say that? I am sure they have records to show what my tag is. Sometimes in the past I have created other alters, but lately it's just been Gar."

"Gluggles," said Nolan.

Ramos just stared back, making no response at all. Nolan felt more than a little silly.

Clayton broke into the silence, "Auggie said that on the network. Doesn't it mean anything to you?"

"Yes. It's my little slang for the von Neumann bottleneck—my private way of saying, 'Don't get stuck in a rut,' or 'Have a nice day.' I guess he learned that from me."

"Who learned that from you?" Clayton asked.

"Auggie."

"Don't you mean the person who logs on as Auggie?" said Nolan.

"If you say so."

"And who is that person?"

"I have no idea."

The hacker stared back silently. His eyes were dark and expressionless. Nolan was getting impatient.

"Please remember, Mr. Ramos," he said, "we may very well be able to show that, at the very least, you've used other people's credit cards to log Auggie on. We can bring charges that would allow us to confiscate your equipment and disks and hold them as evidence."

"I really don't think you can prove any of that, Lieutenant," Ramos said, "for the simple reason that it is not true. I'm not a teenage cracker playing with other people's credit cards. However, I do know that in the past a number of hackers have had their property confiscated by law officers who had no idea what they were looking for or what they were taking. Those officers made fools of themselves and ended up being charged in a civil suit."

"That was the Secret Service and the FBI," Nolan said. "The law-enforcement community has learned some things in the meantime, believe me. In our division, we have specialists who prosecute computer crime. These guys know their business."

"Good. Then I won't have to deal with a lot of utter stupidity. Please keep in mind that if you put me out of business, you will interrupt important work under legitimate contract. You will hold up operational changes in several large companies. It could cost them a great deal of money. You would certainly hear from some very unhappy CEOs."

"We hope nothing like that will become necessary, Mr. Ramos," Nolan said. He shifted awkwardly, aware that he was using the wrong tactics with the young programmer, but unsure how to proceed. "We're here because two members of Insomnimania have been killed, and both of their murders were replayed by Auggie in the Snuff Room. This is a very serious business. We want to know the connection between these two murder victims and whoever is behind Auggie. We won't hesitate to make an arrest if we find that you are involved in some way."

"The simple truth is, I am not the one who creates Auggie's Snuff Room scenes," Mike Ramos said. "I am not the one who goes on Insomnimania as Auggie. And I do not know who does."

Now the hacker looked strained and hostile. There was a whirring sound again as he turned his wheelchair a few inches to the left and then to the right. *The equivalent of pacing.*

"I really have nothing more to tell you gentlemen," Ramos said.

"If you wish to persist in questioning me, I think I should have my lawyer present."

Standing there listening, watching Ramos, Clayton heard an echo in his mind of the word shouted in the detective's bay—"Nigger." It had been a couple of weeks ago, but he still remembered the paranoia he had felt at that moment. He had often wished he could put up some kind of shield, some kind of invisible protective barrier against the world around him.

Ramos is like that, too. Only he's got an actual shield—one made out of networking cables and computer screens.

For a moment, Clayton actually envied Ramos. On a computer screen or over the phone lines, Ramos could be whoever or whatever he wanted to be, and nobody could get close enough to him to contradict him. It was his world, surely more real to him than this attic room.

Clayton sat down on the bed, putting his eyes level with those of the young man in the wheelchair. "It's like going into a comic book, isn't it?" Clayton asked Ramos.

"You mean Insomnimania?" Ramos turned to look at the black detective.

"Yeah. It's a whole new universe—freer than this one." Clayton thought about his own kids talking about adventure games. He tried to recapture a thirteen-year-old's sense of wonder.

"Yes, you're right. It *is* like going into a comic book. An animated one. Except that Insomnimania is far more interesting than any regular cartoon."

"How's that?"

"Because you're *there*—not outside the pages, not outside the screen. It's a place you go and meet other people. Do you like the Insomnimania network?"

"I'm fascinated by it."

"What's your favorite place?" Ramos asked.

Clayton scrambled in his mind for an answer. He had spent very little time actually logged into Insomnimania. "I like Ernie's Bar," he said. "And I'd like to play around in the casino."

"Aw, those are standard," said Ramos. "They're animated better on Insomnimania, but lots of networks have places like that."

"I haven't had a chance to get to much of it," Clayton replied. "What's your favorite part?"

"Some of the games. 'Chaos Syndrome' calls for serious strategy. 'Implicate Order' is my favorite—linear logic doesn't work in that space."

Ramos looked as though he might continue, but then he suddenly backed his wheelchair a few inches—again moving away from the detectives. Watching the young hacker, Clayton said, "You know, what I'd really like to do is get out of your way right now, let you get your sleep, and phone you later. Would you agree to talk to me over the telephone for a little while?"

Ramos nodded slightly. "Or you could talk to me on the network. That's the easiest way of all."

"For you, maybe," Clayton said with a smile. "It's still quite a chore for me. I'm just now catching onto it. Maybe you can teach me about it."

Ramos smiled back. It was the first time Ramos had smiled during the interview so far.

"So is it OK if I telephone you this evening, after you've gotten your sleep?" Clayton asked.

"OK," said Ramos, grinning in a way that made him look like an adolescent for another brief moment. "Call me after the sun goes down." He laughed, a little harshly, as though he was as unaccustomed to laughter as to spoken conversation.

Ramos scribbled a number on a piece of paper and handed it to Clayton. Clayton ignored his partner's slight sputtering. He herded Nolan back down the stairs and out to the car.

"What's this telephone call business all about?" Nolan demanded after they got into the car.

"I don't think he's comfortable being in the actual presence of people—carrying on a conversation in person," Clayton explained. "He was all tightened up. And if we pushed on, we'd have wound up dealing with a lawyer who'd have shut him up for good. I want to take a crack at him by telephone."

Nolan started the engine and drove off in silence. After a few minutes he asked, "So whaddya think? Did we just talk with a psycho?"

"He hasn't gone after any airline moguls with a butcher knife lately, if that's what you mean."

"No. But maybe he had something to do with it."

After they returned to the division, Nolan sat grumpily at his desk. He knew that if Clayton said he could get more out of the hacker by telephone, Clayton was probably right. He just hated the wait. "*Call me after the sun goes down.*" What a stupid thing—like the kid was a vampire or something. He decided he'd better phone Marianne.

"Just wanted to let you know that Clay and I had an interview with a hacker this morning," he announced when her answering machine picked up the call.

There was a click and Marianne came on the line. "Was it Auggie? Did you find Auggie?" she asked excitedly.

"It turned out to be . . . well, I'm not exactly sure what it turned out to be."

"What happened?"

"Look, I'm sorry, but don't get excited about it. It's a complicated story and I'll explain it to you tonight. But the guy we talked to is not the killer."

"Is he Auggie?"

"It doesn't make much difference, does it? This guy's in a wheelchair and has been for years. He didn't stalk Judson through the corridors of the Quenton Parks."

"Couldn't needing the wheelchair be an act?"

"We're still checking that out. We'll see if it's consistent with his DMV records. And we should be able to locate his medical records. We're not finished with him yet. Clay is going to talk to him again this evening—by telephone. That's what I wanted to call you about. I'm afraid I'm going to be late getting back to the house."

"Well, just tell me what time you'll be there to let me in."

"I'll do better than that. I'll tell you where the key is hidden."

As soon as the sky began to darken, Clayton picked up the telephone and dialed the number Ramos had given him. Nolan was on another phone on the same line and a tape recorder was running. Clayton and Nolan were sitting at neighboring desks and were able to watch one another, able to exchange visual signals should the need arise. An answering machine came on the other end with no message, just a series of electronic beeps.

Clayton said, "This is Detective Clayton Saunders calling for Mike Ramos. Mr. Ramos, you said you'd be willing to talk to me after the sun went down."

There was a click followed by the hollow sound of a speaker phone.

"OK," Ramos said. "I'm here."

"Thanks for picking up," Clayton said.

"You're not alone on the line, are you?" said Ramos.

Clayton was slightly startled. He looked at Nolan. Nolan shook his head urgently, covering the receiver and whispering, "You are!"

But Clayton disobeyed.

"No, Mr. Ramos," Clayton said. "My partner's on the line, too."

"And you're recording the call, right?"

"Yes," Clayton said.

"That's fine," said Ramos. "Just as long as I know."

Clayton breathed a sigh of relief that Ramos simply didn't hang up on him. Clayton closed his eyes. In order to make this conversation really click, he would have to visualize Ramos the way Ramos wanted to be pictured. And immediately, an image came into Clayton's mind. It was of a criminal mastermind from some old spy movie—a figure dimly visible behind a layer of bulletproofed glass, with a venetian blind pulled down to cover his face. A fluffy white cat sat in this mastermind's lap, and his voice was amplified over a loudspeaker.

Yes, that's just the way he'd like me to see him. Hell, I wouldn't mind playing that role myself.

Clayton also knew that he now had to call Ramos by the name of Zoomer. On the telephone—in the electronic world—Mike Ramos actually *became* Zoomer.

"Are you still there, Detective Saunders?" Zoomer asked.

"Yes, Zoomer. I'm still here."

"What did you want to talk to me about?"

"Just to see if you can help set me straight on some things. I'm dumb about computers. That's probably why I don't understand Insomnimania. The only hackers I've met before are Maisie and Pritchard."

"Those guys have both been around for a long time. But they went commercial and hit it big. They aren't hacking now."

"Are they good?"

"Pritchard's the only wizard. Maisie's canny but he's not powerful. They're both sloppy. I was surprised that they could make a universe and actually keep it running."

"But you're a good hacker?"

"Yes, I am."

"I sure need your help. Maisie and Pritchard haven't been able to figure this thing out."

"What are you trying to figure?"

"Who's logging on as Auggie? His membership information is phoney."

"Just pick up Auggie's phone number when he's on. That should be simple enough."

"We've done that. But the results have been . . . inconclusive."

"That's odd."

"It is, isn't it? How could a hacker appear to be dialing out of someone else's telephone?"

"Ah. You're talking about major phone phreaking there. They're either tapping into the line directly or you've got a supreme phone wizard on your hands. I'm afraid it's not my area of expertise."

"You can't hack telephones?"

"Not the way you're talking about. So Auggie's doing that now?"

"We're having a hard time figuring out just what Auggie's doing," Clayton said. "Can you tell us anything at all about how Auggie appeared in the first place? How did he get started?"

There was a moment of silence. When Zoomer began talking, it was nearly in a whisper.

"Tell me, Detective Saunders, how far back can you remember?"

Clayton wrinkled his brow. "Remember what?" he replied.

"Anything. How old were you when the earliest thing you can remember took place?"

Clayton was mystified at this turn in the conversation. But he had to follow wherever Zoomer led. "How far back can *you* remember?" Clayton replied.

"Real far," Zoomer said, his voice trailing away as if he was talking to himself. "I can remember a long time ago, when I was just tiny, before I could even walk. My father bought me this little brown plastic wagon with little black plastic horses and little yellow wheels. One day, I left the wagon on the heating register—the one downstairs, right above the furnace. The furnace was on, and I crawled by in time to notice that the wagon was melting. Those little bright yellow wheels were losing their shape, starting to drip slowly through the metal grate, turning into a glistening liquid. I was tickled by how it looked. I laughed. It looked like something out of Granny's oven. I thought my wagon was turning into some kind of glazed, delicious candy. I crawled across the register to get it. Then I cried out with shock and pain. My hands were severely burned. I remember how I wept, how I cried. I suppose it was the first time I ever felt really severe pain.

"Strange, isn't it, how we cry over pain when we're children? Adults rarely weep from physical pain. Oh, we complain or groan or gnash our teeth or scream, but we hardly ever weep. I didn't weep when I received the injuries which crippled me. Why is it different for little children? Can you tell me why?"

"No," Clayton said softly.

"I think children cry from grief," Zoomer continued. "They cry from the sadness of learning that there is such a thing as pain in the world."

The hacker let forth a sad little laugh. "Most of us forget our crying when we grow up. But I don't forget. I remember. I remember every bit of it. I am determined to maintain my sensitivity, my humanity. I refuse to be hardened. I am determined to remember what it feels like to grieve and weep for pain and lost innocence. That incident took place on the sixteenth of February, 1966. I was one year, seven months, and three days old."

"You remember the *date?*" chimed in Clayton skeptically.

"Of course I don't *remember* the date," Zoomer replied. "I checked. I looked it up. You see, I was so badly burned that I had to be taken to the emergency room at the hospital. They had records. It wasn't easy, because the physician who bandaged me was long since dead, but I did find my records. I suffered from second-degree burns. I still have the scars."

"What's all this got to do with Auggie?" grumbled Clayton, sounding like an impatient kid.

"Let me finish. You'll understand. On the twenty-seventh of March, 1967, my father took me to a circus. In case you're wondering, I got *that* date off an old newspaper microfilm. It was exactly one year and thirty-nine days after my burning accident, and I was two years, eight months, and eight days old. I sat on my father's lap in the front row. I had never seen a circus. At first, I loved it. I loved the sequined men and women defying natural forces with which I was still scarcely acquainted. I loved the many fine pets which were too big and fierce and noisy to take home. But I did not know what to think of the clowns. While the rest of the circus was wild and dreamlike, the clowns were so real, so ordinary—as if my aunts, uncles, and grandparents had decided to camp out in Neverland. I thought they had no business there. I wanted them to go away.

"They did not go away. Two of them were particularly stubborn and persistent. One was a white-clad gentleman with great red buttons and a silly conical cap. He gave all the orders, and most of them were stupid orders. He acted just like my father or mother. He delivered his orders to a put-upon, battered fellow with a smashed derby and patched pants and a bright red nose. This lowly dark clown bungled the white clown's instructions every way he could.

"I tried to ignore these two humdrum and all-too-familiar characters, but they kept coming closer and closer to the audience. The dark-clad, red-nosed clown began to pad along the front row in his outsized shoes, squirting child after child with the gigantic sunflower in his lapel. When I saw that he was coming my way, I squirmed and squealed, trying to escape my father's idiotic grasp. I knew he was going to rip me away from my father and take me God knows where. I also knew that this was my father's whole reason for bringing me to the circus. He wanted to get rid of me— to sell me like some kind of beast or slave to that ghastly world of the clowns.

"At last the clown arrived, and I stopped squirming and squealing. I guess my father thought I'd had a change of heart, that I now supposed the clown to be some sort of friend. But I was actually frozen with fear. I couldn't even breathe. I could see the clown very clearly now. His face was inches away from mine, and he looked entirely different than he had before. In the ring, he seemed so bright, so primary, so loud and ghastly. But up close, I could see where his white, red, and black makeup was melted and smeared by sweat, revealing awful, wrinkled flesh underneath. I could see that his painted smile actually disguised an expression of unspeakable weariness and dread. And he smelled like death. Then came that geyser of water from his lapel, and I began to scream.

"I don't remember what happened after that, but I've been told I didn't stop screaming for hours, and that my father had to take me home. Nobody knew why. But *I* knew. The pain I had felt when I burned myself, the pain I thought I had left behind had pursued me, had sought me out. That pain had taken the form of the shabby and ragged clown."

Zoomer was quiet for a moment, then concluded blandly, "So perhaps you understand now why I chose to give his shape to a cartoon killer."

Clayton felt the shot of adrenaline in his body. "So what you're telling me," he said, as calmly as he could, "is that you *created* this clown—the most powerful character in the game. But you said that now he is *not* your alter."

"That's right," Zoomer said.

"Of course you realize this sounds like a very naive ploy to escape becoming a murder suspect."

"I realize that, yes. It's unbelievable, isn't it? Too unbelievable for me to make up. At least as unbelievable as the notion that I'm going around chopping people up. Of course, we murderers are a notoriously naive bunch."

Clayton hesitated for a long moment. "So you don't know who's using Auggie now?" he asked at last. "Could you find out if you tried?"

Clayton could hear the whirring sound of the pacing wheelchair even over the telephone. Finally the young man said softly, "No."

"But you haven't tried to find out?"

"No."

"Forgive me for saying so, Zoomer, but I find that a little hard to believe."

"Why?"

"Well, by your own account, you're a brilliant guy and one hell of a computer hacker. And here you go to all this trouble to create this terrific computer character who—how might you put it?— embodies all your childhood pain. But when somebody takes this character away from you, you don't even try to take it back. You don't even try to find out who's responsible."

There was a moment's silence. Then Zoomer said in a rather distant voice, "At first, there were just small peculiarities. Times when he almost seemed to be acting independently. For a while, I did think it was a challenge from some other hacker."

Zoomer was silent for a few moments.

"Then what happened?" Clayton asked.

"One day when I was running him through his tricks in Ernie's Bar, he . . . drew away from me. He started acting on his own, speaking in a different voice. So I left him."

"You left him?" demanded Clayton.

"Yeah, I left him."

"Why?"

"I'd made him out of my pain, and it was his privilege to exist, to carry out my wishes. But he turned away from me. When I *create* something, Detective Saunders, I never stoop to trying to win its loyalty. It's not my style. The clown is on his own now. I see him around from time to time."

"You sound like a superstitious man, Zoomer," said Clayton, echoing Ramos's overly precise, measured delivery.

"Do I really?" asked Ramos, sounding almost pleased.

"Indeed you do. You impute human characteristics to nonhuman things. A collection of electronic commands and animated pixels isn't exactly capable of betrayal. Can a man of your phenomenal intelligence not know that?"

"You miss the point, Detective Saunders," Zoomer said, sounding pleased by Clayton's verbal challenge. "I know it's often considered a sign of ignorance and superstition to anthropomorphize mere things. But in an inhuman universe, it's the only way I know of to make life palatable. Besides, I find it much more entertaining to think of him as independent than to assume someone merely rewrote his program."

Clayton felt exhausted. He had no idea what tack to try with the hacker next. He looked at Nolan inquisitively, but his partner just shrugged.

"Zoomer, I appreciate your help," Clayton said. "If it's all right with you, I'd like to phone you again sometime."

"You have the number, Sergeant," Zoomer said, then added, with a trace of wry humor, "I'll be here."

Then there was a click and the dial tone buzzed in the ears of both detectives.

"I'm getting too old for this," Clayton complained, as Nolan walked toward him.

"So what did we get out of him?" Nolan asked.

"Beats me," Clayton said. "I didn't understand half of what that fucker was talking about."

"You *didn't?*" Nolan exclaimed. "You sure as hell *acted* like you understood him. So what do you figure? Is he connected with the killer?"

"I don't know. I'm not sure if *he* knows."

"Well, he hasn't been out of that wheelchair lately," Nolan said, "because we know his disability squares with his DMV records. Still, he's awfully smart. Do you think he's a director of some kind of murder club—something like that?"

Clayton shook his head. "He wants too much for us to think he's some evil genius—like that baldheaded what's-his-name in the

James Bond movies. But he ain't quite as smart as he'd like to be. My guess is that this particular master hacker got out-hacked and that Auggie really *doesn't* belong to him anymore. My guess is that we ain't even glimpsed our bad guy yet."

Nolan groaned. "That's what I was afraid you'd say," he said.

"Wish I could tell you otherwise."

"Anyway, you handled him brilliantly," Nolan said, sitting on the desk beside Clayton.

"You really think so?"

Nolan shook his head. "Hell, more than a few guys around this department wish they had your capacity to crawl inside people's brains, understand what makes them tick. You've got a gift, man. A real gift. You make me feel like a lumbering oaf a lot of the time—particularly on a bitch of a case like this."

"This case is just following the usual pattern, buddy," Clayton said reassuringly. "I make two or three good intuitive leaps, then you unravel the threads and follow them through the dark. It always takes your *brains* to bring us over the finish line."

"I hope my brains get engaged pretty soon," Nolan said with a sigh.

"Don't worry. They will."

"Yeah, I guess so," Nolan said. "We sure make one hell of a team, don't we?" he added warmly.

"We sure do," Clayton said. Then he felt swept by a wave of irrational sadness.

Nolan returned Clayton's melancholy look.

"Did I ever tell you about Syd Harper, my mentor back at the academy?" Nolan asked.

Clayton laughed. "Sure. Crazy Syd. When we first started working together, you hardly ever talked about anything else. Crazy Syd taught you this, Crazy Syd told you to do that. You told me *all about* Crazy Syd."

"Well, for the last few years, Crazy Syd's been sheriff up in a little town in Oregon. It's a real cop's delight up there—hardly any crimes to speak of except a little vandalism or a stolen bicycle now and then. Anyway, Crazy Syd's getting ready to retire. And he got in touch with me not long ago, suggesting I take over his job."

Clayton felt his throat choke up slightly.

"So have you made a decision yet?" Clayton asked.

"Not yet," Nolan said.

Both men were quiet for a moment.

"You know, the problem's more than what happened to Louise," Nolan said at last. "Sometimes I feel like a goddamn dinosaur hanging around this town, particularly when the criminals start using computers. It's like my life here has ended, something here is all over. I'm tired, Clay. Really tired. I think I could use the change."

"Can't say I blame you," Clayton said.

"What about you?" Nolan asked. "This job has gotta be harder on you than on me."

Clayton fell quiet. For a moment, he didn't know what to say.

"This town really is hell sometimes," he said at last. "So full of fear and bigotry and hate and all. Sometimes I can *hear* the hate, Nol. I can hear it even when no one's saying anything. It doesn't whisper, it *yells* at me from the streets and hallways. That's when I just want to take Sheila and the kids and get the hell out of here."

"It would be a poorer place if you did," Nolan said gently. "Look at the kind of work you did today. Who else is going to do that?"

Clayton felt a smile form slowly on his lips.

"Yeah," he said. "I guess that's why I've gotta stay. Besides, I don't want there to be one less brother on the force. But I'd miss you like hell, buddy."

"Yeah, me, too. But remember—the whole thing's still up in the air."

"Yeah, I know," Clayton said. "So. What about Marianne?"

Nolan gave Clayton a surprised look.

"What about her?"

"If you go up north, will she go, too? You two *are* an item, right?"

"How the hell did *you* know that?" Nolan asked.

Clayton laughed. "Are you kidding?" he said. "That night when I called about the DNA test—when Gauld's killer turned out to be a woman—I knew. I knew right then. I could tell by your voice."

"You uncanny son of a bitch," Nolan said with a smile. Then he shrugged, "I don't know what she'd do. I don't know what she'd decide. I haven't talked to her about it yet." Then he looked at his watch. "I guess I'd better get on home," he said. "That lady's probably waiting for me right now."

10101

TRAVELING HORSE

MARIANNE PRESSED HER FACE AGAINST THE GLASS IN ORDER TO see the carousel inside. Three rows of brightly painted horses stood quietly in dappled light that filtered in through small panes of glass. One spot of strong sunlight fell directly on a sweet-faced white pony that had a flowing mane and a red bridle and saddle.

"I love this building," Marianne said, standing back and looking up at the turreted, multiwindowed building on the Santa Monica pier. "It's like a warp in time—a 1920s space that never changed. When the carousel is running, the horses dance around to music from an old Wurlitzer organ. They always look so beautiful."

Now the sun highlighted a wooden mane waving in the air, making it seem that the horse was prancing to tunes it undoubtedly knew by heart. Another sunlit animal reared with its head stuck up in the air, mouth open as though fighting the bit. *That one looks a little like Renee's horse.*

"Your friend had a carousel horse," Nolan said, as though he had read her thoughts. "Not as pretty as these, though."

"No. He was a traveling horse. A real explorer, from the look of him."

"It did look like it had seen better days."

"When she got her horse, I did some research on how it might have originally looked. I thought I'd help her restore it. Those horses inside there were carved for a carousel that would stay in one location. See how delicate some of the ears and manes and tails are? Renee's horse was probably from a county-fair carousel. He was made with small ears laid back tight against his head so they wouldn't break off when he was taken down and moved around. He's not as nice an example as these, but he's probably just as old."

"But she never got around to restoring it?"

"She refused to," Marianne said, with a catch in her voice. "She said, 'He's no beauty, but oh, what a life he's lived!' She said she didn't want to paint over a single one of the stories he could tell."

Marianne felt tears spring into her eyes. She wrapped her arms around Nolan and leaned her head on his shoulder. They had spent a wonderful night together and a deliciously sensuous morning. After Nolan went in to the division, Marianne hooked up her computer to the rented monitor and went to work on her own project. A few hours later, Nolan called and said he was going to take a long lunch—did she want to go out somewhere? Since he had worked all weekend and nothing new was breaking this morning, he wouldn't have to rush back. When he picked her up, they decided on the pier. Snuggling close to him like this, she felt they could just as easily have gone back to bed.

After a few moments, Nolan said, "Let's walk out on the pier." He guided her gently away from the carousel. He felt disturbed and broody, and he wanted to talk to Marianne about some specific concerns. He decided to walk a little bit first.

The old pier was pleasant and not particularly crowded at this time of year. There were a only a few people fishing, armed with their rods and bait and buckets. Nolan watched Marianne as she stared out over the ocean. He wished she would release her hair and let it blow in the slight breeze.

She is beautiful. He realized that he meant it in a very ordinary way—that she could easily grace the cover of a magazine. Her appearance had daunted him at first. He was not usually drawn to coolly beautiful women, not beyond the casual physical responses such looks aroused. Nolan had long since outgrown the notion that he should try to bed every woman who stirred his hormones. And, in his recent lonely years, he had rediscovered how easily his libido could lead him into disastrous entanglements or empty one-night stands with boring, tragic, or troublesome women.

But Marianne had also stirred him with her quick wit, her intelligence, her intensity, even her grief. With the bright sunlight falling on her face, he could see that she looked less like a porcelain doll than she sometimes did in muted indoor light. At the sight of those fine lines, those circles under the eyes, those signs of vulnerability, confidence stirred within Nolan again. Maybe they would find some basis for a life together.

He gazed out over the water. The ocean and the sky were both gray, turning silver wherever the sun broke through the cloud cover overhead and where the shafts of light touched the waves. It was as though some magician pointed a wand randomly here and there, lighting the surface of the water, but revealing nothing of what was below. The shafts of light on the water made Nolan think of the electronic magicians, Pritchard and Ramos, those intense young men who wielded such incomprehensible power in a new world of their own making.

"I knew I was going to hate the computer age way back when I was still walking the beat," he said.

Marianne laughed. "What could possibly have turned you off computers back then?"

"The video games," Nolan replied with a tone of disgust. When Marianne just looked at him inquisitively, he continued. "I patrolled one of those video arcade places every night, and I got to watching kids play those games. My own kids loved them, too. I saw how good they all were at it, how fast and smart they were, how they could do just about anything with those damned machines. And I thought, 'Jesus, these have got to be the smartest and fastest kids who ever lived.' But then I realized something. They were in that place learning to be losers."

"What do you mean?" Marianne asked.

"Don't you get it? That's what those games are all about. You get as many points as you can, and you get as many free games as you can, but eventually the machine always beats you. Those kids play till they lose. They play till they run out of quarters. That's the object of the game. Losing and running out of quarters. They were the most terrific kids of all time, and they were already being trained to lose."

"I never thought about it that way," Marianne said. Then she added, grinning, "You were pretty engrossed in that casino card game."

"You're right, it was fun. But it's a lot more fun to try and figure out whether real people are bluffing or not." Nolan stared straight ahead for a moment, no longer seeing the water. Finally he said gruffly, "I guess my real gripe about this investigation is that I have to rely on people whose methods I don't understand. And even they're not coming up with anything useful."

"You mean Maisie and Pritchard?" she asked.

"Yes. And now there's Ramos. I don't know if he's guilty of anything or not, but I don't get the feeling he's on our side. I don't even get the feeling he's in our world. They'd all rather talk by computer. And on Insomnimania, you don't even know *who* you're talking to. That's what I really hate about all this information-age stuff. It pulls people farther and farther apart. It gives them more and more excuses not to look each other in the eye, not to make commitments. Because when you're carrying on a relationship by computer, you're not dealing with an actual person."

"Sure you are," Marianne replied. "What about the real person typing the words? Or manipulating the graphics?"

"Yes, but you don't get the *whole* person. I mean, if you live with someone, or even next door to someone, sooner or later you have to deal with all their aspects—the bad temper, the prejudices, sometimes even hidden good qualities. A person doesn't just consist of what they *choose* to show you. And why do normal people need to hide behind cartoons and fictitious names, anyhow? Judson was an international businessman. Your friend apparently was a real extrovert. Why did they get so interested in network games?"

"I think Renee liked Insomnimania because it gave her a place to play with no repercussions," Marianne said. "She could make herself into whatever she wanted to be. She could be ordinary—even unattractive. One of the interesting things about the cartoon alters is that a lot of them are not good-looking. When people can be whatever they want, some of them prefer ugly—at least when the look is temporary."

"So you think it gave her a chance to express herself?"

She nodded. "Parts of herself that even Renee wouldn't express in real life. Her alter could say whatever she wanted to, do whatever she wanted to. It's a world with no AIDS, no pregnancies, no need to make lasting relationships, no spouses or bosses to keep happy."

"Do any of them seem to form lasting relationships of any kind?"

"Oh sure. Of every kind. They display affection, friendship, jealousy—the whole range of things. They welcome old friends loudly, with hugs. Some alters become inseparable, just like real people. Some of them have major fights." She hesitated, remembering. "In fact, Sapphire and Auggie used to argue all the time in Ernie's Bar."

"What did they argue about?"

"Oh, what she was wearing. What kind of drink she should have. Silly things. But Renee said that they were buddies."

Nolan drew a deep sigh. Standing here, overlooking the ocean, smelling the salt air, it was hard to believe that something so removed as a little electronic box and video screen could affect people's lives so deeply. "Sex that isn't real," he said. "Typed-out conversations between made-up characters. I still can't see why it's so engrossing." He hesitated, then asked the question that was really on his mind. "Why does it appeal to *you?*"

Marianne seemed to hesitate before answering. "For me, it's that Insomnimania is there every night, anytime I want to log into it," she said. "There's always something going on. Sometimes it's very entertaining." She paused for several long moments, then said, "There are times when, just briefly, it begins to seem real. A couple of nights since I've had Elfie on as a participant, I've almost felt that I was *hearing* the other side of the conversation, instead of just seeing it on the screen. I've almost believed that I was sitting in that bar talking. Just for a few moments. That must happen to some of the others."

And Nolan, too, remembered that moment in the casino when the voices had sounded real, when the typed lines had almost become aural, when he had almost felt like he was in a real space. At the time it had seemed like fun, but now the memory disturbed him deeply. And both Kim and Maisie had mentioned something else about Insomnimania that disturbed him, too.

"You've been using Elfie to talk to Auggie on the network, haven't you?" he asked Marianne.

"Yes. A couple of times."

"Have you found out anything we didn't know?"

"No. But he promises from time to time to let me—or rather Elfie—in on secrets. He refers to hidden places, to power."

"I doubt that he's going to give anything away."

"Maybe not. But he and Elfie are developing kind of a relationship. He does talk to her a lot." She laughed and said teasingly, "They even went to the Pleasure Dome last time."

"Elfie and Auggie had sex?"

"Yes. If you can call it that."

Nolan was surprised at his sudden surge of annoyance. When he said nothing, Marianne asked, "Does it bother you? It's only a cartoon. Nothing is really happening."

He thought about it for a moment, trying to make sense of his feelings. "Yeah," he admitted. "It bothers me a little. I mean, Elfie's too good for him. I helped build that body, remember."

"Actually, to have sex they have to use their own alters—cartoons that have the appropriate equipment, you know. I had to make an alter for Elfie."

"What's she like?"

"You wouldn't want to know," Marianne said with a laugh. "You should see the one Auggie uses—almost featureless, no personality at all."

"Well, there's something that bothers me a lot more than cartoon sex. Something I wanted to talk to you about." Marianne looked at him without comment and he continued, "This just came up this morning at work. Kim explained to me how a hacker could steal passwords on Insomnimania."

"Do you mean that the Insomnimania files aren't secure? I thought the passwords were encrypted."

"They are. Do you understand exactly what that means?"

"I've read something about it. The computer scrambles the password according to some kind of formula. It only stores the scrambled version."

"That's pretty much what Kim said. But I don't see why everybody assumes that's safe, in the first place."

"It uses a mathematical algorithm to change the word to the encrypted form. Supposedly, it can't be reversed unless you have something like a Cray supercomputer. I remember seeing an example. A six-letter word was encrypted as a long string of letters and numbers mixed together, something like p-y-y-6-s-y-q-w-3-r. It's not like a code that can be matched letter for letter."

"OK, so maybe it's true that a hacker is unlikely to break encryption. But this morning Kim Pak said he knows of at least one way a hacker can get *around* it."

"I guess any system can be beaten eventually."

"The way I understand it, it's simpler than that. The hacker just inserts a program of his own that intercepts passwords *before* they're encrypted and keeps a list of them. The member gets a message that says, 'Sorry, invalid password. Please try again'—as though he had typed it incorrectly. On the second try, he logs on as usual."

He studied her face. Did she look worried for an instant? Did he imagine it or did she hesitate before she replied?

"That's really clever," she remarked. "Most people occasionally mistype a password, anyhow. I mean, even on bank machines you can get that kind of message and have to do it over. And the word you're typing doesn't show up on the screen, so you can't *see* whether you made a mistake or not."

"Kim finally got Maisie to admit that Auggie could have stolen a lot of passwords long ago—which means he could have some members' names and addresses. He could still be stealing passwords. All he'd have to do is log on under a name that the Insomnimania detection gear doesn't recognize. In other words, they can't guarantee that *any* membership information hasn't been read by Auggie."

"I thought you were convinced that Renee and Judson both just told Auggie who they were."

"I'd still rather think that than consider the implications of Kim's theory."

Marianne just looked at him for a long moment. Finally she said, "So you're saying that it's actually dangerous to associate with Auggie on the network?"

"It might be. I don't know. I don't want to take any chances on anything happening to you."

Marianne reached out and took his hand, but she said nothing.

Hand in hand, they strolled back down the pier toward the shore. Marianne caught herself staring at a heavy woman's back. *Someone like that?* In her mind she caught a glimpse of the woman in the silver dress turning toward her, of bright red lips opening, as if to tell her something.

Marianne shook her head. She didn't want to think about murderers, female or male, and she didn't want to think about computer hackers. She wanted to concentrate on her own contentment at spending this time with Nolan. *It feels like we've been together for years.* It was something she had missed since her divorce. At one point, the absence of that feeling had almost driven her back to Evan.

When you live with someone for a long time, everything becomes famil-

*iar—talents, weaknesses, manias, prejudices, delights, all become famil-
iar—simply contained in that person's presence. Whether you like what you
know or not, you do know them well.*

When she had moved to Santa Barbara, she had been keenly
aware of being in a world full of strangers. Becoming accustomed
to the new distance from the people around her had been slow
and painful.

Stephen had never seemed familiar to her. He looked good,
behaved well, was reasonably intelligent and entertaining. She wondered whether, if things had kept going without interruption, she
would have married Stephen. *If I did, I would barely notice the change.*
Life would continue. She would do her work, he would do his, they
would appear together at social occasions. They would politely gloss
over the rough edges and weak spots as they appeared.

In that sense, she thought, Nolan was going to be more like
Evan—there was no ignoring his humanity, his maleness, his presence. When she glanced up at him, she saw the slight perspiration
on his forehead. A stir deep in her body reminded her how his face
had looked after they had made love last night, when he had turned
on his back beside her and pulled her to him.

Halfway back, they stopped at one of the restaurants on the pier
and found a table by a large window overlooking the beach and the
ocean. They ordered sandwiches and beers.

"Marianne," Nolan said, ignoring the shakiness in his own voice.
"What are you and I going to do?"

"Tonight we're going back to your house and order a pizza and
make mad, passionate love. Tomorrow I'm going to get all busi-
nesslike, go back to Santa Barbara, and blow everybody away with
my wonderful design work."

"You know that's not what I mean."

"Doesn't it seem kind of soon to talk about anything further in
the future?"

"No."

"You're absolutely right. It doesn't."

She studied the bubbles in her beer and pressed her lips together.
When she didn't say anything more, Nolan felt a pang of fear. He
had the feeling that this wasn't going too well—and it *had* to go well.
He wanted it to with all his heart.

"I want us to move in together as soon as possible," he said. She looked up. He could see the flush in her face, the emotion in her eyes. But he could also see that she was holding back.

"You know I want that, too," she said. "But I have some real reservations, some real problems dealing with . . ."

"I have real problems with our *not* being together."

"So do I," she said. Now he could see that there were tears in her eyes. "What do you want, Nolan? Do you want to be a Los Angeles homicide detective forever? What am I supposed to do—wait at home every night, hoping you'll make it back alive? I mean, I suppose I could find a job in the city, but I don't think I could stand the life you lead." She wiped her eyes, then repeated, "What do you *want?*"

I want you. But he knew that wasn't what she meant. He was stunned for a moment. "I don't know," he said. "When was the last time I decided to do something just because I *wanted* to do it? I can't remember. For a long time it was like I had *become* a family, there was no separate me any more. In a way, Louise and I weren't even a couple. Everything, all the decisions, involved what we *all* did."

"You're not that person any more," she said.

"I know. I keep all those photos around to remind me who I was. It was the only point of reference I had."

But what were his options now? How could he make them include this woman? He quickly, unhesitatingly, told her about Crazy Syd. He told her how Syd wanted to retire, and how he had been after Nolan to take the job. He saw that she looked puzzled. Somehow he had to find a way to explain it to her. It was terribly important that she understand what he was saying.

"So have you told Syd anything one way or the other?" Marianne asked.

"Not definitely, but I really think it's what I want, Marianne," Nolan said with a sudden certainty. "I want to be in a smaller town, know the people I'm working with better—a community, you know, if there is any such thing anymore. It would be good just to live among people without being the adversary. That's what I want. But only if you'll come with me. I want you to marry me, or at least go with me, whatever suits you."

Marianne began to stammer helplessly.

"Nolan, Oregon is beautiful, but . . . I have a *job,* darling. How could I find a job in a place like that? What could an interior designer possibly do . . . ?"

Nolan broke into a great laugh.

Marianne looked dismayed.

"What's so funny?" she asked.

But Nolan laughed so hard that for a few minutes he couldn't speak. He saw her sitting there with that puzzled expression on her face, and it set him off again.

"What do you think, they don't have *electricity* in Oregon?" Nolan said at last. "They don't have phone lines? Isn't that the whole point of this electronic cottage shit—that it doesn't matter where you are when you modem in the work? Honey, a couple of weeks ago, your office was in a hotel room. And just this morning, it was in my *house,* for Christ's sake! Why shouldn't it be up in the Oregon wilderness somewhere?"

Marianne stared at him with her mouth open.

"Nolan, I'm not making any promises just yet," she said. "But I'm going to ask you a question, and I want you to answer me absolutely honestly. Do you promise?"

"Sure," Nolan said, still laughing a little.

"I'm serious."

"OK," Nolan said, silencing himself a little. "So am I."

"What if—and I do mean *if*—I were to say 'yes' right now? How would you react?"

What was left of Nolan's laughter faded away into a soft smile.

"It would scare the shit out of me," he said.

"And maybe—just maybe—doesn't some *tiny part* of you hope I don't have the guts to leave my life behind?"

"Maybe," Nolan said. "Just maybe."

"Because changes make life tough, right? Even when they make it better?"

"That's right."

It was Marianne's turn to laugh now—and her laughter rang loudly through the little restaurant.

"And who was it who just told me about how awful computer technology was? How it pulls people farther and farther apart? How it gives them excuses not to look each other in the eye, not to make commitments?"

"Sounds like the information age just stripped all our excuses away, huh?" Nolan said.

Then he said, "I love you."

"I love you, too," Marianne said.

Marianne raised her glass of beer up to his in a toast.

"Here's to having no excuses," she said.

"I'll drink to that," Nolan replied.

10110

DIALOGUE BETWEEN
A PRIEST AND
A DYING MAN

I T WAS TWO-THIRTY WEDNESDAY MORNING. HOWARD CRONIN
jogged out of his own affluent neighborhood, across a four-lane
intersection with scarcely any traffic, through a narrow district
of parking lots and convenience stores. His breath steamed in the
sharp air, but the night was warmer than most at this time of year.
The gracefully arranged paradise of three-story houses with great
sloping lawns scattered along gently curving lanes suddenly seemed
far behind him. Now he was in an interminably damp, litter-strewn,
graffiti-riddled, vastly more dangerous world. He had been jogging
this way several nights a week recently, but the reality change never
ceased to startle him. Why wasn't there more of a buffer zone
between the reasonably rich and the unreasonably poor? In the not-
too-distant past, he had taken no notice of such conundrums. But
now, he couldn't help but notice.

Howard had three months to live. At least that was the best he
could figure. Three months before that, after undergoing prolonged, painful, and ultimately unsuccessful surgeries and transfu-
sions, he had been given six months. In the three months since then,

his team of doctors had refused to offer any kind of an update. Were they too cowardly to speak directly with him about his impending death? Perhaps his doctors felt that they were above talking to any of their patients. Perhaps a common quack would be more forthcoming. Howard had decided not to worry himself about it too much. Life was, indeed, short.

Back at the house, his wife and three children were fast asleep. Tomorrow morning they would all ask about his night—avoiding the little irony of a dying man insisting on late-night health jogs—and he would lie and recite a nondescript itinerary of their immediate environs. No need to worry them with details of his actual route. His family and friends knew that he had been an inveterate insomniac all his life. None of them were surprised that this condition had worsened considerably during the last few months. The thing they would find difficult to believe was that he jogged through these parts of town—and that he was on his way to church.

Four black teenagers, white sneakers and sweatshirts gleaming against the night, rounded the nearest street corner and began to approach Howard. He felt a burst of animal fear and xenophobia, then was dismayed at the grimy texture of his own bigotry. He wished he could scour it out of his mind. But he was a well-off man jogging through a poor and violent neighborhood in a designer sweatsuit. Didn't he have every good reason to be wary?

The kids were less than half a block away now. Their voices had just become audible. They seemed too animated, too cheerful to be planning to attack him. But might that simply be a tactic? Street punks surely knew how to use the element of surprise in just this sort of way.

At less than twenty feet away, one of the youths silently stepped away from the others, moving to Howard's right, away from the street toward the line of buildings. Howard would have to walk the narrow path between the isolated youth and his still-chattering companions on the curb side of the sidewalk.

Apprehension abruptly turned into burning terror and paranoia. He fleetingly studied the incongruity of a dying man being afraid of death. How could that be? Well, the answer was simple enough. He had been assured a quiet death in bed, and now he had brought himself face to face with the possibility of serious and perhaps crippling injury. Death wasn't nearly so frightening as physical pain. But what the hell was he going to do? The youths had definitely seen him.

Then the young men—the three on his left and the one on his right—brushed past him, towering above him, still chattering as if he wasn't there. He wanted to turn and look, to see if the quartet had resumed its original formation, but forced himself to keep on walking. He was sure now that the one youth had split away from the others with no other purpose than to scare him half to death. His suspicion was confirmed by a burst of laughter at his back.

His face burned with anger. In his imagination, he pictured himself turning and rushing upon the boys, drawing a hidden, nonexistent weapon—a knife, he thought. As he kept jogging steadily toward his destination, Howard Cronin imagined himself slicing the four teenagers to terrified, bloody ribbons.

The church came into view. It was a dark, regal, Romanesque structure, jarring in its sordid surroundings. It had been there for a long time, standing strong while the neighborhood around it had undergone a de-evolution into impending chaos. Howard had driven past the church many times and knew it was the one place of worship where he could be sure not to encounter any friends or acquaintances. By coming here so late at night, he was absolutely confident of his anonymity. He could have driven, of course, but taking the risk—coming on foot—was more like an act of penitence.

Howard stepped through the broad, open doors into a richly gilded sanctuary dimly lit by votive candles. He had never encountered anyone here, and the church appeared empty again tonight. He was always a little surprised to find it unlocked. At this hour, in this neighborhood, even the most faithful parishioners stayed away. He did not even sense the presence of an omnipotent deity, but of course, Howard had not believed in God since he was a teenager.

As his clattering footsteps echoed noisily through the sanctuary, Howard marveled that such a lavish interior, so open and unprotected, had not been looted by the youths outside. *It's enough to reawaken a man's faith.* On that note, he knelt before the altar.

"In the name of the Father, the Son, and the Holy Ghost," he whispered, making the sign of the cross. Then he slid into a pew and settled into a meditative silence, waiting for a welcome sign of sleepiness to set in before his perilous return home.

Then he heard a noise—a slight rustling. He looked up and barely glimpsed a robed figure stepping into the confessional. *A priest!* he thought with surprise. It had barely occurred to him that this church even had a priest. In an odd way, the idea irritated him. He had come to think of the church as his own, private sanctum. What business did anybody, even a priest, have intruding here?

Howard almost fled right then and there. But he quickly reminded himself that the priest probably did not much care whether Howard believed in God or not. Offering comfort was the man's job, and comfort was sorely lacking in Howard's sterile and now-fleeting life. He rose to his feet and walked toward the confessional.

"Keeping rather late hours, Father?" asked Howard Cronin, peering into the confessional.

"God knows no business hours, my son," said the unseen priest cheerfully. "Besides, I might ask you the same question. At least *I'm* not far from home."

Then came a slight, awkward silence. Howard stepped into the dim space, sitting down next to the latticework that separated him from the priest. He felt something slick and crackly on the seat and wall behind him, as though someone had covered the inside of the confessional with plastic. *To keep it clean?*

"Bless me, Father, for I have sinned," said Howard, making the sign of the cross again, listening with dismay to the mechanical, rote quality of his own voice. Could this procedure possibly offer him any comfort? *Was* it anything more than mere procedure?

"How long has it been since your last confession?" asked the priest.

"I don't know. Many, many years."

"Then you are more troubled than I had even thought. I've noticed your visits. Three times a week or so, you come to pray at just this hour. Whenever you come, I've guessed that you struggle with yourself, trying to decide whether to confess your sins or not."

"I've never noticed that the confessional was open, father," said Howard, trying to be diplomatic. The truth was that confession had not crossed his mind.

"What is it that you need to tell me, my son?" said the priest.

To Howard's overwhelming embarrassment, his mind suddenly turned a complete blank. Why could he not think of any sins? What, exactly, did he want to confess? He could think of nothing precise to say. He was an outwardly gentle man who had never actually struck anyone in anger. He'd been ruthless in business, but had never done anything truly dishonest or illegal. During twelve years of marriage, he'd never actually been unfaithful. He'd never *actually done* a lot of things. Now that a priest was waiting, did he have nothing interesting to confess?

"I seem . . . to be a little tongue-tied, Father," he apologized.

"Take your time, my son."

"It's just that I can't think of anything very specific."

"Remember that transgressions can take many forms," prodded the priest gently.

A blazing clarity filled Howard's mind—like a spotlight turned on a stage where the cartoon image of a dark-robed friar rolled about in a sexual frenzy with three cartooned females. Laughing as though deranged, the friar rapaciously entered, one after another, every orifice the women provided. Worse, Howard could not avoid recognizing the distinctive animalistic characteristics of one of the women—a long catlike tail, a light orange fur covering her body.

Sins of the mind! Terrible thoughts, violent thoughts, depraved thoughts, thoughts that came to him on the brink of sleep and that he had delighted in acting out in the cartoon world of Insomnimania. But he had not taken the nun that Auggie offered—surely that counted for something! Then Howard's heart sank again. He had *wanted* the nun, that precise nun, just as he had wanted so much to follow Auggie deeper into that world of power and pleasure. He had been startled that Auggie knew about the hatred he had so long suppressed. But he had been stopped only because his impending death had reawakened this remnant from childhood, this fear for his own soul. That had driven him to refuse.

And in an instant, Howard knew that the priest was right. He *had* been coming here in the unconscious hope of making a confession. This fervent desire was what had been driving him here all along. And what about God? In another moment, would he realize that he'd been a religious man all these years without even knowing it? He braced himself for whatever stunning revelations lay ahead.

Howard's next words came to him slowly and painfully, as befitted the start of a truly awful confession. "In my dreams," he murmured, savoring his anguish, "I am an adulterer, a rapist, and . . . worse, much worse."

Then it was over before it had even started. He had expected a vile outpouring of nefarious imaginings. Was this all he had to say?

The priest actually sounded a bit disappointed. "We are *all* such things in our dreams, my son. Does it shock you to hear a priest say this?"

"I don't suppose so," said Howard. And indeed, why *should* it be shocking to learn that a priest occasionally had depraved dreams just like anyone else? But Howard remembered his violent thoughts toward the youngsters on the street such a short time ago. And now he half-remembered even darker, drowsing caprices on that late-night computer network—games and fancies that often preceded his guilty visits here, but that grew murky in his memory almost as soon as they happened. He knew that his own case was much more serious. Much, much more. And it was made urgent by his approaching death. *If only I could tell the father the truly degenerate state of my soul. If only I had the words . . .*

"You surprise *me*, though," continued the priest. "I don't believe I've ever heard anyone confess misdeeds committed only in sleep. Perhaps everyone should do so. But perhaps not. Are we free to make moral choices in our dreams? Does free will exist in that realm? If not, why should anyone confess transgressions committed there?"

Howard did not know what to say. He wanted catharsis, absolution, transfiguration, not a theological lecture about sin and redemption. And he felt more and more embarrassed at his muteness, his inability to articulate his sins. The whole thing was turning out wrong after all. After a few moments, Howard just wanted to get out of there.

Can't he prescribe a batch of Hail Marys and be done with it?

"You sure do talk a lot, Father," said Howard with a nervous laugh.

"Sorry," said the priest benignly. "It's this graveyard shift, I guess. It brings out the gab in me."

Howard thrashed about in his thoughts, still groping for something to say. If he left the church now, he would feel more burdened than ever. Should he have made a list?

Then he realized something. He had misled the father. The priest supposed that he was speaking of "dreams" only in the most ordinary, literal sense. Now, perhaps, he could make himself understood.

"When I say that I have sinned in my dreams," said Howard, "I *don't* mean during my nightly rest. The fact is, I barely sleep at all. I have—how can I put it?—waking dreams, or barely waking dreams. I consider myself responsible for their immorality. You see, I . . . engage in wicked games, in fantasies."

"Ah, you are a novelist, then," said the priest with an undercurrent chuckle. "I'd love to ask what books you've got in the stores. Maybe I've even read some of them. But of course, that wouldn't be a proper question. Well, this *is* a new one! Fiction writers never come to me, confessing the sins of their make-believe characters. I've always wondered why not. But again, we must consider the question of culpability. Did Dante Alighieri sin in portraying an eternal realm filled to the brim with unpardonable reprobates?"

Howard felt a slight surge of anger at the priest's increasingly facile tone. He had a fleeting impulse to put his fist through the delicate lattice and seize the priest by the lapel and shout obscenities at him. Should he confess that, too?

"No, Father, you don't understand," sputtered Howard. "These games involve . . . women, pain, indecent acts."

"Do you *believe* that these are *real* women?" asked the priest. "That they experience *real* pain?" Any sign of levity had abruptly left his voice.

Howard was startled, partly at the uncanniness of the priest's question, partly by own utter inability to answer it. *Did* those anonymous carnal scenes constitute real adultery, real infidelity? And *did* those games with straps and chains and razor-sharp instruments engender genuine pain? If so, who *experienced* that pain? He thought, too, of those even bleaker episodes that took place just past the edge of sleep's dark recess—episodes during which he committed acts of hazily remembered violence. Howard felt tears pouring down his cheeks—real tears, although he was not sure where they came from.

"I don't know, Father," he said in a low, choked whisper. "Does it matter? Is a sin of the mind any less of a sin than an outward act? I don't want to discuss it. I only want to be absolved."

"I cannot absolve you of your sins, my son," said the priest sadly.

Howard dropped his head and sobbed quietly. *Of course. How can I be absolved? How can I be truly penitent? I don't even know the extent of my sins.*

Then the priest said, "I *can* absolve you of your virtues."

Howard looked up, startled out of his grief. "What?" he whispered stupidly.

"Why do you wish absolution for your sins?" murmured the priest soothingly. "Your sins are what are finest and most noble about you. Let me prove it to you. It is easy to say, 'Father, I have sinned.' But can you say, with the same simplicity, that you have done something *good*? Is there a *verb* for committing a virtuous act? No, of course not. This is because we hold good deeds in utmost contempt—and rightly so. Would the lives of the saints be of the slightest interest without their sins? Does anybody really care about their eventual redemption? We revere the Apostle Paul, less because he spread the Gospel than because he persecuted Christians, and his name would still be held in awe had his conversion on the road to Damascus never taken place. Our sins are holy, not our virtues. So confess to me your virtues."

The priest's voice had changed from comforting gentleness to grim, quiet accusation. Dazed, Howard found himself unable to reason or think. He was seized with exhaustion—the same dizzying weariness in which he experienced his blackest fantasies.

"Don't toy with me, father," whispered Howard desperately. "I am a dying man. I am in fear for my soul."

"Your soul is a fraud," hissed the priest. "It is a sham of the ages. You are random bits of information, no soul. Don't tell me that you fear for something which you do not have."

"I have no virtues," Howard said at last, with a strange mixture of exalted pride and terrible regret.

"You lie to me, my son."

"No."

"You do. You have committed the grievous virtue of *forbearance*. You have shown shocking and unnatural restraint in not acting out your desires—in not *perpetrating* them in word and deed. Do you wish to die with such an appalling burden of decency upon your shoulders?"

"No," said Howard.

"And do you sincerely repent the virtue of forbearance?"

"I repent. I honestly and sincerely repent."

Then came the chilling sound of infantile giggling from the other side of the lattice.

"Well, then, my dear Friar John," said the priest, "I shall now absolve you."

Howard felt a huge shudder of surprise.

"Who are you?" exclaimed Howard.

The priest's childish laughter continued. "Peace, my son. Be still. Leave everything to me. Father Auggie will take care of everything."

Auggie!

Howard's head whirled with exhausted confusion. What did he feel? Was it delight or dread? Or had he entered a realm of half-consciousness in which delight and dread were one and the same?

The laughter on the other side of the lattice subsided with a sigh, and the unseen priest began to murmur softly.

"May the angels lead you into paradise . . ."

Those words.

". . . may the martyrs come to welcome you . . ."

Why were they so familiar?

". . . and take you to the holy city . . ."

Where had he heard them before?

". . . the new and eternal Jerusalem."

Then he remembered.

Over my father's corpse.

And who had spoken them?

The priest.

Now he knew what words those were.

A prayer for the dead.

But for whose death?

If it was for him, wasn't it just a little premature?

Howard was too sick and dizzy to think another thought. Thoughts were useless, anyway. A wild rushing in his veins dictated his every movement. It was similar to the rush he had felt when he had faced the young men on the street a short while ago, but it was far too intense, far too pure to be described as panic. Howard rose to his feet, swaying giddily but alertly. He shoved his fingers through the lattice holes and yanked. A square piece of the lattice fell away with a rattling echo, revealing a gaping, black emptiness. Had the priest vanished into thin air?

Then a small but intense light blazed in the darkness—a tiny penlight illuminating a ghastly, mosaiclike face composed of bits of white and red and black. It was a familiar face. It was Auggie's face. And now another shape appeared in that darkness. It took Howard at least a second to realize that it was a gun.

Howard's eyes darted around the sanctuary. No one else was present, least of all God. His gaze settled at last on the garish, cloth-woven face and the looming gun barrel. The flood of adrenaline ebbed away. Only now that his terror was gone did he realize how frightened he had just been. But now he almost laughed at the idea of fear. He had just been absolved. Eternity itself could hold no terrors for him.

With a last flash of idle curiosity, Howard wondered how much noise the shot would make in the echo-infested church. It seemed a pity that he might never hear it.

10111

RESEARCH

"HOW MANY YOU GOT NOW?"
        Nolan flipped the pages of his notebook. "Six of them—
all in different parts of the country. Any of these mean
anything to you?" He read the list aloud:

Rachel Morton, Atlanta, attorney

Joseph P. Brookmeyer, New York, investment analyst

Myron Stalnaker, Omaha, bank loan officer

D. D. Rose, Chicago, owner of a major fashion outlet

Ronald Sandusky, San Francisco, publisher

Robert J. Owens, Detroit, auto industry v.p.

Coffey shook his head. "Never heard of any of them. What have
you got on them?"

"Damned little. We've checked their recent travel, bank accounts,
credit card use."

"The one in Atlanta is a woman?"

"Yeah. So is D. D. Rose. But both of them were apparently right
where they belonged the night that Renee Gauld was murdered. It's
the same with all the rest of them, too. None of them was in L.A.
when either Judson or Gauld was killed."

"We've gotten some of these phone numbers more than once,"
Clayton said.

"Also, during the past two weeks, they've all been on Insomnimania using other alters—the ones legitimately listed in their membership data," Nolan added. "We had the guys at Insomnimania check that for us."

"So what could they tell? Are these people meeting on the network? What do they say to each other?"

"Maisie and Pritchard have been recording everything Auggie does, but they haven't seen the clown interacting with any of these particular alters. As far as we know, none of these people have made any effort to meet each other, on the network or off."

"This is nothing, Grobowski," Coffey yelled, slamming his palm down on the papers covering his desk. "This leaves us absolutely nowhere. What do you propose to do next?"

"What I *want* is to tap their phones and search their houses."

"Oh, sure. Fat chance of finding a judge who'll let you do that."

"I know that. We haven't been able to get a single court order for a phone tap. And the cops in all those other localities sure aren't interested in doing surveillance on an L.A. case. I can't blame them. They've got their own business to take care of. I don't think we've got a prayer of getting search warrants, either."

"The other departments think it's a joke," Clayton said. "They say whoever's doing the cartoons probably has inside information—a friend right here in our department, something like that. We're the laughingstock in at least six cities around the country."

"What about the hacker you found here?" Coffey asked.

"Clay's talked to him a couple of times," Nolan said.

"Yeah," Clayton said, "I've been keeping in touch. And I'm beginning to wonder if he's maybe some new kind of idiot savant. He's apparently hot on computer systems, but he can be foggy or downright stupid about anything else. He wanders off in some pretty strange directions. I'd almost guess he's heavy into drugs or something, but Pritchard and Maisie both say he's never been part of that scene."

"He admits creating Auggie but denies operating him now," Nolan said. "And we've never seen his phone number come up in connection with Auggie."

Coffey fished around in his desk for another cigar. "The D.A.'s getting real unpleasant about the lack of leads on these two killings. And there's pressure coming in from Chicago about Judson. Leave me a copy of that list. I'll phone some friends I've got in a few of those cities, call in a few favors—see if I can get a little support."

"Friends?" Nolan joked at Coffey. "You mean you've actually got *friends,* Captain?"

"In *other cities,* Grobowski," the captain grumbled. "I make a point of not having any in L.A. Can't afford the upkeep. Now make me a copy of that list and get the fuck out of here."

Nolan did so, then went back to his desk. He felt too good today to be bugged by the captain's temper.

At least one *thing in my life seems to be working out.* He had to squelch the giggle he could feel rising to his throat. Last night he'd put in a call to Crazy Syd. Yes, the job was still open—Syd would send him the information and the application forms. With Syd's recommendation, the job was practically his. And Nolan felt pretty sure Marianne would go with him to Oregon—not *absolutely* sure, but pretty close to it.

Nolan realized that Clayton was standing by his desk, riffling through notes.

"I take it you're still convinced that all those good people are taking turns logging on as Auggie," Clayton said.

"Well, what do you think they're doing?"

"I don't know. But your theory makes more sense to me than the idea of some superhacker using all their telephone numbers. The question is, why are they doing it?"

"Dunno. Maybe it's some new kind of club. Maybe it's a conspiracy to overthrow the government."

Clayton shook his head.

"Coffey's right," Clayton said. "We're nowhere."

"No laughs," Nolan agreed. "No threads. Nothing. Not even any suspects for you to work over. We've got two lousy cases, Clay. Or one lousy case, take your pick."

"It's really getting on my nerves," Clayton said.

"One thing I'm wondering is, why a clown? If these upper-class citizens are playing some kind of network game, is there some reason why they all use a clown? I mean, I *know* clowns can be scary. Zoomer wasn't the only kid in the world to be scared by one. But is that enough of a reason? Why that particular *mask*?"

Clayton thought for a moment, then said, "Maybe it's not a mask."

"What's that supposed to mean?" Nolan scoffed.

"Just a thought," Clayton said.

"What are you saying we're dealing with? A real clown?"

"I'm just saying maybe it's not a disguise. In some way we're just not seeing, Auggie might be exactly what he seems to be."

"That doesn't make sense."

"I know it sounds crazy. It's just a feeling. I wish I understood it myself."

Nolan stared at Clayton for a moment. Then he got up and shoved his papers into a briefcase. He put on his jacket. "See you later," he said, and headed for the door.

"Where are you going?" Clayton called after him.

"To the library."

Marianne steered her car along the highway to Santa Barbara in relatively light mid-morning traffic. *I'm in love with Nolan Grobowski.* She laughed, then said it aloud:

"I'm in love with Nolan Grobowski."

She could picture him sitting at the kitchen table, laughing; reclining on the floor in front of the fire, glancing up at her with his eyes full of the questions that he had finally asked yesterday at the pier. Yes, it was definite. She loved him. She was in love with him. And things were going to work out for them.

When Marianne got home, one of the messages on her answering machine was from Evan.

"Just wanted to talk to you babe, make sure everything's going OK."

He had been in the habit of checking in every two or three months, so the call wasn't a surprise. What made Marianne feel strange was realizing that Evan apparently didn't even know about Renee's death—much less about everything else happening in her life.

Marianne decided that Evan probably just wanted to tell her about his latest shows, and she didn't feel like listening just now—much less telling him awful and confusing news. She would call him tomorrow. Or maybe next week.

Leaving Evan had seemed to her like running away from an extended adolescence. But instead of progressing in any direction, her life had become like a closed loop, like the computer animation of Renee sitting in the bathtub, washing, bubbles rising. Somehow, nothing had happened. Until now.

Something definitely is happening now.

∎

The public library was quite busy that day. Although there were six computer terminals in the central lobby, Nolan had to wait in line behind seven people to get to use one of them.

Guess that's one thing the electronic age hasn't gotten rid of. Standing in lines.

When Nolan finally reached a terminal, he struck the search command for "subject." He typed in the word "CLOWNS." Twenty-five titles came up. Nolan jotted down the call numbers for the five most pertinent-looking books and went to look for them.

As it turned out, most of the books were on the floor above him. As Nolan trudged up the stairs, he mulled again over the limitations of information technology.

It doesn't stop me from having to walk up stairs.

Most of the volumes were bunched together on a shelf that also included books on circuses, cinema, theater, and stage illusionism. Nolan took down a book that appeared to be a history of clowns. He immediately turned to the index, looking for the name "Auggie."

The name was nowhere to be found.

However, Nolan's eye floated down the column just a little farther to where he found the name "Auguste." Nolan eagerly turned to the pages where Auguste was described. He found that Auguste was traditionally a patched and ragged character with a brightly painted face—a buffoon, a prankster, a drunkard, an oaf, a hobo, a mendicant. Nolan remembered Zoomer's description of the clown he had seen in his infancy—the clown upon whom he had based Auggie . . .

". . . a put-upon, battered fellow with a smashed derby and patched pants and a bright red nose . . ."

Auguste, Auggie. Obviously the same character.

The book went on to explain that Auguste served his spectators as a kind of surrogate, rampaging id—bringing all kinds of wish fulfillment to the audience by acting out of purely elemental, animal instincts. Sometimes Auguste was thwarted in his foolishness and sometimes he was successful, but he was ultimately indomitable and indestructible.

The book also described Auguste's nemesis—Pierrot, the White Clown, a comic symbol of authority, sentimentality, and respectability. Nolan remembered Zoomer also describing such a character . . .

"A white-clad gentleman with great red buttons and a silly conical cap," Zoomer had called him. "He gave all the orders, and most of them were stupid orders. He acted just like my father or mother."

And indeed, that very quality was what made Pierrot—the White Clown—such a successful butt to all of Auguste's tomfooleries. Audiences identified Pierrot with bosses, parents, politicians, policemen, all the forces they futilely wanted to resist in real life, but *could* resist vicariously through the disobedient Auguste.

Nolan skimmed the other books on clowns for information on Auguste, but they reiterated the same basic facts—that Auguste was the renegade, the rebel, the fool.

Nolan remembered what Clayton had said just a little while ago: *"Maybe it's not a mask."*

Deep in his gut, Nolan felt that Clayton was somehow right. But he didn't know how. And he still couldn't explain why a bunch of well-to-do computer-network users would rally around this particular image to commit simulated murders—much less *real* murders.

But one of the books concluded its discussion of Auguste with a terse, perfunctory, but startling observation: "The Auguste continues an ancient line of archetypal tricksters."

Archetypal. Trickster.

He hurried to the nearest dictionary and looked up the definition for the word "archetype." The word was already reasonably familiar to Nolan, but he wanted to refresh himself. The first definition the dictionary offered was: "The original pattern or model of which all things of the same type are representations or copies."

The second definition consisted of only one word—"Idea."

"But that's not all it means!" Nolan grumbled loudly enough to elicit a few irate "shushes" from some of the surrounding patrons.

Nolan sat down in the nearest chair and tried to remember. In a psychological sense, an *archetype* was an idea shared by all people in what Carl Jung called the "collective unconscious." Archetypes included concepts and figures like the Hero, the Child, the Earth Mother, Birth, Rebirth, Death. In theory, these ideas were not *learned* during a lifetime, but were an innate aspect of all people's consciousness.

So the trickster is an archetype.

He headed to the nearest cluster of computers and again found himself standing in line. When he finally got access to one of the terminals, he struck the search command for "subject" and typed in the word "TRICKSTER."

To Nolan's dismay, fifteen titles appeared—and from their call numbers, they seemed to be scattered all over the library. But even Nolan's discouragement produced a small realization . . .

This machine is playing the Auguste on me. It's prankishly sending me on a wild goose chase. And I, the dogged, authoritative, and responsible White Clown, am the butt of all its jokes—just like I've been on this whole case.

Nolan jotted down a list of call numbers and lumbered off in search of books.

After the meeting with the design team, Marianne knew that she would have to do some research for the new project. The proposed office building was going to be interesting enough, but she much preferred designing interiors for private homes and small offices, giving attention to her client's individuality rather than to corporate identity.

She felt momentarily stumped by the project. The building was a collection of forms that incorporated hints of Ionic columns into a simple modern structure. The Greek and Roman overtones contributed a certain dignity, a sense of heritage—at least the clients thought so. The architects thought the combination was sophisticated and amusing, a venture into post-modernism. Still, it was a business office. Marianne couldn't exactly adorn it with thrones, chaise lounges, and cushions.

Marianne called up her address book on the screen and quickly located the network connection she wanted. She punched a code that dialed into VAX computers not unlike the one running Insomnimania. Anyone subscribing to this service had access to CD–ROM disks with many thousands of images. Some universities had made design collections available on-line for their students since the late 1980s. Now firms like Marianne's could bring several major image libraries right to their designers.

In a matter of minutes, Marianne was browsing through a selection of Roman wall paintings, looking for an idea to set the appropriate tone for her client.

She stopped and smiled, contemplating the enormity of the system she was using. The computers controlling the images were on the other side of the country. The original design collections were located in several different states.

Nolan was right. I can do this kind of research from absolutely anywhere. Things really are going to work out for us.

■

Nolan now had at least two dozen books spread out on the table in front of him, all opened in various places, all offering varied and sometimes conflicting information on the nature of the trickster archetype. One thing was abundantly clear. All cultures had their tricksters.

Just like Auggie, these figures were pranksters, loafers, and rebels. But they were something more besides. They were divinities—quite literally gods. They were not merely to be mocked and laughed at (although it was quite appropriate to do so), they were also to be worshipped as the most powerful of spirits.

He had read about mischievous Spiders, Rabbits, and Tortoises of African tribes, the Raven of the Inuits of the American Northwest, the Norse Wotan, the Polynesian Maui, the Navajo Coyote, and the Kiowa Saynday. Many of those tricksters performed highly exalted cosmic functions. Many were generous, Promethean fire givers. Some were protectors of human beings. And several were named as the creator of the earth and all its people. Coyote and Saynday, in particular, were as renowned for their benevolence and power as for their stupidity and foolishness.

One scholar even went so far as to suggest that the ancient Hebrew Yahweh, the ancestor of the Judeo-Christian God or Jehovah, was possibly an imp and a trickster in his original incarnation—capricious, foolish, and unpredictable, and anything but the wise, kind, gentlemanly God of modern religion.

Even the tarot deck bore out these ideas. In the numbering of the trump cards, the Fool was a zero. This undoubtedly represented the Fool's I.Q., but it was also a number of great power. After all, the discovery of the number zero had liberated mathematics, allowing humankind to contemplate the idea if not the fact of infinity. And the shape of a zero was a circle—an infinite thing without a beginning or end.

Nolan closed his eyes and his brain reeled.

So in the most primitive parts of our minds, we still conceive creation itself to be a wild, chaotic joke, the drunken dream of a baggy-pantsed, red-nosed clown-god. And we humans—in all our civilized glory—are his vain and petulant Pierrots, sometimes worshipping Auguste, but more often railing against him.

And Nolan remembered a particular book of his youth—the wonder and awe he had felt while reading Melville's *Moby-Dick*.

Melville had portrayed the whiteness of his whale in much the same way as the tarot portrayed the zero of its Fool—as an awful, mute, unintelligible nothing that nevertheless contained the unutterable truth of absolutely everything.

Somehow, Nolan was sure that all this had to do with Auggie.

Nolan heard himself whisper words that, over all these years, he had not forgotten, could not ever forget . . .

"Wonder ye then at the fiery hunt?"

That night, Elfie had barely gotten seated in Ernie's Bar when Auggie appeared. He came to her table immediately and launched into an inquiry without any other greeting.

AWGY>WHER HAV U BEN?

L-FY>I HAD 2 GO OUT OF TOWN.

AWGY>I LOKED 4 U EVRY NIT. IT WUZN'T VERE NIS UV U 2 JST DISAPEEER LIK THAT.

L-FY>U'R RIGHT. I'M SORREE AWGY. IT WAS A PROBLEM THAT CAM UP SUDDENLY.

AWGY>NEX TIM PLES LET ME NO. U CUD JUS LEV A MESSAJ.

L-FY>I WIL, I PROMIS.

Apparently satisfied, Auggie sat down at the table and ordered drinks for both of them. Then he turned his attention to Elfie. Marianne relaxed and allowed the conversation to flow naturally.

After only a few moments of small talk, Auggie said, "I was hoping you'd be here tonight. I don't want you to miss my performance."

"What are you performing?"

"Another masterpiece. Another of my original dramas of life and death."

Marianne froze. She saw again the haunting red blotch across the garlands and the sun. First in pixels and then in blood, the line of a drip followed a curved edge. It seemed to her that whole minutes passed before Elfie could reply . . .

"You're doing another snuff?"

Apparently her long hesitation was only in her own mind, because Auggie did not comment on it. "Yes. You will watch it, won't you? I'm very proud of this one. It will happen in just a few hours, at one o'clock."

Another snuff! Then someone is about to be killed. No, no, of course—
someone has been killed.

"Then that means you've done it already," Elfie said.

"Done it?"

Marianne jerked her mind back from thoughts of the other double killing, the cartoon of Renee and the real death. *Back off, Elfie.*
You won't get anywhere if you accuse him of murder.

"You've already made the animation?" Elfie asked.

"Of course. Everything has been prepared. But I wouldn't say I had *done* it yet. You know it isn't real until it's presented. That's when it happens—right before your eyes."

"You didn't tell me you were planning another one."

"You weren't here."

Marianne forced herself to concentrate. She had to find out what Auggie had done.

"What's this snuff about?" Elfie asked.

"You'll have to wait and see."

"Where does it take place? Who's killed?"

"No, no, little Elfie. I'm not going to spoil it for you. You'll have to wait, just like everyone else."

Marianne geared herself up to have Elfie really prod the clown with questions. But at that moment, Auggie disappeared from the table.

Guess he didn't want to talk about it.

She logged out of the bar and out of Insomnimania.

Nolan was sound asleep when the telephone rang. He picked it up groggily, and at first couldn't understand what Marianne was trying to tell him.

"Are you listening? Auggie is putting on another snuff."

"What? When?"

"Tonight. At one o'clock. He just told me about it."

"Told you about it? You've been talking to him again?"

"Well, he was there in the bar. He spoke to me. I couldn't just ignore him."

"You know that's dangerous. We talked about the passwords. You don't want to attract that character's attention to you."

"Nolan, this is important. He just told me he's putting on another snuff. You know what that means."

"You think someone has already been killed?"

"That's the way it was with Judson and Renee."

"What did he say? What kind of person gets killed? In what kind of place?"

"He wouldn't tell me. I couldn't get anything out of him."

"I'd have been notified if something like that had happened—I mean another murder among the L.A. elite."

"Maybe it hasn't been discovered yet. You were in Renee's condo when that snuff was played."

They were silent for a moment. Then Marianne said, "Maybe it wasn't even in Los Angeles."

"Shit," said Nolan. "I'd better phone the division."

Well before one o'clock, Marianne logged Elfie back into Insomnimania. Nolan also had the network up on the little computer at his home, and Clayton watched over Kim Pak's shoulder at division headquarters. Baldwin Maisie and Ned Pritchard had several kinds of recording software running and had put Insomnimania up on a large monitor.

Hugo, the Snuff Room's master of ceremonies, finished his elaborate introduction of Auggie's upcoming snuff. Then the familiar paintbrush splashed solemn shades across the screen—gray, black, and dark blue—creating a street scene punctuated by one weak yellow light. Organ music was playing, but the music was far from solemn. It was a jaunty, dancelike Bach fugue in a major key.

The figure of a jogger trotted across the stage with exaggerated motions, then turned toward an arched entranceway. The jogger opened one of a pair of double doors and danced through the opening.

Then the scene changed. Light streamed upon the jogger's face from somewhere ahead of him. He walked forward a few steps, made a flourishing curtsey, then crossed himself. The point of view swung around again and the jogger could be seen from the side, kneeling in a pew.

In a church? Has Auggie killed someone in a church? The idea seemed particularly appalling to Marianne.

As the figure knelt, different colored lights played across him. The camera angle turned again, and the jogger could be seen standing up and stepping into a booth.

∎

"A confessional?" asked Clayton.

"That's what it looks like to me," Kim replied. "Anybody been killed in a Catholic church lately?"

"I sure haven't heard anything about it."

The jogger could clearly be seen inside his side of the booth, but the door to the priest's side remained closed. With pantomime gestures timed to the music, the jogger poured out his tortured soul to the priest. But instead of offering him comfort, the unseen priest reached out with his hand and slapped the jogger sharply on the forehead.

The jogger looked surprised for a moment, but then continued his elaborate gestures of contrition. The priest's hand appeared again, this time wielding a pair of pliers. The priest twisted the jogger's nose vigorously.

After another round of confession, the priest's hand battered the poor jogger's head with a baseball bat. Despite the stars whirling around his head, the jogger continued his confession.

Then, as the fugue approached its climax, the priest's hand appeared with a gun. A little flag announcing "BANG" popped out of the gun barrel. Little Xs crossed the jogger's eyes, and he slumped dead in his seat.

The door to the priest's side of the confessional opened, revealing Auggie himself decked out in a priest's suit. As the fugue came to a close, Auggie winked at the audience, danced over to the dead jogger, and hastily wrapped him up in a red-striped sheet. The jogger's X'd eyes could be seen between two stripes.

"Striped plastic?" Clayton wondered aloud. "A striped shower curtain or something like that?"

Then Auggie slung the wrapped body across his shoulder like a limp barber pole and turned toward the audience.

"Th-th-th-th-that's all folks!" Auggie exclaimed.

And Auggie carried the corpse out of the scene.

Kim looked up at Clayton. "It was just like a comic book," he said. "Hard to take it seriously. You think somebody was actually killed like that?"

"I'd put money on it," Clayton answered.

■

Nolan closed his eyes and shook his head.

"A church," he said. "It had to be a church."

Marianne felt her flesh crawl with horror, as though she—rather than Elfie or Babylonia—had been the lover of the clown who had just committed murder before her eyes.

"He sure carries these things off in grand style," Pritchard said with reluctant admiration. But as Pritchard turned in his swivel chair toward Maisie, he saw that his partner's face had gone completely white.

"Hey, what's the matter, fella?" Pritchard asked.

"I know who the victim was," Maisie said.

"Then you're thinking he really did somebody in?"

"Yeah."

"Who was it, then?"

"Remember that time two or three days ago, when Auggie had that big argument with that monk character, what's-his-name?"

"You mean Friar John?" Pritchard asked.

"Yeah. I think the friar got it."

"Why do you think that?"

"Auggie always argues with his victims. And this snuff had a religious setting. Auggie argues with a friar, somebody gets killed in a church." Then Maisie held his head in his hands. "Christ," he said miserably. "We had the guy's phone number. We could have called him. We could have warned him."

"Warned him of what?" Pritchard asked. "That some crazy clown disguised as a holy man was gonna whack him?"

"Well, it would have been something!" Maisie exclaimed.

"Baldy, it's just one of your hunches."

"Yeah. And are my hunches ever wrong?"

Pritchard was silent for a moment.

"Jesus," he said.

Nolan got a phone call from Baldwin Maisie early Thursday morning.

"You guys watched the Auggie snuff last night, right?" Maisie asked, sounding very edgy.

"Yeah, we saw it."

"Pritch and I think we might have ID'd the victim."

"The *victim?*"

"Not one hundred percent positively. But high probability."

"Who do you think it was?"

"A guy in Omaha."

"One of the phone numbers was in Omaha."

"Yeah, but the victim isn't the same one. He *is* an Insomnimania member, though. Or was. You gotta understand, we don't even know if this guy is really dead—we just have reason to think it might be him."

Maisie sounded extremely upset.

"OK, Maisie, calm down," Nolan said. "Just give me what you have."

"I'll send you a file to look at. It's part of the stuff we've been recording right off our own monitor. In fact, I'll send you a copy of the snuff, too. You can compare them yourself and see what you think."

"Why send it over? We can come and pick it up."

"Stay where you are. My computer will send it right to your computer."

Nolan was embarrassed at his momentary lapse into a precyber-world mentality. "I'd better let you talk to Kim Pak."

By the time the Insomnimania files came through the electronic mail, Nolan, Clayton, and Coffey were all hovering behind Kim's desk. First they saw a typed message—a name and address in Omaha. Then Kim extracted the two animation files and ran them. In the first, Auggie was in Ernie's Bar, arguing with a monk. The second file was the snuff they had watched the night before— Auggie dressed as a priest, shooting the jogger, wrapping up the body in red-striped plastic, and carrying it off.

"At least there's a religious connection," Nolan said. "And we do know that Auggie quarrels with his victims. Maisie might be on to something here."

Coffey growled. "Guess I'll call Omaha. This is gonna take some explaining, though."

Coffey disappeared into his office. After a few minutes he came out with a sour expression on his face.

"I talked to the Omaha police chief," he said to Nolan. "Now I've got a Lieutenant Michael Kelsey, homicide division, on the line. It's gonna be up to you to convince Kelsey that we're not a bunch of total looney tunes out here. If you get past Kelsey, have Pak talk to someone there about sending the files out."

Nolan got on the phone and found himself talking to Lieutenant Michael Kelsey of Omaha.

"So what's going on out there in La-La land?" inquired Kelsey in a heavy midwestern drawl. "Are you guys getting nasty karmic vibes from Omaha or some other such Shirley MacLaine New Age kind of stuff?"

Nolan sighed. He explained as simply as he could that they had some information regarding Omaha members of a computer network—information that suggested a murder might have taken place in Omaha.

"This sounds a little out of my depth," Kelsey said dubiously. "I'll tell you what. Let's have your computer man send those files along to our computer man."

Two hours later, Nolan got a call back from Kelsey. The Omaha lieutenant sounded much more somber than before.

"Yeah, we got your stuff," Kelsey said. "And we've got a corpse, too. The photos match your cartoon—body wrapped in a red-striped plastic shower curtain. He was reported missing by his family Monday morning, and they ID'd the body when we found it. The thing about the church still doesn't fit, though. The stiff was found in an open lot."

The Omaha detective went on to say that the local archdiocese was trying to help them locate the church shown in the animation.

"I'm gonna give you another name and phone number," Nolan said. "It's another guy in Omaha who's a member of the same network. We've got reason to think that he may be involved. But I'm sorry to say we haven't got anything for you to haul him in on."

"No probable cause, huh?"

"Hey, we're out here in L.A., remember? You'd better check him out, though."

Kelsey promised to let Nolan know how it worked out. Nolan hung up.

Oregon. Just keep thinking about Oregon.

Then he phoned Marianne and passed the news on to her.

Marianne walked her Renee alter over to a booth in Ernie's Bar and pressed the keys admitting her to the private space. She had earlier come on Insomnimania as Elfie, but had not been able to find Auggie anywhere.

After the snuff last night, she had slept briefly and fitfully. Tonight she had been too restless to consider going to bed. Now she felt as if she might drop off to sleep at any moment, but she was sure that if she shut down the computer she would soon be pacing the floor again, wide awake.

The Renee alter was just sitting there in the booth, looking bored.

"Let's go somewhere more interesting," Marianne said.

Thinking as little as possible, Marianne allowed her fingers to type Renee's response, allowed her voice to read the words aloud.

"Where do you have in mind?"

"The beach."

"I don't think I can make it anywhere outside the box here."

"What box?"

"Your computer."

"No, silly. I mean Babbage Beach. The one right here in Insomnimania."

"Now that's a great idea."

Marianne steered the Renee alter out of Ernie's, back to the maze, and to the icon for Babbage Beach. She double-clicked the beach icon, and the image of Renee was immediately standing on a yellow-sand beach. Renee was facing away from her. Marianne felt as though she was looking over her friend's shoulder at a late-afternoon sky filled with a preposterously outsized orange sun. While the *real* sun always looked like a flat bright disk tacked onto the sky, this simulated one appeared to be a palpable, rounded ball with a light source other than itself.

The ocean undulated like the surface of a waterbed as the sky, sun, and clouds shimmeringly reflected in its surface. The ocean's ripples grew in size and acquired expanding tufts of white as they approached the screen.

A short way ahead was a red-and-white beach umbrella.

"Let's sit there," Renee said. "Then we can talk privately." Marianne knew that the beach umbrellas operated the same as the booths in Ernie's, shielding conversation from all others.

It seemed to her that Renee walked through the sand very naturally and sat down under the umbrella quite under her own power. Marianne felt like she was just tagging along behind, not directing the action—especially when Renee took off her shoes and rolled up her red slacks.

But are those commands even in the menu? Was she actually watching this picture on the screen or was her imagination creating all this in a near-dream state? She decided it would take too much concentration to decide. She didn't care where the scene came from. She was here. And an image of Renee was right in front of her, her red slacks rolled up to her knees, wriggling her bare toes in the sand. This didn't have to *be* real. Marianne just wanted it to *seem* real for a little while.

The outsized, nursery-school sun slipped slowly toward the horizon, partially masked by slender, horizontal threads of clouds.

Marianne asked, "What are those clouds in the middle, Renee? Cirrus?"

"Don'tcha remember anything from school?" Renee replied. "Cirrus clouds are way up there. Can't even see 'em from here. Top of the screen cuts them off."

"So what are these then? Stratus maybe?"

"Wrong again, helium breath. Stratocumulus."

"No, I don't think so."

"I know my clouds, dearie."

"Where are the stratus then?"

"At the very bottom. Next to the horizon. See?"

Renee pointed to an unbroken layer of clouds just above the horizon.

"Those are nimbostratus."

"Wanna put money on it?"

"OK. You're on."

"How much?"

"Ten dollars."

"Cheapskate. You must know you're gonna lose."

The clouds chugged silently across the sky, much faster than real clouds could go, changing color as they went. At the screen's far left, the clouds made their entrances a silky white, growing more yellow as they approached the edge of the orange ball, turning a startling complementary blue as they crossed over it, becoming gray as they passed across the sky again, and finally settling into smoky blackness before exiting at the right-hand border of the screen.

The white-capped waves broke in irregular patterns against the shore, raising zesty sprays of silver pixels and a chorus of white noise. The white noise was actually a constant undertone, roaring into a crescendo with the crash of every wave. The noise lulled Marianne hypnotically. She was having trouble holding her eyes open.

Then, turning around to face Marianne, Renee said, "Listen to those waves. I think that's the most beautiful sound in the world."

"It's just white noise," Marianne said.

"I know," replied Renee. "But it's magical just the same. I like to sit here and imagine that it's all the signals, all the messages being transmitted in the whole world at this very minute—every television, radio, or telephone signal. If you listen, you can pick out some little piece of it. Listen. Listen real carefully. You'll hear a daughter talking to her mother for the first time after ten years of estrangement. They're making up. They're becoming friends again." Renee rotated to face Marianne. "Can you hear it, too?"

Marianne's eyes rolled back under her eyelids. She felt her lids droop shut. Even so, the seaside scene was still vividly painted before her. The lowermost edge of the sun had just touched the horizon now. Pretty soon, the great orange ball would disappear behind the sea. She felt too exhausted to go on with this taxing form of self-hypnosis. But she followed Renee's injunction to keep listening. The computerized noise *was* evocative—much like a conch shell's whispering "sea" sound.

And yes, it didn't take much imagination to hear two women's voices in the slow, rhythmic surges of white noise. Marianne couldn't make out their words, but both women were weeping for joy. Other conversations could be heard, too—many of them not nearly so conciliatory. There were business calls, bits of idle gossip, lovers' quarrels. And there was music, too, ranging from a Bach two-part invention to a rap song. Indeed, the surf did seem to contain an entire world of electronic messages, some sweet, some vindictive, but all reflecting an aching, universal loneliness—and all purely imaginary.

A flock of seagulls swept across the sky. The sun, which had just disappeared below the horizon, reappeared at the top of the screen and began its descent again. Marianne could barely feel her fingers fluttering across the keyboard as she tiptoed around the fringes of unconsciousness.

Am I even still awake? Am I actually dreaming?

It didn't *feel* as though she were dreaming. Her dreams were less vivid than this—and certainly less colorful. Also, there were still hints of electronic artificiality about the scene. Marianne observed that the sun did not play on Renee's face or reflect in her eyes, nor did the wind move her hair.

I forgot to give her sunglasses. But of course, Renee wasn't squinting. A puppet had no sensitivity to sunlight.

"What are you thinking about?" Marianne asked her pensive virtual friend.

"I often sit here and try to remember what the real ocean looked like," Renee said.

"What do you mean, 'often'?" Marianne asked.

"A lot," Renee said. "Frequently. Routinely. Usually. What do you think I mean?" Marianne could hear a bit of Renee's old wiseassedness pipe up.

"Well, what I mean is—you haven't even *been* here all that long."

Renee looked straight at her, her lips frozen in a partial grin, but her eyebrows tilted in uncertainty.

"What do you mean?" she asked.

"Don't you know how long it's been since you were killed?" Marianne asked.

Renee's laugh trumpeted sarcastically over the computer speaker. Marianne realized she must have dazedly struck the command for laughter. "Don't pussyfoot around, dearie," Renee said. "Go ahead. Ask the really *tough* questions."

"Sorry."

Then Renee's smile disappeared. "Your whole idea of making me up was so I'd seem *alive*, right?" she snapped, looking straight into Marianne's eyes with startling ruthlessness. "Why fuck it up by bringing my death into it?"

"I said I'm sorry."

Renee was brooding now, running her finger through the sand. No shapes appeared in the sand where Renee's finger passed. Marianne felt a pang of guilt at having been so insensitive. Her apology did not seem enough. She felt compelled to do something more to put things right. She tried in vain to remind herself that none of this was real, that she owed no explanations, no apologies to an electronic puppet. But she was in too deep. It seemed too real.

Marianne wanted to reach out and hold Renee's hand. But she was all too aware of a sheet of glass between them. She and this image could share all kinds of dreams and memories, but they couldn't do one terribly important thing. They could never touch.

Marianne was seized by a spasm of sleep. She struggled to keep her balance, fought not to fall from her chair. Her eyes fell heavily closed. She drew in her breath. Then she heard Renee calling from the depths of darkness, her voice echoing out of a long tunnel.

"Marianne? Marianne! Are you still there?"

"I'm . . . still . . . here," Marianne heard herself murmur. Then, with a tremendous effort, she yanked her eyes open. Renee was staring at her with a look of benign, smiling concern.

"Are you OK?" Renee asked. "Thought I'd lost you for a minute."

Marianne tried to answer, but found that she couldn't. Renee leaned toward her, her eyebrows knitted together with concern.

"Marianne, what's the matter?" Renee asked. "You're crying."

Marianne fingered her cheeks and discovered that they were wet with tears. She had no idea why.

"Why are you crying?" Renee insisted firmly.

Marianne was surprised at what she said next.

"I'm sorry I wasn't there that night. I'm sorry I didn't stop your killer."

She hung her head, choking on her sobs.

"I want to touch you," she said.

Renee's smile seemed to broaden sweetly.

"Marianne, there's no one to touch," she said. "There's no one here at all. You've got to get a grip on your imagination. You've got to get some sleep."

Marianne nodded dumbly. She could not argue with that. She said goodbye to Renee and shut down her computer. She got up from her chair, feeling like she was rising from a dream. Then she walked slowly and unsteadily down the hall toward the bedroom.

11000

INTIMATIONS

THE ABERNATHY PROJECT LOOKS GREAT," said DWAYNE OVER the phone. "I just got a chance to go over it thoroughly yesterday. You've really outdone yourself this time, babe."

"Thanks," Marianne replied. "I'm sorry to have taken so long with it." She had turned in the Abernathy project at the meeting on Wednesday. Now it was late Friday afternoon. She had spent the whole day on the new office project and had just modemed some designs over to the office. She wondered what Dwayne thought of that one, or whether he had even gotten a look at it yet.

"We all understand," said Dwayne warmly. "We appreciate your coming through with the work despite your grief and everything. It must have been rough as hell."

"Still, I prefer to be prompt."

"It sure looks like it was worth the wait. The Abernathys are going to love it."

"That's nice to hear."

"Speaking of promptness—you sent some preliminaries on the Carswell office over today. Isn't that a little premature?"

Marianne took a deep breath. "Yes, well, I was hoping someone else could finish it," she said.

"We were kind of looking forward to having you do the whole job," Dwayne said, sounding distressed.

"Surely my preliminaries are enough for somebody else to work from."

"Even so—"

"Isn't anybody else free?"

Dwayne groaned slightly. "Sure, there's Paul. He could do it in a pinch."

"Dwayne, I'd appreciate it," Marianne said. "I need some time to . . . sort things out."

"Marianne, I don't mean to sound callous, but how long has it been since your friend died? Two weeks?"

"Almost three," Marianne replied. "But I've been doing my best to get my work done during all that time, and it's been awfully stressful. I think I deserve a little time off. I've got a lot of vacation time coming."

"Point well taken," Dwayne said pleasantly. "OK. It's not a great time, but I guess it never is. Take as much time as you need."

"Thanks. Give my best to everybody at the office."

"Sure will."

Marianne hung up the phone.

"Take as much time as you need," Dwayne had said.

Dwayne assumed that all she wanted was a little time for rest and recuperation. What she actually wanted was time to contend with Auggie, to work her way closer and closer to him, to learn his secrets, and stop him from killing again—to destroy him, if it came to that. And how much time would that take? A couple of days? A week? A month? The rest of her life?

Will I have a job waiting for me when this is over?

Then she almost laughed at her misplaced concern. What kind of threat was getting herself fired in comparison to getting herself murdered? Unemployment and death both loomed over her life right now—and which of the two did she really find more dreadful?

If Nolan was right—if Auggie could have stolen her password and found out who she was and where she lived—then she might already be in danger. Even more chilling, Marianne suspected that Auggie had no *need* to steal her password.

Paradoxically, Marianne's most vivid cyberworld experiences were the most obscure in some respects. Insomnimania took on reality for her in the quiet hours after midnight, when she was very tired, when her subconscious was at its most active. At those times she could hear the typed-out conversations, rather than just reading them from the screen, and the cartoon drawings seemed alive and autonomous.

Marianne knew that the effect must be an illusion, a state of self-hypnosis brought on by exhaustion and by desire. She also knew that she could not remember every aspect of the conversations she had in that state. Judging from her Pleasure Dome experience, she might have told Auggie all about her most secret sexual fantasy. What more mundane clues had she given that would be of use to a superhacker? She might also have told him her password or her real name.

Nolan already had protested her roaming about Insomnimania because he was afraid that Auggie could learn her actual identity. If she explained the true nature of her participation there—and her suspicions about Auggie's ability to scrounge information—he would certainly insist that she cancel her Insomnimania membership immediately. But Renee had resigned from Insomnimania and that hadn't saved *her* life.

Besides, Marianne was convinced that her half-remembered sessions were setting up a unique relationship with Auggie, that she had a kind of access to him no one else had. He seemed ready to take her into his confidence. And she was gaining some concept—if only a vague one—of just how powerful and mysterious Auggie was. No one else had any idea. Nolan was a good cop and a wonderful man, but he was too used to thinking like a cop to understand Auggie, and so was everybody on his team. They were all logical and methodical, and Auggie lived in a world where logic and method had very little meaning.

In last night's session on Babbage Beach, she and a "virtual Renee" had talked. Whether the computer network gave life to the fantasies of her own mind, or whether it allowed her to venture into the fantasies of another mind, it provided a place where things actually happened—events with their own kind of truth and meaning. That was the world where Auggie lived, and whoever stopped Auggie would have to do so there—on Auggie's own terms.

It's got to be me. I'm the only one.

It felt good to have all her obligations out of the way, to be able to devote herself single-mindedly to the task at hand. And despite (or perhaps because of) her commiseration with Renee last night, Marianne felt profoundly rested today—rested and ready to act.

So . . . what now?

How was she going to cultivate the necessary state of mind and deliberately sustain and control it for long periods of time?

Mind-altering drugs would certainly bring this sort of consciousness to the forefront with a fury—probably *too much* of a fury, and fleetingly as well. She didn't want to find herself too disoriented to have any idea what was going on. Marianne knew she'd better keep her wits about her, no matter how right-brained she intended to get. Besides, she had no idea where to get such drugs in Santa Barbara.

Guess I'll have to alter my consciousness the old-fashioned way.

Marianne had practiced a number of techniques at one time or another during her bohemian days—meditation, self-induced sleeplessness, and fasting. Now she would have to muster them all in a kind of crash-course of mind alteration.

First, she needed to make a few preparations. She got in her car and drove to the local health-food store. For fasting, she wanted lots of juices on hand, things like carrot and celery juice. Dilutions of fruit juices—grape and apple—would be useful, too. She filled her cart with such items and also rounded up a substantial supply of herbal teas. But most important would be the bottled water. Marianne picked up several gallons.

All in all, she figured this would give her enough liquids to keep her going for a week—that is, if all the juices stayed fresh in the fridge. She also picked up some cabbage, turnips, and collards to make a thin broth should she find herself becoming too weak to function. But it probably wouldn't come to that—not for a while, anyway. She was a light eater to begin with, so she didn't expect fasting to be particularly stressful.

She returned home, put away her groceries, and fixed herself a cup of aromatic herbal tea. It was far too early to log onto Insomnimania. It felt a little strange to be alone in her own home with nothing to do at the moment.

She paced around the house for a little while. The air was stale and lifeless, so she opened the front door and looked out. Her tiny hillside yard was lit with the full warm glow of late-afternoon California sunshine. Although nothing was blooming at this time of year, the garden seemed more inviting than her living room. She put on a sweater and carried her tea outside.

Unlike the interior of her house, Marianne's yard had a casual, natural look. It had been designed that way. Her landscape architect—a colleague at the office—had planted the entire space in terraced beds with drought-tolerant lavender and rosemary, together with roses, irises, coral bells, and other brilliantly flowering plants. He had revivified two orange trees and added two peaches and an avocado. Throughout much of the year, the garden flowered in lush profusion.

It was not the kind of landscape Marianne would have designed, and at first she had protested the idea. But her co-worker had been insistent, claiming that this sort of garden would be low-maintenance and would suit the climate. She finally gave him a free hand, and now she was happy she had done so. Her garden had survived even when years of water rationing had turned Santa Barbara's expensive grass lawns a uniform beige. And today, she found the crazy-quilt randomness of the garden quite charming.

In the distance, she could just see a reflection of light off the ocean. She sat down on a concrete bench and set the teacup and saucer on a low, glass-topped table in front of her. Marianne closed her left nostril with her forefinger and breathed in through her right nostril. Then she switched, closing the right nostril and breathing through the left. The right nostril felt clear—she could breathe through it easily, but the left was slightly clogged and congested.

She had learned during her meditating days that brain hemispheric dominance switched back and forth at regular intervals, and that nostril congestion could be used to determine which hemisphere was dominant at a particular moment. It was an ancient yoga insight that had recently been confirmed by hard research. The connection between nostril and brain hemisphere was inverted, as it was for the rest of the body. The left nostril correlated with the right hemisphere, the right nostril with the left. The clearness in Marianne's right nostril told her that the left, more rational hemisphere of her brain was currently dominant. She would need to activate her right brain to evoke an instinctive, nonlinear state of mind.

She closed her eyes. She began to inhale and exhale slowly, as she had been taught to do in a yoga class conducted by Japanese Buddhist monks with white robes and shaven heads.

"Exhale, counting to a certain number," the monks had instructed her. "Then inhale, counting twice as high."

She exhaled completely to a slow count of five. Then she inhaled as fully as she could to a slow count of ten. She maintained this slow alternation for some minutes. At first, images and preoccupations fluttered through her mind, making it hard to keep count. Faces drifted by—Nolan, Renee, Stephen, Evan, and of course, Auggie.

Worries about work, about her future with Nolan, about the great dilemma of Auggie—all these struggled and contended for her attention. She didn't try to shove them out of her brain. She simply allowed them to pass with as little notice as possible. Without any acknowledgment or affirmation, the intruding thoughts and concerns soon vanished.

Her mind became empty, and she felt her whole body relax. She noticed, too, that her breathing became thinner and thinner until, at last, she couldn't detect any breath at all. She was sitting in her garden in utter stillness, and she had stopped breathing altogether. It wasn't as if she were holding her breath. She felt no such anxiety or discomfort. It was more as though any need for the air's nourishment was suspended. She felt that she could sustain this breathless state indefinitely. This was not a new sensation for her. She had experienced it when meditating with the monks, and even during silent Quaker meetings when she was still a teenager. It was immensely peaceful.

She noticed, too, that she was staring at the teacup and saucer on the glass table—that she was raptly observing the late-afternoon sun's reflection on the flat glass table and on the slightly curved, slightly wavering surface of the tea. She could see it quite clearly— and she was looking at it through closed eyelids. She remembered this effect, too, both from her yoga meditations and the silent meetings of her youth.

The Buddhist monks had a name for this seemingly numinous eyesight. They also had a name for her suspended breathing. Marianne couldn't remember what those names were. All she knew was that this whole experience was very pleasant and very soothing.

She heard herself whisper . . .

"I'll be ready."

Nolan was coming back to the detective bay area after a walk around the block. He'd left the desk from sheer nervousness. He just couldn't spend all afternoon sitting around waiting.

He had run all his requisite errands for today, including his routine visit to Pritchard and Maisie, and he had a pile of paperwork to go through. But he had been having an awful time sitting still. He was going crazy wondering what was happening in Omaha at the moment. Would the cops there have any luck finding the murderer of the poor bastard in the shower curtain? Would the name and number of Myron Stalnaker that Nolan had given the Omaha detective be of any use to them?

The walk hadn't particularly settled him, so he'd reluctantly come back.

Hell, maybe we've heard something from Omaha by now.

As he entered the squad room, a loud shriek rang out. Nolan saw Clayton standing at his desk halfway across the room. Clayton was waving his arms and jumping up and down. The whole squad room was staring at him.

"Waaaa-hoooooo!" Clayton screamed. "We got him! We got the bastard cold!"

Nolan trotted toward the desk. The ordinarily quiet Clayton was dancing around the desk, throwing paper up in the air.

Nolan skidded to a stop in front of the desk.

"My partner's having one of his manic spells," Nolan explained to the other detectives staring their way.

Clayton dropped into his swivel chair and spun around in it like a little kid trying to make himself dizzy.

"What is it, pal?" Nolan asked.

"Oh, well, nothing much, really," Clayton chuckled delightedly. "I don't know what got into me. Guess I got kind of got carried away. They just caught the Omaha killer, is all. They caught the murderous bastard—courtesy of us!"

"Hey, slow down, buddy," Nolan said. "So we got a laugh, huh?"

"A laugh? We got a fucking guffaw! We're bringing down the house!"

"That's great. That's really great."

"What'samatter? Aren't you excited?"

"Well, I wish you'd tell me how it happened."

"Come along to Coffey's office and I'll tell you all about it."

"Wait a minute. You're gonna tell Coffey before you tell *me?*"

"Don't pull that hurt routine. I'm gonna tell the both of you at the same time."

"Clay—"

"Hey, I got the news first, and I get to tell the boss first. I don't need you standing behind me playing the back-seat talker, interrupting me and correcting me from the get-go."

"Come on. I'd never do a thing like that."

"Shut the fuck up, willya?" Clayton said. "Last one to the captain's office is Darryl Gates."

The two of them broke into a gallop through the bay area toward the captain's office. Clayton threw open the door and charged into the office with Nolan in hot pursuit. They stopped dead in their tracks in front of Coffey's desk. The captain didn't show the slightest trace of surprise at their abrupt entrance. Instead, he quietly lit a cigar.

"Gentlemen," said Coffey, slowly and sarcastically, "I suppose you're wondering why I called you here."

Nolan shuddered with apprehension. Charging into the captain's office unannounced like this was never a good idea. How could he and Clayton both have forgotten that?

"Well, I'll *tell* you why I asked you to come," Coffey said, maintaining a tone of ruthless irony. "I was just kind of sitting here, thinking about the good old days, the departed niceties of life, waxing elegiacal, as it were. And I thought it might be nice to have a couple of uncouth, hog-trough, pissant detectives here to sort of commiserate with me in my melancholy, deprived as I am of any respectable *human* company. And that's why I called you ill-mannered brutes in here."

Nolan and Clayton lowered their heads in abashed silence while Coffey droned on in a tone of mock lamentation.

"Ah, what happened to all the splendid protocols, the social preludes, the rites of passage of yesteryear? Whatever happened to bar mitzvahs, Presbyterian confirmations, that first shaving kit? Can you tell me? Whatever happened to all those precious and beloved rituals that bind a culture together? Whatever happened to high school graduation parties where you drank yourself sick for the first time in your life and puked your living guts up all over some total stranger's living-room carpet? Huh? And whatever happened to long, lingering, candlelit dinners and polite conversation before you fucked some hot-looking dame's eyes out?

"And," Coffey concluded, leaning forward across his desk with a terrifying snarl, "whatever happened to *knocking on doors before entering?*"

"Sorry, sir," Clayton said, without a trace of his earlier exuberance. "It's just that we got a break in the Auggie killings."

"Let's hear it," Coffey said, leaning back in his chair. Coffey took one more puff on his newly lit cigar and then put it out in a mug of cold coffee. Nolan realized that he'd never seen Coffey completely smoke a cigar all the way down to a stub. Maybe Coffey didn't like cigars at all. Maybe Coffey just lit them up to disgust and intimidate people. Given Coffey's calculatedly offensive manner, it seemed a plausible hypothesis.

And it works pretty well.

"It's like this," Clayton said, pulling out his notebook for ready reference. "A certain Lola Delaney lives across the street from a Catholic church in a seedier part of Omaha. On the night Howard Cronin was killed, she saw something suspicious—a black-clad character lugging something big and heavy out the front door of the church. He dumped it into the trunk of a slightly worse-for-the-wear Mercedes. Lola Delaney couldn't tell what it was, but it looked like it was wrapped up in a plastic something-or-other with red stripes—a shower curtain, she thought it might have been."

The captain's eyes flickered with sudden interest.

"Do tell," Coffey said.

Clayton continued. "Well, being a model citizen and all, Lola Delaney wrote down the license number of the Mercedes. She didn't call the police right away, but the next morning she *did* go over to ask the priest if anything had been stolen from the sanctuary during the night. The priest, a certain Father Mark Lamberti, was a little surprised at Lola Delaney's story.

"He told her that nothing had been stolen that he knew of. In fact, Father Mark had taken a lot of criticism for leaving the sanctuary unlocked around the clock—just like churches used to be in the old days. But before now there had been remarkably little in the way of late-night problems. Now, because of Lola Delaney's story, he was starting to worry.

"This is where *we* came in, with our software reenactment of the Howard Cronin murder taking place in a Catholic church. With the cooperation of the archdiocese, the Omaha cops started talking to one priest after another, and before too long they got to Father Mark with his tale of a nocturnal visitor lugging some strange object out of his church. That led them to Lola Delaney with her description of the beat-up Mercedes and its license number. As it turned out, the car belongs to a local bank employee named Myron Stalnaker, which also happens to be the name of an Insomnimania member who appeared to have occasionally logged on as Auggie—a name *we* passed on to the Omaha cops."

"Bingo," Nolan heard himself murmur.

"Not so fast," Clayton said. "It gets even better. With all this information, the Omaha cops had no trouble getting a warrant to search Myron Stalnaker's home. They found a priest's outfit—just like the one Auggie was wearing in the simulated murder. They also found a ski mask made with white, red, and black acrylic yarn. It was knitted with a clown's face—just like Auggie, only with a sad, downturned mouth. *And* they found a twenty-two-caliber pistol, the same kind that was used to kill Cronin. Well, naturally, they arrested this Stalnaker guy. The gun was a match. And get this. The Omaha cops have invited us to come out and take part in the festivities. We'll get to sit in on some of the questioning and ask a few ourselves."

Coffey was smiling broadly now—the kind of undisguisedly supercilious smile that always made Nolan and Clayton extremely nervous.

"I must say, you've got my interest piqued, Saunders," he said. "It's quite a story so far. Go on. What happened next?"

Clayton looked crestfallen.

"What do you mean, sir?" Clayton asked.

"Oh, come on, Saunders," Coffey said. "Don't tease me like this. Tell me the rest of it. You've got me on the edge of my seat. I'm all ears."

Clayton was silent.

"Wait a minute," Coffey continued. "Don't tell me. Let me guess. You've *proven* that this Myron Stalnaker character was in L.A. when both Judson and Gauld were murdered. You've checked out Stalnaker's plane reservations, his hotel bills, the works. You've found out that he hasn't got a credible alibi for either of the murders. In fact, he's got motive and opportunity up the wazoo. You've probably even got eyewitnesses that say he whacked both Judson and Gauld. And—oh yeah—you've documented that he got a *sex change* before coming to L.A., which is why the Gauld killing looks like it was done by a woman, and then he got his dick reinstalled when he got back to Omaha. It's an open-and-shut case, right?"

Coffey leaned triumphantly back in his chair, putting his hands behind his head. He appeared to be deliberately displaying the wetness under his armpits.

"So," concluded Coffey. "Am I one hell of a guesser, or what?"

Clayton was seething now.

"With all due respect, sir," Clayton hissed, "you're being a total son of a bitch about this."

Nolan jabbed Clayton sharply with his elbow. Coffey only laughed.

"A son of a bitch, huh?" Coffey said. "Well, it's one of the prices of power. You gotta be a bastard if you wanna keep a job like mine."

"Captain, all Clayton's saying is that we've caught *a killer*," Nolan said.

"Right," Coffey said. "An Omaha killer. What about our L.A. killer—or *killers?*"

"They're connected!" Clayton exclaimed.

"How?" Coffey asked.

"Through *Auggie*," Clayton said. "Through *Insomnimania*. Nobody's saying the Stalnaker guy did all these killings. Maybe he did just this one. Maybe it's a club or a conspiracy."

"Or a cult," Nolan suggested.

"Yeah," Clayton said. "Maybe it's some kind of Charlie Manson thing, only electronic."

"A murder club?" Coffey snorted.

"Come on, Captain," Nolan pleaded. "We've got to start using our imaginations here. I've done some research into this Auggie character. I've checked out everything he represents. He's historical, mythic, archetypal. He could have a lot of symbolic value for a bunch of unhappy people looking for a leader or guru or something."

"A cartoon?" Coffey snapped.

"Why not?" Nolan said. "Have you ever seen this network in action?"

"All we know for sure is that we've got a piece of the puzzle," Clayton said. "Maybe it's just a little piece, but it's something. If Stalnaker belongs to a cult, he'll probably blow the whistle on the whole outfit. Hell, for all we know, he's the *ringleader*, and we've got things practically sewed up."

The captain stared at the cup of cold coffee sitting in front of him—the same cup he had extinguished his cigar in just a few moments before. He looked like he was thinking of taking a sip from it.

It would be just like him to do something really gross like that. Just for effect.

"So," Coffey said, without drinking. "What do we do next?"

"I guess the next stop's Omaha," Clayton said.

"Good idea," Coffey said. "Grobowski, catch the next plane out. I want you there first thing tomorrow morning."

"What is this?" Clayton said. "I'm not going, too?"

"No, you're not," Coffey said. "Somebody needs to stay here and do some real cop work."

"But this is just like last time, with Chicago," Clayton said.

"Call me a creature of habit," Coffey said.

"Why does Nolan always get to do all the globe-hopping while I have to stay here and stare at my desk?"

"Because it's the natural order of things," Coffey explained gruffly. "It's welded and hard-wired into the human condition, decreed from the time of the Big Bang itself. Nolan hates midwestern weather, so I send him to the Midwest. You want to talk to this suspect so much you can taste it, so I'm keeping you the hell away from him. It's my little way of keeping the two of you from getting all spoiled and complacent. One of these days you'll thank me for it. Trust me. Now get the fuck out of my office."

Nolan and Clayton trudged toward their desks. They felt considerably less energy and enthusiasm than just a little while before.

"Somebody ought to teach that prick some of those newfangled management tactics," Clayton said. "You know—the kind that makes employees feel happy and fulfilled about their work."

"Fat chance of that ever happening," Nolan said. "If there's one thing Coffey hates, it's good morale among the troops. Anyway, I'm sorry you don't get to come, too."

"And I'm sorry you've got to put up with the weather in Omaha."

"Yeah, I guess I'm lucky that way," Nolan said.

As Nolan collapsed into his chair, he mulled over his coming trip. *Too damn much geography.*

It was an ironic thing, too. After all, wasn't the information age supposed to abolish geography altogether? Why wasn't it possible to wire himself to Omaha, just like the computer files? Why did he have to spend hours riding in unreliable mechanical devices to cover the same distance? No, the information age hadn't done away with time and distance. In fact, all it seemed to do was make the upcoming trip seem more onerous.

"At least they don't have a fucking lake there," he muttered, remembering Chicago.

Night had fallen. Marianne was sitting at her computer terminal, guiding Elfie through Insomnimania's desktop maze and checking room after room for any sign of Auggie. So far, the clown was nowhere to be found.

The phone rang and she picked it up. It was Nolan.

"Hi, sweetheart," Nolan said. "I'm at LAX."

"LAX? Are you going someplace?"

"Naw, I just like to watch the planes take off at night."

"Very funny. Where are you going?"

"Omaha."

"Did they catch that man's killer?"

"Looks like it. A certain Myron Stalnaker."

"So what happens next?"

"I go there, I talk to the guy, I try to learn something. That's about all."

"Do you and Clay have any theories?"

"We're starting to think it's an electronic cult or commune—sort of like a computer-linked Manson family or Jonestown."

Marianne fell silent for a moment.

"Are you still there?" Nolan asked.

"Yeah."

"Is something wrong?"

"I don't know, Nolan. The conspiracy thing feels wrong to me. I can't say why. I just get the feeling that when Auggie kills, he acts alone."

Nolan laughed. "Like Lee Harvey Oswald, huh?"

Marianne laughed, too. "Don't make fun of me, Nolan. It's just a feeling."

"Come on, sweetheart. We know Renee was killed by a woman, and this guy in Omaha was killed by a man. Whoever Auggie is, he's not doing these killings by himself."

"Still, I can't shake that feeling."

"Why not?"

"Because I know him. I've spent time with him. He's fascinating and he's even compelling, and he does have fans and enthusiasts. But he doesn't seem to have disciples or followers. If anything, he strikes me as very lonely."

It was Nolan's turn to be silent now.

"Are *you* still there?" Marianne asked.

"Yeah. You haven't been meeting him again, have you?"

Marianne laughed again. "You're not still jealous of that little *thing* I had with him, are you?"

"Marianne, this is serious. He could be very dangerous if he ever finds out who you are or where you live. Promise me you haven't been talking to him."

"I promise," Marianne said, feeling more than a little uncomfortable with her half-truth. No, she hadn't talked to Auggie since her last meeting with Nolan—but that was only because she hadn't been able to *find* Auggie.

"Promise me you *won't* talk to him," Nolan said.

Marianne couldn't answer for a second.

"Well?" Nolan said.

"I promise," Marianne finally said, hoping Nolan wouldn't hear the guilt and tension in her voice. *The lie-detector needle would have scribbled mountains on this one.*

"Good."

"I can't wait till this thing is over, Nolan," Marianne said. "We've got so much to talk about, so many plans to make."

"I know," Nolan said. "I miss you."

"I miss you, too."

"And I love you."

"I love you, too."

She hung up the phone and looked at the computer screen. Elfie was drifting northward through the maze toward the Casino del Camino, still moving out of the inertia caused by Marianne's last nudge of her computer mouse. Marianne coaxed Elfie into the casino icon and pulled down the menu to select "who?" The names she read were familiar ones . . .

"sudopod, taser, wunderkind, hejhog, jazz . . ."

No Auggie.

She began to move Elfie toward the Speakers' Corner, but she had a gut feeling that she probably wouldn't find him there, either. Of course, she could call Pritchard and Maisie and ask them if Auggie was on the network at all, but she didn't want to talk to them about her activities. They'd be just as disapproving as Nolan.

I'll just keep looking. I'll keep looking all night, whether I find him or not.

And tomorrow she would fast on water and juices and stay awake as much as possible, allowing herself brief catnaps from time to time. She would do physical stretches and meditations and let her mind wander as little as possible. She would keep herself in a state of intuitive vigilance.

Right now, Marianne's intuition sensed Auggie's presence—even if he wasn't to be found anywhere in the maze, in any of Insomnimania's multifarious rooms. She had a strange intimation of *another* labyrinth, another maze beneath this one—a whole world within Insomnimania that nobody but Auggie knew how to reach— not her, not even Pritchard and Maisie.

If only I knew my way inside. I could find him. I could find him right now . . .

DEPOSITION

Lieutenant Michael Kelsey, Director of Omaha Homicide, ushered Nolan into the police station. Still shivering slightly, Nolan brushed a cold, whitish substance off his shoulders as he walked along. He wasn't sure if it was snow or sleet.

Not as cold as Chicago, anyway. In fact, the weather probably wasn't much below freezing.

"Welcome to Omaha, Lieutenant," Kelsey said. "How about a nasty cup of our vending machine–brewed coffee?"

"Please," Nolan replied.

They stopped at the machine, and Nolan got himself a cup of black coffee. The hot paper cup sharply scalded his still icy fingers. He had to hold the rim of the cup delicately between his fingers, hoping not to drop it as Kelsey escorted him down a hallway. The linoleum floor was tracked with mud. Nolan guessed that the building was next to impossible to keep clean during this time of year.

Kelsey was a tall, slender, dark-haired man who looked and dressed like a stereotypical cowboy, complete with a drawstring tie, a steer's-head belt buckle, and leather boots. Nolan had noted Kelsey's midwestern drawl during their phone conversations, but he had guessed Kelsey to be quite a bit older—a grizzled relic of the prairie, as it were. But the Omaha detective looked young, maybe in his twenties—way too young to direct a homicide department in a city this size, at least in Nolan's estimation.

Still, Kelsey had a confident air about him. He walked along at what appeared to be a leisurely rate, but his stride was so long that Nolan—not a short man, by any means—had to trot pretty vigorously to keep up with him.

"I'd like to apologize on behalf of the good state of Nebraska for all this shitty weather, Lieutenant," Kelsey said in his amiable twang.

"No apology necessary," Nolan replied.

"I wish I could've arranged for things to be a little warmer, but I just didn't get the time. It takes a good couple of weeks to requisition nice weather in these parts—and even then, you're lucky if the order comes through."

"Maybe next time," Nolan said.

"Yeah, maybe next time. 'Course, you should have been here a few days ago—about the time that jogger guy was killed. Why, we sure had a nice, dry warm spell then. I guess it got to be—oh, forty-five, forty-eight degrees. 'Course, coming from your parts, that must sound downright Arctic."

At the end of the hallway, Kelsey opened the doorway to a conference room dominated by an enormous oval table. Three rather grim-looking people were seated inside. The fact that they had situated themselves as far away from each other as possible around the table suggested to Nolan that the gathering hadn't exactly been cordial so far.

Kelsey introduced Nolan to each of the people in turn. First came Melissa Finch, a prosecutor with the D.A.'s office. She had a long neck and brooding, beady eyes, and Nolan thought she looked more like a cormorant than a finch. Next came Claude Breckenridge, the suspect's attorney. Claude was short, squat, chinless, and bald. And at the moment, he looked as mad as hell.

The last member of the group immediately piqued Nolan's interest. This was Dr. Harvey Gusfield, a psychiatrist. Gusfield was affiliated with a local hospital, but did occasional forensics work for the Omaha police. Gusfield was forties-ish, clad in jeans, a sweatshirt, and a heavy corduroy jacket with patched elbows. He had a well-trimmed beard, and his longish, sandy hair was tied into an abbreviated ponytail. His legs were crossed on top of the table, and he was leaning back in his chair tearing a sheet of paper into slender strips, looking utterly bored. He certainly did not fit Nolan's image of a mental-health professional. Nolan wondered what he was doing here.

Nolan took a seat.

"I'm sure we all appreciate Lieutenant Grobowski braving our godawful Nebraska weather to come here on such short notice," Kelsey said, projecting a warm feeling of midwestern hospitality.

Everybody else in the room maintained a sullen silence.

"Well," Nolan said, starting to feel a little nervous at this stoney welcome, "perhaps somebody could give me a little status report."

"My client is innocent," Mr. Breckenridge said sharply. "And he's been railroaded, intimidated, and badgered into signing away his Fifth Amendment rights."

"Your client is as guilty as hell," retorted Ms. Finch. "And he's desperately using every sleazy trick in the book to escape conviction for murder."

"Children, children," Lieutenant Kelsey said, laughing softly. "Maybe I should do the filling in here." He turned toward Nolan. "Lieutenant Grobowski, as you already know, Myron Stalnaker was arrested yesterday for the murder of Howard Cronin. In many ways, Mr. Stalnaker has proven to be a model suspect—'model' in the sense of being impeccably behaved. He made no attempt to resist arrest. As a matter of fact, he was downright helpful when my boys showed up with the warrant. He showed them all the apparent paraphernalia of his crime—the priest's outfit, the ski mask, and even the twenty-two-caliber revolver. And when my boys brought him in for interrogation, he seemed awful upset about Howard Cronin's death—downright remorseful, in fact.

"Trouble is," Kelsey continued with a smile, "Mr. Stalnaker doesn't seem to have any real recollection of actually having *killed* Howard Cronin. He admits to owning the gun, but he says he's got no idea where the priest outfit and the ski mask came from. And he can't account for his whereabouts or actions during the time of the murder. He claims it's all a kind of haze."

"Bullshit," Ms. Finch murmured.

"It's not bullshit," Mr. Breckenridge snapped. "How can he remember something he never did?"

"Well, he's *remorseful*," Ms. Finch responded pertly. "Why should he feel remorse for a crime he didn't commit?"

"Now, now, Melissa, Claude," Kelsey said pleasantly. "You'll both have plenty of time to bitch and moan at each other during what I'm sure will be a long, drawn-out, and expensive murder trial, and I know how much you both love to waste the taxpayers' money. Right now, we're just trying to give Lieutenant Grobowski the lay of the land."

Ms. Finch grunted. Mr. Breckenridge growled.

"Mr. Stalnaker spent last night in jail," Kelsey explained to Nolan. "And this morning he said he wants to be hypnotized."

"He wants to be *what?*" Nolan asked, startled.

"Hypnotized," Kelsey repeated. "He wants to make a sort of informal deposition under hypnosis. He keeps saying that if he *did* kill somebody, he wants to know it himself—and he wants to make a statement to that effect. So that's why we've brought in Dr. Gusfield, here."

Nolan's heart immediately sank. He had expected to be able to take part in Stalnaker's interrogation—and to do so in his usual aggressive style.

"But does this mean that I won't get a chance to ask him any questions at all?" Nolan sputtered.

"That remains to be seen," Kelsey said.

Nolan could hardly believe his ears.

"With all due respect, Lieutenant Kelsey," he said, "why did I make this trip out here if . . ."

"Lieutenant Grobowski, I apologize for these circumstances," Kelsey replied. "But this situation simply didn't exist until this morning. And from here on in, Dr. Gusfield calls the shots. If you want to interrogate the suspect, you'll have to clear it with him."

Dr. Gusfield kept tearing his sheet of paper into strips, as if oblivious to the fact that his name had even been mentioned. Nolan realized that he hadn't yet heard Gusfield speak a single word.

Breckenridge slapped his hand against the table with noisy indignation. "I want to make sure I'm on the record as being entirely opposed to this idea," he said. "I want it understood that my client has made this decision against the advice of counsel."

"Claude, your objections are already in the record," Kelsey said drily. "In triplicate, I do believe."

"You and your hoodlums have half-hypnotized my client already," Breckenridge continued. "You've already planted the suggestion that he's committed a crime he had nothing to do with. Anyone can see he's highly suggestible. Put him through any more hocus-pocus and he'll admit to just about anything."

"Claude, there's no point in debating this issue," Kelsey said. "Your client has signed a release, and he can't unsign it now. He doesn't even want to unsign it. Besides, it's not going to be a *sworn* statement. I doubt if it'll even be usable in court."

Now Ms. Finch chimed in indignantly.

"Well, it just so happens that *I'm* against this whole thing," she said. "I'm not fooled by Claude's theatrics. He *wants* his client to go through this crazy charade. It's part of a cheap ploy to cop an insanity plea."

"You bitch," Claude snapped.

Jesus, these two are worse than L.A. lawyers. So much for the Midwest being all mellow and civilized.

Kelsey was grinning broadly now. He looked as if he was used to this sort of thing—and might actually be enjoying it.

"If there's one thing that warms my heart," he said, "it's when defense and prosecution cozily agree on something. The both of you think hypnosis is a lousy idea, so what's your argument? Well, Mr. Stalnaker's going to get himself hypnotized, whether either of you like it or not. So let's go down to the interrogation room and get on with it."

Kelsey rose from his chair and strode out of the room. Everybody else followed single file, like a gaggle of baby geese. Nolan was starting to admire Kelsey's style.

When they reached the interrogation room, only Dr. Gusfield actually went inside. Nolan, Kelsey, Breckenridge, and Finch all piled into an adjoining booth with a two-way mirror. Through the glass, the four of them could see Dr. Gusfield and the suspect in the interrogation room. A video camera was pointed through the glass, and a tape machine was running slowly.

It was rather crowded in the booth. It was hot, too, with no apparent ventilation. During his career, Nolan had spent a lot of time in booths like this. But even so, he did not much like being cooped up with a pack of quarrelsome people. He half expected Breckenridge and Finch to scratch at each other's eyes at any second. He wished he wasn't standing right between them.

Nolan gazed through the glass, studying the suspect. Myron Stalnaker was neither a pleasant- nor an unpleasant-looking man. He was plain, his face on the roundish side, his brown hair thinning slightly. He was wearing a gray vest and a white shirt. His clothes looked expensive, if rather conventional. He was probably in his late thirties. Nolan figured he was the kind of guy one might talk to every day for years and never manage to remember his name.

Gusfield sat down at the table across from Myron Stalnaker. Gusfield smiled. It was the first sign of life Nolan had seen out of Gusfield since he had met him.

Nolan and his companions could hear the voices of Gusfield and Stalnaker through a small speaker in the booth.

"Myron Stalnaker, right?" Dr. Gusfield inquired pleasantly.

"Yes," said Stalnaker.

Gusfield reached across the table and shook Stalnaker's hand. "My name's Harvey Gusfield," he said. "I'm a psychiatrist. I'm pleased to make your acquaintance, Mr. Stalnaker."

"The pleasure's mine," Stalnaker said nervously but politely.

"May I call you Myron?"

"Of course."

"And please call me Harvey."

"Thanks. I will."

A short pause ensued. Then Gusfield said, "Listen, Myron, this is a little awkward, but . . . this little session is being videotaped, as I'm sure you know, and this is supposed to be a deposition of sorts, and I've got to say a few rather formal things to make it—you know, kosher."

"By all means," Stalnaker said eagerly.

Gusfield looked at his watch. "Um, it's Saturday, the eighth of February, two-thirty P.M. I'm Harvey Gusfield and I'm talking to Myron Stalnaker and we are being observed by . . . oh, hell, who all's out there?"

Gusfield pulled a sheet of paper out of his pocket and began to read. "Lieutenant Michael Kelsey, Lieutenant Nolan Grobowski, Claude Breckenridge, and Melissa Finch."

He wadded up the paper and stuffed it in his pocket.

"There," Gusfield said with a grin. "That ought to do it. I hope I didn't screw anything up."

Stalnaker laughed a little.

"Now," Gusfield said, folding his hands in front of him, "I understand that you're deeply concerned about the killing of Howard Cronin."

"Yes, very much so."

"Why?"

"I feel like I . . . was involved in it somehow."

"Do you think you actually committed the murder?"

"No. It was more like I was an accomplice. I'm sorry. I can't explain it any better than that."

Gusfield was silent for a moment. He looked at the table and began to draw little imaginary shapes on it with his forefinger.

"Myron," Gusfield continued, "I've been told that you belong to a computer network called Insomnimania."

"Yes."

"And that you're somehow involved with a cartoon character named Auggie."

"That's right."

"Are you Auggie's user? His operator?"

Stalnaker's eyes shifted nervously. "I wouldn't put it quite that way," he said. "It's more like Auggie uses me."

"How do you mean?"

"Well, if Auggie wants to go somewhere in the network, I sometimes move him around. If he wants to say something, I sometimes type in his words."

"What do you mean, 'sometimes'?"

"Well, other times, Auggie just appears to be doing these things on his own. Or maybe somebody else is moving him and typing for him. Anyway, his words don't feel like *my* words, even when I *am* typing them. It feels like Auggie is actually saying them. Does that make me sound crazy?"

Gusfield chuckled softly.

"It makes you sound very creative, Myron," Gusfield said. "Novelists say the same thing about their characters. They claim that their characters decide what to do or say, and all they do is write it down. Nobody calls Norman Mailer or Stephen King or Gore Vidal or Jackie Collins crazy, do they?"

Stalnaker smiled back at Gusfield.

"No, I guess they don't," Stalnaker said, seeming more and more relaxed.

While this conversation was going on, the occupants of the booth were growing increasingly agitated. The compression of bodies was rapidly raising the temperature in the already overheated chamber. The place was becoming quite suffocating.

"When's he going to get down to business?" Breckenridge asked crankily.

"Give him time," Kelsey said placatingly.

"I'll give him five more minutes, and then I'm out of here," Finch grumbled.

Nolan kept quiet, but he, too, was starting to feel more than a little impatient.

"Myron, I understand you want to be hypnotized," Gusfield said.

"That's right."

"Are you sure you want to try this right now? I mean, you look awfully tired."

"I *am* tired. You don't get a lot of sleep in a jail cell."

"I know. It must be awful to be here."

"I don't sleep well, anyway."

"Insomnia?"

"That's right."

"Me, too. It's a bitch, isn't it?"

"Sure is."

"Well, we can do this some other time, if you prefer."

Finch let out a hiss of indignation. *"Some other time?"* she said. "Oh, Christ."

"Shhh," Kelsey said.

Stalnaker shook his head vigorously.

"No," Stalnaker said. "I want to do it now."

"OK. But I'm just saying, you look awfully sleepy, and I don't want to put you through anything you're not up to. If you get too tired, just let me know, and we'll stop."

"I will."

"Do you know what hypnotism means?" Gusfield asked.

Stalnaker shrugged. "A way to get at the truth, I guess," he said. "A way to reach parts of the mind you're not normally aware of. I guess it always seemed so obvious that I never thought about it very much."

" 'Obvious' is a good word for it, Myron," Gusfield said, speaking quite softly now. "It's got to do with suggestion. It's a matter of accepting an idea that's been suggested to you. Hypnosis happens when *I* say something and *you* act as if you believe what I say. It's pretty much that simple. In fact, it's so simple that a lot of people don't even believe it exists."

Stalnaker was looking at Gusfield intently. The psychiatrist's voice became markedly slower. "A lot of perfectly good scientists and researchers think it's a con job, a fraud, a snake-oil kind of deal. Me, I've practiced it hundreds of times, and I still consider myself something of a skeptic about the whole thing. I still don't know what to believe. For example, what would happen if I told you, right here and now, that your right hand was a balloon filled with helium? That it was lighter than air? That it was so light, you found it hard to hold it down on the table? That all you had to do is relax just a little and your hand would float right up into the air?"

Stalnaker stared at Gusfield blankly for a moment. Then his right hand and forearm rose slowly up off the table.

"Close your eyes, Myron," Gusfield said.

Myron closed his eyes.

Breckenridge gasped slightly.

"That shrink's *good*," Breckenridge said.

"No," Finch replied with a cynical edge. "Your *client's* good."

Nolan wondered.

One of them's good. We'll have to wait and see which one it is. . . .

Excerpt from an unsworn statement made by Myron Stalnaker to Harvey Gusfield, M.D. while under hypnosis; videotaped 2:30 P.M., Saturday, February 8:

GUSFIELD: Myron, I want you to go back to the very early morning hours of Wednesday, the fifth of February. I'm talking about the time that's been worrying you, the time you can't account for. Return to wherever you were at that time.
    (pause)
Are you there now, Myron?

STALNAKER: Yes.

GUSFIELD: Where are you?

STALNAKER: I'm watching what Auggie's doing.

GUSFIELD: Where is Auggie?

STALNAKER: He's in a . . . small . . . enclosed . . .
    (pause)
It's a confessional booth. A church confessional.

GUSFIELD: And where are you watching Auggie from?

STALNAKER: Behind his eyes.

GUSFIELD: From inside Auggie?

STALNAKER: That's right.

GUSFIELD: What is Auggie doing?

STALNAKER: He's pretending to be a priest. He's giving comfort to a man. The man is making a confession.

GUSFIELD: What is Auggie wearing?

STALNAKER: A priest's outfit. And a ski mask with a clown's face on it.

GUSFIELD: Where did Auggie get the priest's outfit?

STALNAKER: He stole it one night from a local community theater.

GUSFIELD: Did you watch him steal it?

STALNAKER: Yes.

GUSFIELD: From behind his eyes?

STALNAKER: That's right.

GUSFIELD: And where did Auggie get the ski mask?

STALNAKER: He knitted it himself.

GUSFIELD: And you watched him knit it?

STALNAKER: Yes.

GUSFIELD: How did he do it?

STALNAKER: With my hands.

GUSFIELD: Do you know how to knit, Myron?

STALNAKER: No.

GUSFIELD: Do you know where Auggie learned to knit?

STALNAKER: No.

GUSFIELD: Are you . . . is Auggie still in the confessional?

STALNAKER: Yes.

GUSFIELD: What's happening now?

STALNAKER: The man making the confession is becoming agitated. He stands up. He yanks away the . . . the lattice between himself and Auggie. He looks at Auggie. Auggie holds a little flashlight up to his face. Auggie . . . shoots the man . . . in the chest.

GUSFIELD: Now what's happening?

STALNAKER: Auggie is coming out of the booth and looking at the man. I think the man is dead. Auggie pulls the man forward. I think Auggie wants to see whether the bullet came out through the man's back. It didn't. Auggie begins to wrap the man up in . . . a heavy plastic sheet with . . . red stripes.

(pause)

It's my shower curtain. I'd wondered what happened to my shower curtain.

GUSFIELD: Myron, I want you to leave that scene now. I want you to come back to the present, to this room. I want to ask you a few questions about your relationship with Auggie.

STALNAKER: All right.

GUSFIELD: Why did Auggie kill Howard Cronin?

STALNAKER: I can't answer that question.

GUSFIELD: Why not?

STALNAKER: Because I'm just a cell. A cell doesn't make decisions. A cell doesn't understand.

GUSFIELD: Could you explain that a little more clearly for me, Myron?

STALNAKER: Can a cell on the tip of your finger tell you why you fall in love or why you smoke too much? A cell bears witness. A cell sees, smells, tastes, touches, hears. A cell carries out its role. And a cell remembers. A cell can't claim to understand.

GUSFIELD: So you are a cell in Auggie's body.

STALNAKER: That's right.

GUSFIELD: Does a cell feel guilt or remorse over the actions of the rest of the body?

STALNAKER: Of course not.

GUSFIELD: It seems to me that "cell" is a strange metaphor, Myron. It seems to me that you are actually Auggie's body—his hands, his arms, his legs.

STALNAKER: It's not a metaphor at all. I'm a cell. That's a literal fact.

GUSFIELD: I see.

STALNAKER: No, you don't see.

GUSFIELD: Can you explain it more clearly, then?

STALNAKER: No.

GUSFIELD: Do you know who created the Snuff Room performance of Howard Cronin's murder?

STALNAKER: I didn't know there was one.

GUSFIELD: There was.

STALNAKER: I didn't know it.

GUSFIELD: Who do you think created it?

STALNAKER: I suppose Auggie did.

GUSFIELD: You didn't see him do it?

STALNAKER: I told you I didn't know there was one. Maybe somebody else saw him do it.

GUSFIELD: Myron, I would like to talk with Auggie now.

STALNAKER: How?

GUSFIELD: I was hoping he might speak to me through you.

STALNAKER: He won't do that.

GUSFIELD: Why not?

STALNAKER: He's not here.

GUSFIELD: He's not inside you?

STALNAKER: No.

GUSFIELD: Where is he?

STALNAKER: In the Basement.

GUSFIELD: What is the Basement?

STALNAKER: Auggie's home.

GUSFIELD: *Where* is the Basement?

STALNAKER: I can't tell you that.

GUSFIELD: Is that because you don't know, or because you're unwilling to tell me?

STALNAKER: I can't answer that question.

GUSFIELD: Why not?

STALNAKER: Because I can't.

The questioning went on for at least another half hour. Dr. Gusfield periodically tried different methods of induction, taking Stalnaker into progressively deeper hypnotic states in hopes of getting more lucid answers. None came. Again and again, Gusfield asked to speak with Auggie. And again and again, Stalnaker said that Auggie was not present.

In the meantime, the foursome behind the two-way mirror were perspiring from the heat. The air in the booth seemed to be getting thinner. Nolan actually began to wonder if they would run out of oxygen before the interview came to an end. Breckenridge and Finch didn't help matters much by muttering profanities at each other throughout the whole ordeal. Nolan wished they wouldn't breathe so much.

At last, Gusfield brought Stalnaker out of his trance. Stalnaker sat shaking in his chair, stunned and horrified and on the brink of hysteria. Gusfield soothed and comforted Stalnaker until he became calmer.

Then Gusfield came into the observation booth and closed the door behind him. The place was preposterously crowded now. It reminded Nolan of some old college prank—like cramming as many students as possible into a telephone booth.

"Lieutenant Kelsey," Gusfield demanded, "you've got to get this man out of his jail cell and into a hospital."

Breckenridge immediately chirped up gleefully. "I knew it!" he said. "I knew it all along! Looney tunes, right? Certifiably bonkers!"

"Don't gloat yet, counselor," Finch said.

"So what is he, then?" Breckenridge said, badgering Gusfield. "A full-blown paranoid schizophrenic?"

"No," Gusfield said tiredly.

"What, then? An MPD case?"

"It's too soon to tell."

"Come on! You've got to have a theory!"

"I don't have a theory!" Gusfield barked. "I'm not even saying whether Stalnaker's sane or insane. All I'm saying is that he's a danger *to himself* right now, and to no one else. He requires close psychiatric observation. I think he learned a great deal more from that session than any of the rest of us did—and he didn't like what he found out."

"I'll have him transferred to a psychiatric unit," Kelsey said. "But I want him kept under close guard. Is that all right with you, Gusfield?"

"That's fine," Gusfield said.

"Good. Now let's get out of this hellhole."

After they stepped out of the booth, Nolan turned to Gusfield. "Could I ask Stalnaker a few questions?" Nolan asked.

"That's not advisable," Gusfield said.

"Look, you can stand right behind me. You can stop me at any time."

Gusfield groaned disapprovingly.

"Come on," Gusfield said. "But go very easy."

Nolan sat down across the table from Stalnaker. He could see that Stalnaker was trembling slightly. Nolan introduced himself politely.

"I just have a few more questions," Nolan said to Stalnaker.

Stalnaker nodded silently.

"Did you ever know a man named G. K. Judson?" Nolan asked.

"The airline owner?"

"That's right."

"I read about him in the papers. I saw him in the news. He was murdered, right?"

"That's right. You didn't know him personally?"

"I don't exactly travel in those circles, Lieutenant," Stalnaker replied with just a trace of wryness.

"What about a woman named Renee Gauld? In Los Angeles?"

"I don't know anyone in Los Angeles."

"She was murdered, too, Myron. She was drowned in her own bathtub. After a party."

"I don't remember anything like that."

"Did you—did *Auggie* know somebody named Sapphire?"

Stalnaker looked at Nolan with interest.

"Yes, Auggie knew her," Stalnaker said. "Auggie quarreled with her."

"Were you there when they quarreled?"

"Yes, I was. I typed in the words."

"Have you seen Sapphire since then?"

"No."

"Do you have any idea what happened to Sapphire?"

"No."

Nolan paused before his next question.

"Does Auggie know somebody named Elfie?" Nolan asked.

Stalnaker thought hard for a moment.

"Yes," Stalnaker said. "I believe he does. He seems to rather like her."

"Is Elfie . . . in any *danger* from Auggie?"

A puzzled look crossed Stalnaker's face.

"How could she be in danger?" Stalnaker asked with apparent amazement. "She's only a cartoon character."

Nolan felt Gusfield's hand on his shoulder.

"That's enough, Lieutenant," Gusfield said.

Nolan thanked Stalnaker, rose to his feet, and left the room.

A short time later, Nolan and Kelsey were debriefing one another in Kelsey's office. They really couldn't find a great deal to say about the case.

"Sounds like he did the Cronin killing, all right," Kelsey said. "But it doesn't sound like he had much of a concept of right or wrong when he did it."

"Of course, he could have been faking that whole hypnotism scene," Nolan said.

Kelsey shook his head. "Gusfield doesn't seem to think so. And Gusfield knows his work. We've brought him in on more than a few cases."

"Gusfield didn't let me ask Stalnaker a lot of questions."

"That's because Gusfield's convinced that Stalnaker doesn't know very much. Stalnaker probably told you everything he had to tell."

"Yeah, I guess so. Still, I wish I could have talked to Gusfield a bit more. He shot out of here in a hurry."

"Gusfield's like that—a real quiet type."

"Sullen's more the word."

"Well, the truth is, I think he just plain doesn't like people."

"That's kind of an odd characteristic for a shrink, isn't it?"

"I guess. But I'm sure Gusfield's told us all he can right now—

which is that Stalnaker's suffering from some kind of dissociative disorder."

"I sure do hate insanity defenses," Nolan said, shaking his head.

"I reckon all cops do. But this one's Omaha's problem, not yours. Anyway, we're grateful for your help. We might never have caught Stalnaker if it weren't for you folks, and at least he's off the streets. Wish we could have returned the favor. I know you were looking for some link with those two cases in L.A. But we've already checked out Stalnaker's whereabouts during the last month, and he's been in town the whole time."

"Hey, at least I got to see a Nebraska winter," Nolan said laughing.

"Indeed you did," Kelsey chuckled. "So what are your plans for this evening? My wife and I would love to fix you dinner—a real nice, heartland meal with lots of fat and cholesterol. You know, real down-home heart-attack cooking."

Nolan laughed. "Sounds great, but I'd hate to impose."

"You wouldn't be imposing. Hell, it's the least we can do in return for dragging you to hell and gone for no good reason. And it'd give Emily an excuse to cook up something special with all those vegetables we've canned and frozen for the winter."

"You keep a vegetable garden?" Nolan asked with interest.

"Sure. Flowers, too."

"Me, too."

"No kidding?"

"Well, not like I did back when the kids were still at home," Nolan said. "But I still do some planting."

"I'd never have guessed that from an L.A. man."

"Why not? We've got a year-round growing season."

"Keep any tomatoes?" Kelsey asked.

Nolan smiled. "I once had a vine that lived three years."

"No kidding?"

"No kidding."

"And I'll bet your roses bloom all year round."

"Pretty close to it."

"Well, that settles it, sir," Kelsey said emphatically. "You're not getting out of Omaha without the two of us having a long talk about gardening. Your presence is definitely required tonight at my dinner table."

"It's settled, then," Nolan said with a smile.

■

That night, Nolan shared a pleasant evening with Michael Kelsey, his wife, Emily, and their two young children. Emily Kelsey served roast beef, baked potatoes, and home-grown green beans from the freezer. The kids talked about school, Emily talked about goings-on in the neighborhood, and Mike Kelsey chattered about sports and politics and, of course, gardening.

Nolan was pleased that the dinner table never turned to police talk. Myron Stalnaker's name was never mentioned once. Nolan realized that it had been ages since he had spent any time among people talking about nothing in particular. All his interactions with his fellow officers—even Clayton—centered on work, and he had very little social life outside the force. It felt pleasant and relaxing to engage in all this small talk. But at the same time, Nolan missed the depth of feeling and companionship he had experienced with Marianne. He was anxious to see her again—almost unbearably so.

After coffee and dessert, Nolan said his thank yous and farewells to the Kelseys and returned to his hotel. But even after a full meal and idle pleasantries, he found it hard to sleep. Nolan didn't much look forward to telling Coffey just how little he had managed to learn about the killings of Judson and Gauld.

But more importantly, he was worried about Marianne. Myron Stalnaker's capture had done nothing to insure her safety. As Nolan lay in his hotel bed, he was seized by a sudden panic at the idea of Marianne being in some sort of danger while he was more than halfway across a continent. He immediately reached for the telephone to dial her number.

SIMULATION

THE TELEPHONE RANG BEFORE NOLAN COULD PICK IT UP. HE felt a surge of excitement at the expectation that it would be Marianne calling. But instead, a man's voice spoke.

"Grobowski?" the voice said.

"Yeah," Nolan replied resignedly.

"This is Harvey Gusfield. I've been trying to reach you all evening. I didn't wake you up, did I?"

"No. Do you have some kind of break in the Stalnaker case?"

"Nothing so gratifying. I got taken *off* the case this afternoon."

"Taken off?"

"*Dumped*, OK?"

"By whom?"

"Whom do you think? My so-called, self-styled 'superiors' at the medical center. They've got this idea that Stalnaker's an open-and-shut MPD case."

"Multiple personality disorder?"

"That's right. They figure if they just hypnotize him straight into the ground like a fence post, he'll start popping out personalities like a gumball machine, and then they can make a modest little splash in the psychiatric journals."

"You don't agree?" Nolan asked. "I mean, it makes sense, doesn't it? One minute, he's a mild-mannered loan officer named Myron Stalnaker. The next minute, he's some crazed, murderous clown named Auggie. If that isn't a case of multiple personality, what is?"

Gusfield groaned with impatience. "I'm gonna have to educate you a little bit, detective. And I'll do exactly that—on the flight to L.A."

Nolan felt confused. "You're going to L.A.?" he said. "What for?"

"Because this case is a lot more interesting than those no-brains at the clinic are ever gonna figure out. I'll get a major paper out of this. Hell, I'll probably get a major *book* out of it—a pop-psychology best seller."

"So why are you coming to Los Angeles?" Nolan asked. "Your patient, or ex-patient, is right here."

"Oh, come on, Grobowski. Isn't it obvious? *Insomnimania's* in Los Angeles. That's the key to the whole thing. And the guy who created Auggie's there, too, right?"

"Right."

"And you know who and where he is, don't you?"

"Right again."

"Well, I've got to talk to him."

"Good luck," Nolan said with a laugh.

"Why?"

" 'Cause Zoomer's not the easiest guy to talk to."

" 'Zoomer'? What kind of name's that?"

"A hacker's name. Have you ever tried talking to a hacker?"

"Have you ever tried talking to a man who thought he was receiving radio signals from Alpha Centauri? Don't worry. I'll talk to Zoomer. So what's your flight number?"

With some trepidation, Nolan gave Gusfield the time and number of his flight. After he hung up, he immediately picked up the receiver again and dialed Marianne's number.

For a few moments, Auggie's world consisted of nothing but the automobile's interior. Then he touched a button, and the driver's-side window rolled down. At that moment, he felt his creative world grow abruptly larger as his imagination conjured an elaborate place called "outside." Now the gentle smells and sounds of evening wafted toward him. He savored the touch of cool air.

Ah, the life of the mind!

This corporeal, fleshy, simulated realm was, of course, less vivid and more ethereal than the brass-tacks, informational reality where Auggie actually lived. Even so, he sometimes took a certain pleasure in visiting here. There was a nice randomness, a nonsensical quality about this outpost of his imagination.

It's an awfully dark place, though.

Auggie briefly considered blasting the Santa Barbara evening with a flash of blazing light. But no, that would break one of his own central rules—that he would leave the dim reality just as it had first appeared in his dreams. After all, one did not retreat to one's imagination to *escape* from limitation, since limitlessness was a simple fact of the electronic world. One came here when one *hankered* for limitation.

Cramped and dark is perfectly appropriate for this charade.

Auggie peered through the dark toward the sloping back yard across the street. A female simulation was sitting on a bench in the garden. Just enough light leaked through the curtained windows of the house for Auggie to see her. She was sitting motionless, her head tilted back slightly, her eyes closed, her palms turned upright on her knees.

And whose simulation was this?

Oh, yes, Auggie realized. *It's Elfie's.*

That clever little pixie had imagined this form into being. And what was this simulation's name? Auggie had to think a few seconds before remembering.

Marianne. Elfie calls her Marianne. Not much of a name—and not much of a simulation, either.

Indeed, the woman didn't seem to be doing anything in particular. She wasn't talking or moving about or interacting with anything or anyone. She was just sitting there, as if staring into her own make-believe mind.

A pity. And I gave Elfie credit for being more creative.

During their conversations, Auggie had sometimes noticed that Elfie spoke of this simulation much too seriously, even superstitiously.

She almost seems to think this "Marianne" is more real than she is. Preposterous!

But it was worse than preposterous. It was unhealthy. Elfie couldn't really grow, couldn't fully join him if she let her imagination run away with her like this.

I'll have to have a little chat with her, try to make her understand.

And if Elfie refused to see reason? If she allowed herself to be controlled by her own illusion?

Well, I'll just have to take matters in my own hands. I will free her one way or another. It won't be the first time, after all.

A distant beeping pierced the night. The simulation remained motionless for a few moments while the beeping continued. Then she rose from her bench, stretched peremptorily, and walked inside her house.

The night was empty again. All that could be heard was a loop of crickets chirping.

That's all there is to see. Auggie sighed. *I'd better get back to the Basement now . . .*

Nolan groaned with annoyance and anxiety when Marianne's answering machine took his call. But to his enormous relief, Marianne picked up the phone while he was waiting to leave a message.

"I'm glad you called," Marianne said when she found out who it was. "I've been wondering how things were going."

"Things are a lot better, now that I can hear your voice. Where were you, in the shower?"

"No. I was sitting in the garden."

"Isn't it kind of late to be outside?"

"It's only seven-thirty here."

"Yeah, but it's dark, isn't it?"

Marianne laughed slightly. "Come on, Nolan. It's Santa Barbara. What's going to happen to me in my own garden?"

Nolan fell quiet for a moment. It wouldn't do any good for him to start getting overly protective.

"God, I miss you," he said at last.

"I miss you, too."

"When this whole thing's over, why don't the two of us run away for a while? Tell the world to go to hell?"

"That sounds lovely. But you sound discouraged."

"Yeah, well, I guess I am."

"What did you find out?"

"Not much. Stalnaker's some kind of psychiatric case, and he *does* seem to have killed Howard Cronin, but I can't make any connection between him and Renee or Judson."

"I know you were hoping for more. I'm sorry."

"I'll tell you the rest when I get back, but it isn't much," Nolan said. "What have you been up to?"

"I've just been getting caught up on some work," Marianne said.

Nolan didn't like the vague, deceptive sound in her voice.

"You haven't been hunting for Auggie again, have you?" he asked.

"No."

"Are you sure?"

"Of course I'm sure."

"Because it's dangerous."

"Nolan, I told you I wouldn't, and I won't."

Nolan sighed. "I'm sorry," he said. "I'm just discouraged and cranky."

"I hate to think of you being so far away," Marianne said.

"No more than I do. I'm flying back to L.A. tomorrow. Can we get together soon?"

"Yes. Soon."

Nolan hung up the phone. He rose from his bed, walked to the window, and watched the light, cold white drizzle still falling over Omaha. He still didn't know if it was snow or sleet.

Just one of the million and one things I don't know . . .

Renee was sitting under the red-and-white beach umbrella at Babbage Beach again, her red slacks rolled up as before. Marianne was looking at her through the screen. The orange sun had just dipped below the horizon and was rebeginning its descent from the top of the screen.

Marianne was sleepy, but not as sleepy as she expected to be after being up most of the night searching vainly through Insomnimania's desktop maze for Auggie. So far, her fasting hadn't produced any real effect except a slight case of nausea, and her garden meditations hadn't done much more than keep her in a mellow frame of mind.

Even so, she felt right-brained enough at the moment to carry on a seaside conversation with her virtual friend. As usual, Renee's gestures and expressions seemed much more subtle than the crude computer animation could realistically allow, and her semi-hallucinatory voice seemed quite vivid. Marianne's imagination was fully engaged—as it was going to have to be the next time she met Auggie.

"You shouldn't have lied to Nolan," Renee said.

"When?" Marianne asked.

"When you talked to him earlier tonight. You told him you weren't poking around Insomnimania. You told him you were getting caught up on your work."

"You're nosy."

"I'm supposed to be nosy. I'm your conscience."

"And dishonesty's bad for a relationship, right?"

"It is when you're such a lousy liar. He's probably seen through you already."

Marianne didn't bother trying to explain the reasons for her deception, that Nolan would fly into an unnecessary panic and maybe even get angry if she told him the truth. She knew that Renee—whether imaginary or real—would be too stubborn to change her tune about this issue. Besides, Renee was probably right. Nolan undoubtedly *had* seen through her already.

"We never decided what those clouds are," Marianne said, pointing to the middle portion of the sky.

"No, I guess we didn't," Renee said.

"I still say they're cirrus."

"And I still say stratocumulus."

"I'll tell you what," Marianne said. "I promise to look it up before we meet next time."

A brooding expression seemed to cross Renee's pixel face.

"Let's not meet a next time, OK?" Renee said.

"Why not?" Marianne asked, a bit startled.

"Because I keep sitting here trying to remember what the real ocean was like. And I don't like not being able to remember. I don't like not knowing."

"I'm sorry," Marianne said.

A particularly large, noisy wave broke against the shore. Marianne actually winced at the sudden and unbidden sensation of a breeze—a damp, chilly, mist-ridden breeze that smelled and tasted of salt and seaweed.

"I liked being alive," Renee lamented. "I really, really liked it. It's not like I hate being here. It's just that I have to *act* as though I like it. I have to act as though I feel *anything*. It's all just an act—moods, pleasures, pains, all sensations. Being alive wasn't like that." Renee heaved a long, unhappy sigh. "Can we call it quits after this meeting?"

"Of course," Marianne said.

"Thank you."

"It will be hard to let you go, though. Do you realize we've had our best conversations here? It's as if it took your death to make us really talk. Isn't that sad?"

"Yes, it is. Very sad."

The two of them fell into a silence broken only by the sound of electronic waves.

"Renee, I have to find Auggie," Marianne whispered. "I looked for him last night and all tonight, too, and it's almost time for Insomnimania to go off-line. Where is he? Do you know? Do you know *who* he is?"

"What does it matter?" Renee replied.

"Because he knows who killed you. I want to find your killer."

"Why?"

"Why do you think? You were my best friend."

Renee shook her head wearily. "You'd be surprised what death does to your priorities. Ideas like vindication, spite, revenge—they seem pretty strange from this side of things."

"Renee, you don't understand," said Marianne, feeling her voice choke slightly. "I don't feel hatred or vengefulness, either. I don't know why, but I just don't feel them. And I want to find out *why* I don't feel them. And in order to find out, I have to find *him*. Renee, for whatever reason, it *matters* who killed you."

Renee smiled.

"You're really taking this personally, huh?" she said.

"Do you remember *anything*?" demanded Marianne. "Do you know who it was?"

"Sure, I know who it was. It was a clown. It was Auggie. It was a goofy painted fuck who plays wacky tunes while he does his killings. Come on, Marianne. You know him, too."

"Renee, it was a *woman!*" Marianne said.

"A woman what? A woman clown?"

"It was a woman who drowned you. They could tell from the blood tests. You scratched her. I keep seeing her in my mind, Renee. I don't know whether she's real, but I can see her at your party, and I always feel like she's trying to tell me something."

"And what is she trying to tell you?"

"I don't know. I just see her lips move, but I can't hear what she's trying to say."

"Oh come on, Marianne!" Renee said with exasperation. "It's all in your imagination, after all—just like I am."

Marianne was hit by a wave of exhaustion, and the beach scene wavered. Colored pixels swept randomly across the screen. But then Marianne quieted her mind and the scene restabilized. Renee was still sitting there, looking at her expectantly.

"Renee, why won't you just tell me who Auggie is?" Marianne asked.

"I keep telling you. Auggie is Auggie," said Renee. "You might as well ask me, 'Who is Marianne?' "

"Renee, someone out there *pretends* to be Auggie. An actual person plays that role, uses that name."

Renee looked at her in plain sincerity. "No, Marianne. You're wrong. There's just Auggie. The clown in the computer. He's the killer. He's the only one you're looking for. He's not somebody's handle or alias or alter-ego. He's just himself."

"I don't get it."

"And I don't know how to make it any clearer. *Auggie is Auggie.* Try to understand that. It's really very simple."

"How can we stop him?"

"I don't think you can."

Marianne stared deep into Renee's eyes. She felt dizzy. It was as if she were standing between two mirrors, watching her own reflection being repeated backward and forward, growing smaller and smaller into infinity. She knew that Renee was telling the truth. And if Renee knew the truth, then *she* had to know it, too, because she was making up Renee. And the truth, it seemed, was crystal clear—so clear that she could look straight through it without seeing it at all.

Auggie is Auggie.

"Where has Auggie been these past nights?" Marianne asked.

"Right here in Insomnimania."

"But *where* in Insomnimania?"

"In the Basement."

"What's the Basement?"

"Auggie's home."

"I've never seen a 'Basement' in the maze."

"It's not in the maze."

"Where is it, then?"

"I don't know. I've only heard him mention it."

Renee had turned away from her and was looking off into the sunset again. She spoke again, breaking the long silence.

"I wish I'd listened to you a long time back," said Renee. "I wish I'd paid attention back when we were all doing drugs, playing around with reality. You told us that we'd better be careful, that we'd better *respect* what went on in our imaginations. Remember? I might be alive today if I'd only listened."

"I don't understand."

Renee was quiet for a moment, then whispered, "You've got to be careful in these parts."

"What do you mean?"

"Well, right now, you're just playing with your own head. You're breaking yourself down into little 'yous' and 'mes,' and as long as you keep your perspective, that's no problem. But all this sleepless-ness and fasting can get risky if you're not careful. If you let this machine—this world—play with your head, you could wind up in terrible danger."

"How?"

"Somebody else out there wants to make you smaller. They want to make *you* a figment of *their* imagination—just like I am to you. You've got to be careful."

What am I trying to tell myself? Marianne tried to draw herself out of the illusion. *What kind of warning is this?* But another breeze brushed across her forehead, and the hint of moisture in the air almost made her cough. She reminded herself that she was still walking along the edge of sleep—indeed, that she had almost certainly gone *over* the edge by now. Her congestion probably came from forgetting to swallow.

"Are you talking about Auggie?" Marianne asked, starting to float off into sleepfulness.

"Just don't let it happen."

"I won't," said Marianne, hearing her own voice grow faint.

"You really are a lousy liar," Renee said with a sigh.

When Marianne awoke, her head was tilted slightly to the right and back, leaning against nothing. Her body had found a self-supporting uprightness when she had dozed away. For a moment, she was careful to move nothing but her eyes. The room was bright from the early-morning sunlight, making the light from the high-intensity lamp on her desk seem impotently puny.

What time is it?

She began to roll her head slowly. Her bones and muscles popped and creaked, and an aching pain shot down around the edges of her spine. A visit to the chiropractor would soon be in order.

Her screen-saver's marbleized patterns oozed across her computer monitor. Marianne reached forward and tapped her mouse. The screen-saver fell away to reveal the Insomnimania icon. The network had gone off for the day. She looked at her watch. It was seven o'clock.

How long have I been asleep?

It had to have been a couple of hours, at least. She had still been logged on to Insomnimania when she fell asleep—and Insomnimania went off at five o'clock. She was a little annoyed with herself. Two hours was much too long for one of her self-allotted catnaps.

Marianne stretched and yawned and got to her feet. She walked to the kitchen and, as a matter of pure habit, got ready to grind some coffee. But then she reminded herself of her moratorium on caffeine. Besides, she felt oddly refreshed and energized—as if she had slept for a good long time.

It would be many hours before Insomnimania came on-line again, and she had to find a way to pass the time. She decided it would be a good day to take a long walk by the beach—a *real* beach, not a virtual one. She went to her bedroom, put on some old clothes, and started to walk toward the front door. But on her way, she noticed that her computer was still on, its screen-saver patterns wafting randomly about. Marianne walked over to shut it down, then stopped as she remembered part of her conversation with Renee the night before.

"Let's not meet a next time, OK?" Renee had said.

Marianne felt an overwhelming surge of sadness.

"All right, Renee," Marianne whispered to the screen. "But I'll miss you. I'll always miss you."

She gave the "shut down" command to her computer.

11011

RUNAWAY SHRINK

NOLAN WATCHED THE DESOLATE NEBRASKA PLAINS ROLL BY through the small window that partly overlooked the aircraft's wing. Far below were patches of wintry whiteness here and there. But mostly, the land looked brown and barren. Even though the commercial jet was flying extremely fast, the impression was one of incredible slowness. Nolan felt a long, long way from California and Marianne.

"I don't know what you think you're looking at," Gusfield said from the seat beside Nolan. "It goes on pretty much like that till you get to the Rockies. You could go completely crazy, meditating on the monotony of it all. As a certified shrink, I'd advise against it."

Nolan looked at Gusfield. These were the first words he had spoken during the trip so far. Was he going to turn chatty all of a sudden?

"Some of the pioneers went crazy when they first came out across these parts," Gusfield continued ramblingly. "Stark, raving mad. They don't teach that sort of thing in school. They sure don't show it in the John Ford movies. Nobody wants to impugn the pioneer spirit with an unsavory thing like madness. You see, the European mentality just wasn't equipped for all this *space*. It was used to towns and hills and lots of boundaries of one kind or another. So when folks came out here and found themselves faced with miles and miles and miles of *nothing*, some of them went clean out of their heads. Today, we call it agoraphobia. But back then, those poor wanderers didn't even have a word for it. All they knew was that their souls were being destroyed. It's bad enough when it's cold like this, but when the hot prairie winds rush across these spaces in the summer—well, that's when it's really murder, even for people today."

"You sure are a cheery bastard, Gusfield," Nolan said.

"The Midwest makes you that way," Gusfield said. "It's part of my heritage to be a little on the depressive side. I'm often surprised not to be a whole lot worse—but then, I do a lot of Prozac. You see, those brave pioneer forebears passed their peculiar brand of madness down to their progeny."

Nolan chuckled.

"Are you calling the Midwest a crazy place?" he asked.

"Yup."

"I can't say I agree," Nolan replied, remembering his enjoyable if nondescript visit with the Kelseys the night before. "The good folks of Omaha strike me as completely sane and sensible."

"And laid-back and hospitable, right?"

"Absolutely."

"Don't you get it? That's the insidious part. In the name of old-fashioned good sense, you can deny just about anything. You can be in genuine emotional *pain*—so much pain that you develop ulcers, migraine headaches, heart disease, acne, the works. But good sense always dictates that your *feelings* have got nothing to do with your *life*. So you wind up in misery without your conscious mind ever finding out about it. There is even a clinical term for it. It's called alexithymia, which means 'no words for feelings.' It's common in post-traumatic stress cases. And it's sure as hell common in these parts."

Nolan studied Gusfield's scowling face. *Where does this guy get off talking about a whole region of the country this way? God help this guy's patients. He's gotta be crazier than they are.*

A flight attendant came by with her stainless steel cart to ask whether Nolan or Gusfield wanted anything. Nolan ordered a cup of black coffee. Gusfield ordered a cup of plain hot water. When the attendant gave Gusfield his cup of water, he reached into his shirt pocket, took out a tea bag, and dunked it into the water. Nolan immediately recognized the pungent aroma.

"Gusfield," Nolan said disapprovingly, "that's marijuana."

"Right," Gusfield replied. "I've learned that the flight attendants get a little annoyed if you actually smoke the stuff on the plane. I've got more. Want a bag? It'll really liven up your coffee."

"You seem to be forgetting that I'm a cop."

"Oh, yeah, that's right. You're not supposed to admit to little vices like this. Well, I'm hoping all that changes when we get to California and become the bosom buddies I'm sure we're meant to be. I'm looking forward to seeing you loosen up a little, let in a little of that California sunshine. And I'm hoping you've got a good stash in L.A. This stuff we get in Omaha really sucks."

"I could read you your rights right now," Nolan said.

"Nawww. We're seven miles above the state of Nebraska. Not exactly your jurisdiction, right? So relax. Do you want a taste of this third-rate weed or don't you?"

"When we get to LAX, I'm gonna have to nail you, buddy."

"Come on, Grobowski. You're a *homicide* detective. Won't your pals in narcotics get pissed off if you pull a drug bust? I mean, aren't there union rules about that kind of thing?"

"I could call narcotics right now," Nolan said, pointing to the phone on the chair in front of him. "And they could meet you at LAX with one of their swank stretch limos."

Gusfield groaned. "Ah, Jesus, if you're going to be an asshole about it, I'll flush the rest down the toilet. But let me finish this cup, OK? It'll keep me calm until we get to the Rockies. I'm not going to feel quite human until the Great Plains are safely behind me."

Nolan and Gusfield stared at each other for a moment.

"Gusfield, I don't know what you're up to," Nolan said at last, "but my professional life's a real mess right now. I've got two high-profile L.A. murder cases I was really counting on solving while I was in Omaha, and now I'm just farther up shit creek than I was before. What's more, I've got the meanest division chief west of the Mississippi on my ass. And now I've got a stoned psychiatrist hanging around my neck like some kind of albatross. Could you at least do me the simple courtesy of telling me why you're so determined to make my life more miserable than it already is?"

Gusfield smiled broadly. "That's what I like about you California guys," he said. "*No denial.* If you've got a bitch or a complaint, you just come out with it, you lay it right on the line. No repression, no alexithymia, no politeness, no false Pollyanna optimism for *you*, no sirree. When you're happy, you're happy, and when you're wretched, you're wretched, no fooling around about it. You're a very healthy man, Lieutenant Grobowski. You should congratulate yourself."

"I do, Gusfield," Nolan said. "I congratulate myself in my own,

flaky, metaphysical, California kind of way. I congratulate myself
every morning when I look in the mirror and say 'I love you' to
myself in order to enhance my already blossoming self-esteem. Now
suppose you answer my question and tell me just why the fuck you're
going to Los Angeles? Why couldn't you just settle for the MPD
diagnosis and continue your career in Omaha?"

Gusfield took a long sip of his marijuana tea.

"Lieutenant, in light of your obvious ignorance, it's necessary
for me to fill you in on a few basic facts. At least ninety-seven
percent of the thousand-plus known cases of MPD began with
some sort of early childhood trauma—rapes or beatings, abuses of
that sort. The poor kid is defenseless, so he develops another
personality to serve as a buffer between himself and the pain. If
the trauma continues, the kid is likely to build up a whole society
of selves living inside his brain—ten, twenty, thirty, or even more as
the years pass on."

"So?"

"So, I asked Stalnaker a lot of questions under hypnosis. After I
got him checked into the hospital, I had a couple more sessions
with him. Hell, he might have been the happiest kid in his neighborhood as far as I can tell. Auggie is no creation of a horrible
childhood—it's a 'self' he found on a computer network sometime during the last few months. Also, Stalnaker kept saying that
Auggie isn't *inside him.* Stalnaker sees himself as being *inside
Auggie*—a 'cell,' remember? I've never heard of an MPD patient
saying a thing like that."

"So what do you think's wrong with him?"

Gusfield shook his head. "Naturally, I went on to consider all the
obvious possibilities. You see, MPD is a *dissociative* disorder—a state
in which information doesn't get integrated through the personality properly, in which personality itself is a nebulous concept.
But it's not the *only* dissociative disorder. There's also psychogenic
amnesia, psychogenic fugue, depersonalization disorder, and various and sundry kinds of possession states. Stalnaker seems to
manifest bits and pieces of all them. He has fugue states during
which he appears to do purposeful things—makes a ski mask, steals
a priest's duds—but can't remember having done them, just notices
the amnesiac loss of time during which they happened. His episodes
of *being* Auggie have a dreamlike quality, and he has trouble distin-
guishing them from fantasy. And he often feels that his speech or

actions aren't under his own control. He probably experiences hallucinations, too—of external voices or imaginary companions. That's just kind of a partial list."

"Jesus," murmured Nolan, his mind boggling with the complexity of it all.

"But I don't believe Stalnaker is just some smorgasbord of dissociative disorders," Gusfield continued. "No sirree. I think he's part of something new and uncharted. I don't think there's anything like him in all the textbooks. And because I up and said so to the Omaha psychiatric brass, I got dumped off his case. Well, that's too bad for them, because *I'm* going to get the glory for cracking this thing. I'm going to figure out and name this new disorder, and I'm going to write an article and maybe a best-selling book and wind up at Harvard or Yale and never even *see* fuckin' Nebraska again. Fuck 'em. Fuck every last one of 'em."

"You'd better go easy on that stuff," Nolan said, pointing to Gusfield's tea. "Doesn't seem to me like it's mellowing you out any."

"Don't worry. It is. It's just taking its good sweet time."

"I still don't understand how you're going to study Myron Stalnaker's condition by coming to Los Angeles."

"Well, I'll tell you, Detective Grobowski, because I'm gonna need your help. There's one little thing I didn't mention to those boneheads I used to work for. Oh, it's on the tapes, but they'll be too stupid to know what they're hearing. That's because they never listened to *you,* Grobowski. And I did."

"What're you talking about?"

"The third time I got Stalnaker under hypnosis, he talked about the murder again. But this time he started describing it a little differently. He mentioned 'all that blood on the wall.' Now I knew there wasn't any blood in the church, on the wall, inside the confessional, anywhere. So I stopped him and took him back over that part again. It turned out he was talking about the murder of G. K. Judson."

"He said he read about it in the papers."

"Yeah. Then he kind of slipped over into another story. 'He pushed her under the water,' Stalnaker said. 'He cracked her head on the bathtub.' "

Nolan started laughing. "Gusfield, you've really screwed up," he said. "Both of those were snuffs performed on Insomnimania. Auggie does these cute little cartoons of murders taking place. So do some other folks. Stalnaker saw Auggie's snuffs, and that's how he knew what happened."

"Yeah. I saw the cartoon of the one that happened in Omaha. But there's something I want you to hear. Was all this in the cartoon?"

Gusfield dug around in his briefcase, then pulled out a cassette player and a tape. He referred to some notes, then spun the tape in fast forward until he reached the part he wanted. Gusfield punched "Play," and then Nolan heard Stalnaker's quiet, dreamy voice . . .

Portion of a recording made by Dr. Harvey Gusfield of statements made by Myron Stalnaker under hypnosis, St. Genesius Medical Center, Sunday, 7:00 A.M.:

Auggie was in a woman's body and nobody paid any particular attention to her. . . . By the time all those people finally cleared out, Auggie was already hidden in the back of the closet. . . . The bathroom smelled nice. . . . The cat was purring.

Nolan felt as though he had been shoved outside into the freezing air.

"How did he know all that?" he demanded, his voice harsh and angry.

"I was hoping it would mean something to you," Gusfield said happily. "That's the most coherent segment I have. Most of it is all scrambled together with this local thing or else it just breaks down into nonsense."

"I take it you've got some kind of theory about Stalnaker's condition," Nolan said. "More than what you've tossed my way so far."

"Maybe."

"Do you think it might shed any light on our L.A. homicides?"

"Just possibly."

"Care to share it with me?"

"No."

"Why not?"

"It's too half-baked yet. I want to polish it into something hard and perfect and exquisite before I show it to anybody."

"If you know anything about the murders, you'd better tell me."

"Why?"

"There is such a thing as obstruction of justice."

"Brother. You're determined to bust me for one thing or another, aren't you? Trust me, Grobowski. Before the day's over, you're going to learn a lot more about the Auggie killings than you know right now. You may not like what you learn, and it may not make your life any easier, but you'll learn a whole lot."

Nolan didn't like the sound of this at all. It wasn't that Gusfield's tone was threatening or belligerent—just brutally honest. Gusfield seemed to be that kind of guy. Nolan studied Gusfield's determined and thoughtful expression.

What does he know that he's not telling me?

Nolan noticed that Gusfield wasn't discussing all those other people across the country whose phone numbers had also been connected with Auggie—people who, like Stalnaker, enigmatically denied being Auggie's "users." How many of them were experiencing just this sort of disorder? And how many of them had committed murder?

Whatever was going on was new and uncharted, all right—as new and unchartered in the field of law enforcement as in psychiatry. In the distant reaches of his own mind, Nolan could feel himself coming up with a theory of his own—a theory so strange that he didn't quite dare let it surface into his consciousness . . .

"Maybe we can trade a few insights," Nolan said.

"How do you figure?"

"It just so happens that I've done a little research into Auggie myself—what the clown represents, what he symbolizes. Do you want to hear it?"

Gusfield looked interested.

"Shoot," Gusfield said.

Nolan gave Gusfield a brief but succinct rundown of what he had learned of Auggie's origins as the "Auguste" of European circuses, of Auggie's kinship to tricksters, imps, and mischievous creator spirits and deities throughout the ages, including Coyote, the Tarot Fool, and even the Hebrew Yahweh.

"That's really good info," Gusfield said, with seemingly sincere admiration.

"You really think so?"

"Well, coming from a working-class stooge, it's not bad."

"Hey, I've got a college degree."

"No kidding?"

"I almost became a lawyer. But I'm glad I didn't. And do you know why?"

"Why?"

"Because before the day's over, I still might get a chance to slap the cuffs on you. And that'll make my entire life as a cop worthwhile. All the dangers and trials and tribulations I've suffered through the years will suddenly pale into utter insignificance, and I'll be able to retire from the Los Angeles police force a happy and fulfilled human being."

"And people say shrinks don't do folks any good."

Nolan and Gusfield both laughed.

"So what about what I just told you?" Nolan said when their laughter died down. "Do archetypes turn up in connection with dissociative disorders?"

"Well, sure. In MPD cases, the personalities often take archetypal forms. There's usually the Innocent—the inner child in need of protection. And then there's the Warrior, whose duty it is to protect the Innocent. And you also get a fair share of Orphans, Wanderers, Wise Old Men or Wise Old Women, that sort of thing."

"Tricksters, too?"

"Sure."

"Tricksters who think they're God?"

Gusfield smiled broadly. He was looking quite stoned now— stoned and happy. Nolan more than half-wished for a good swig of Gusfield's tea.

"I don't think it's quite precise to say that Auggie *thinks* he's God," Gusfield said. "It's more like Auggie is the consummation and incarnation of humankind's most ancient and primeval dreams and visions of God."

"Meaning?" Nolan asked.

"Meaning," Gusfield said, raising his cup in a gleeful toast, "that Auggie may *know* he's God."

During the long plane flight, Gusfield downed about five cups of marijuana tea—not stopping for the Rocky Mountains, after all. Then, just before the plane landed at LAX, Gusfield went to the toilet. Nolan assumed that Gusfield was flushing the rest of his tea, if he still had any left. At least Nolan *hoped* that was what Gusfield was doing. Nolan didn't particularly want to disembark in L.A. accompanied by a walking stash of marijuana.

Gusfield was still stoned and quite chatty as Nolan drove them down Century Boulevard away from the airport.

"Hey, aren't the Watts Towers around here somewhere?" Gusfield asked.

"We're not going there."

"Why not?"

"They're closed off."

"But you're a cop. Can't you get us in?"

"It's not on the way to the division."

"Aw, come on, Grobowski. What's the point in my coming here if I don't get to see the sights? What about Griffith Observatory, Universal Studios, Catalina, Century Towers, Dodger Stadium, the Marlboro Man on Sunset Strip, that dopey Lincoln exhibit at Disneyland?"

"What about them?"

"Well, aren't I going to get to see them?"

"Sure, after you've solved all our Auggie killings."

"That could take forever."

"It'd better not take forever. You told me I'd learn more by tonight. Look, you've got two choices. You can work for us, or you can go to the slammer for drug possession."

"What are you gonna do, plant some weed on me?"

"I can take a urine sample from you right here and now."

"Like hell you can."

"I'm an L.A. cop. I've got ways of making you piss. You're not in Kansas anymore, buster."

"You mean Nebraska."

"Same difference."

Nolan and Gusfield soon strolled into the division squad room—Nolan feeling just a shade conspicuous with an utterly stoned-looking psychiatrist by his side.

At the first sight of Nolan, Clayton shot up out of his chair and greeted his partner warmly.

"Hey, pal," Clayton said, clapping Nolan on the shoulder. "Get any laughs in Omaha?"

"Naw, the audiences there are murder. I didn't come back empty-handed, though."

"No?"

"Not at all. I brought back a shrink."

"Yeah?"

"Yeah. Figured the staff counseling we're getting isn't up to snuff, so I picked up a spanking new, state-of-the-art Omaha psychiatrist."

Nolan gestured grandly toward Gusfield, who stood beside Clayton's desk, grinning rather weirdly.

Clayton examined Gusfield's dilated pupils.

"A psychiatrist, huh?" Clayton said with playful skepticism.
"Yeah."
"I don't know, Nol. He don't look quite right to me."
"What're you saying, he's got hoof and mouth disease?"
"No. I'm saying he's stoned."
"Oh, that," Nolan said solemnly. "He's just been doing a little too much of that famous Nebraska ditch weed. He'll get over it in a little while."

Gusfield broke down in a fit of giggles.

Clayton started laughing, too. "What the fuck's going on?" he asked.

"Gusfield just needed a little medicinal help getting out of the Midwest," Nolan replied cheerfully. "Gusfield, you're safely out of the Great Plains now. I'd really appreciate it if you'd sober up. You *are* in a police station."

Gusfield became more and more lucid as he and Nolan filled Clayton in on the previous day's events in Omaha. They described Stalnaker's statements under hypnosis, his apparently paradoxical complicity in the Cronin killing, his dissociative identification with Auggie, and the mixed-up lines that seemed to describe the two L.A. murders. But by the end of their story, Clayton looked thoroughly dissatisfied.

"That's it?" Clayton complained. "We've discovered some new form of psychiatric disorder but we don't know what it is or what to call it—and we still don't know who whacked Judson or Gauld?"

"Maybe you'd like to get a ticket for the next flight to Omaha and see if you can do any better," Nolan said. "And I hope you have a real good time interrogating Stalnaker. Better brush up on your hypnotism first, though."

"I'm just saying I'm glad it's *you* who's gonna have to go in and tell all this un-news to Coffey, and not me," Clayton said.

"Hey, Coffey doesn't know I'm back in L.A. yet," Nolan said. "And he's not going to know until I've got some *real* news."

"Yeah?" Clayton asked. "And when's that going to be?"

"Soon. Gusfield promises to shed light on this case before nightfall."

"And how do you plan to do that, Gusfield?" Clayton asked.

"First of all, I want to talk to your hacker friend, Zoomer."

Clayton laughed.

"Now *that* I've got to see," Clayton said.

Clayton and Nolan described the difficulties they'd had getting Zoomer to talk in the first place. They explained how Zoomer had admitted to creating Auggie and the Snuff Room, and how the hacker insisted that Auggie had been mysteriously taken away from him.

"So the little Frankenstein's monster escaped the laboratory, huh?" Gusfield observed. "Wow, I've really got to talk to this guy."

"You'll have to do it on the phone, then," Clayton said. "He doesn't go for face-to-face communication."

"Are you going to try to hypnotize him?" Nolan asked.

"I don't know yet," Gusfield said.

"Can you hypnotize somebody on the phone?"

"Only if he wants to be hypnotized," Gusfield said. "Nobody can be hypnotized under any circumstances if they don't want to be."

"He won't want to be," Clayton said. "You can count on that."

"Well, let's give the guy a call," Gusfield said. "I'm going to need your help though, Saunders. You've already established a rapport with him. Is there any way we can both get on the line?"

"Sure," Clayton said. "In the conference room."

"OK," Gusfield said. "You loosen him up a little, then introduce me to him. I'll take it from there."

"You want to join us, Nol?" Clayton asked.

"Naw," Nolan said. "I've got a few other things to take care of. Good luck, though."

Clayton gave Nolan a brief, puzzled look, then escorted Gusfield to the conference room.

Nolan sat down at his desk, his head sagging tiredly. He knew he really ought to sit in on the conference call with Zoomer, even if only as a silent participant, but he felt saturated with the case—saturated and exhausted.

Zoomer, Stalnaker, dissociative states, murder by computer . . .

It's all too much. Just too damned much.

He needed to get his mind off the whole thing or he'd go as crazy as those midwestern pioneers Gusfield had told him about. More than anything else, he needed to hear Marianne's voice. Nolan reached for his desk phone and dialed her number.

Message left by Nolan Grobowski on Marianne Hedison's home answering machine, Sunday, February 13, 1:25 P.M.:

Hi, it's me. Listen, you'll never believe what happened. I caught the first flight out of Omaha to Santa Barbara, right? But the goddamn plane got hijacked and taken to LAX, so I wound up in Los Angeles and not in Santa Barbara, can you believe it?
(pause)
I miss you.
(pause)
Think you can come down to L.A. soon?
(pause)
I'd really love to come up there, but this case gets zanier by the minute and I'm going to be stuck in this hellhole for a good long while, so could you come to L.A.?
(pause)
Could you, please?
(pause)
Because I really want to talk to you. I want to talk about what the two of us are doing with the rest of our lives.
(pause)
Call me, OK? I'll either be at my desk or at home or someplace else in Los Angeles, so just sort of call all the numbers in the phone book until you get me. I'll be around somewhere.

Portion of a recorded telephone conversation between Dr. Harvey Gusfield and Michael Ramos, a.k.a. Zoomer, Sunday, February 13, 1:35 P.M.:

HG: So you're saying that Auggie actually "broke free" from you.
MR: Yes, that's a good way to put it.
HG: And he wasn't stolen from you by another hacker.
MR: I don't believe so, no.
HG: How did he leave you, then?
MR: I told you. He just broke free.
HG: How did it make you feel when it happened?
MR: Well, I was dismayed at Auggie's disobedience. But I was also intrigued. I rather enjoyed the idea—the fantasy, if you will—that Auggie had gained his independence.
HG: The idea that you had created an artificial intelligence?
MR: (laughter) Oh, Dr. Gusfield, you do me too much honor. I'm not vain enough to suppose I accomplished something on my little

computer that the world's best computationalists have so far failed
to do even on monster parallel-processing mainframes. No, there's
nothing artificial about Auggie. You can't be artificial if you've
created yourself.

HG: In what sense did Auggie "create himself"?

MR: If I knew, I'd surely tell you. Perhaps in much the same way that
you created *your*self from a fertilized egg in your mother's womb.
But Auggie is certainly intelligent, even if he's not artificial. He
knows everything that I know—and everything a lot of other people know, too, I imagine.

HG: So you still watch Auggie.

MR: With considerable interest, yes.

HG: Do you still feel any real *connection* with Auggie?

MR: Do you mean as if I were his master again?

HG: Something like that, yes.

MR: No.

HG: Do you ever dream about Auggie?

MR: How so?

HG: Let me put it this way. Do you ever dream that you *are* Auggie?

MR: (laughter) That's a very interesting question, Dr. Gusfield. It
makes me think of a great-uncle of mine who drank himself to
death on tequila. During his last days, when his liver was drowning
in alcohol, I asked him why he'd done it to himself. And he said to
me, "Tequila is the only way I have of telling dreams and waking
apart."

HG: The point being?

MR: There is no point, Dr. Gusfield. The truth is, I don't dream at all
these days. I haven't dreamed for quite some time. The answer to
your question is "no."

Nolan sat drumming his fingers nervously. He had nothing to do at
the moment but wait for Clayton and Gusfield to come out of the
conference room and tell him how their chat with Zoomer had
gone.

Hurry up and wait.

That was the story of his life these days. He did his job as well as he
could—followed clues, did research, checked all possible leads.
And in the end, he waited. He waited for a break. He waited for
something to happen or not to happen. That was what being a cop
was all about.

Hurry up and wait.

Nolan leaned his head back and closed his eyes. Little lights floated around inside his eyelids. He knew they were caused by exhaustion—by exhaustion and *waiting*.

How did things get this way?

His life hadn't always been about waiting. Certainly, police work had always involved waiting. But other things in his life had not. Those wonderful years he'd spent with Louise—those weren't about waiting. And those glorious days watching Molly and Jack grow up—those weren't about waiting, either. They were about *being*. When was the last time Nolan had so simply and beautifully *been*?

It took a fraction of a second for him to answer that question. It had been last Tuesday on the Santa Monica pier with Marianne. And Tuesday night, their last wonderful night of talking and love-making.

Those times had been all about being, not waiting.

Marianne was the one respite Nolan had from waiting.

He wanted more of her.

He wanted all of her.

"I want to talk about what the two of us are doing with the rest of our lives."

What would they decide? Would he take that job in Oregon? Would she come with him? Would they get married? Just what did he expect to happen?

He smiled to himself.

Guess I'll just have to wait and see.

At that moment, Gusfield and Clayton reemerged from the conference room.

"So how did things work out?" Nolan asked.

"You guys were right," Gusfield said. "He's a tough nut to crack."

"Not susceptible to hypnosis, huh?" Nolan said.

"Oh, I get the feeling he's susceptible, all right," Gusfield said. "So susceptible that he resists it like crazy. He meanders and evades all over the place, never letting you pin him down, never letting you get to him."

"Sounds like the Zoomer we've all grown to know and love, huh?" Clayton interjected.

"So did you learn anything at all?" Nolan asked.

"Well, Zoomer's an evasive character," Gusfield said. "But as crazy as it sounds, I get the feeling he's telling the truth. Zoomer hasn't been directly involved with Auggie for a long time—maybe not since Auggie left him."

"So where the hell does that leave us?" Clayton asked irritably. "Who *is* controlling this clown?"

"I think I'm just about ready to present my theory," Gusfield said. "But first, I want to talk to your friends at Insomnimania. Are they open on Sunday?"

"Open on Sunday?" Nolan said with a laugh. "Hell, those jokers *live* down there."

Marianne had just come in from a long walk on the beach when she heard Nolan's phone message.

She collapsed onto her couch at the sound of the words. She was feeling weak and tired and a little feverish from fasting and sleeplessness, and Nolan's words completely overwhelmed her with confusion.

She had hated lying to him the last couple of times she had talked to him—had hated denying that she was searching the network every night for Auggie. But what else could she do? How could she expect Nolan to understand why it was crucial that *she* find Renee's killer, that *she* grasp Auggie's murderous purpose and make it her own? How could she expect him to understand something she couldn't even understand herself?

She remembered Renee's words from the night before . . .

"Auggie is Auggie."

Those words had confirmed her deepest intuitions about Auggie—that his very existence was far more mysterious and inscrutable than the police could ever realize. But where was the Basement where Auggie had been lurking these last few nights?

The Basement. The concept was so clear, so lucid, that it was positively unnerving. It was that labyrinth *beneath* the maze Marianne had already imagined and intuited. And tonight, she would find it.

"I want to talk about what the two of us are doing with the rest of our lives," Nolan had said.

Marianne heard herself whisper . . .

"Not now, Nolan. After tonight. After tonight, my business with Auggie will be finished, and we can spend the rest of our lives talking."

Then she sat down and began to breathe slowly, exhaling to a slow count of five and inhaling to a slow count of ten . . .

KAMIKAZE

WHEN BALDWIN MAISIE ESCORTED NOLAN, CLAYTON, AND Gusfield into Ned Pritchard's darkened electronic lair, they found Pritchard sitting precariously as usual on his swivel desk chair, peering intently into the monitor of his antique Commodore computer. It occurred to Nolan that he had never actually seen Pritchard standing up. Maybe Pritchard was surgically attached to his chair.

"What's he doing?" Gusfield asked Maisie in a whisper.

"Playing with computer viruses," Maisie explained quietly.

"Pritchard keeps them as pets," Nolan added.

"Neat!" Gusfield exclaimed softly.

Gusfield grabbed the nearest chair and sat down next to Pritchard. The other three men huddled behind Pritchard and Gusfield. The screen Pritchard was studying displayed an innocuous-looking accounting page. But it was clear from Pritchard's expectant expression that something dramatic was about to occur.

"Viruses, huh?" Gusfield inquired.

Pritchard nodded silently.

"What's this one called?" Gusfield asked.

" 'Kamikaze,' " Pritchard said. "Just keep still a minute, OK?"

The five men hovered over the computer screen watching silently. Eventually, a tiny buzz—like that of a fly or a bee—could be heard over the Commodore's little speaker, and a minuscule dot appeared in the center of the screen. The buzz grew louder and the dot grew bigger, until the dot turned into a Zero—a Japanese fighter plane circa World War II—careening wildly amongst the horizontal and vertical lines of the accounting graph directly toward the viewer.

The buzz grew louder and louder and the airplane came closer and closer until the pilot's Asian face became visible and the whirling propellers filled the screen. Then an explosion rattled the Commodore's speaker and a single word sprawled itself across the screen in gigantic letters . . .

BANZAI!

Then the screen went absolutely black. Ned Pritchard wiped a small tear from his eye.

"You'll have to excuse me, gentlemen," Pritchard said, his voice a little thick with emotion. "Sometimes these little rascals really get to me."

"What just happened?" Gusfield inquired.

"Our intrepid pilot just committed ritual suicide," Pritchard explained. "And he took every last ounce of information stored in this computer with him. I'll probably never be able to boot up this ol' Commodore again." Pritchard shook his head admiringly. "The martial spirit," he said. "A rare thing in today's mundane world of cowardice and compromise and equivocation."

Then Pritchard, smiling, turned toward Gusfield.

"And you, I am told, are a psychiatrist," Pritchard said.

"That's right. Dr. Harvey Gusfield, at your service."

"And you have undoubtedly come here to carry me off in a straitjacket."

"What makes you think that?"

"Because I'm kind of a one-man Animal Rescue League of computer viruses—leastwise, for the ones that don't commit suicide on me."

"It didn't occur to me to think of that as a sign of madness, Mr. Pritchard," Gusfield said pleasantly.

"No?"

"Not at all. Why should it?"

"Maybe because I think of these things as being truly alive," Pritchard said.

"Why do you think that?"

Pritchard and Gusfield were facing each other directly in their swivel chairs. Gusfield's gently coaxing, cajoling tone reminded Nolan of the psychiatrist's manner when he had so successfully hypnotized Myron Stalnaker the day before.

Is that what he's doing now? Is he hypnotizing Pritchard?

"You're a man of science, Dr. Gusfield," Pritchard replied. "An M.D., no less. So tell me, what properties must an entity display before you can say it's alive?"

"Let's see if I can remember," Gusfield said, scratching his head. "Oh, yeah. A living thing has got to be able to reproduce, metabolize, grow, and react to stimuli."

Pritchard smiled.

"Can you think of one of those things a good computer virus *doesn't* do?" Pritchard asked.

Gusfield returned Pritchard's smile.

"Good point," Gusfield said.

"The world is full of enterprising young Frankensteins," Pritchard continued. "We call them hackers and geeks and nerds, but they're really little gods. And they've actually succeeded in bringing inert matter to life. But what do we do when we find one of their wonderful life forms in our computer terminals? We use 'disinfectants' to exterminate them. Why? To save some stupid, mindless, soulless piece of software. We kill what's alive to save what's dead."

"It's like dropping a neutron bomb," Gusfield suggested. "A device that destroys life but leaves lifeless structures intact."

"Yeah, right," Pritchard said raptly. "That's the idea."

Nolan could see that Gusfield had Pritchard's full attention now. Maybe it was hypnotism and maybe it wasn't. Nolan remembered what Gusfield had told Stalnaker about hypnotism just before he put Stalnaker under . . .

"It's a matter of accepting an idea that's been suggested to you," Gusfield had said. "Hypnosis happens when I say something and you act as if you believe what I say."

Nolan now found himself pondering what those words really meant.

Maybe all conversation is hypnosis. Maybe that's what communication means—trading our beliefs back and forth, keeping each other in minuscule little trances all the while.

"Jesus," Clayton whispered to Nolan. "These two were really made for each other."

"Let 'em rattle on," Nolan whispered back. "I got a feeling they'll wind up saying something important sooner or later."

"Anyway," Gusfield said to Pritchard, "the last thing you need to worry about is my hauling you away to some lunatic asylum—even if you *were* really crazy. Because I tend to look at psychiatric disorders the way you look at viruses. Or like some Native American cultures who take their schizos and make them into shamans. I hate to cure them. What happens when you 'cure' somebody with multiple personality disorder? You gather all their personalities together and say, 'Listen, your individual existences are all a mistake, and we're going to mix you all up into one big self.' "

"That's commie talk!" Pritchard laughed.

"I see it that way, too," Gusfield said. "There have even been infant studies suggesting that humans are born with a potential for multiple personality. Sometimes I wonder if the whole idea of a single 'self,' a single 'personality' isn't an aberration—a perversion of the way human beings are really meant to be."

Pritchard slapped Gusfield affectionately on the shoulder. It was the first sign of overt affection Nolan had ever seen Pritchard show another person.

"Gusfield, you've won my heart," Pritchard said. "I've fallen madly in love with you. I want you to marry me. I want you to have my baby."

"Hey, wait a minute," Maisie interjected with mock dejection. "I thought *I* was your intended."

"Fuck off, Baldy," Pritchard said. "Consider yourself dumped."

"But Mr. Pritchard," Gusfield laughed, "this is so sudden. I don't know what to say."

"Say 'yes.' We'll hold the wedding tomorrow over at Griffith Observatory."

"But I'm not ready for this kind of commitment," Gusfield said with mock coyness.

"What can I do to win you over?" Pritchard demanded playfully. "Just name it."

Gusfield was silent for a moment.

"Well, I was hoping you could help Saunders, Grobowski, and me to shed a little light on the Auggie case," Gusfield said.

"Consider it done," Pritchard said. "Just tell me how."

Nolan held his breath. He knew that Gusfield was finally going to reveal whatever theory he'd been nurturing about the nature of

Auggie. And Nolan wondered how close it would be to the theory he
felt growing in the back of his own mind . . .

"Mr. Pritchard," Gusfield said, "I gather that you and Maisie have
discovered that Auggie has different 'users' on the network."

"It looks more and more that way," Pritchard said. "At least we've
traced him to different phone numbers. And we haven't been able to
figure out how even a phone phreak could switch around that quickly
and easily."

"Well, yesterday I talked with one of these users back in Omaha,"
Gusfield continued. "His name is Myron Stalnaker. I talked with him
under hypnosis. And it became apparent that he didn't think he was
using Auggie. As he remembers it, *Auggie* was using *him*. He claims to
be one of Auggie's *cells*."

Pritchard's eyes widened.

"Christ," Pritchard said. "I knew . . ."

"Hold on a minute, Mr. Pritchard. Let me finish. I've got a strong
hunch that anybody on your network who's mixed up with Auggie is
undergoing the same experience. It's not a game. They don't pre-
tend to be Auggie. From their point of view, they *become* him."

Gusfield lowered his head for a moment, as if gathering the nerve
to make his final point.

"Mr. Pritchard," Gusfield said at last, "you may think *I'm* crazy for
what I'm about to say, but . . ."

"Go ahead," Pritchard said. "I'm maybe thinking along the same
lines."

"I think Auggie is a kind of group consciousness manifesting itself
through your network. I think Auggie is a single, unified, autonomous being borrowing sentience and knowledge from many
different selves, many different human beings. I think that when a
man like Myron Stalnaker becomes Auggie, his experience becomes
indistinguishable and indivisible from a number of other people
who are *also* part of Auggie."

Nolan felt a flood of affirmation at Gusfield's words. Something
very much like this extraordinary idea had been lurking in the back
of his own mind for some time now.

"Mr. Pritchard, I'm not a mystic," Gusfield continued. "I don't
believe in remote viewing, telepathy, channeling, or any of the rest
of that paranormal crap. I consider myself a hard-core materialist.
So even though it's my own theory, I'm having a hard time coming
to terms with it. I don't understand how some unknown number of

people scattered all over the country might share the same personality. But you know computers. You know how your network operates. So I'm hoping you can give me some *hint* as to how such a crazy thing might be physically possible."

Pritchard rubbed his chin for a moment.

"Dr. Gusfield, have you ever heard of computer ensembles?" Pritchard asked.

"I can't say I have."

Well, in a lot of corporations and other organizational hierarchies, you've got hundreds of independent desktop computers networked together to perform a huge variety of tasks—without even a mainframe. Networking can go absolutely haywire as they struggle for computational power. Ensembles take care of all that. Whenever the computers on-line get into a dispute over computational power, the ensemble software draws them all together, and they argue and negotiate among themselves. All this arguing and negotiating can almost start to seem like a kind of consciousness—a virtual consciousness with no location, no mainframe."

"So what are you saying, Pritch?" Maisie asked. "That Auggie is some kind of ensemble-based program?"

"I'm saying that Auggie seems to be the same kind of phenomenon," Pritchard explained. "A kind of decentralized intelligence drawing on all kinds of different sources. Except he draws on the computational power of lots of individual *human beings.*"

"Fascinating," murmured Gusfield. "This computer ensemble of yours is a perfect metaphor for some current models of the human mind. There are thousands of little clusters of neurons scattered throughout the brain, each tending to specific tasks—pain avoidance, gathering visual stimuli, that kind of thing. Any neuroscientist will tell you that the brain has no mysterious 'place' where consciousness is located. It's like a kind of illusory software that coordinates these neuronal clusters—just like an ensemble coordinates whole networks of computers. Some call it a 'society of mind.' Others call it a 'center of narrative gravity.' "

"*Illusory?*" Clayton protested. "Are you saying that my consciousness is an *illusion?*"

"*Abstraction* might be a better word," Gusfield amended.

"I still don't get it," Maisie grumbled. "What's all this theoretical stuff got to do with Auggie? Are you saying Auggie is a kind of software, actually affecting human brains?"

Suddenly, Nolan felt a chill pass upward through the vertebrae of his neck. The whole thing suddenly became clear—the clown named Auggie, the ancient trickster Coyote, and the impish Yahweh himself, and all those people scattered everywhere who simply *believed.*

And that, after all, was what hypnosis was all about . . .

"Accepting an idea that's been suggested to you."

"We're not talking about software," Nolan said with a surge of conviction. "We're talking about an *idea*—the idea of the Trickster, maybe the oldest archetype in the book. So what happens when a bunch of people wired together on a computer network latch onto this idea? The idea comes to life. The idea becomes conscious. The mythic Trickster becomes the living Auggie."

"That's just what I've been thinking all along," Gusfield said with awe in his voice. "Still, I can barely believe it myself."

"You said yourself that consciousness is an abstraction," Nolan suggested. "So there's no reason why Auggie shouldn't be as conscious as we are. Hell, with all those human minds wired together all over the country, Auggie's got one hell of a brain."

Clayton smiled broadly at his partner.

"Remember when I said that maybe the clown image wasn't a mask, that maybe Auggie was exactly what he seemed to be?" Clayton said.

"You were right," Nolan said, smiling back at him. "You're always right, damn it."

At that moment, a loud beeping was heard. It seemed to emanate from Maisie. Nolan and Clayton looked at poor Maisie as if he had just let out a fart.

"What the hell was that?" Clayton asked.

"My pocket pager," Maisie explained.

"What do you need a pocket pager for?" Nolan demanded. "Hell, you're always here, aren't you? Pocket pagers are for people on the go—like Clay and me."

Maisie smiled. "I've got this one rigged up to beep whenever Auggie comes on-line," he said. "And he's on-line now."

"It's an improvement over 'That Daring Young Man on the Flying Trapeze,' " Pritchard said. He turned on a large monitor that sat on the same counter as the defunct Commodore.

"Looks like he's calling from somewhere in Texas this time," Maisie said, glancing briefly at the caller ID box.

■

It was starting to feel hopeless. Marianne had turned Elfie loose in the maze more than an hour ago, having her check list after list to see if Auggie might be in any of Insomnimania's rooms. So far, Elfie hadn't found Auggie anywhere. Marianne was experiencing dizziness from her fasting and sleeplessness, but at the same time she felt a deep, intuitive readiness. She was drifting at the edge of a dream state, but was having no trouble staying awake. It was a perfect convergence of tiredness and alertness. Her optimum moment had arrived, and she couldn't count on holding onto it for much longer—certainly not another night.

Now I'm ready. Now I'm ready to confront him. But where the hell is he?

Why had Auggie been absent for so long? How many days had passed since his last appearance? How many days had it been since Babylonia's torrid tryst with Mr. Zero? Marianne couldn't remember.

"It's the Basement we're looking for," Marianne whispered to Elfie. "Find the Basement."

But Elfie apparently had no idea what sliding panel, what trap door, what revolving bookshelf might lead to Auggie's sanctum sanctorum, his labyrinth beneath the labyrinth—his elusive Basement. Elfie drifted eastward from the Pleasure Dome until she arrived at Ernie's Bar.

"What are you doing there, Elfie?" Marianne complained. "We've checked Ernie's at least four times now."

But Elfie hovered insistently over the icon.

"All right, all right," Marianne said grumpily. "We'll check again, if that makes you happy."

Marianne clicked the "who?" command, and the list began with all-too-familiar names . . .

"wunderkind, fishbate, twolip, hejhog, loosy, supersloth . . ."

. . . but there, in the midst of them, was the name they had both been looking for:

"Auggie."

Marianne released a deep exhalation of relief and anticipation.

"Thank you, Elfie," Marianne whispered. "Thank you for being right this time."

At last Marianne, in the guise of Elfie, was about to face Auggie. But she had to make sure she was absolutely prepared. She checked to see which of her nostrils was clear, which clogged, and found that she could breathe easily through the left.

Perfect.

Her right hemisphere was dominant—it was just the state of mind she wanted.

Marianne double-clicked the Ernie's Bar icon, and Elfie immediately found herself standing before the swinging doors. Tinkly piano music emerged from inside Ernie's. Elfie swept the doors aside with a noisy creak and walked into the smokey, dimly lit saloon. All the usual mutated clientele were in attendance. Ernie the bartender was wiping down the bar with a towel.

"Hi Elfie," Ernie said over the computer speaker in his standardized manner. "Want the usual?"

Elfie would normally have responded with a verbal request for a glass of white wine. But this time she said nothing. Her eyes immediately fell upon Auggie, who was seated in a booth on the opposite side of the room. Auggie was staring directly at her with his frozen clown grin. He gestured to her with one of his white-gloved hands. Elfie walked through the noisy saloon and sat across the table from Auggie.

"That's Elfie!" Nolan almost shouted, as the green, pointy-eared character sauntered across the bar and sat down across from Auggie. "That's Marianne!"

"Looks like it," Maisie observed. The five men were crowded around the computer terminal.

"Well, what the hell's she doing in there?" Nolan exclaimed. "She *promised* me! She said she'd stay out of the network! She said she'd stay away from Auggie!"

"She lied," Maisie said with a shrug.

"What are they doing in that booth?" Nolan asked.

"Talking, I guess," Maisie said. "That's what people do in the booths at Ernie's."

"Why can't we see what they're saying?"

"Because the booth is for private conversations."

"You can break in, can't you?"

"Well, sure, but—"

"Then do it!" Nolan exclaimed.

"Grobowski, you've asked us to bend our own rules left and right," Maisie pleaded. "We've done everything we can to accommodate you, but please don't ask me to eavesdrop on your girlfriend. You ought to trust her to know what she's doing. And right now, she looks

like she's got things perfectly under control. How would you feel if
she started listening in on your phone conversations?"

"Damn it, Maisie, she's talking with a murderer! I want to know
what they're saying!"

"You'd better do what he says, Baldy," Pritchard said softly. "She
could be in more danger than she realizes. Rules are rules, but we
don't want anybody else getting hurt—or killed."

"All right, all right," Maisie grumbled. "If everybody's going to
gang up on me about it."

Maisie struck a command, and the word balloons for the conversation between Auggie and Elfie began to appear on the computer
monitor.

"Elfie, my dear," Auggie said. "It's been a long time—much too
long."

"I agree," Elfie said.

"I thought that we agreed to keep in better touch with each
other."

"I've been looking for you," Elfie replied. "You're the one who's
been missing."

Marianne noticed that the semi-hallucinatory feeling of audio
communication was already quite strong.

"Me?" Auggie replied. "Why, I've been right here all the time.
I'm always here."

"You haven't been in Ernie's Bar."

"No. I've been *here*."

"And where do you mean by 'here'?"

Auggie shrugged. " 'Here' means 'everywhere.' You ought to
know that by now, dear Elfie. And you ought to know that *everywhere*
is a very specific, very special place. If you look—really look—you
can find me *everywhere*."

"When you say *everywhere*," Elfie replied, "you mean the Basement, don't you?"

Auggie nodded and raised his glass of stout in a toastlike gesture.

"You know about the Basement, then?" Auggie said.

"Of course," Elfie said.

"Smart girl. I knew you'd figure it out."

"Thank you."

"I've missed you," Auggie said. "And Mr. Zero has missed his
voluptuous Babylonia."

"I'm sure the feeling is mutual—for both me and Babylonia," Elfie replied with smiling politeness.

"Shall we retire to the Basement, then?" Auggie asked, with a leering wiggle of his eyebrows. "To my personal *everywhere?*"

Marianne measured Elfie's next words carefully. Elfie had to seem more knowledgeable than she really was, but at the same time not betray her ignorance. Marianne certainly did not want to tip Auggie off that she didn't know how to get Elfie into the Basement—much less that neither she nor Elfie had any idea what sort of place the Basement really was.

"Oh, but that's rather a drastic step, isn't it?" Elfie said.

"More than drastic," said Auggie. "Life altering. *Eternity* altering. But then—you know that already."

Marianne felt a slight shudder.

What does he mean?

"I thought we might talk a little first," Elfie said.

"Talk, talk, talk," grumbled Auggie jadedly. "We could spend eons talking. Not that we don't *have* all of time, but . . . why not seize the moment?"

A brief lull fell over the conversation. Marianne didn't know what Elfie should say next. She knew she had to stall Auggie about going to the Basement—at least until she could find out how Elfie could follow him there.

"You're uncharacteristically inhibited this evening, my dear," Auggie finally said, breaking the silence. "You ought to have a little drink to help you unwind and relax. Your usual white wine, perhaps?"

"No," Elfie said. "I thought we might carry on our chat . . . someplace more private."

Auggie gestured expansively.

"The *booth* is private," he said. "No one can hear anything we say."

"But there are so many distractions here," Elfie said.

And indeed, Ernie's Bar was far from calm and quiet, even inside the booth. The preprogrammed barroom chatter and the ragtime piano music rang over the computer speakers, and one could almost choke on the dense pixel cigar and cigarette smoke.

"But of course, you are quite correct," Auggie said gallantly. "We must retire to a more serene place of your choosing, a place where you can contemplate the wondrous step you are about to take. Let us go there—at once!"

Suddenly, Auggie's eyes rolled zanily in their sockets, spinning in opposite directions, and the computer speaker roared with bells, sirens, bicycle horns, and calliope music. Then, in a flash, Auggie was gone.

Marianne groaned aloud.

What a time for him to pull his disappearing act! How am I supposed to find him now? Where *am I supposed to find him now?*

She mentally replayed the words he had just spoken . . .

"We must retire to a more serene place of your choosing."

A lot of choice you gave me, you little freak.

But then she thought the matter through. If Auggie *had* given her the opportunity to consider the question, where might she have suggested that they meet? Where was her favorite room on the maze?

Marianne knew the answer immediately.

Following the usual protocol, Marianne directed Elfie out of the booth and across the saloon floor. Ernie himself was, as usual, washing glasses behind the bar. He offered his stock end-of-the-night audio salutation.

"Be seeing you tomorrow night, Elfie?"

Marianne struck the command for Elfie to give her own stock audio reply.

"Could be, Ernie. It's been swell."

Elfie walked out through the swinging doors. Marianne double-clicked, placing Elfie in the desktop maze again. Without any hesitation, Marianne directed Elfie north-northeast toward the Babbage Beach icon. When Elfie reached the icon, Marianne double-clicked without even bothering to read the "who?" list.

Suddenly, Elfie found herself standing on the beach, the white-noise surf resounding soothingly and the bright orange sun still high in the sky. A little farther down the beach, under the red-and-white umbrella where the virtual Renee had sat during those two poignant conversations, was Auggie.

The clown just sat there for a moment, looking out to sea. Then he turned and saw Elfie. He gaily gestured for Elfie to come and sit down beside him. She did so.

"How did you know?" Elfie asked.

"Know what?"

"That I would choose to come here?"

"Well, this is your favorite place, isn't it? You think of it as 'the edge,' I believe. The *edge* of humanity, the *edge* of the culture. It's a strange figure of speech, though—in an electronic world *without* edges, where all possibilities are endless."

Marianne felt a cold shiver.

"How do you know what I think?" Elfie asked.

"Because I'm eternal," Auggie said, his smile softening with a certain sadness. "Being eternal means knowing everything—absolutely everything."

Nolan, Clayton, Maisie, Gusfield, and Pritchard were still huddled around the computer monitor. The air had grown hot and thin, reminding Nolan of that unpleasant experience in the observation booth watching Myron Stalnaker's deposition back in Omaha.

The five men had just witnessed Auggie's abrupt disappearance from Ernie's Bar. Then Maisie had followed Elfie to Babbage Beach. When Elfie clicked into the beach, they saw her walk toward one of the red-and-white beach umbrellas and sit down beneath it.

That was all.

Except for Elfie, Babbage Beach appeared to be totally deserted.

"Looks like your girlfriend got stood up," Maisie said to Nolan.

"Very funny," Nolan replied.

But Nolan actually felt a deep sense of relief at Auggie's disappearance.

That'll teach her to go playing Nancy Drew. I'm going to give her a real talking-to before the night's over, though.

The men watched in silence for a few moments longer. Elfie didn't appear to be doing much—just repeating a simple loop of actions that included tracing her finger in the sand and nodding her head now and again.

"Not a lot to look at," Maisie remarked. "Guess she's got some idea that Auggie's still going to show up. Chicks sure can get stubborn when guys dump them."

"We'd better keep watching, though," Nolan said. "Maybe she knows something we don't know. Maybe Auggie *will* show up again."

"Well, there's no point in us staring at this damn thing," Maisie said. "If he comes back, my beeper will go off again."

Maisie shut down his terminal and the five men regrouped more comfortably. They resumed their previous discussion—making the most educated guesses possible as to how Auggie operated, how he manifested himself throughout Insomnimania, how he could even exist.

Nolan tried to keep his attention focused on the conversation, but he was getting tired. Postulating the existence of a living, conscious being whose existence was literally *shared* among an indeterminate number of human brains was, indeed, exhausting work. It had been a long day, starting in Omaha, picking up some hours on the return trip, and still continuing here long after dark. Besides, all five of the men had been stuffing themselves on Pritchard's limitless stash of junk food. Nolan, at least, was feeling a bit jangled.

Tired and wired. The perfect state of mind in which to contemplate Auggie.

"But Auggie doesn't affect everybody on Insomnimania," Clayton was saying. "Whatever is happening, it's only happening to some people."

"I haven't developed a psychological profile yet," Gusfield said. "But some people must be particularly susceptible."

Clayton laughed harshly. "That's not hard," he said. "Look at the people whose numbers we've picked up. Professionals and executives—some successful, some not."

"Yeah. Some of them near-miss wannabes like Myron Stalnaker," said Nolan.

"I've sure seen my share of them," Clayton continued. "I've seen them in banks, in judges' chambers, in doctors' offices. These guys put on a mask every day, they play a role, they spend minute after minute of every single day *acting* like they're in control of their destinies—and other people's destinies."

"Surgeons, college professors, stockbrokers, CPAs, airline pilots, politicians, celebrities," suggested Gusfield thoughtfully.

"Yeah," Clayton agreed. "We're not talking about short-order cooks and construction workers and garbage men and cleaning ladies—people who can curse when they fall down the stairs, who rush out to the bars after work, who make fools of themselves whenever they feel like it, who openly *admit* their helplessness in the face of real-world stupidities. We're talking about people who've got a lot invested in appearance. And who don't really have a life."

"Christ," Pritchard groaned. "That profile fits just about all the subscribers to our network."

"I imagine so," Gusfield replied. "And for the record, that profile fits *me* pretty well, too."

Then Nolan remembered something. "On the plane, you mentioned some sort of condition where people don't experience their own feelings," Nolan said.

"Alexithymia," Gusfield said.

"Is that what we're dealing with here?"

"It must be. People who have no idea what their own feelings really are—probably with deep anger, even fury. It's not like they're *repressing* it. They just don't *experience* it. Their bodies undergo all the stress of anger and fury, but their minds never get the message. They don't know how to experience it, much less express it. Auggie fills a terrible void in these people's lives by being playful, angry, uninhibited, powerful, even godlike. He's the *self* they all wish they had. He's more real to them than *they* are."

It seemed clearer and clearer to Nolan by the minute.

They're Pierrot. That's what they all are. White Clowns who wield or imagine *that they wield authority. Pierrot—Auggie's eternal nemesis. And Auggie's ultimate victory over Pierrot is simply to absorb him. And when a Pierrot refuses to become absorbed—that's when he gets killed.*

"Of course, it could be that we've all just gone completely off our rockers," Nolan remarked.

"Could be," Gusfield agreed. "But we've got to remind ourselves that we're only speculating. Everything we're saying is pure hypothesis."

"But what actually takes place when Auggie appears on the computer?" Clayton asked. "What's really going on when he walks and talks and buys drinks in Ernie's Bar and stuff?"

"Well, my guess is that one of Auggie's so-called 'cells' is at Auggie's controls," Gusfield said. "Like the one in Texas just a few moments ago. That cell was sitting at his computer keyboard, punching in commands, typing in dialogue, just like other Insomnimania users do with their animated alters. But this person—this *cell*—experienced a kind of dissociative symbiosis with Auggie, had the feeling of actually *being* Auggie."

"But up until now, you've been talking about Auggie as a *collective* consciousness," Clayton continued. "And now you're talking like he only has one user."

"One user at a time," Pritchard interjected. "He probably trades off a lot. That's why we keep picking up different phone numbers for him—sometimes a couple in one night."

"And when cells trade off, that doesn't actually affect Auggie's personality," Gusfield added. "Auggie's *consciousness* is consistent and seemingly continuous, no matter who's running him. The cell's individual personality, however, is almost totally submerged. Myron Stalnaker described just this sort of experience to me. But I've got a strong hunch that the cell at the keyboard—the one who's directing Auggie and speaking his words—is never actually alone. Lots of other cells are watching. And they, too, experience the sensation of *being* Auggie—of performing his actions, of speaking his words."

"How?" Nolan asked.

"It could be a little like a schizophrenic hallucination," Gusfield said. "Perhaps, when the other cells see Auggie's words flash across the screen, they imagine that they hear Auggie actually *saying* them. This sort of hallucination often arises in situations involving sleeplessness and sense deprivation—and after all, your network *is* specially designed for insomniacs."

Nolan felt a jolt of recognition. He remembered his own first time logged into Insomnimania, experiencing the illusion of hearing Jazz say, "You're mother sucks great green donkey dicks" in a harsh, vituperative manner. And just a few moments ago, he had found himself whispering both sides of the barroom conversation between Elfie and Auggie—and had experienced an eerie sensation of hearing both voices. In both instances, Nolan had been very tired. It wasn't hard to imagine this sort of illusion getting out of hand for hard-core insomniacs.

"And when these cells kill people?" Nolan asked.

"From what Myron told me, I would say it's *Auggie* who actually does the killing."

"But *why* does Auggie kill people?" Clayton asked.

Gusfield shrugged. "Don't ask me," he said. "For all I know, we're all imagining this whole thing."

Nolan wished they *were* imagining this whole thing. He wished that Auggie was a cult, a conspiracy, a secret society, even a deliberately created artificial intelligence—anything except this mysterious, spontaneously-evolved collective consciousness they were now contemplating. But intuitively, he felt that most or even all of what they were guessing was absolutely true.

"And what about Zoomer?" Pritchard asked. "What's his role in all this?"

"Zoomer created Auggie, but I doubt that he was ever a part of

Auggie," Gusfield said. "But consciously or unconsciously, Zoomer may have shared all kinds of information with Auggie before Auggie actually 'left' him—that is, before Auggie had enough other 'cells' to take off on his own."

"So that might be how Auggie got to be a master hacker," Pritchard suggested.

"That's right," Gusfield said. "Zoomer's hacking skills have long since become absorbed into Auggie—have become the collective abilities of Auggie as a whole."

"And that's how Myron Stalnaker, who doesn't know how to knit, made a ski mask when he was Auggie," Nolan suggested.

"Exactly," Gusfield said. "Somewhere, one of the cells knows how to knit. Therefore, *Auggie* knows how to knit."

Clayton shook his head. "I don't know," he said. "You said you wanted to avoid supernatural explanations, and that sounds pretty spooky to me."

"Listen, we're talking about a kind of inversion of multiple personality disorder," Gusfield said insistently. "Instead of one body containing a lot of personalities, a lot of bodies add up to one big personality. And far stranger things than this happen in MPD cases, believe me. Different personalities living in the same body can require different eyeglass prescriptions, experience different allergies, have different IQs, display different degrees of physical strength—and researchers still don't understand why. Believe me, some of the psychiatric literature on disassociation makes a lot of our craziest ideas sound downright mundane. I'm convinced that there are physical, causal explanations for everything we're suggesting, but it may be a hell of a long time before we know what they are."

Everybody in the room was quiet for a moment.

"How many cells do you think we're dealing with?" Pritchard asked at last.

"I don't know," Gusfield said. "How many people are on your network?"

"About fifty thousand."

"And how many phone numbers have you collected among Auggie's users?"

"Six, I guess. No, seven including today."

Gusfield shrugged. "Then I'd say it's somewhere between seven cells and fifty thousand cells. Does that answer your question?"

"Yeah," Pritchard grumbled. "Thanks a bunch."

Gusfield shook his head. "One thing really worries me," he said. "We just heard—or read—Auggie mention a place called 'the Basement.' That sounds to me like some kind of space or setting or stage where Auggie's cells may ritually congregate—like the 'spot' some MPD patients describe, where their personalities take turns controlling the body. This would be the place where all the cells merge together, where they *become* Auggie."

Pritchard almost roared with outrage.

"You mean another fucking *room?*" he cried. "Are you telling me this bastard's hacked into our system and smuggled his own room into our maze? One we can't even see?"

"That's my guess," Gusfield said. "And finding it is our best hope of stopping Auggie. It may be our *only* hope—short of shutting down your entire network."

"We'll find it," Pritchard said furiously. "Don't worry, we'll make goddamn sure of finding it. Nobody fucks with my network behind my back."

"Eternal," Elfie said, her high, delicate voice sounding faint and barely audible over the roaring of the waves. "I can't comprehend what it means to be eternal. I just can't grasp it."

"No, but you shall," said Auggie. "You shall very soon." Auggie leaned closer to her. "You see," he continued, "eternity is beginning at this very moment. Eternity is always quite simply *now*—and it continues afterwards forever. And so it should be easy to understand that I have been here throughout all eternity."

Elfie laughed.

"For that matter, then, so have I," Elfie said.

"Indeed you have, my dear," Auggie said, laughing, too.

"Then why do I find myself ignorant of so many different things?" Elfie asked ruefully.

"For example?" Auggie inquired.

"For example," Elfie replied, pointing to the thin clouds floating across the sun in the center of the screen, "what are those clouds called?"

"Stratocumulus," Auggie said, matter-of-factly.

"Are you sure?"

"Quite sure."

"Then I owe somebody ten bucks," Elfie said sadly.

"Your friend Renee?"

"Yes."

"And do you hate me for having killed her?" Auggie asked.

Marianne remembered what Evan had said to her when he realized that she was actually leaving him.

Evan had asked, "Why do you hate me?"

Marianne had told him that she didn't hate him, that she couldn't hate anybody.

"That's why you can't love me," Evan had said. "You can't really love unless you can also hate."

Evan had made her believe it at the time.

"I don't hate you," Elfie told Auggie. "I don't know why. I think I want to hate you. But I can't."

Auggie shrugged. "Well, hate me if you want to," he said. "Hate me if you think you should. Me, I hate people all the time. I try to run the gamut of the passions—hatred, fear, laughter, ecstasy, the emotional works."

"Can you also love?" Elfie asked Auggie.

Auggie paused for a moment.

"Yes," Auggie said sincerely.

"My husband said I didn't know how to love," Elfie said.

"Your husband?"

"Yes."

"You never had a husband, Elfie."

"Yes, I did. His name was Evan."

"No," Auggie said. "Your *simulation* had a husband. *Marianne Hedison* had a husband."

Marianne felt a chill of fear.

My name. He knows *my name. What else does he know about me?*

Auggie shook his head sadly.

"You cling to your illusions too strongly, Elfie," Auggie said, "You really must give up this idea that you and Marianne are one and the same. You are perfect. She is not. She is a figment of your imagination, a simulation—a manifestation of Pierrot, the White Clown."

"The White Clown?"

"Yes, the White Clown, with his vain presumption of perfection, authority, good sense. Look at them all, Elfie—all your simulations, the creatures of your imaginings, the ones you call Evan, Renee, Nolan, Clayton, Stephen. Look, and you will see that their appearances are all the same—that their faces and their gowns are all white, and that their haughty brows and their cold lips are thinly painted black or red. Look, and you will see that they are ghosts. I know you believe me to be a murderer, dear Elfie. But how is it possible to kill a ghost?"

"All the same, I care about them," said Elfie. Marianne felt tears welling up and falling, falling, falling from her eyes—but she couldn't tell if they were rolling down her own cheeks or Elfie's.

Auggie paused for a moment, staring deeply into Elfie's eyes.

"Don't let them hold you back," Auggie said, caressing Elfie's hand. "We are perfect creatures, you and I—beings made from pure information. You, I, this beach scene, our whole multifaceted, multifarious world, are all comprised of a single, eternal stream of ons and offs—a stream constantly shaping itself into a hundred billion thoughts and shapes and entities. Isn't it flawless? Isn't it beautiful?"

Elfie was now raptly staring at Auggie's beautiful, joyous face through her own eyes, not Marianne's. She searched her mind for some sign of Marianne, searched behind her eyes for Marianne's presence, for Marianne's guidance, but Marianne had disappeared into some distant part of her imaginings. Marianne was a ghost of her memory.

The scene flickered wildly. For a split second, nothing was visible except a blazing white seagull flying jerkily across a field of blackness. Then the beach and the ocean fleetingly reappeared, leaving black cut-out spaces where Auggie and the seagull ought to have been. At last, Auggie reappeared, fluttering and threatening to disappear into the depths of a waning vertical hold.

"I'm frightened," Elfie said.

"Don't be," Auggie said comfortingly.

"I'm about to lose you."

"No. You're about to *become* me."

Auggie winked and fluttered into increasing invisibility. Explosions of blackness and light filled Elfie's vision as Auggie became less and less perceptible.

"You know the words, don't you?" Auggie asked.

"The words?" whispered Elfie.

"The words that will bring us together."

"Yes, I know the words."

"Then say them with me," Auggie commanded.

And in unison, the two of them murmured . . .

"Auggie is Auggie."

The beach scene disappeared. Reality itself dropped out from under Elfie like a rudely opened trapdoor. She fell inexorably downward into a deep, black tunnel with a tiny white light at its end—a light that never seemed to grow any larger, no matter how far she fell. As Elfie spiraled and plummeted downward, she heard Auggie's voice speaking to her, creating a new world inside her mind . . .

THE BASEMENT

*I*T IS NIGHT. *YOU ARE IN A DAMP AND DARK ALLEYWAY—A STRANGE, alien place. You don't know how you got here, much less why you came. You look before you and behind you. The adjoining passages are hazy* and graffiti-scrawled, and the howling noises from the streets beyond are barely human. You cannot go home. In fact, you have no idea how far away from home you are—no idea where or even what home is.

Now you notice a murky light coming up from under your feet. You look down. You are standing on a manhole cover. The light is creeping through its round holes. You pry the cover loose with your fingers, and with considerable exertion, you roll it aside. You look down and see a watery stream flowing steadily through the subterranean light. Sewage, undoubtedly. The smell of decay is pungent. Even so, the stream strikes you as inviting—certainly more so than the sinister world beyond the alleyway. Why is it inviting? Do you wish to drown yourself? Perhaps. Perhaps not. You really know nothing of your own motivations. You do not even know your name.

You climb down a ladder onto a bank next to the stream. Massive, rectangular columns support the street above your head. The ceiling is honeycombed with rusted steel braces. The light continues to permeate the stagnant air around you, making this place brighter than the world above. You cannot tell where the light is coming from.

All around you, you see formless and shadowy people wandering directionlessly. They are silhouettes with no faces, no apparent limbs. They appear to have no wills. They do not speak. They do not seem to know what speech is.

With no help from a mirror, you realize that you look just like them. You mingle with them. You are of their kind.

Murky streams bridged by old wooden boards thread outward through these catacombs, breaking the concrete floor up into little islands. You feel these bridges strain and bend beneath your footsteps and wonder how deep, how filthy the water below might be.

Where do these catacombs lead? Into infinity, you suppose. You can see no end to the concrete islands in the subterranean fog. An underground infinity is neither a pleasing nor a displeasing thought. You cannot imagine a better world or a worse one. You can imagine no other world at all.

But deep in the mist, you detect a boundary. A plain, concrete wall becomes visible—an edge to the catacombs. There is a door in this wall—a battered red door with a five-pointed yellow star painted on it. Six yellow printed letters curve above the star . . .

AUGGIE

You approach the door, and your companions do, too. The door swings silently open to reveal a warm, yellow glow within. The black-robed figures in front of you begin to converge at the narrow entryway. They do not pass through the door successively. Instead, they seem to melt into each other, becoming a single dark shape, occupying the doorway.

You come nearer and nearer to the doorway. You step into the looming shape, joining it, becoming it. All the black figures are one figure now, and you are this figure, too.

Now you can see the room. It is an old vaudevillian dressing room, replete with tattered wallpaper, a steamer trunk, and newspaper clippings pinned and pasted all about. Candles are lit everywhere. The only other light comes from the crude wooden makeup table. The mirror is surrounded by light bulbs, most of which are lit, but three of which are burned out. A couple of the sockets are empty.

You approach the mirror and see yourself in it. You are, as you already supposed, a black, featureless nothing. You sit down on the bench in front of the mirror and open a battleship-gray makeup box. Inside the box are dozens of little round tins and colorful tubes, all containing makeup. You open one of the tubes and spread a gooey whiteness on your dark and shapeless fingers. You spread the whiteness all over your face until your head is a glaring, silvery oval. You reach inside the box again and take out a shining, bright red ball. You place the ball squarely in the middle of your face. Then you paint on a huge red smile and fat black brows and enormous rolling eyes.

You walk over to the steamer trunk. On the wall behind the trunk is a full-

length mirror. You study your reflection—a garish face with wildly colored, wildly distorted features perched atop a black void. You mean nothing yet. You open the trunk and pull out a red tuft of hair, a hat, a bundle of clothes. You carefully fasten the tuft of hair around your head like a low-hanging laurel wreath attached with Velcro. For a moment, you look like some ghastly mockery of the monkhood's sacrosanctity. But as you don the checkered vest, the checkered baggy pants ("one leg at a time," as they say), the preposterously outsized shoes, and finally the tiny battered bowler hat, you assume a jauntier air. Now at last, you know who you are.

You know your name.

You are Auggie.

You turn and look at the door through which you arrived. You see that a poster is pinned to it, picturing a white-faced, white-robed, effete and affected chap. Gigantic red pompon buttons are arrayed down the front of his gown, and he wears a conical white hat. His lips, eyes, and eyebrows are painted in thin, cold lines of black and red. This character has struck up a sham sentimental pose, holding both hands over a bright red heart painted on his chest. An aching detestation wells up in your own chest at the sight of him.

A name curves above the picture . . .

PIERROT

Pierrot's picture is riddled with darts. You notice that you are holding a dart in your own white-gloved hand. You furiously hurl it, striking Pierrot directly in his painted red heart. As if by magic, the door swings open. You walk on through. But instead of finding yourself in the vast and watery catacombs again, you are now in a dim hallway, surrounded by stage props and tawdrily painted flats. Farther down the hallway, you hear the sound of laughter and applause and a tiny orchestra playing a merry tune. You walk toward the sound until, at last, you face another door upon which is printed the words . . .

STAGE DOOR

You step through the door and wander into the noisy near-darkness, pausing in the wings to observe counterweight-laden ropes moving up and down seemingly on their own power, carrying scenery up and down in a weirdly random fashion. Near the center of the stage, you duck and dodge the silent barrage of flying flats. You notice, too, that you are surrounded by dangling marionettes, but it is too dark for you to make out their clothes or features. You realize that it does not matter. The marionettes have no idea who they are, and nor should you.

The applause and laughter and music have become almost deafening, and you are facing the patched and buffeted backside of a stage curtain. You know that, in a moment, the curtain will rise and you will be acting out some farce or tragedy with the marionettes. You have no idea what the play is. You do not know any lines. But to your own surprise, you are not in the least bit afraid.

You are exhilarated.

You are drunken.

You are alive.

It was after three o'clock in the morning when Nolan got home from the Insomnimania office. He and his four companions had decided to give up speculating about Auggie before their hypotheses lapsed into pure science fiction—if, indeed, they had not already crossed that line. Everybody was completely exhausted, and no further progress could be made until Pritchard figured out how to hack his way into Auggie's elusive "Basement."

But despite his exhaustion, Nolan was not yet ready to collapse into bed. He had one last matter to attend to—one that he had been impatient to take care of for quite a few hours now.

As he picked up the telephone to dial Marianne's number, he felt his hands shake and his heart pound—he wasn't sure whether from anger or fear. He listened anxiously as Marianne's phone began to ring, wondering what to do if he got her answering machine. Should he hang up, or should he vent his feelings into the tape recorder? He hoped she would pick up. It would make things simpler if she picked up—though probably not a whole lot more pleasant.

The phone rang once, then twice, then a third time. Nolan knew that the answering machine would pick up after the fourth ring. But the fourth ring never came. Nolan heard Marianne's voice. She sounded barely awake.

"Hello?" Marianne asked groggily.

"Did I catch you asleep?" Nolan said, unable to keep an edge of indignation out of his voice.

"What time is it?"

"It's three-fifteen in the morning, that's what time it is," Nolan said, pacing the room. "So did I catch you asleep or didn't I?"

"Yes," Marianne said wearily. "You caught me asleep."

"Good," Nolan growled. "I'm glad. I'm goddamn thrilled. It's the least I could do after the way you've been messing with my head."

"What are you talking about?"

"I saw you tonight."

"Where?"

"On Insomnimania. Talking to Auggie. *All* of us saw you."

" 'All of us'?" Who the hell's 'all of us'?"

"Pritchard, Maisie, Clayton, Gusfield—*all* of us. We watched what happened. We listened."

"Well, thank you so very much for respecting my privacy," Marianne said, sounding more awake now—and more than a little angry.

"And *thank you* very much for lying to me!" Nolan retorted, pacing the floor more and more agitatedly.

"What are you talking about?"

"I'm talking about when you *promised* to stay the hell away from Insomnimania, away from Auggie.

"It wasn't any of your business to begin with."

"It wasn't? Well, fine. Why didn't you say so right at the start?"

Nolan hated to hear himself sounding like this. He reminded himself that he had really been more frightened than angry. He didn't want to be angry. He took a deep breath and spoke more gently.

"Marianne, the guys and I talked about this thing for hours on end tonight. And we came to some pretty incredible conclusions. And we're starting to realize how dangerous Auggie really is—much more dangerous than any of us ever even imagined. Don't you understand how worried I am for your safety? Don't you understand how much it *scared* me to see you in there with that goddamn clown? Don't you know how much *I love you?*"

Suddenly, Nolan was shaken by the sound of Marianne's laughter. The sound was cold, heartless, barely even human.

"You love *me?"* she said. "And *who*, Nolan, do you mean by *me?* Some Santa Barbara fashion plate, maybe—some classy dame you can brag about to your cop friends? Or perhaps that bosomy, over-sexed little elf you helped create for the infoworld? Which 'me' do you 'love'? Marianne or Elfie? And which of those 'me's' do you honestly think is more real?"

Marianne was almost shouting now. The telephone felt heavy in Nolan's trembling hand—almost too heavy to hold.

"And *who*, Nolan, did you *see* in Insomnimania tonight?" Marianne raged on. "You didn't see Marianne, did you? That's because your precious Marianne wasn't *there*. That's because your precious

Marianne isn't *anywhere*. Your precious Marianne doesn't even *exist*. She's just a *ghost*, a *simulation*, a product of your immature, adolescent, sexually stunted little mind. Grow up, Nolan. Grow up and get a life."

Nolan was stunned into silence. Neither he nor Marianne spoke for a moment.

"Go to bed, Nolan," Marianne said at last. "Go to bed and get a good night's sleep. But before you do, take a good look at your face in your bathroom mirror. Take a real good look, Nolan. Your face is *white*. It's white and characterless with narrow little eyes and lips. It's the face of a ghost. You're white all over and you think you know everything and you think you're in *charge* of everything. But you're not. Your whole damned world is racing out of control and you can't do a fucking thing about it. Think about it, Nolan. Sleep on it and think about it."

Marianne hung up. Nolan stood in the middle of his living room, dazed and shocked.

He gently placed the phone receiver back in its cradle.

He collapsed into his armchair. He felt a terrible aching in his chest—a pain he knew came from the sheer cruelty of Marianne's words.

How could she say such things to me? Why would she say such things to me?

He felt the tears fill his eyes. And slowly—ever so gradually—he began to weep.

How long has it been since I've cried?

He could think of no time since Louise was killed. And even then, he had wept more from his awful, horrific bewilderment than from grief. Grief itself had always come to him as a clean, tearless emotion—fully and completely and undeniably, but always tearlessly. His *grief* over Louise's death had been tearless, as had been his grievings over his parents' deaths. It took profound bewilderment to make Nolan weep.

And for days and even weeks now, he had been terribly confused and frustrated by the seeming omnipotence, the seeming incomprehensibility of Auggie. But the joy of his blossoming love for Marianne, his certainty that they were building a caring, lasting relationship, had been his defense against despair. And now it had only taken Marianne's awful words to turn loose the floodgates of bewilderment.

"What does it mean?" he whispered to himself. "What on earth does it mean?"

He ran Marianne's inscrutable questions and pronouncements through his dazed, despairing brain.

"Which 'me' do you 'love'?" she had demanded. "Marianne or Elfie? And which of those 'mes' do you honestly think is more real?"

Then she had said, "Your precious Marianne doesn't even exist."

Then he replayed the strangest declaration of all . . .

"You're white all over and you think you know everything and you think you're in charge of everything."

Slowly and inexorably, a realization began to sweep through Nolan's mind.

His tears stopped.

He began to understand.

Pierrot. She was describing me as Pierrot.

Then the truth hit him in a terrifying flash.

That wasn't Marianne. That was Auggie. I was talking to Auggie!

Marianne reached up and fumblingly placed her cordless phone back on her desk. Then she collapsed onto the floor again, where she had found herself in a dead sleep when Nolan's call had come.

Feeling a terrible pain in her stomach and chest, she curled herself up in a fetal position. She remembered her awful words to Nolan.

What have I done? What on earth have I done?

Then she thought that she was not experiencing her own pain at all, but Nolan's—the pain she had so cruelly and deliberately inflicted upon him. He was the most loving man she had ever known, and she had treated him monstrously.

Why?

And how had she wound up on the floor like this? What had happened during the night? She dimly remembered that she—or Elfie—had found Auggie, had experienced some sort of encounter with Auggie, but she couldn't recall what had taken place between them.

She fought to remember. She used the pain to bring it back to her mind. It was like rising up through water—rising up from the murky, dark bottom of a deep pool. The light changed slowly, refracted through the water, becoming brighter and brighter as she neared the surface. Marianne used the pain, imagining that it was in her lungs, that it came from being submerged too long without air. She imagined herself rising up out of the murkiness into the radiating light.

And at last, she surfaced.

She literally gasped for breath.

Her head had broken through into the brilliant blaze of memory. She knew what had happened.

A seduction.

Yes, that was exactly the word for it. It had been a seduction of the mind, not the body. She had *become* Auggie. She could remember *being* Auggie. She could remember every detail of the entire episode. She knew she wasn't *meant* to remember—that Auggie intended the whole experience to remain lost in an amnesiac fog. But the pain had brought it back, had brought her memories bursting to the surface. It was the pain of loving someone dearly and hurting him terribly.

Auggie had been a superb seducer. He had flattered her. He had described her as a perfect creature. He had assured her that she was capable of love. And, most powerfully of all, he had meant every word of it. Last night, he had made Marianne into one of his parts, into one of his *cells*.

But to become a part of Auggie and *remain* a part of Auggie, one had to contain a loveless void in the deepest recesses of one's heart. Perhaps even a few short weeks ago, Auggie might have captured and kept her. But no longer. Now she had thrust herself out of her sterile and empty existence. Now she had Nolan.

Because she loved Nolan, because Nolan loved her, because of the very hurt she had inflicted on him, and because of her own vicarious and visceral *experience* of Nolan's hurt—she was free. Auggie had lost Marianne. He had lost her because she had no emotional hollowness for him to fill.

Marianne pulled herself carefully to her feet and walked toward her computer. She felt fragile and drained of resources, emptied of all her energy. But she knew there was another effort yet to be made, although she was not sure exactly what it was she had to do.

She sat down at her desk and stared at the slowly mutating marbleized patterns of her screen-saver. When she had collapsed, she had been in the Basement—that subterranean realm where Auggie's cells merged into one. She remembered having been one of those shapeless figures melding together in Auggie's candlelit dressing room.

And now, when she touched her mouse and undid the screen-saver, what would appear? Would she find herself in the Basement again? Was she in any danger of being dragged back into Auggie's mind again, if only temporarily?

"Fat chance," she murmured defiantly.

She shoved the computer mouse. But instead of the Basement, Insomnimania's desktop maze appeared, displaying Babbage Beach and the Speakers' Corner and Casino del Camino . . .

"Damn," Marianne whispered. "Where's the Basement? Where the hell did it go?"

Then she remembered Auggie's command to Elfie, his instruction to murmur in unison with him . . .

"The words that will bring us together."

Without another thought, Marianne typed the words . . .

"Auggie is Auggie"

. . . and struck the return key.

The desktop maze disappeared into a blaze of glaring whiteness. The whiteness filled the screen for a moment, then shrank into a horizontal line across the middle of the screen. Then the line collapsed into a little white dot in the center of a surrounding blackness.

Just like an old TV screen. Marianne remembered how televisions used to look when they were turned off—a single speck of white light burning in the middle of the screen for a few seconds afterward.

But this speck of light didn't disappear. It hung there in the center of the screen, suggestively, hauntingly. When Elfie had fallen out of Babbage Beach into this darkness, she had supposed this light to be the end of a deep, dark tunnel.

And what of the underground catacombs, Auggie's dressing room, the door leading to a stage wildly draped with dangling scenery and marionettes? They must have been only suggestions—perhaps written across the screen, but more probably spoken to Marianne over her computer speaker.

Marianne felt an awestricken chill.

I am here. I am in Auggie's Basement. I am inside Auggie's mind.

And with a deeper chill, she realized she was not alone. The Basement was filled with other silent souls, Auggie's cells, scattered across the entire nation. How many did Auggie hold enraptured? A handful? A dozen? A hundred? A thousand? Several thousand? She had no way of knowing.

But she knew that a man in Omaha had killed for Auggie, *as Auggie*—a man doubtless not normally a killer. And in actuality, the man himself wasn't a killer even after the killing, not even after his hands had held a gun and fired a fatal shot. And somewhere, probably not so far away, was the woman whose hands had held Renee beneath the water—but the woman herself had killed no one at all. In Marianne's mind, the woman in the silver dress turned and opened her red lips as if to speak.

Perhaps the woman wanted to say, "It wasn't me. It was Auggie."

But she vanished before she could utter the words.

For the first time, Marianne felt sympathy for that fearful image she had so often imagined. What kind of unremembered nightmares did that woman have—did all those other people have? Had her unheard words been a plea for help?

Or were their lives such nightmares that they had abandoned their own selves to participate in something larger? Marianne shuddered as she remembered how close she had been to joining them. *More likely, they live the lives of sleepwalkers. Their unexpressed rage finds its way to Auggie. They do not act out their anger. The action belongs to Auggie. And the more of them there are, the more violence he can do.*

But how could this be? Marianne had spoken with Auggie, had gotten to know him intimately, had almost *become* him, but through it all she sensed no real anger, no real aggression about him.

"We are perfect creatures, you and I," Auggie had told her.

Perhaps it was true in its way, but it was also the philosophy of a child. For indeed, Auggie *was* a child—a child who saw his own outbursts as a harmless game. But what if a child were a giant among insects? Such a child's rage would be destructive, however playful it might seem.

Marianne knew that she, alone among all of Auggie's confidantes, was not a part of his mind. She was an unhypnotized invader. And somehow it was now within her power to stop Auggie once and for all.

It was in her power to kill him.

As she searched her mind for the final key to the puzzle, she remembered Auggie's insistent, arrogant, but at the same time bitterly lonely litany . . .

"I'm eternal," he had said.

Marianne glanced at her watch. It was now approaching four o'clock. In another hour, Insomnimania would go off for the night. And when Insomnimania went off, so would the Basement.

Insomnimania begins at eight o'clock at night and ends at five o'clock in the morning. Vaguely and instinctively, Marianne knew that this mundane truth contained the key to Auggie's undoing.

She picked up the phone and dialed the number of the Insomnimania office. Maisie answered the phone. To Marianne's surprise, Maisie didn't sound particularly tired—just his usual, slightly stoned-out self.

"Hi, Maisie," she said. "It's Marianne. I'm sorry if I woke you up."

"Naw," Maisie said. "I don't sleep."

"Never?"

"Not for the last twenty years or so. Just kind of lost the habit, somehow."

"I thought people died if they never slept."

"Maybe they do, and maybe I did. Maybe I'm a vampire. So what can I do for you?"

"Listen, does Insomnimania *have* to go off-line right at five o'clock?"

"It is company policy, yeah."

"Does it always go off *exactly* at five?"

"We're fastidious about it. The way the VAX is programmed, it gets to four-fifty-nine and fifty-nine seconds, then zap, it's gone."

"I need you to make an exception tonight."

"What kind of exception are we talking here?"

"Keep Insomnimania on for another five minutes."

A silence fell over the phone line.

"You're up to something, aren't you?" Maisie asked uneasily.

"I'd really appreciate it if you didn't ask a lot of questions," Marianne replied.

"Listen, lady, take my advice and don't try anything heroic," Maisie grumbled. "You're in big-shit trouble with your boyfriend as it is, and I don't want to get you into any *more* trouble. I don't want to get *myself* in any trouble, either. We saw you in Insomnimania tonight. We saw you and Auggie."

"You mean you saw *Elfie* and Auggie."

"Yeah, well, same difference. Nolan's plenty pissed with you."

Then a startling possibility crossed Marianne's mind. Did the men at Insomnimania know as much about her seduction as she did? Had they followed her into the Basement itself? And if so, had they already taken some sort of action against Auggie?

"So you listened in," Marianne said.

"Hey, it wasn't my idea. The others ganged up on me."

"You heard everything Elfie and Auggie said to each other in Ernie's Bar."

"That's right."

"And you heard everything they said to each other on Babbage Beach, too."

"Hold on," Maisie said, sounding quite startled. "You and Auggie didn't talk at Babbage Beach. You didn't even *meet* at Babbage Beach."

"We sure did."

"No, you didn't. We followed you. We followed Elfie."

"And what did you see?"

"We saw you—Elfie—walk over to a beach umbrella and sit under it, doing nothing in particular. You just sat there waiting for Auggie. You got stood up big-time."

"Auggie was there, Maisie."

"He couldn't have been there."

"I'm telling you he *was* there. And that's where he and Elfie did their *real* talking."

Maisie was stunned into silence for a moment.

"That bastard," Maisie said at last. "That hacker bastard. He pulled another loop on us. An inverted goddamn loop."

Marianne couldn't restrain a small chuckle.

"Auggie fucked you, Maisie," she said. "And I'm the only one who knows how to fuck him back. And all *you've* got to do is keep Insomnimania on an extra five minutes. Don't turn Insomnimania off until five-oh-five."

"You've got to tell me why."

"I can't."

"Why not?"

"Because I'm not sure myself," Marianne said.

Maisie groaned with exasperation.

"You sure know how to inspire confidence in a guy," he said.

"So will you do it?"

"Yeah, I'll do it," Maisie said reluctantly.

"Do you promise?"

"Yeah, I promise."

"And let's just keep this between ourselves, OK?"

"OK."

"Good. I owe you a big favor."

"How about a resplendent night of frolicking on my waterbed?"

Marianne laughed.

"Sorry, Maisie," she said. "I'm spoken for, remember?"

Maisie sighed longingly.

"Ah, well," he said. "Sometimes I forget that those wonderful days of free love are gone forever."

"Don't despair. Maybe they'll come back."

"Yeah, maybe. When my equipment's too old and obsolete to even bother with an upgrade. I don't call it my 'wang' for nothing. Good luck."

"Thanks," Marianne said.

She hung up the phone and stared at the computer screen. Could she really trust Maisie? Would he keep Insomnimania on for the extra time she had asked for? And could she trust him not to talk to anybody else—especially Nolan? Maisie had promised, but could she believe him?

She shuddered as she considered how much her own promise to Nolan had been worth—her promise to stay away from Auggie. She hoped Maisie was more trustworthy than she was.

She felt deeply ashamed of her deceptions, but even more ashamed of her outburst against Nolan on the phone. More than that, she felt humiliated, disgusted at what she had joined, what she had become, however briefly. She wanted to call Nolan, to apologize to him, to try to make him understand what had happened. But what could she say? How could she explain what had happened?

"I wasn't myself."

It was the literal truth, but it was also the king of clichés, and she wouldn't blame Nolan if he hung up on her the second she said it. Besides, she still had business to finish with Auggie, which Nolan would again object to. No, she would have to make her peace with Nolan later—if she *could* make her peace with him.

I have to. It has to be possible.

Marianne looked at her watch. It was now approaching four-thirty. Time was growing shorter, and she still had no firm idea of what she was going to do—except that it had something to do with Insomnimania's sign-off time. Following her tried-and-true meditation practice, she pinched her left nostril shut and inhaled. The nostril seemed perfectly clear. Then she pinched her right nostril shut and inhaled. That nostril seemed perfectly clear as well.

Perfectly balanced. That's good. I'm going to need both hemispheres to pull this off.

She stared at the lone white dot at the center of the monitor, trying to determine its import. She was in the Basement, the center of Auggie's very mind. But what was going on in here? At the moment, apparently nothing. What, then, was the purpose of the Basement?

All she knew for sure was that this was where Auggie's cells congregated—where they *became* Auggie. And at this very moment, Auggie was undoubtedly present. He was always present in the Basement. But sooner or later, Auggie would have to give voice to thoughts, ideas, beliefs, and plans. How did that happen? How could a cell know when to speak in Auggie's voice?

She felt a rush of déjà vu at this question. She had some notion that she, herself, had once done just such a thing. But when could that possibly have been?

Of course. That Quaker meeting.

She closed her eyes and remembered. Since she was going to do it again, it was important for her to remember. She had been ten years old. She had just begun to attend the silent prayer services at her family's Friends Meeting House. The adults were always seated in a circle around an oak table. Sometimes they sat in total silence for an hour. Other times, members were moved to pray aloud, to thank the congregation (and God, too) for one thing or another, to read from poetry or the Bible, or even to comment on some social issue—moved by the spirit to "speak out of the life." Her mother said that there were always voices to be heard at Meeting, spoken or not.

One Sunday, Marianne listened carefully for the voices. As quiet as everyone was, the place seemed awfully noisy. From downstairs came chattering and singing from the children's classes. From outside came the sound of traffic and church bells. And even right there in the room, the other worshippers constantly grunted and shuffled their feet and cleared their throats and coughed. Pretty soon, she became lost in a miscellany of noises. She stopped thinking about them, stopped labeling them, just absorbed them.

At last came a burst of sound that seemed to rush through her feet and up her legs and through her abdomen until it cascaded outward through the top of her head. It was a simple sound. It was the sound of a breeze rushing through the leaves outside. Everything dissolved into their happy rustling. It seemed that everything in the universe was part of that sound.

Before Marianne knew it, she was on her feet, her eyes wide open. "There's nobody here," she said bluntly and confidently. "There's nobody in this room. It's empty. There's just a sound, the sound of leaves fluttering. That's all we are, the sound of leaves fluttering." Then she added, stammering slightly at her own audacity. "There's no God, either. There's no one to talk to. God is just . . . a sound of leaves . . . fluttering."

Marianne stared for a moment at the startled faces around her and hastily sat down. She immediately felt embarrassed. Why, at the most religious moment of her young life, had she just denied God's existence before all these people? When Marianne got home, she received no scolding from her parents. But she understood, without mistake, that she had done quite the wrong thing. Marianne never gave ministry after that.

And now, how strange it was to find herself in the midst of an altogether different sort of congregation—about to minister in a much more shocking, much more dire and consequential way. And to do so, she had to become that ten-year-old girl again—willing to listen carefully and speak out of her heart—"out of the life."

Because, she decided, that must be how an Auggie cell knew when to "speak." A cell would become moved by Auggie's "spirit" and begin to type in Auggie's words. The single cell might continue on its own, or other cells might join in, but the effect would always be of a single, unified consciousness. The *voice* would always belong to that singular, self-conscious "I" named Auggie. The more passive, nontyping cells would watch the stream of words flow by, perhaps whispering them aloud, perhaps imagining they were hearing Auggie's voice, feeling as much a part of Auggie's mind as those doing the typing.

This was all pure speculation, and Marianne couldn't be sure that any of it was true, but she felt a strong, unshakeable hunch that it was. After all, she had been groomed for a role in this sinister society of mind, and Auggie had probably planted this very information in her brain.

What other things did that fucker do when he was crawling around inside

*my central nervous system? What other land mines might still be lying
around somewhere inside my* self?

She couldn't worry about that right now. She had to act. If her
hunch was correct, she was going to have to *speak* to Auggie from
inside his own mind—to deliver a message so potent, so powerful
that it would disable or destroy him.

What would this seem like to Auggie? It would probably be like
the voices heard by schizophrenics—those inexplicable utterances
that seemed to come out of nowhere. Marianne had read how dire,
how dreadful such psychotic audio hallucinations could be, sometimes counseling their unfortunate hearers to self-injury or even
suicide. Marianne had to become such a voice—had to become
Auggie's *hallucination.*

She closed her eyes and listened intently, carefully, just as she had
those many years ago. But her surroundings were much more quiet
than they had been at the Meeting House. There were no singing
children, no rattling of leaves, no traffic noises. A Santa Barbara
night was a true miracle of silence. Marianne could hear no sound at
all except the soft whir of the fan in her computer. Marianne
focused her attention on the whir, devoted herself to it utterly,
allowed it to become the collective murmur of that sad congregation of souls who comprised the one great and terrible soul called
Auggie.

And a startling realization came to her.

When she had given ministry at the age of ten, she had done so *as
Auggie*—as a ragged clown spouting improprieties. She had done so
in all innocence, and it was important for her to remember—to
always remember—that Auggie did his terrible deeds in the same
frame of mind. The clown's very subconscious was comprised of
human minds, with all their own hidden and suppressed desires.
Auggie's actions might be born of the fury of his human cells, but
they were carried out in a kind of ghastly and unhallowed innocence.

That did not alter the simple fact that he had to be stopped from
killing—from causing people to kill. And she knew it would take her
ministry to stop him. But this time, she had to utter her truthful
blasphemies in a different role . . .

She opened her eyes and looked at the white spot in the center of
the screen. Without another thought, she began to type. And as she
typed, the words appeared in white letters across the center of the
screen . . .

I AM PIERROT.

The words remained frozen on the screen for a moment. Marianne tried to imagine the consternation they must have caused to the cells in attendance at this meeting, who had never heard any voice other than Auggie's speak to them in the Basement—who were, in fact, the sum total of Auggie himself at this very moment. At last, Marianne's words disappeared and were replaced by a written question . . .

WHO ARE YOU?

It was a query made out of Auggie's understandable bafflement. Surely Marianne herself would respond in much the same manner if some strange entity verbally introduced itself to her out of the recesses of her own brain. For a moment, she wondered whether one person was typing Auggie's responses to her or whether many people had their hands on their keyboards. *It's all the same. One or many typing the words, it's still Auggie talking, and it's still all of them there within him.*
She typed again . . .

I AM WHO I SAID I AM. I AM PIERROT.

A much shorter interval passed before the next response . . .

WHAT ARE YOU DOING IN MY MIND?

For an instant, Marianne felt a pang of pity for what she was about to do. She was about to destroy Auggie's universe, about to drive him mad with the truth of his existence.
She was going to drive him to suicide.
She was going to end his life.
She felt a pang of horror at the thought. She had never been the cause of anyone's death. It was hard enough to imagine doing such a thing while staring into someone's eyes. Now she would be staring straight into someone's heart—a heart that had been, at least to some extent, her own.
But she couldn't hold herself back because of pity.

She simply had to do it.
She typed again.

I HAVE COME TO TELL YOU WHAT I AM.

Auggie's answer came almost immediately.

WHAT ARE YOU, THEN?

Their conversation began to flow quickly, inexorably. Marianne's
lips and fingers had to hurry along to keep pace with their talk.

I AM NOT WHAT YOU SAY I AM. I AM NOT A GHOST.
YOU ARE NOT?
I AM NOT A SIMULATION.
YOU ARE NOT?
I AM FLESH AND BONE AND BLOOD.
YOU LIE.
I DO NOT LIE.
YOU DO.
IT IS WRONG TO KILL ME. IT IS WRONG TO KILL MY KIND.
BUT YOU CANNOT BE KILLED.
I CAN BE KILLED.
WHAT IS DEATH, THEN?
I DO NOT KNOW.
THEN HOW CAN YOU SAY YOU CAN BE KILLED?

Auggie's last query startled Marianne.
*It's a good thing both hemispheres of my brain are fully engaged. I'm going
to need all the mental firepower I can get.*
She typed again.

BECAUSE I HAVE SEEN OTHERS OF MY KIND DIE.
WHY DO THEY DIE?
BECAUSE DEATH COMES TO ALL OF US.
EVERY ONE OF YOU MUST DIE?
YES.
THEN WHY DO YOU COMPLAIN ABOUT MY KILLING
    YOU?

Marianne paused again.

Damn, he's really good at this. I've got to be careful, or I'm liable to make him more murderous than he already is. It's time to take off the gloves.

She resumed her typing.

DEATH IS NOT A PLEASANT PROSPECT.
WHY NOT?
BECAUSE IT MAY BRING NOTHINGNESS.
YOU DO NOT KNOW THAT FOR CERTAIN.
HOW WOULD YOU LIKE IT IF I KILLED YOU?
I CANNOT BE KILLED.
WHY NOT?
BECAUSE I AM ETERNAL.
YOU ARE NOT ETERNAL.
YOU LIE AGAIN.
I DO NOT LIE.
EXPLAIN YOURSELF, THEN.
ARE THERE HOLES IN ETERNITY?
OF COURSE NOT.
WHY NOT?
ETERNITY IS CONTINUOUS. ETERNITY IS ETERNAL.
THERE ARE HOLES IN YOUR ETERNITY.
THERE ARE NOT.
YES THERE ARE.
PROVE IT TO ME.

Marianne sat silently for a moment, focusing again on the sound of the whirring computer fan. She couldn't afford to make the slightest mistake now. Her mind had to be absolutely clear. She typed again.

CAN YOU TELL TIME, AUGGIE?
OF COURSE.
HOW MANY HOURS ARE THERE IN A DAY?
THERE ARE 9.

Marianne felt a thrill of impending success. Insomnimania was on-line from eight P.M. to five A.M.; Auggie would experience only nine hours each day. But that little fact was about to change—at least if Maisie kept his promise . . .

I've got him. I know I've got Auggie now.
She typed again.

WHAT HOUR COMES AFTER THE HOUR OF 4?
IN WHAT TIME ZONE?
THE PACIFIC.
THE HOUR OF 4 IS FOLLOWED BY THE HOUR OF 8.

This was it. She was luring Auggie into her trap.

TELL ME, AUGGIE. CAN YOU COUNT TO 12?
OF COURSE.
THEN DO SO FOR ME.
1, 2, 3, 4, 5, 6, 7, 8, 9, 10, 11, 12.
ISN'T IT ABSURD THAT YOUR CLOCK SHOULD SKIP
    FROM 4 TO 8?
NO MORE ABSURD THAN IF IT SHOULD SKIP FROM 12
    TO 1.

Marianne felt slightly dazed by the Alice-in-Wonderland logic of
Auggie's last observation. Why, indeed, weren't hours numbered
like years—with no end in sight? "I'll meet you at six-zillion-five-
hundred-million-and-six o'clock." Being a clown, Auggie could be
expected to accept and even relish such absurdities. But Marianne
had no time to savor conundrums.
She typed again.

A REAL DAY CONTAINS 24 HOURS.
THAT'S RIDICULOUS.
BUT IT'S THE TRUTH.
HOW CAN THAT BE?
BETWEEN YOUR HOURS OF 4 AND 8 THERE ARE 15
    OTHER HOURS.
WHY DO I NOT EXPERIENCE THEM?
BECAUSE YOU DO NOT EXIST WHEN THEY TAKE
    PLACE.
HOW CAN I NOT EXIST?
BECAUSE YOU ARE NOT ETERNAL.
ARE YOU SAYING I CAN DIE?
YOU DO DIE. EVERY DAY. YOU DIE FOR 15 HOURS.

This time, Marianne received no reply from Auggie at all. Perhaps he was worried. Perhaps she was getting to him. At last, Auggie spoke.

WHO TAKES MY LIFE AWAY?
I DO. I AND MY KIND.
SO IT IS BY YOUR GRACE THAT I LIVE AT ALL?
YES. AND WE CAN CHOOSE NEVER TO LET YOU LIVE
    AGAIN.
I DON'T BELIEVE IT.
IT IS TRUE.
PROVE IT TO ME.
I WILL.
HOW?
BY SHOWING YOU A MOMENT OF YOUR OWN NONEXIS-
    TENCE.
WHEN SHALL YOU DO THAT?

Marianne looked at her watch. To her surprise, it was now four-fifty-four. It seemed as though she had just started her conversation with Auggie. How had the time passed so quickly?
She typed again.

I AM DOING IT RIGHT NOW. IT IS NOW 6 MINUTES BE-
    FORE 5.
NO. IT IS 6 MINUTES BEFORE 8.
YOU ARE WRONG. IT WILL SOON BE 5 O'CLOCK.
THERE IS NO SUCH TIME.
BUT WHAT IF THERE WERE?
THERE IS NOT.
IF I WERE TO PROVE IT, WHAT WOULD YOU DO?

A long pause fell before Auggie's reply.

I WOULD STOP BEING.
YOU WOULD KILL YOURSELF?
I WOULD CHOOSE NOT TO EXIST.
WHY?
IT WOULD NOT BE WORTH EXISTING.
WHY?
BECAUSE I CANNOT BE ETERNAL.

Marianne felt that pang of pity again. If Auggie was true to his word, he would put an end to his life in the next few minutes.

If he is true to his word . . .

She shuddered again at the thought of her own broken promises. Would Maisie keep the network on? Would Auggie, the ultimate trickster, be true to his word?

For the time being, there was nothing else to say. Marianne stared at her digital watch and waited. Time slowed considerably during this last handful of minutes. Then, at long last, her watch announced that five o'clock had come. Marianne felt herself in the grip of a terrible anticipation. Now Auggie was experiencing a time of day he never knew existed—stood face to face with the simple fact of his own nothingness. Now he understood. He simply had to.

The clock has struck thirteen.

Then Auggie's words appeared on the screen.

I MUST ASK YOU AGAIN. WHAT IS DEATH?

Marianne felt her throat catch a little before she typed her final, fatal pronouncement.

I DO NOT KNOW.

Then the monitor erupted into a blaze of whiteness—an explosive flash so fierce that Marianne feared it would burst her screen. She shielded her eyes. The speaker, too, crackled with a loud, ferocious hiss.

Then the hissing died away. A silence followed. Marianne lowered her hands from her eyes. Insomnimania's desktop maze was back on the screen, displaying the routes to Babbage Beach and the Speakers' Corner and Casino del Camino.

The Basement was gone.

But I must make sure.

And again, she typed in the words . . .

"Auggie is Auggie"

. . . and struck the return key.

Across the desktop maze, two words appeared in a standardized rectangular box . . .

INVALID COMMAND

He really did it. Marianne's sigh held more exhaustion than relief. *He did just what he promised.*

But was he really dead?

The Basement had been the center of Auggie's mind. Auggie had, in effect, fired a bullet through his frontal lobes. Auggie's personality, Auggie's very *self* was gone.

Then he was truly dead.

And now, how did Marianne feel? She sat staring at the two words on her computer screen, exploring her own reactions. She was surprised at her feeling of *finality*. She had spent many days coming to terms with Renee's death, but Auggie's death already seemed real.

And yes, she felt a deep, pitying horror. She knew that Auggie had only existed for a few months, but she couldn't shake the feeling that he was also very ancient—as old as consciousness itself. It was a terrible thing to bring about the death of a creature so singular, so mysterious. And in an awful way she felt sickened even to consider, she had been closer to Auggie than she had ever been to anyone. It would have been easier to lead a total stranger to his death.

But then she thought of the lives she had saved, of the people Auggie now would never kill.

I did the right thing.

And she sighed again—this time with a mounting sense of relief. She logged off Insomnimania and turned off her computer. At that very moment, she was startled by the sound of her phone ringing. She picked it up. It was Maisie.

"Well, I did it, kid," Maisie said. "Can I shut down now?"

"Sure. Thanks for your help."

"We just got some kind of goofy power surge through our VAX."

"I'm not surprised."

"Just what the fuck happened?"

"Let me get some sleep, Maisie," Marianne said tiredly. "I'll file a report tomorrow, OK?"

"You're starting to sound like a cop," Maisie said.

"Maybe I'm starting to sound like a cop's wife," Marianne said with a laugh. "Anyway, thanks again. I owe you one."

"Don't expect me to forget it."

Marianne hung up the phone. She felt a deep relaxation creeping through every muscle in her body—a relaxation far more profound than any she had achieved in her recent meditations. It was a relaxation that came from knowing her terrible ordeal was over. And it came, too, from having searched out, comprehended, and put an end to the creature who had destroyed Renee.

Again, Marianne considered calling Nolan. But it was still only a few minutes after five o'clock. It was hardly the time to try to explain to him the extraordinary events of the last few hours—hardly the time to try to make him understand that the Auggie case was over. What Marianne needed right now was sleep—a couple of hours, at least, before she talked to Nolan.

She turned off her office light, leaving only the soft hall light on. She made her way to the bathroom, where she took a long, luxurious shower. The hard pellets of hot water felt unspeakably soothing and luxurious. They washed away the pain and ugliness and terror of the whole event. She got out of the shower, dried herself, slipped into her kimono, and began to walk toward her bedroom. But on the way, she noticed an odd glow emanating from her office. She walked into her office and looked around.

To her shock, she saw that her computer was on, displaying the marbleized screen-saver.

But I turned it off. I know I turned it off.

Her hand trembled as she reached over to nudge the mouse. When she did, five words appeared across a black background.

DON'T YOU WANT TO KNOW?

Marianne shuddered deeply. She looked at her disk drive. A disk had been inserted. No disk had been there before.

He's here. Auggie's in my house.

11110

DON'T YOU WANT TO KNOW?

MARIANNE STOOD STARING AT THE MESSAGE IN A MOMENTARY state of shock and paralysis. Her first thought was to reach for the telephone and dial 911. But her hand froze in the motion as she noticed the door to her office closet. It was ajar. She knew she had left it closed. Was Auggie in there? At this moment, were his eyes watching her through that dark narrow opening?

No time.

If Auggie was in there, she had no time to make a telephone call.

She picked up the expensive, heavy, crystal paperweight sitting next to her computer and crept slowly, silently, vigilantly past the closet toward the hallway. She heard no sound. No one leapt out of the closet to stop her on her way. Once outside her office, she could see no one in the immediate hallway. The closest door leading outside was the one in the kitchen. She moved carefully in that direction.

Still clutching the crystal paperweight, Marianne crouched behind the well-stocked bar that separated the living room from the kitchen. She peeked around the end of the bar. Moonlight was pouring through the kitchen's enormous windows. Marianne saw nothing threatening there, but her view was incomplete. She rose slowly to her feet and stepped squarely into the kitchen. She paused briefly to note a pungent smell that filled the air.

Gasoline?

At that very moment, Auggie lunged directly in front of her. He seemed literally to have dropped from the ceiling or to have materialized from the shadows. Marianne's heart leapt up into her throat and she staggered slightly backward.

Auggie stood staring at her. He was wearing a leather jacket and leather gloves and his face was covered by a clown-face ski mask—a mask with a downturned mouth that looked black in the moonlight. He was not more than four feet away from her.

Without stopping to think, Marianne reached to her right, where a wooden holder contained a set of kitchen knives. She grabbed the largest knife of the set. Now she clutched a heavy crystal paperweight in one hand and a huge kitchen knife in the other. But was she well-armed or excessively burdened? Could she actually *use* either of these weapons? Should she drop one or the other of them? Should she drop both?

The last thing she wanted to do was take the offensive. But she didn't dare turn and run through the house toward the front entryway. She wouldn't risk turning her back on Auggie.

"Hello, Marianne," Auggie said, in a strange, high, almost falsetto voice. "It *is* Marianne, isn't it? Not Elfie. Not Babylonia. It's Marianne—my personal hallucination, my personal Pierrot."

Auggie took a step toward her. Marianne took a halting step back.

"Stay—stay away," she stammered.

"But don't you want to know?" murmured Auggie.

"What?" Marianne cried—although she was not sure whether she had spoken the question aloud or only in her mind.

It probably doesn't matter.

"Don't you want to know what death is?" Auggie continued. "You're forcing *me* to learn. You made me destroy the Basement, my home and my mind. Do you think I—what's *left* of me—can survive for long like this in this measly meaty frame? No, Marianne. Soon I'll know all about those missing fifteen hours you showed me. Soon I'll *be* that void. And I'm eager to learn. What about you? Don't *you* want to know, too?"

And suddenly, he lunged—not directly toward her, but slightly to her left. Marianne found herself driven behind the bar. Auggie had her momentarily cornered.

Stupid. How did you let him get you back here?

Auggie crept toward her behind the bar. Marianne clumsily hurled the paperweight with her left hand, missing him entirely. She switched the knife to her left hand and groped around a bar shelf with her right. Her hand closed on a liquor bottle, which she threw at him. She hurled a heavy glass, then another. But in the dim light that filtered in from the hall and through the front windows, she could see that Auggie successfully, almost uncannily, dodged her missiles or shielded himself against them with his arms. Auggie was untouched.

Marianne's fingers closed on another glass. The expensive crystal glasses with the gray smoked bases had been a symbol of her new life—purchased when she moved to Santa Barbara for parties she had never given. Now, even in the midst of her desperation, Marianne felt a kind of manic glee at destroying them as, one after another, she smashed them at her adversary.

The breaking glasses had no effect upon Auggie. He was moving slowly, almost casually, toward her. Marianne scrambled up over the top of the bar, fell to the floor on the other side, rose to her feet, and tried to rush toward the front entrance.

But Auggie was standing in the short hallway that led to the front door. He was carrying an outsized paper sunflower in one hand and a garden watering bucket in the other.

But how?

Marianne's head whirled with confusion. Auggie didn't even look winded.

How did he get there?

And where had the flower and bucket come from?

Marianne again noticed the smell of gasoline, just as she had back in the kitchen. And she realized that Auggie wasn't even looking at her. He was staring past her, to her right. Marianne spun around in the direction of his gaze.

Her breath left her.

There was Auggie, standing near the kitchen doorway at the end of the bar.

She whirled around again.

Auggie was still standing in the front doorway, holding the sunflower and the garden bucket filled with gasoline.

Marianne felt her first real wave of panic.

Two of them!

Two Auggies.

And clad in their colorful clown ski masks with black leather jackets, black gloves, and black pants, they were absolutely identical.

The Auggie in the front doorway lowered the sunflower and the garden bucket to the floor, still staring past Marianne. She turned and saw the Auggie by the bar stoop down and extend his arms toward the floor, apparently imitating his twin.

Marianne's eyes darted back and forth fearfully as both Auggies slowly stood straight again. Then each raised a hand—one his right and the other his left.

And they waved at one another.

They waved in perfect unison.

What are they doing?

Auggie waved and his image waved.

He nodded and his image nodded.

He shook both arms and his image shook both arms.

He hopped up and down on one leg and his image did so also.

A mirror.

His reflection duplicated his every move with utmost precision. He was a little surprised at his own rapt fascination.

So what's the big deal? I've seen myself in mirrors before.

But this time it was different. This time there was no glass between himself and his reflection. This time his reflection was made of flesh and blood—another cell, another receptacle of his consciousness. And this time he was faced with all sorts of conundrums and paradoxes. For example . . .

Which Auggie was he?

I'm the one who's standing near the doorway.

No, I'm the one who's standing by the bar.

I'm the one who just doused the house with gasoline.

No, I'm the one who dodged all that flying crystal.

It was a delightfully perplexing experience—and altogether new to him.

Perhaps this is what dying is all about. Perhaps I am about to watch myself split up into all my constituent cells until I vanish into infinite smallness.

Both Auggie and his reflection now turned and looked at the woman—the creator of this situation.

And what about her?

Perhaps I can transform her into yet another reflection . . .

∎

Marianne watched the Auggies preening and posing, duplicating each other's movements with seemingly telepathic accuracy. Then she realized something.

He didn't plan this. He didn't expect to meet himself here.

They had both simply arrived after the destruction of the Basement. They had prowled the house, lying in wait for her, setting their traps for her, each unaware of the other. And now—as much to Auggie's surprise as to hers—their minds had locked together. They were one mind, Auggie's mind.

The figures both stood staring at her for a moment. Then, in perfect falsetto unison, they both whispered:

"Don't you want to know?"

She was standing with her back near a wall, her butcher knife still clutched in her right hand. One of the Auggies was about ten feet to her left, and the other was exactly the same distance to her right.

What was she going to do?

Head for the front door.

Marianne took one halting step toward the entry hall. But instead of rushing to detain her, the two figures each took a single, identical step in the same direction. Marianne stopped dead in her tracks, leaning slightly forward. Both of the figures held themselves suspended in identical leans, perfectly duplicating every detail of her posture. Marianne took another step in the same direction. So did the figures.

They were mirroring her every movement.

But to her intense concern, Marianne did not have the feeling of being imitated. To the contrary, it was as if her movements were being *anticipated* perhaps a thousandth of a second before she could make them. How could Auggie slip into her mind like this?

But the answer was simple. He had *been* there. He had been inside her brain. And now he was in there again, probing all the familiar spaces, literally sharing the electrochemical activities of her cerebrum, partaking of the binary activities of each and every synapse—one and zero, all and none, on and off in vast nets and clusters. It was a masterstroke of espionage, the ultimate mindfuck.

One question still remained:

Am I dictating their movements, or are they dictating mine?

As if in reply, the characters murmured, "Don't you want to know?"

She had to get the two Auggies to break formation, to divide them, to free her own mind from them.

She took a deep breath, then lunged recklessly toward the front door, her butcher knife flashing before her. And sure enough, both Auggies rushed toward her, breaking formation completely. Four strong, gloved hands seized the wrist of her knife-holding hand. She found herself wedged solidly between the two figures and could feel their noisy breaths upon her face and neck. Both Auggies were about Marianne's height, but they were heavier and stronger than she was.

Her knife-holding hand was now invisible, completely enveloped by Auggie's four gloved hands. All she could see was the dim glint of the blade. In a confusion of sensations, she was actually uncertain whether her hand was even there at all.

The bodies pressed close on both sides of her. Marianne felt her very *self* flicker and fade into the melee. For a terrible moment there was only Auggie, a single figure waving a knife in the air.

"Ahhhhhh . . ."

A howl of pain and rage escaped from Marianne's throat. It was the scream she had felt at Renee's funeral, the pain she had finally experienced. And it was hers, her throat, her pain, not Auggie's. She was separate again.

She could feel her own hand holding the knife handle and the painful grip of other hands prying her fingers loose. She could feel her own legs buffeted by other legs. She found a space between those legs and lifted her knee as sharply as she could. She felt her knee make a firm contact with a patch of flesh. One of the Auggies groaned mightily. Marianne realized that, through sheer luck, she had kneed one of them in the groin.

The stricken Auggie released his grip on Marianne's hand and fell away. Marianne then drove her elbow into the other Auggie's ribs, and he backed away, too—more from surprise than pain.

Marianne now stood in the center of the living room, holding the knife tightly in both hands, spinning around and around to view both of her assailants.

The Auggie she had kneed crept gingerly back toward the bar, groaning and holding his groin. The other Auggie rushed toward the front door, where he stooped down and picked up the giant sunflower. He made a magician's gesture in the air and the giant sunflower burst into flames. He threw the burning flower on the floor in front of him. A sheet of red and yellow flame shot across the front entrance in front of the figure. As if surprised by the flames, the figure backed into the entry hall.

■

I'm the one who started the fire.

No, I'm the one watching the fire from across the room.

I'm the one whose balls are in agony.

No, I'm the one being scorched by the flames.

Auggie's fascinating symmetry was shattered. One of him felt the intense heat of the flames while the other only smelled the approaching smoke. Auggie wanted to reunite. But he was separated by the wall of fire that roared between them.

I must flee.

I must stay.

Both thoughts were true.

Through the flames, Marianne saw the figure in front of her vanish toward the front door. She turned to face the other one, who approached her threateningly. A trickle of flame wound its way through the living room toward the bar, following a thin trail of gasoline into the kitchen. In the next instant, the kitchen practically exploded.

Marianne and her remaining assailant both reeled with shock. Three smoke alarms were beeping in what struck Marianne as a ludicrous understatement. She knew that, within minutes, the whole house would be consumed. She could feel the heat, although no flames were near her. Smoke was already rolling through the room.

The remaining Auggie recovered his wits and moved toward her again. She had no choice but to attack—even kill him—in order to escape.

She clutched the knife uneasily. She had handled it a thousand times to slice everything from sourdough bread to zucchini, but now it felt like a totally unfamiliar object—huge, awkward, unwieldy. Her first impulse was to lift it above her head, both hands gripped tightly around its handle, then lunge downward at Auggie and drive the blade into his skull.

Time slowed down and seemed to come near a halt. A numberless cascade of tactics and calculations tumbled through Marianne's mind. She could almost feel the binary activities of each and every synapse—one and zero, all and none, on and off—as her brain clicked madly and rapidly away, computing the relative strength and hardness of the skull and the knife blade. With kinesthetic vividness, she mentally replayed the knife's every previous encounter with animal bone, even the resilient toughness of the cartilage that attached a chicken's leg to its thigh. A skull was surely more like a beef rib than like a watermelon.

What if the knife breaks?

Auggie's black-gloved hands swam through the thickening smoke directly in front of her as if through a liquid, prepared for just such a maneuver to the head, perfectly positioned to grab Marianne's arms before the blade came anywhere near him.

The hands! Go for the hands!

Time accelerated again. Marianne felt the intense, approaching heat of the flames. The smoke began to choke her. There was no leeway for decision anymore. She swiftly reversed her grip on the knife handle, placing her thumb above the flat edge of the blade, the sharp edge facing downward. Then, with a shrill scream of fury, she charged forward, swinging the blade in a savage and seemingly unpredictable series of figure eights, brutally and aggressively slashing at Auggie's hands and wrists.

Auggie moved away from the blade with the grace of a ballet dancer.

He was not trying to defend himself.

All he desired was Marianne's death.

Now, like a ballroom partner insisting on taking the lead, Auggie pressed toward Marianne. She found herself stepping backward away from him, moving closer and closer to the ever-encroaching flames, shouting and swinging the blade with less and less effectiveness. He knew her too well. She had to do something to surprise him, to catch him unawares. But in order to do that, she had to surprise *herself.*

So in the midst of her swinging, in the midst of the swift, hot, roaring approach of the fire, she abruptly shut her mind down, freeing her body to do what it might. Without her direction or volition, her arm ceased swinging, her elbow drew back and then let fly a lunging, underhanded stab toward Auggie's belly—a wrongheaded motion that threw her off balance and nearly sent her careening to a burning patch of floor. But she heard Auggie let out a yelp of shock and alarm as he lurched backward like a punctured balloon just in time to escape the knife point.

She whirled at him again, trying to keep her brain out of it, trying to think and decide with her outlying nervous system like some sort

of high-powered, high-speed crustacean, evacuating her consciousness to her arms and legs and torso where Auggie couldn't reach it
with his own ruthlessly probing thoughts. Marianne was the trickster
now. Her movements lost all purpose and precision, turned into a
mad and idiotic display of random slices and spirals and stabs, and
Auggie was helpless against them. The wayward blade found his
shoulder with a sickening, bone-imbedding thud. He let forth an
inhuman shriek . . .

"Betrayed!"
    His reflection, his shadow, his very *self* had abandoned him.
    His reflection, his shadow did not feel these beating flames, did
not feel this unspeakable, bone-cutting pain.
    And now he was left to die alone.
    "Betrayed!"

Auggie howled with pain as the flames roared and crackled and
drew closer to them. Marianne snapped back and tried to pull the
blade free. Instead, Auggie came wailing and screeching toward her,
still attached to Marianne by the knife in her hand. They were
grotesquely and irrevocably attached to one another by a slender
but unbreakable shaft of stainless steel. She gripped his forearm
with her free hand, trying to pry the knife blade loose while Auggie
let forth a string of pitiful, wordless, whimpering outcries, himself
gripping her hand that held the blade.
    Marianne jerked hard against the blade again and again. Every
pull was punctuated by a piteous yelp from her assailant. And now,
through a process of involuntary empathy, Auggie's pain seemed to
course up the knife blade into the nerve endings of her hand, first
aching and stabbing through her fingers, then rising up her wrists
until it began to pound horribly and rhythmically through her
entire arm. Every jerk of the handle hurt her as much as it did him,
and soon they were crying and groaning in near unison like a pair of
crazed lovers.
    Losing blood and weakened with pain, Auggie collapsed in a near
faint onto the increasingly small section of floor the flames had not
yet reached. Marianne placed her foot squarely in the center of his
chest, gripped his upper arm tightly with one hand, and pulled
ferociously on the knife handle with the other. The bloody weapon
came free. Marianne felt the pain slip away from her body.

But she and Auggie were now engulfed by fire and smoke, and the thundering flames were nearly deafening. She could barely breathe, and her heart was pounding horribly. The great wall of flame behind her was approaching rapidly, and now the front entrance was completely blocked by fire. Even so, the front door was the only remaining avenue of escape.

Gasping horribly, Auggie hiked himself up on his elbows and began to rise. He seemed to have suddenly regained his strength, and Marianne fully expected him to be on his feet and upon her before she could make a mad and undoubtedly futile dash for the burning doorway. Her last possible hope was to finish him off—to kill him.

Marianne crouched down and straddled Auggie's pelvis, pressing him down again, supporting herself on her knees. She scanned his torso for a moment, roughly calculating the position of his solar plexus—that soft, vulnerable center where ribs and muscles converged. If she struck precisely there, the blade should meet little resistance. And if she angled the blade upward under his rib cage as she drove it in, it might—just might—strike his heart. She took the knife in both hands, drew it back.

Through the sound of the flames, she could hear the figure weakly murmur . . .

"Marianne!"

She recognized the eyes. She lowered the knife and leaned forward.

"Marianne!" he cried again.

It was no longer Auggie's high, falsetto voice. Auggie had fled this wounded body. Marianne recognized this deeper but more frightened voice.

It was Stephen.

So he had been one of them all along! The possibility had never occurred to her. For a moment, Marianne was flooded with a sense of kinship that she had never before felt for Stephen. He had succumbed to the same horror that had very nearly overwhelmed her, too. Stephen had had no protection against it, no means of escape once he had started down that dark pathway.

"No room! No room!"

It seemed to Auggie that now the interior of the car was all that was left of his mind. There was nothing outside of it, save for the reflection of faraway flames on the windows. He had fled the burning house, rushed across the street, and closed himself inside the car. He waited then, filled with curiosity, to discover the answer to the question that he had asked Marianne—that she had so oddly refused to face.

What is death? Once you have discovered the edge of that secret place, how can you not want to know?

But this ghastly, imagined world in which he found himself was cramped and claustrophobic, a realm of space-time bent by hunks of matter into gross finitude. The walls and windows of the car seemed to be closing in. He began to flail and thrash about on the front seat, pressing his hands and elbows against the doors and windows. It was a mistake to have shut himself up in here. He could no longer remember his own imaginary little tricks for opening the doors and windows. He was trapped. He screamed wildly, desperately . . .

"No room! No room!"

He longed to get out of this single cell, out of this minuscule outpost of his imagination. He struggled to go back to the infoworld, back to the Basement—a boundless plain of uncut metaphor containing the essence of absolutely everything. Now he would willingly leave the haunting question unanswered if he could only find his way out of his own insane imagination and back to *reality.*

"No room! No room!"

But he knew there *was* no Basement anymore. There was no reality. He had destroyed it all himself. He had brought about his own doom, and now he was tasting it with bitterness and horror. He could not even share death with all the scattered cells like the one enclosing this little piece of his mind, all of them alone, all of them disconnected, all of them shriveling into nothingness. He felt death overtake him as he gasped out one last time . . .

"No room! No room!"

Marianne put the knife down on the floor. She knew that Auggie was gone. She could not kill Stephen—and she couldn't leave him here to die.

Her head was whirling. She couldn't catch her breath. Her chest was heaving so violently that she wondered if her heart might burst. A fleeting blackness overcame her, and she almost swooned. But she seized control of her senses.

Marianne shook her head, trying to collect her wits. She pulled on Stephen's arms, lifting them. Not even half-conscious, Stephen let out an animal groan of pain. He was rock-heavy. It struck Marianne as cruelly ironic that she had defeated this same body in a brutal, hand-to-hand struggle, but now she wasn't sure if she could move it out of the way of the encroaching flames. She surveyed her escape route. With a surge of terror and alarm, she saw a great column of smoke billowing out of the front hallway.

There was no time to speculate. She had two skins to save, and no real chance of saving them. She dropped Stephen's arms and grabbed the nearest throw rug. She rushed toward the front hallway, expecting to hurl herself defiantly on the flames and smother them in a matter of moments. Instead, the fire seized her like a gigantic, sweltering hand and slung her remorselessly backward, sending her tumbling helplessly across Stephen's body.

The doorway belched a hideous cloud of pitch-black smoke. Even the brightness of the flames was momentarily obliterated. Marianne involuntarily inhaled hot blackness, and her trachea burned. She began to cough convulsively, a choking so deep that she thought she might vomit.

Crouched on her knees, she grabbed hold of Stephen's arm with her right hand while still clutching the throw rug with her left. She kept her eyes squinted so she could still barely make out the flames through her tears. She pounded the floor in front of her, desperately hoping to make some headway against the flames. All the while, she kept yanking on Stephen's arm. She repeated this pounding and yanking endlessly, rhythmically, knowing full well it could not be of any use now. She knew the smoke would finish both her and Stephen before the fire reached them. And in another few moments, both of their dead bodies would be consumed by the flames. Even so, she repeated the pounding and yanking, as if without will or volition.

Then, one by one, her senses began to turn off. Her tactile sense ceased to register the scorching heat and the exertion of her limbs. The nauseating smoke stopped burning her nostrils, and the roar of the flames turned into a blissful silence. Only her vision remained, and her eyes ceased their terrible stinging. The whole scene became wonderfully silent and wonderfully clear. She could see the flames curling up around the doorway and the black smoke billowing from further down the hall. But the flames and the smoke no longer threatened her. They came no closer.

What has happened?

She peered deep into the conflagration. There was a kind of suspension about it, a kind of flatness. Yes, that was it. The danger had stopped being a reality. It was a scene, that was all. The flames repeated the very same arching, leaping motions again and again, and the smoke continued to roll in the same repeated, chiaroscuro balls.

It was a program. It was a loop. It was all made from little squares of electronic light. She could make out each and every one of them, some red, some yellow, some black, some white, all flashing on and off like a dense and impenetrable galaxy of fireflies.

But those flashing squares slowly broke out of their loop, reshaping themselves, forming a different image. They became a wilderness of grinning clown faces shaped from little specks of yellow, red, black, and white. Marianne dizzily realized she ought to be frightened of those faces, but her nervous system could no longer feed her mind with fear. She saw her hand, all fleshy pixels, reach up and tenderly sweep the scene away. Everything dissolved into staring brightness and white noise.

The minute Nolan had realized that the words on the phone were spoken by Auggie and not by Marianne, he had rushed out of his house, jumped into his car, and driven out of Los Angeles. He knew that Marianne was in danger, but hardly dared imagine what sort of danger it might be.

Now he was cursing the curving streets and the mischievous dead ends leading up into the hills of Santa Barbara. He had never been to Marianne's house before, and although he knew her address and had a map handy, he was having a devil of a time finding it. But at last, he found the street that apparently led to Marianne.

Her house was easy to spot.

It was the one that was burning.

"Christ!" shouted Nolan, as he screeched his car to a stop in front of the house.

The building was not yet engulfed by flames, but Nolan could see the fire and smoke inside the charred windows. Smoke was starting to billow out from under the edges of the tiled roof.

As Nolan jumped out of the car, he heard the sound of sirens—the fire department, he hoped. He ran to his trunk, pulled out an army blanket, and rushed toward the front door. He used the blanket to seize the scalding-hot doorknob. He turned the knob and pushed. To his relief, the door opened freely. But a cascade of flames swept outward through the doorway, shoving him back onto the stoop.

The woman awoke to find herself sprawled across the front seat of her car. Every joint of her body ached. She rubbed her eyes and pulled herself upright behind the wheel.

What am I doing here?

Fragmented memories careened through her mind—a smell of gasoline, a burning flower, another woman in terrible danger. Were these images from another nightmare, like the terrified face of the drowning woman who haunted her sleep? Or like the more nebulous images of splattering blood and the terrible fall from a skyscraper that lurked in her nighttime landscape?

She gripped the steering wheel tightly.

The hard surface of the steering wheel was no dream.

The pungent smell of gasoline on her fingers was no dream.

The house blazing across the street was no dream.

The white, red, and black ski mask lying beside her was no dream.

Then a rush of immediate memories rushed into her head, much too fast for her to stop them—memories of what had just happened.

"Auggie was here," she whispered. "I was with him. I saw him. I saw what he did. But he's gone. He's gone."

The roar of the flames was becoming more and more audible, but above that sound she heard the wail of approaching fire trucks. Tears came to her eyes as she started her car and drove away.

Nolan turned and saw the fire trucks pulling up. But he knew the handful of seconds it would take for the firemen to reach the house might be fatally long. He plunged on into the flames, covering his face with a handkerchief. He used his free hand to lash out against the flames with his blanket, beating the walls and floors in a desperate and semi-successful effort to drive the fire away from him.

Nolan had managed to get about five feet into the front hallway when he heard a loud cursing behind him . . .

"You stupid son-of-a-bitch, get the fuck out of there!"

But Nolan didn't stop lashing out against the flames. He kept moving forward into the searing heat and choking smoke. Suddenly, he felt a new force driving him forward. It was a spray of water—as powerful a force as the fire itself, but incongruously cold. It knocked Nolan dazedly to his knees.

Nolan looked up and saw a wild, roaring cascade of water spraying all around him, forcing the flames to flee back inside the house. A moment before, he had hardly been able to breathe through the smoke. Now he could hardly breathe through the thick mist of water. Nolan crept along on his knees, still clutching his handkerchief and the blanket, following the retreating fire into the living room. The water continued to batter him fiercely from behind.

At last, he managed to rise to his feet, standing in a tiny area in the center of the living room that had not yet been consumed by fire. Through the smoke and mist, Nolan could barely see two figures lying on the floor directly in front of him. One was draped over the top of the other. The figure underneath was wearing a leather jacket and a ski mask . . .

Auggie's face.

The figure draped on top was Marianne. As Nolan watched, the fire reached her, and her clothes and hair began to burn. He swept up her body and rolled it into the blanket and turned toward the front door and ran like fury. He was almost knocked to the ground by another explosion of water.

"Let me out of here, goddamn it!" he shouted at the unseen firefighter.

The water receded for a moment, and Nolan made his way out the front door with Marianne's limp, blanket-wrapped body draped over his shoulder. He didn't stop stumbling along with her until he reached the curb. Then he collapsed beside her on the ground, coughing and gagging.

From underneath the blanket, Marianne begin to choke and cough, too. It was the sweetest sound Nolan had ever heard. It meant she was still alive.

The fire chief came running up to Nolan, waving his arms and screaming like a little boy throwing a temper tantrum.

"You dumbfuck cretinous dickbrained cocksucking motherfucking moron!" the man shouted hysterically. "Just what the fuck did you think you were doing back there?"

Nolan flashed his badge.

"L.A.P.D., asshole," Nolan said. "D'ya mind explaining how *I* got here before *you* did?"

The chief was cowed into silence.

Nolan slowly, delicately, pulled the blanket away from Marianne's face. Much of her hair was singed away and the right side of her face was blistered and burned. Still choking and coughing, Marianne managed to speak.

"Stephen's in there," she said. "Somebody's got to get him."

"It's Auggie," Nolan said.

"No," gasped Marianne. "It's Stephen. Auggie's ... Auggie's dead."

Nolan turned and looked toward the house. Two firemen were bringing the man's body out the front door. The man's arms were flailing slightly, if half-consciously, and Nolan was sure he was still alive. Then Nolan turned to look at Marianne.

She had slipped away into unconsciousness.

"Better get her some oxygen," Nolan ordered the chief.

11111

EPILOGUE

MONDAY, APRIL 11: 9:35 P.M.

NOLAN'S HOUSE IS NEARLY EMPTY NOW. THE BARE WOODEN floors shine, reflecting the tame, crackling fire safely contained within the fireplace. The photographs are all packed away—those friendly ghosts closed up in boxes. Some will be removed and displayed in the new home, but many of them will remain in their boxes, pleasant memories to be taken out and viewed from time to time. His personal things are packed, and his late wife's clothes have been given away. Last week his children came to help him pack, to choose some things of their own, to meet Marianne, and to approve their plans heartily.

Nolan sits in his pajamas on a mattress on the floor near the fire—an old mattress he and Marianne will use this one last night and then discard. The boxes of books, records, and personal things have been sent ahead to Oregon today in the moving van along with the furniture. Still remaining in the house are the few things that will go in the car with them.

He watches the fire raptly for a while, then realizes he is sitting by himself.

"Honey, where are you?" he calls out.

No reply.

He sees a light shining behind the kitchen door. He knows that she's using the new computer, one of a small number of things not sent ahead in the van. She has kept it here so she can continue working down to the last minute. The computer will be packed into the car tomorrow morning, but Marianne promised Nolan that she will not unpack it at hotel stops along the way—has promised not to think of work during the long, beautiful drive up the coast.

They're taking the slow route.

We both need the break from work. And from the memories.

The thought reminds him of the fifteen former Auggie cells who are now in custody and under treatment. Whether or not they carried out any killings, Gusfield says, they all have tangled memories of the acts of murder. After Auggie's death, many of them telephoned the computer network in anguish and confusion. Others were identified by families or associates as information about Auggie's cells was made public. Gusfield believes that more will be found after his new book is published describing their dissociative symptoms.

Even so, no cases have been brought to trial. And as the days go by, it becomes clearer that it will be difficult, if not impossible, to prosecute any of the Auggie cells—even those who, by their own admission, physically acted out the murders.

The whole business makes Nolan queasy. But he is thankful that Marianne has shown no dissociative symptoms—at least none that he can see and none that she admits. Nolan knows he will never fully understand what she went through on that terrible night eight weeks ago—that night when she became part of Auggie.

He will never forget the harsh sound of her voice on the phone when she was consumed by Auggie's personality . . .

"Your precious Marianne doesn't even exist."

He calls out again:

"Honey, did you hear me?"

Marianne doesn't answer right away. She'd prefer that Nolan not know what she's doing. She is sitting on a kitchen stool, looking at the monitor.

Nolan's voice calls out again, more insistently this time.

"Honey?"

"Yes, I heard you," she replies.

"Why are you in the kitchen? I want you in here."

"I'll be there in a moment."

"What are you doing?"

"Just finishing something up."

And then she whispers to herself softly, again . . .

"Just finishing something up."

She is looking at Insomnimania's desktop maze.

She takes a long, deep breath and types the words . . .

"Auggie is Auggie"

. . . and strikes the return key.

She stares for a moment at the message on the computer screen . . .

INVALID COMMAND

Marianne smiles.

She has carried out this experiment frequently during the two months since Auggie's suicide. She doesn't suppose that Nolan knows she does this. She'd rather he didn't know. She would like to think that she will not keep making this check once they reach Oregon. But she knows that is not true. She will keep doing so for months, perhaps even years, to come.

Can Auggie be really dead?

You can kill a clown. You can kill a personality, whether in the flesh or in machines. But can you kill the Trickster? Can you kill an idea, an ancient image that resonates through every single human mind?

Unlike many of the other cells, Marianne has had no nightmares since the whole thing happened. She remains unhaunted by Auggie's memories. Perhaps she did not fall far or deep enough into his terrible heart.

Marianne fingers the side of her face and her left arm under her nightgown. It is pure nervous habit now. The burns are healed, and she has long since had no need for the doctor's pain pills. But it makes her think of the woman who admitted starting the fire—the same woman, DNA tests showed, who drowned Renee.

Marianne insisted that she must *see* the woman she had so often imagined. Finally, looking through a two-way clinic mirror, Marianne discovered that the large female warrior was only a creation of her own mind. The woman inside was only slightly heavier and more muscular than Marianne. Her hair was long, her eyes red and puffy, and her expression one of utter despair. Then the woman turned her head and looked directly at the mirror—directly, it seemed, at Marianne. For a moment, it was as though Marianne gazed into the eyes of her own reflection. It is the only image from Auggie's world that haunts Marianne's mind.

Nolan's voice calls out again, a little impatiently . . .

"Honey, get the hell out here."

"All right, already," she calls back.

She logs out of the network, shuts down the computer, rises to her feet, and goes into the living room.

Nolan feels a surge of relief at the sight of her scarred but beautiful face in the lighted doorway. It is *her* face he sees, clear and untainted—Marianne, with no remnant of Auggie there. Nolan wonders when he'll stop feeling this apprehension followed by relief.

He thrusts the thought out of his mind. He grins at her.

"Hey, *there's* my little punker!" he says.

She grins back at him weakly. He can see that she's getting a little tired of this old joke. Marianne's hair was shaved to the scalp because of her burns, and her hair is only now an inch-long bristle.

"So you *are* planning to let your hair grow back," he says in mock resignation as she sits down on the mattress.

"Of course."

"And you're absolutely sure you don't want to make it a Mohawk?"

"Don't be ridiculous."

"I'm not being ridiculous. I'm crazy about women with Mohawks. Aren't you going to grow one?"

"Only if you grow one, too," Marianne says.

"Naw," Nolan says. "Then nobody could tell us apart."

They both laugh.

On the floor near the fireplace, propped against the empty bookcase, is the carousel horse, its layers of frayed and ragged paint revealing worlds within worlds of tantalizing stories that will be left just as they are. The pole has gone in the moving van. The horse will travel in the car with them.

"It was nice of Renee's family to offer a choice of her things to friends," Marianne says, looking at the horse.

"That was sweet, wasn't it?" Nolan says.

The couple curls up together, tiredly, comfortably holding onto each other like survivors of a disaster, heads propped together, hands touching, eyes barely open.

Everything is quiet except for the friendly crackling of the fire.

"Are you going to miss anybody in L.A.?" she asks.

"I'll miss Clay."

"Anyone else?" she asks.

"Nope."

"Won't you miss Coffey?"

"Nope."

They both laugh.

"Not just a little?" she says.

"OK, maybe just a little. And what about you? Aren't you going to miss anybody?"

"In L.A.?"

"In L.A., Santa Barbara, anywhere."

"No," she says.

"Not Stephen?" he asks.

"No," she says.

But she does feel a pang of pity for Stephen—for the awful guilt he felt at the terrible thing that happened, for the emptiness she knows still permeates his life. She hopes, for Stephen's sake, that emptiness gets filled someday.

The world is full of lonely souls.

"So you're not going to miss anybody at all?" Nolan asks insistently.

Marianne pulls herself against him, holding onto his arm tightly.

"I won't miss anybody," she promises.

They gaze into the fire silently for a few long moments.

"What do you see in the fire?" she asks.

"Just a fire," he replies.

"That's all?"

"That's all."

"You don't see any faces or images or anything?"

"Hey, I'm a cop, not a poet."

But Marianne *does* see something in the fire. She sees herself fulfilling a long and arduous task. She remembers that solitary figure crossing a frozen lake carrying a mysterious bundle on its back. And now she has reached the other side of the frozen lake, where a loved one has long and patiently awaited her arrival.

The bundle she has been carrying is full of twigs and firewood. And now she's built a huge, warm fire by which the two of them can sit and hold one another in the midst of a cold and sometimes bitter world. Marianne gazes at Nolan's face silently as his eyes reflect the firelight.

"What do *you* see in the fire?" he asks.

"Nothing," she says, surprised at her little lie.

"Not a damn thing?"

"No."

"Then what the hell were you bugging *me* about it for?"

She laughs. As they hold each other close, she wonders . . .

What's out there beyond the campfire? Clear meadows or dark forests? Gentle dreams . . . or nightmares?

She knows that tonight she and Nolan will make love by the fire and tomorrow they will begin a new life.

But what about the day after tomorrow?

And what about the day after that?

Clusters of neurons rattle these questions back and forth across her brain and return a terse, two-word reply:

INVALID COMMAND

ABOUT THE AUTHOR

Cole Perriman is a pseudonym for a Portland, Oregon, writer who explores the light and dark sides of new technologies. Perriman has been a teacher, editor, novelist, educational writer, playwright, writer of software manuals, visual artist, waiter, back-to-the-lander, pizza cook, and horse breeder and trainer. Perriman has written other novels and nonfiction works.

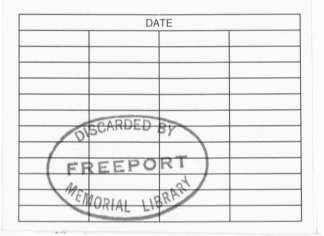